Paul's main loves have always been family, friends, music, reading and travel. He had always wanted to write a novel, but at the same time, was always too busy. Finally, in his later years, Paul has been able to write his first book. He hopes to write more soon, each under the titles of Queen songs, in memory of his favourite band. I hope you enjoy it…

This, my first book, is dedicated to Sharon, my inspiration, my world, the love of my life.

Paul Evans

WHO WANTS TO LIVE FOREVER

AUSTIN MACAULEY PUBLISHERS™

LONDON * CAMBRIDGE * NEW YORK * SHARJAH

This is a work of fiction. Names, characters, businesses, places, events, locales, and incidents are either the products of the author's imagination or used in a fictitious manner. Any resemblance to actual persons, living or dead, or actual events is purely coincidental.

A CIP catalogue record for this title is available from the British Library.

ISBN 9781035831913 (Paperback)
ISBN 9781035831920 (ePub e-book)

www.austinmacauley.co.uk

First Published 2024
Austin Macauley Publishers Ltd®
1 Canada Square
Canary Wharf
London
E14 5AA

I would like to thank all my friends and family who have helped me along the way to finally writing my first book. Most of all, I would like to thank Debbie, who, way back in 2012, convinced me it was then the time to do it...

1

The first few weeks following the amicable, yet tearful separation had been little short of a nightmare. Bird and Bloke had been an institution on the karaoke circuit of Surrey and Sussex. The Bird, sometimes known as Ellie and I had been thrown together by a mutual friend and a mutual lust in May 1999, and had been the rock of relationships for twelve and a half years. We had seen other couples come and go, marriages collapse, new relationships formed, but still we ploughed on. I lost count of the number of times one or both of us had advised one of our friends that they had to move on when such things ended. It sounded weak and hollow, but what else can you tell someone who's heart has been broken, and who's new best friend was the bottom of the next vodka bottle?

Even now, many years later, there are still certain things I cannot do without thinking of her. If I hear The Coors singing Runaway on the radio, I switch channels, as I can still picture her looking at me as she sang it in The Castle, Reigate, during what Copa Karaoke called the Sunday Service. Indeed, run away is exactly what Bird and Bloke did just a few weeks later, albeit just down to Cornwall for a few days break from work, not to mention her ex who wanted to rip my head off and put it on a stick. Bizarrely, it always makes me smile when she sings Def Leppard's Love Bites, but that, as they say, is another story.

I don't think I could ever return to Paphos or Kissonerga in Cyprus, where we spent our first real holiday together... Ellie's first ever venture abroad, where we dumped the cases, hit the bar in Blazing Saddles, she hitting the cocktails and having a late afternoon nap that lasted until the next morning, when she awoke with the mother of all hangovers.

The one thing I strived to get myself past, was the thought of never seeing my beloved West Country again. In the years leading up to my relationship with Ellie, I had spent many happy weeks, on my own, touring Devon and Cornwall, simply turning up on somebody's B&B doorstep, staying the night and moving on the next day. That was to be our first holiday together. I had already planned a week in June 1999, so I simply asked her to join me. It was a week of fun, laughter, copious amounts of alcohol and much, much more. I couldn't bear the thought of never again driving down a country lane, turning a corner and spotting the blue Atlantic just five minutes away. There was always something magical about that sight. I think there always will be.

Probably the hardest part of the break-up was learning to take my own advice. How many times had I told friends to move on? During the winter of 2011/2012, I began to realise it was not as easy as it sounded. We parted in early December, and that Christmas was pure Hell. It was the first I had ever spent totally alone. I celebrated with a bottle of Scotch, several beers and re-runs of Morse and Frost on the Freeview Channels. The Bird and her family were just ten minutes' walk away, in The Plough, my local, enjoying the usual family Christmas dinner.

Of course, I had been invited, but politely refused. I don't think I could have handled the false happiness and joviality. Plus, I'm fairly certain everyone would have felt uncomfortable. I left a drink behind the bar for each of them, wishing them all the very best for the New Year. I meant it as well. They were, still are a lovely family and I will always have a soft spot for them, and for Ellie.

Two months later, at the end of February, Marie snapped me out of the nightmare. I had known her, casually, for about three years. She worked in the finance department of Brannigan Helicopters, the company who had employed me since the long hot summer of 1975. On one of our regular Friday lunch-time visits to the village pub, the Station Hotel, Nutfield, Marie had suddenly mentioned that if ever I fancied a break in the sun, I would be more than welcome to join her at her parents' villa in Cape Verde. I asked if the invitation included my significant other and all I received in return was that certain look. It was the look girls give when they're after something a man is not willing to give. I politely refused, but said I would bear it in mind for the future. In the words of Joe Cocker, who knows what tomorrow brings?

Despite the fact that Ellie and I hadn't made a big thing of the split, somehow word had reached the office where I worked and Marie picked up on it. One cold, wet, miserable Wednesday afternoon that February, she breezed into my office, perched on the corner of my desk, showing more than the usual amount of thigh for the time of year and said, "You need a holiday young man!"

Now firstly, I have to say for Marie to call me 'young man' was stretching the truth considerably. I was, at the time, just turned sixty-one, some twenty-five years her senior... But this did not seem to deter the lady. Secondly, she was absolutely right, I *did* need a holiday! I hadn't seen the sun, or felt its warmth on my skin since the previous July, when Ellie and I had spent what was to be our last ever holiday together in Paphos. With very little hesitation, I looked Marie in the eye and asked where she was taking me, and when.

Ten days later, I was on a flight out of nearby Gatwick Airport, all set to enjoy the experience of a life-time. The moment I met Marie's parents, I could see why I was attractive to her. They lived in a time-warp to be honest. Diane and Jack would not have looked out of place in a hippy commune in the 1960s. She grew all her own vegetables while he tended the chickens, pigs and numerous other farm animals, all of which kept them virtually self-sufficient throughout the year.

Diane would swan around the kitchen all day in a gold and red kaftan, preparing the most amazing meals I had ever tasted, and believe me, I am a very fussy eater, while listening to Jethro Tull and Pink Floyd. Jack would spend all his spare time tinkering with either his Cessna light aircraft or one of his three boats, The Who and The Kinks blasting from the stereo. There was also a familiar haze in the air, both in the kitchen and the boat-house. I felt at home ten minutes after I arrived.

From the way Marie had talked about her family, I was well aware they were not exactly hard up... Not short of a bob or two, so to speak. But I was blissfully unaware of just how well off they truly were. I was about to find out it was even better than I thought. On day three, I was told to pack a few things for three days away. 'Away from all this?' I thought. Why would anyone want even a few days away from paradise? OK, so I'd heard of Californians and Australians who loved touring the UK for a break from the blistering sunshine, even enjoying the rain and snow, but they pretty soon tired of it and returned home.

Very few of them actually 'did Europe' a second time and I don't believe it was financial reasons. I certainly never heard of any of them staying the distance and making Great Britain their home. It was a pretty safe bet that, assuming they were 'doing Europe', their next stop would be the Greek Islands.

The very next morning, the four of us were packed and loaded into the Cessna, heading for their Safari Park just outside Kiffa, the capital of the

Assaba Region of Mauritania. Now although I consider myself widely-travelled, having been all over Europe, seen New York, been sun-burnt in the Copacabana and sailed the Fjords of Norway, I had never experienced anything like life in West Africa. Ellie and I had flown to Cairo on a day trip from Cyprus once, so I knew what to expect temperature-wise, but had yet to experience the sheer beauty of the wild open spaces, seeing animals in their natural habitat for the first time in my life, and discovering that racial discrimination and even slavery still existed.

I had been cocooned in my own safe little world for so long. Even though the seven black men and women who worked for Jack and Diane ate, drank and spent their evenings with us, they still considered themselves slaves. They were paid a very good salary and lived very comfortable lives but for whatever was built inside them, Jack was still 'Yes sir Mister Boss'. It was one Hell of an eye-opener for me. Again, we enjoyed some amazing meals. I'm a very fussy eater and anyone back home in Surrey would tell you I would happily live on pizza and curry if I had to, so I never once asked what it was, I was devouring every evening, but I can only say it was delicious.

By day, we would feed and water the animals. By night, Marie and I would sleep on a canopied double bed, situated on the veranda. I swear it's true. Many of my friends at home have seen the photos. We would smoke, drink the local wine and stare up at the stars until we could stay awake no longer. If I thought Cape Verde was paradise, this was one step closer to Heaven. I never wanted to leave. But of course, I had to. Life goes on and after all, this was just a holiday. Unlike that chap on the television, I couldn't simply give up everything I had at home and move out there to care for white tigers, etc. I was due back at work in three days.

Apart from the obvious excitement of experiencing something different and new in my life, plus the joy of spending time with Marie, Diane and Jack, the one thing I realised as I flew home on the first Sunday in March, was that I hadn't thought of The Bird even once during the entire week. I felt I was ready to move on. I still wasn't sure how I would react if I heard Runaway on the radio. And I was still fairly certain I would never again prop up the bar at Blazing Saddles, or Cleo's in Coral Bay, Paphos, but I *did* make up my mind to re-visit Cornwall in June. I will be forever grateful to Marie for helping take those first brief steps towards my future.

2

I calculated that in my life-time, I had spent something like six months touring my beloved West Country. I had experienced the amazing Eden Project, travelled the delightful Dart Valley Preserved Steam Railway, seen the normally highly-respected National Trust ruin the once-beautiful Land's End with commercialisation, had a bizarre experience in Lyme Regis with a comb! I also learned the correct way to pronounce Mousehole and St Austell where, with the help of Ellie, I managed to save the most enormous toad I had ever seen. I've amassed so many wonderful memories and photos that it would be impossible to list them all.

However, the one thing I can categorically state is that it matters not how many times you visit, there will always be more wonderful spots to experience in amazement and wonder. Hence my decision to return in the summer. And so it was, that on 3 June 2012, in the midst of all the madness that was the London Olympics, I packed my Renault Clio iMusic and headed 'home' once again. Please don't misunderstand me. I was immensely proud of our boys and girls in both the Olympics and the Paralympics. I even had the pleasure of meeting Chris Hoy at a 'Meet and Greet' event promoted by one of my American colleagues. Thank you, Erica, it was most entertaining. The sad fact is that outside of my beloved Manchester United, I'm simply not a sports fan.

I had intended to avoid any of the places that brought back memories of past relationships, but I found Lyme Regis impossible to resist. Not only was it one of the most beautiful spots en route to the West Country proper, it also held several fond memories. I recalled it being the first place I had ever seen a white lady working in an Indian restaurant—it turned out she owned it—but it was also the scene of a somewhat bizarre comb incident. I know strange things happen to all of us from time to time, but that was one of the strangest for me.

Ellie's dad was one of the nicest men you could wish to meet. I had never really thought about it before, but all my previous relationships had been with girls who only had one parent, a mother. John was more than happy for me to call him dad, we often joked about it as he was only about fifteen years older than I. He sadly passed away a year after Ellie and I separated and I will always regret losing the only "dad" I ever had, without ever being able to say a proper good-bye. Never-the-less, we had plenty of laughs during the thirteen years I knew him. Even before the illness, he was rapidly losing his hair and I often joked about his need for the little black comb that always rested on the table in the hallway.

One Sunday morning in the summer of 2005, Ellie and I called in to see mum and dad, to let them know we were off on our almost annual tour of the West Country. A couple of days later, after a few drinks and an excellent Indian meal in Lyme Regis, we checked into a little B&B along a side road, just off the main hill leading up from the harbour. It was aptly named the Traveller's Rest. As soon as we walked into the hallway, I looked down at the table, smiled at Ellie and said, "It's just like being at your mum's." For there on the polished table was a little black comb. We both laughed. I know it sounds silly, but remember, we *had* been drinking. The daftest things appear funny after a few drinks.

The rest of the week passed without incident. At least, nothing I care to enter into print over. Upon our return, we called in to mum and dad's for a quick 'hello', all thoughts of the comb incident long forgotten. But as soon as we stepped into the living room, dad took one look at me and accused me, in jest, of stealing his comb. He swore blind it was in its usual place just over a week ago. In fact, around the same time as our last visit. I think I joked about taking and selling it at a car boot sale. To which he replied, quite seriously, that it had definitely been there the previous week. He specifically remembered replacing it the day they returned from their holiday. Jo suddenly burst out laughing. I guessed why, but her parents simply thought she'd lost the plot.

"Where was it you went to?" She asked, cautiously.

"Lyme Regis," came the reply. "We stayed at a little bed and breakfast called the Traveller's Rest."

As I say, despite the little tingles that ran down my neck that morning, nothing was going to stop me calling in at Lyme Regis on the way and topping up my already bulging photo collection. The place had changed very little, which I think is fair to say about almost anywhere west of the New Forest. Prior to my departure, I had carefully checked my Ordnance Survey map of Devon and Cornwall, determined to find new and wonderful delights to experience. Having said that, I should point out one of the local by-laws. You *have* to visit St Ives… By law! OK, so maybe that law is only in my head but I take it very seriously. I know many people will tell you it's far too commercial to be the real Cornwall, but I for one *love* the fact that little old ladies open up the windows of their brightly-coloured cottages and sell you the best pasties ever.

I love walking the lanes up and down the hill, spotting the talented local artists working and displaying their wares. My walls at home were littered with them, and none cost me more than a fiver. Worth every penny. I will never forget the first time I saw St Ives. It was way back in the 1960s, when a little steam train used to take you under the cliffs on the short branch from Lelant on the main line, through Carbis Bay. On that first trip, I was keeping the cost down as much as possible, so instead of taking the train, I picked a spot about 200 yards from Lelant station, where the footpath crosses the railway, turned left and walked the line. Illegal I know, possibly even dangerous if it wasn't for the fact that you could hear an 0-6-0 steam loco approaching from a good quarter mile away, plus they only travelled at about 20 mph. Why, even the driver gave you a friendly wave when he saw me step off the track to 'let him through'. They were innocent days.

By the Thursday of that week in 2013, I had 'done' the South Coast, by-passed Land's End, for the reason I explained earlier and made my way back home-wards along the North Coast. It was my intention to check all the little lanes off the main coast road, drive down to the bays, find a pub and spend the last couple of days exploring the coves and bays, then the nights sampling the local beers and ciders. The plan was to visit Cheddar Gorge on the Saturday, then make the last leg home on Sunday.

That Thursday morning, while driving East along the B3285, I spotted— only just- a lane leading down to a tiny village called St Matilda's Bay. It was, by a matter of yards, the first village over the border from Devon. I only learned its name as I arrived there, as there had been no obvious signs for it. It was a name I had missed on the map, and certainly had never visited on any of my previous trips. If St Agnes Bay and St Hilda's Bay were anything to go by, it had to be worth a visit. I could just about spot the sea in the distance, about two or three miles away, but I soon discovered why the first mile-post I spotted had a '7' on it. At one point I found myself heading *away* room the coast-line. I could even see it in my rear-view mirror. But then, that is the nature of driving in Cornwall. Nothing was ever quite what it seemed.

The road, if you could call it a road, was one of the narrowest I'd driven in all my forty-four years behind the wheel. Luckily, I had spotted the one-way street sign at the entrance, so at least I knew I wasn't about to come face to face with any other vehicles. I assumed, quite rightly as I later discovered, that you entered St Matilda's Bay by this route, and came out further along the B3285. Never-the-less, I still took the drive very steadily, at around 15 or 20 mph. I had learned by experience that you could never trust other road-users.

For example, if a local farmer could make it from one field to another by travelling 200 yards the wrong way along a one-way street, he would do so, rather than wasting all that time, not to mention the fuel, by going the correct way around. Add to that the tourists who, more often than not, ignored road signs, and I knew it was safer to err on the side of caution. It was worth the drive though. Once I passed through the tiny village of Harwick—it boasted a population of 192—I spied the sea once again, this time glimmering in the late morning sunlight. I never failed to feel a warm glow pass through my body each time I discovered one of these hidden treasures. One of the strangest things I have seen while driving was the speed camera between Harwick and my ultimate destination. Only a complete idiot or a boy-racer... Following a sharp 's' bend, I found myself easing down a 1 in 3 winding hill road into St Matilda's Bay. A convenient lay-by allowed me to pull over and admire the view, almost in its entirety.

At first glance, I could see 4 or 5 cottages, what appeared to be a pub, and a glorious sandy beach littered with rocks and boulders, presumably from various land-slips decades or maybe even centuries before-hand. I paused for a cigarette, one of my many vices I have to admit, and ran off a few shots from my Nikon. For a brief moment, as I sat back in the driver's seat, I thought of Ellie. She would have loved that sight. But the feeling passed. I put out my cigarette, taking care to put the end in an old packet I always carried. Nobody could ever accuse me of ruining the landscape. I drove on for a further 3 miles, passing 3 or 4 classic thatched cottages, until I spotted a left turn off the lane.

I turned the corner into a cul-de-sac and came face to face with the Mariners Arms. Hurriedly checking my mirror, I flicked on the right-hand indicator and pulled into the car park. As I did so, a glance further down the hill told me there was another pub just a few minutes' walk away. Bearing in mind the size of St

Matilda's Bay, considerably smaller than Harwick—Population 192—I had to assume I was not the first summer tourist to have spotted it. Two public houses in any village of maybe 10 or 20 residents seemed a little excessive. Either that or they were all alcoholics, which I doubted.

I took out my Cornish guide book and turned alphabetically to 'S'. It transpired that St Matilda's, known locally as Tilda's Bay, had been a small but thriving mining community until the last of the Harwick and St Matilda's mines closed some 20-odd years previously, in the mid nineteen eighties. It was now a reasonably popular visitor spot for those who had no need for bars and clubs or surfing. Reading between the lines, I suspected they were aiming at the over 50s. Tilda's offered 2 public houses, the Mariner and the Beachcomber, both of which offered bed and breakfast—'very reasonable' my guidebook said—a souvenir shop with ice cream parlour selling 'genuine' local Cornish Ice Cream, and a large free car park. I was unable to find the car park.

There were also guided tours of the former tin mines on Tuesday's and Thursday's. I parked and locked the car, deciding upon an early lunch and maybe a pint. I hadn't eaten since an early breakfast just outside Newquay five hours earlier and it was now just after mid-day. I couldn't help noticing the car park was virtually full, about thirty cars, and wondering how many were tourists and how many had made the short journey from one of the nearby towns for a quiet lunch break by the bay. One glance through the window of the saloon bar told me it would be as well to save lunch until after the rush. I didn't fancy sharing my table with a couple of suits.

Apart from anything else, I really struggle not to imitate the accent, quite badly I imagine. The only other alternative was to stroll a few yards nearer to the beach and see if The Beachcomber had anything better to offer by way of seating. It didn't. Despite its proud boast of a new conservatory, which doubled the size of the restaurant covers from thirty-two to sixty-four, it was still crammed. Plus, obviously, everyone wanted a sea view. I wandered back a few yards—I had been nearly on the beach by this time—and entered Connie's Ice Cream Parlour. I couldn't be absolutely sure if I was genuinely hungry, or if my taste buds just needed reviving after the morning's cigarettes.

Connie welcomed me with a big beaming smile, although I could not be certain she actually *was* Connie, as the name tag on her left breast read Rachel. I opted for a very basic '99'... Delicious home-made Cornish ice cream, complete with the obligatory Flake, and took it down to the beach to watch the sea roll in and the children play. All very peaceful and relaxing. To me, it was just another day, like any other day by the coast. Blue sea, sandy beach, mild breeze with a slightly cloudy sky. The lack of sunshine didn't bother the children in the slightest, totally oblivious to the chill in the air as they ran in and out of the rolling waves, squealing with delight. I was always in awe of children's resilience in the British weather. I used to look on in wonder as they casually strolled past my house in the middle of January, on their way to school, in several inches of snow, wearing shorts and tiny skirts.

They just never seem to feel the cold, do they? Back on the beach, the adults had wind-breaks erected, remained fully clothed and many had their hands wrapped around hot mugs of tea or soup. As I sat on one of the huge rocks that were scattered all over the tiny beach, I felt the wind growing stronger as the clouds became darker. As several of the adults wandered past me, heading for their cars, I heard them muttering things like, "Trust me, there's a storm on the way," and "Typical bloody British summer." I have to be honest and say the weather never bothered me one iota.

Of course, I preferred the warm sunny weather, but I was just as much at home in pouring rain or a thunder storm. During some of my earlier ventures into the West Country, you would often find me wandering along the cliffs in torrential rain, head-phones on, singing old rock tunes at the top of my voice. I glanced at my mobile phone to check the time—I never wear a watch—it was just after one o'clock and by this time my stomach was beginning to rumble. I do like my food, as anyone who knows me will confirm. I decided to take a few photos of the beach, the under-cliff, the pubs, etc. before the darkening clouds took away too much of the natural light. Then I would head back to the main road and find somewhere to stop for lunch.

Apart from anything else, it would be a lot cheaper away from the coastal pubs. Having spent many of my younger years in Brighton, I was well aware of the fact that a pint on the beach was often as much as fifty pence dearer than a short walk inland. I began to walk up the steps that led to the circular road that fringed the cliffs before vanishing inland once again. I was, at a guess, about ten seconds away from Connie's ice cream parlour when I heard the first scream. I turned around to check the source of this high-pitched wail and nearly froze in horror at the sight before me. I knew I had only seconds to live…

3

I'd known major disaster in my life several times before, even experiencing it personally, albeit on an indirect level. Way back in 1961, the tiny volcanic island of Tristan Da Cunha had to be completely evacuated following the eruption of Queen Mary's Peak. As a British colony, we gladly welcomed the islanders to our shores, and some of them were re-located to a former gypsy camp near Redhill, where I was living at the time as a ten-year-old. To be precise, I was living in an awful council flat, just on the edge of Earlswood Common.

It had only one fire, in the living room, no central heating and you could see clear daylight under the window sills of at least two rooms. The draught that whistled through there in the winter had to be felt to be believed... The island's children were gradually drafted into our schools and I became very close friends with a boy 2 years younger than myself, whose name was Erik. We remain friends to this day, despite his moving to the Midlands, where he helps to run a very successful building company with his cousin. He had the opportunity to return home some years later, but by then felt that main-land UK was now his home.

Of course, there have been many other major disasters, some very recent, notably Hurricane Katrina, which took the lives of nearly 2000 men, women and children in the state of Louisiana. Not forgetting the Taliban-controlled plane crashes into the twin towers of New York's World Trade Centre. And who could ever forget the earthquakes and tsunamis that have taken the lives of close to a quarter of a million Asians in the 21st century?

Even here, in Cornwall's gentle community, they've had more than their fair share of disaster: The Lynmouth flood of 1952 that killed 34 people and left 420 homeless, not to mention severe structural damage in the area. And then 52 years later, Boscastle suffered a similar fate, although this time, thank-fully, with no loss of life or serious injury. Strangely, both occurred on exactly the same date, 16 August.

On this day in June, the site before me sent shivers down my spine. Across the beach was a wall of water fifty or possibly sixty feet high... Heading straight for me. All these thoughts were running through my head in the first three seconds following that initial scream. Within those three seconds, I had probably run about ten or maybe twenty metres, all the while assessing my options and taking quick glances over my shoulder. Connie's was out of the question, being little more than a large garden shed. I seriously doubted I could reach The Beachcomber, and even if I could, precious milliseconds would be lost trying to open the door.

With what I estimated to be about five seconds gone, in the midst of the panic and madness that surrounded me, I spotted what might just be a life-line. To my right, just inside the gateway to the last cottage before the beach, the garden was lined with what looked like the kind of metal railings you see at the end of an alley-way to prevent cyclists and running children accidentally spilling out onto a busy road. Over the roar of the approaching tidal wave—It had, by then, covered most of the beach—I yelled, "In here!" At the top of my voice, hoping at least *some* of the people making their escape alongside me would hear and follow. The roar of the tidal wave was deafening, like nothing I had ever heard. With seconds to spare, I grabbed a little girl, possibly about nine or ten years old. She was already screaming in vain for her mother. My grabbing her only made things worse.

As I thrust her against the railing, I could only hope I'd done the right thing. As a huge fan of Cornwall and its' history, and a regular visitor to its museums, I had to trust my judgement. I remembered reading somewhere that the first giant wave of water, the one that did the most damage, was normally over in less than thirty seconds. As the deadly wave smashed against the low cliffs at the edge of the beach I pointed at the railings and yelled again to anyone who could hear me, "GRAB THAT, TAKE A DEEP BREATH AND PRAY!"

At the same time, I quickly wrapped my arms around the little girl, then around the railing, linking my fingers, well-known to be one of the strongest grips possible. I didn't pray. Whoever or whatever watched over us on this Earth had clearly let us all down over the centuries, notably during the afore-mentioned disasters... Or acts of God as they were sometimes cruelly known. The last thing I remember seeing was that little girl clasping her fingers together in copy-cat fashion, and mouthing 'mummy'. It had probably been a scream but no sound could be heard over the roar of that deadly wave.

The whole of the beach and the lane was probably screaming but it fell on deaf ears. A nuclear explosion could not have drowned the sound of the water that would inevitably take many lives, quite possibly mine. One thing I *did* learn on that dreadful day, was the truth about your life flashing before you in your dying seconds. All of my 'final' thoughts were of Ellie, my family and friends, all of whom I hoped would miss me to a certain extent and remember me fondly…

4

Try to picture yourself as some destructive giant in a fairy tale, walking the land, destroying everything you see with your enormous footsteps... Imagine accidentally stepping on a child's toy and crushing it beyond recognition... If you can do that, you will know how I felt when I opened my eyes and saw what was left of Tilda's Bay. Had I chosen to buy my ice cream an hour later, I would have been dead. Connie's parlour resembled a pile of coloured matchsticks.

Had I decided on a steak and ale pie for lunch, instead of enduring my hunger a further two hours, I might just have been one of the few people I could see still propping up the bar in The Beachcomber, clearly visible as the entire front of the pub had been ripped off in the killer wave, or whatever the tabloids would choose to call it. Had I stayed on the beach another two or three minutes, the authorities would have struggled to recognise me. That was the fate of the seventy-nine bodies found by the under-cliff later that afternoon.

As I rose to my feet sometime later—It felt like hours but in reality, was probably less than a minute—I saw total devastation. Not just Connie's and the pub, but all along the narrow line I had travelled down just a couple of hours earlier, there were broken fences, bricks, rubble, smashed glass, over-turned cars, 2 abandoned motor-cycles, the remains of The Beachcomber's restaurant extension, its tables and chairs smashed to tiny pieces—again, I assumed, the patrons had managed a last-minute escape, deep inside the bar... It was like a scene from one of those old nineteen sixties Hammer Horror zombie movies, with ten or twelve bedraggled men and women staggering about—I can only assume they were the same people running up the hill alongside me a few minutes earlier—and many more lying in the remains of St Matilda's Bay, their summer clothes ripped to shreds, dead or dying...

Possibly the strangest sight that afternoon was as I turned to face the sea, which now resembled a mill pond—so calm, you couldn't even have surfed in it—was the sandy beach. The clouds were dispersing, the golden yellow sun peeping through, almost as though the past two or three minutes had never existed. As I glanced down at the beach, I could barely believe my eyes. In all my years of visiting the West Country, I had never seen anything so beautiful... The gentle waves were trickling onto a beach of clear pale-yellow sand, completely devoid of rocks, pebbles, boulders... Or people. Thank God, or whatever, that from my angle, some ten or twenty feet above sea level, I could not see the under-cliff.

You have to remember all of this was happening in a space of just a matter of minutes, probably no more than three or four. During that period, I had looked down to see the little girl, now clinging to my leg, shaking uncontrollably, still whispering 'mummy' over and over again. Her grip was so tight it physically hurt. Next to me stood the three other people who had heeded my plea to join me on the metal railings. We were, no doubt, all in a state of shock. One of the ladies next to me was laughing. I was too. It was the laughter of relief, hysterical almost, to know we were still alive and kicking while many others had perished. The other couple were clinging to each other, tears streaming down their faces, unwilling to let go of each other, possibly in fear of another deluge that may tear them apart for the last time.

By instinct, I reached for the water-proof case that held my camera. There was no guarantee it was *that* water-proof, but it had to be worth a try. As I pulled the camera from its holder, I stroked the little girls' head, her shoulder length blonde hair clinging to her face as tightly as her arms were to my leg. I aimed the camera at the beach and clicked. It appeared to be in good working order. The picture appeared on the reverse screen. I ran off several more shots of the coast-line, before turning to the lane, snapping away at what was left of Connie's, the two pubs, the cottages beside me and the devastation that once was a quiet country lane leading to a pleasant secluded beach in this most beautiful part of our nation.

I heard the rumble before I spotted the helicopters. Two Air-Sea Rescue Sea Kings were heading our way. It took no time at all to realise no ambulances would be able to reach us by road, so the air ambulance was the only option. I never saw them land on the wide expanse of sand beneath us. I had collapsed two minutes earlier. My final thoughts, before I passed out, had been to wonder where the little girls' parents were...

5

As I opened my eyes, I saw two faces staring back at me. One I recognised, the other I did not. Gradually, a relieved smile appeared on Ellie's face, but the face of my other visitor told a different story. In the first few seconds of my awakening, the old man's facial expression did not waver. I didn't know him. I couldn't read that look. Who was he?

"Thank God you're OK," said Ellie with a beaming smile. As I said earlier, we may no longer be the most important thing in each other's lives, but we still cared. Had the situation been reversed, I would have been the first person at her bed-side also.

"How did you…?"

"Your passport of course," came her reply. It had been something we had talked about several times during out twelve years together. I had always been a lover of the sea and took great delight, even at a short ferry trip to the Isle of Wight. I'm pretty certain Ellie was not that big a fan, but she tolerated it and the trip was worth-while. The island is truly one of the beauties of the South. For our other trip to the off-shore islands, we took to the air. I had already been to Jersey once before, many years earlier, as a delivery driver. That time I had taken the ferry from Weymouth, an eight-hour boat trip that I enjoyed a lot more than most of my fellow travellers.

The English Channel can certainly have its moments. It was the roughest crossing I had known, so when it came to trying to get Ellie to 'Britain's sunniest island' I knew it would be fly or nothing. We flew. All of this leads to the reason she was at my bedside. On at least one of our West Country tours, we had spotted reasonably inexpensive flights to the Scilly Isles, notably from Plymouth, and decided to try it sometime, when we could afford it. We never did. Therefore, I seriously considered making the trip on my own that time, hence my reason for bringing my passport, which still had Ellie down as principal contact in the event of any emergency. In fact, I only changed the contact details this year when I renewed it and coincidentally had someone else worth adding...

We chatted for several minutes, as old friends, with her showing genuine relief that I seemed to be unharmed apart from several dark and quite painful bruises, and me promising to show her the photos when I came home. I discovered it was seven a.m. the next day. I had been out cold for more than twelve hours. There were vague recollections of being hoisted into the air by a rescue sling and I seemed to recall voices saying things like, "ETA fifteen minutes", but to be honest, most of the previous fifteen hours or so were a total blur.

Satisfied that I wasn't about to depart this Earth and leave her all my worldly possessions—I really must update my Will sometime—she popped out to grab a cup of coffee and, no doubt, a sneaky cigarette or two, leaving me with the old man. He certainly wasn't a doctor, and he didn't look like a vicar or priest, though a dog-collar could possibly have been buried beneath the woollen scarf that covered his neck.

"I wanted to thank you, Mr Evans, for saving our little Minnie," were his opening words, as he reached across and clasped my right hand in both of his. They felt cold to the touch, whereas mine were very warm. I managed a smile as I guessed he was probably talking about the little blonde girl who had clung so tightly to me throughout the previous days' ordeal.

My smile was more from the satisfaction that something good had come out of that day, rather than for his thanks, welcome as they were. It transpired she was staying at her grandparent's house for the half-term holidays. The house had been at the far end of a row of cottages, the opposite end of the village from where I had been half-drowned. It was undamaged and both grandparents were fine, though still very shaken. The old man did not look as happy as he should have been at his grand-daughter's safety... And then I recalled her whimpering cries of 'mummy'...

At that time, I was completely unaware of the full horror of the events of the day before. Considering those of us in the hospital were still suspected of being in shock, or being treated for it, it was thought unwise for any of the survivors to see the morning's newspapers. Had we read them, we would have read countless stories, and seen endless photographs of the utter devastation of St Matilda's Bay. We would have seen what was left of the two pubs—The Beachcomber would later that year be miraculously re-opened—the remains of

Connie's 'matchstick' parlour, the broken windows and cracked stone-work of the four cottages closest to the sea, the rubble-strewn county lane I had driven down with such pleasure and anticipation the day before... And worst of all, the under-cliff...

Where there had once been a row of brightly painted beach huts, looking out over the part-sand and part-rock beach, covered in wind-breaks, towels, buckets and spades, parents, children, lovers... There was now just a pile of rocks, pebbles, even the larger boulders that had rested sporadically on the beach for centuries, broken huts like coloured drift-wood... And seventy-nine dead bodies... Fifty-two adults and twenty-seven children, aged between a few months and thirteen years old. The only child to survive that nightmare had been this old man's little grand-daughter, Minnie. It would be a day that would haunt the poor little mite for the rest of her life... But at least she lived through it, which was more than could be said for so many others.... And then an even greater fear struck me, sending shivers down my spine...

"Her parents...?" I asked, tentatively.

Minnie's father had left them within weeks of her birth, back in August 2001—she was now nearly twelve years old—unable to stand the pressure of father-hood. They had never married. Minnie's grand-parents had never even met the man, my visitor explained. Little had been heard from him since that day, but monthly child support cheques had never failed to arrive, and he always remembered Minnie's birthday and Christmas. No phone calls though, not a single one. So was that just an absent father doing his duty, or was there still some love buried deep in his heart for a daughter he would be unlikely to recognise if he passed her in the street. Not all bad then, thought I. He would have to be told, of course, but how would he take it? While I admit to never having been the greatest father that ever lived, and an even worse husband, I always loved my boys and couldn't imagine going all those years with little or no contact. And the child's mother?

I can't explain why, but I suddenly thought of the only 'named' person I had spoken to in the bay... Connie, or Rachel maybe... This was something I had never before experienced, the violent death of someone you actually knew, if only for a matter of seconds...

It was at that moment the old man, who I would come to know as Tom, broke down. His hands let go of mine, went to his face and he began uncontrollable sobbing as his face dropped to the bed-clothes. I knew at that moment, that Minnie's mother—Maria, I later learned was her name—had been on the beach. Possibly Minnie had been on her way to Connie's for an ice cream, or maybe to her mother's car to retrieve God-knows-what... Maybe a sun-hat, or her swimming costume, another towel... Who knew? The only thing I knew for certain was that at that precise moment, whatever was left of Minnie's mother was now lying alongside seventy-eight other bodies in a nearby mortuary. I prayed to whoever, or whatever, that Minnie never got to see the photographs in the morning papers.

The next few days, weeks and months, possibly years, were going to be bad enough for her already without having to witness a photographic recording of the horror that her mother had known in those few brief seconds the day before. I rested my hand on the back of Tom's head and cried with him, hoping Maria's death had been quick...

Following a hearty breakfast—That's hearty as in cold fried egg, burnt bacon, congealed baked beans and a cup of brown liquid?—I resumed my conversation with Tom, who apparently had just enjoyed exactly the same thing in the café five minutes from the hospital. When I say 'exactly', I have to admit from the old man's description to a few subtle differences. I'm sure you can work those out for yourselves. Tom had also spent another few minutes with Minnie who, as yet, had barely spoken. I could only imagine how much stronger the shock factor would be for one of such tender years.

At least for someone as long in the tooth as myself, I'd seen it all before. Not first-hand maybe, but certainly in some of the scariest news reports known to man. By this time, I was reasonably certain I was OK, and going to *be* OK, although the hospital insisted I, and the other survivors, remained under observation for a further two days in case of delayed concussion, or shock. I strongly suspected many of us would never fully recover from the horror of the day before. Tom asked if I was well enough to come along to the children's ward and say 'hi' to his grand-daughter. I certainly *felt* well enough, but figured I ought to check with the nurse first. He offered to go and find someone for me.

While he was gone, I couldn't stop thinking about the name, Minnie. It was hardly a 21st century name for a girl. In fact, I'd only ever known two Minnie's in my life-time, and one of them was a mouse! The other, strangely enough, was my maternal grand-mother, the lady who, along with her cousin, my Great Auntie May in Brighton had spent most of the nineteen-fifties helping my mother to raise yours truly. Quite a coincidence. I thought, especially considering *my* Minnie's love of the 'unknown'. Within my circle of friends and family it's a well-known fact that my grand-mother had an uncanny knack of predicting the future, but in a kind of off-the-wall way. No crystal balls or tea leaves for her.

For example, when she woke up on the morning of 22 November 1963, the first thing she said was, "Such a shame about Mr Kennedy getting shot. I always thought he was *such* a nice man…" And that was seven hours before the good people of Dallas even woke up. Then almost three years later, she was tucking into breakfast, alongside my mother and I, when she suddenly started chuckling, then said, "I'm so pleased for that chappie from West Ham scoring all those goals. I always *did* like him…" And we all know what happened later *that* day.

Sadly, she also managed to break all the cardinal rules of clairvoyance by telling me I would live to the ripe old age of eighty-four. Now that's fine by me… at the moment. It gives me a feeling of something approaching invincibility. But I'm not too sure how I'll feel about it in twenty thirty-five, going to bed each night, wondering if I'm going to wake up the following morning…

With the kind permission of my nurse, at ten-thirty that morning, I rose from my bed and put on the most revolting dressing gown it had been my dubious pleasure to set eyes upon—but at least it covered the even more hideous pyjamas—and follow my new friend Tom to the children's ward. The nurse tried to convince me I should go in a wheel-chair but I managed to talk her out of that one, promising to stay close to the wall in case I should feel unsteady on the way. I didn't… As soon as I saw Minnie, I could tell she was suffering. It could only be the shock of coming so close to her death under that wall of freezing cold sea water, as she had not yet been told of her mother's death.

I wondered if she had asked for her 'mummy' yet, as she had done so many times while clinging on to me and the railings. Apparently, she had hardly spoken since waking this morning, so I was unsure what, if anything she had said, or knew, or thought she knew. According to her grand-father, all she had mentioned was ice cream and the nice man. He had no idea who the nice man could have been, possibly me, but there again it could just have easily been the man who rented her mother a deck-chair that morning, it was impossible to say.

In some kind of delirium in the night, she had also asked for 'daddy'. He had not, as yet, been traced, although a plea had gone out in all that morning's newspapers, "Martin Davies, your daughter Minnie is safe and well but, etc…"

As I approached her bed, I couldn't help but notice how pale she looked. Extremely pretty—her blonde hair had been washed and brushed that very morning—but so pale, so very pale, almost white. In the short time I had seen her 'yesterday', for less than two minutes, I was not aware of her looking this ghostly white, it surely had to be the shock. Most children, especially those that spend time at the beach, have a natural colour to them. This delicate little girl's was non-existent. She looked up and saw me walking towards her and, for the first time that morning, according to her grandfather, a smile beamed across her little face.

At the same time, she noticeably gained colour to her cheeks. It all happened so quickly, almost as quick as that horror wave, that before I knew what was going on, she had leapt from the bed, run towards me and jumped into my arms. Luckily, I *did* have the strength my nurse was unsure of, or I would have toppled over! Her grip around my neck was even tighter than it had been the day before, if that were possible. For the second time that morning I saw a tear starting to form in Tom's eye, but he controlled it. Children are often scared of crying 'grown-ups', they don't always understand that adults sometimes cry because they are happy.

Tom was clearly overjoyed to see his little Minnie smiling again, albeit thanks to a relative stranger. I held her closely, though not quite as tightly, to comfort her and show her that whatever else was going wrong in this big bad world, she was safe with me. It felt strange to me. In many ways I could understand her amazing reaction to seeing me, but I was even more amazed to find how much comfort *I* took from that hug, to know that someone like me, who was never that fond of children—I could never claim to be the world's greatest dad—could mean so much to this one little girl I really didn't know at all. Her first words to me sent a cold chill down my spine…

"Are you going to be my new daddy?"

That one hit me like a thunder-bolt! Admittedly, it wasn't the first time I'd been asked that question, but on the previous occasions it had always come from a child whose mother I had been dating for maybe a month or two. Not guilty to the best of my knowledge… It is a perfectly natural thing for a child to ask, especially one who had been without a 'daddy' for several months or even years. I would always answer that it depended how well his or her mother and I progressed. To date, it never did. That was one reason I was always careful to give the 'mummy and I are just good friends at the moment, but you never know' answer.

But with Minnie, it was a completely different kettle of fish. She had only cards and presents to show there was a father around, somewhere… And, as yet, she didn't know her mother was dead. Had she even asked of her mother yet? Surely, she must have. I could only assume the medical staff had not thought it appropriate to tell her just yet. I held her close once again, stroking her back and replied, "Oh I'm much too old to be a daddy, but I'm a very good friend of your granddad's—I glanced over to see him smile and nod in agreement—so I'm sure you'll see lots of me, Minnie."

I believe it was at that moment I began to plan my future…

6

Apart from a brief spell in the mid-noughties when I was redundant for just over a year, I'd been at Brannigan Helicopters for something like thirty-eight years, starting in the summer that saw Bohemian Rhapsody at number one for about six months. That may be a slight exaggeration but it certainly seemed like it. Thanks to my mother's sound advice, I entered the company pension scheme after the first year, ensuring a fairly comfortable retirement in later life... As in about now. In addition, the redundancy settlement after thirty years was not inconsiderable, so to put it bluntly, I was never going to be a Broke Bloke. Even when they welcomed me back into the fold, it was on an even higher salary than before, plus overtime and performance bonuses, so all in all, everything in the financial garden was pretty rosy thank you very much.

About a year prior to the incident at St Matilda's Bay, my director came to see me asking if I was willing to stay on after the recognised company retirement age of sixty-two. As I had recently acquired single status again, and having absolutely no interest what-so-ever in gardening, fishing or golf, I had no hesitation in saying 'yes' to a further three years. The money was good, which meant several more holidays in the sun, and I'm also one of the few people outside the sports and entertainment world who actually enjoys his work.

Plus, if I'm completely honest, anything is better than a lifetime of watching re-runs of Heartbeat and The Royal on day-time television. I wasn't even keen on them the first time around so why would I? Combining the look on Tom's face and the feeling of Minnie's heart pounding against my chest was making me seriously re-consider...

I cannot in all honesty say I hadn't considered my future in recent years. Prior to my separation from Ellie, we had considered several options. Both of us had fallen in love with Cyprus and seriously thought about buying a small place on that sunshine island to see out our days. Cornwall, obviously was another possibility. I somehow could not see me ending my days in Smallfield... Not

31

that there's anything wrong with the village, but I always had this yearning for the sea. Having spent much of my childhood in Brighton, I loved the fact that the ocean was never more than a few minutes away on foot. I might even get myself a dog...

Life-changing decisions were made over the following three days. It was now Friday and I was due back in the office the following Tuesday. I knew I had to move fast. I was afraid if I didn't grab this opportunity right there and then, I probably never would. Minnie had eventually fallen asleep on my shoulder and to be honest, she felt like a dead weight, so I rested her carefully back down on her hospital bed and asked Tom to join me outside—I was in desperate need of a cigarette—making quite sure the nurse was aware that should Minnie wake up, she should let the little girl know we were only a few minutes away. I never wanted that pretty little girl to be scared of anything ever again.

One thing I *wasn't* enjoying was all the 'hero' garbage the tabloids were pushing out. Not only was my name being splashed all over the front pages, but they had also located an unbelievably bad photo of yours truly. It had been taken after a drunken night somewhere in Crawley. God only knows where they got it, but in this day and age of social networking, there are probably dozens of them out there. This particular one looked as though I was on drugs! Following one of the scariest nights of my life way back in the bad old days which I prefer not to dwell on, I vowed never to touch anything stronger than the odd spliff, and I've kept to it.

I'm not a lover of publicity, however good it may be, I just do not like being the centre of attention. Apart from anything else, knowing how the British love putting people on pedestals, only to knock them off of them, I couldn't wonder how long before the 'Bad Boy Comes Good' exclusive hit the news-stands. It wouldn't take much for some bright spark, trying to make his way in the gutter press, to discover my former 'life of crime'. In truth, it was one charge of driving on bald tyres—guilty as charged—and a spot of vandalism—not guilty, completely accidental—both more than forty years earlier when I was just an impressionable teenager.

As for the press, I know they have a job to do and for the most part, do it pretty well in my opinion, although some aspects of it leave much to be desired. I've never quite understood how in a country where a person is presumed innocent until proven otherwise, how is it the press are allowed to name a person—notably the rich and famous—before they even reach a court of law? It's a well-known fact that mud sticks. Once you have a charge like assault or rape hanging over you, your life can never quite be the same as it had been before. There will always be someone out there thinking: No smoke without fire!

Having enjoyed not one, but two cigarettes with Tom, and promising to pop back in to visit Minnie later in the day, I headed back to my hospital bed. I needed some peace and quiet—some 'me' time—to formulate my plan of action. Plus, nurse was wagging a finger at me, reminding me I was supposed to be resting, not 'gallivanting around the hospital grounds up to all sorts'… whatever that meant. I was seriously considering fulfilling a life-long dream and making the move to what I had always felt was my spiritual home… Cornwall. How hard could it be?

There were four important points I needed to explore thoroughly before making any major decisions:

- Would I be happy living in the tranquillity that was St Matilda's Bay? That one was simple—A resounding yes!
- How would I feel about no more presenting karaoke shows, something I'd enjoyed doing for eighteen years? Yes, I would miss it, but weighing up the pros and cons, Tilda's was ahead… Just.
- Could I continue my employment with Brannigan Helicopters? The simple answer to that was 'yes', as long as my management were happy with me being about nine hundred miles from our Head Office. As I was already about seven hundred miles away from it, and only needing a laptop and Blackberry to carry out my daily tasks, I was reasonably sure I could overcome that hazard.
- How would I feel about being 250 miles from all my friends and family? That was the tough one, the one that would keep me awake that night until—the last time I looked at the clock—nearly four in the morning.

I believe it was Confucius who said, "Man who go to sleep with problem, wake up with solution." I always thought that had the makings of a very good dirty joke but I'm sure that wasn't what the wise old man meant. However, I *did* wake up with a clear head and the absolute certainty of my future.

I hadn't had the chance to speak to Minnie again the previous evening, despite my efforts to get in to see her. Apparently, Tom had finally got up the courage to give her the bad news about her mother—obviously not the full horror—and the poor love had gone into hysterics. The nurse told me she was inconsolable and didn't even want to see her grandfather, let alone me or anyone else. At around seven o'clock, for the second night running, she had been given a mild sedative and cried herself to sleep half an hour later. You couldn't help but wonder just how much one so young could take.

By the time I entered the ward she was well away in a world where her mother, possibly even her father was with her, caring for her, holding her, loving her, driving her to school, playing with her in the garden, taking her on holiday... but I could still see the salty tear stains on her little cheeks. I leaned down and gently kissed the one nearest to me. "Good-night pretty girl," I softly whispered. Her eye-lids flickered but remained closed. I went back to my own ward.

On the way, I stopped at the public pay-phone to check Ellie had arrived home safely and give her an update. I made no mention of my thoughts and possible plans for the future. There would be plenty of time for that later. In any case, no decisions had yet been made, so no point stirring up a hornet's nest until I was one hundred per cent sure of my intentions. As I approached the bed, it occurred to me to check what was left of my possessions. I hadn't even *thought* about those until that very moment. Did I still have my camera? My phone? My wallet? And what about my car? Had it survived? Was it floating out into the Atlantic on its way to Dublin, or New York, or...? I opened the locker door next to my bed. Sure enough, my phone was in there, good start. Picked it up, turned it on... Nothing. Next, my wallet. All present and correct.

Cards OK, of course, but the notes looked like they'd been through the washing machine and the faded photo of Ellie that I still carried was beyond repair. I decided now was as good a time as any to move on. The photograph would not be replaced. I picked up the water-proof case that held my precious Nikon camera. Even though I was unsure if I would ever want to see those photographs, re-live the nightmare... I had to know. I slid the on/off switch across and hey presto, the little red light flashed and my beloved camera bleeped its own personal 'hello' to its owner. Still unsure, I pressed the button for 'slide show'. It immediately displayed a shot, taken several days earlier at the famous Cornish donkey sanctuary in the Tamar Valley. I looked no further.

When the time was right, I would go through them all, but that day may have been weeks away yet... I certainly wasn't ready to run through horrific photos of the mass destruction of Connie's, the pubs, the beach, the broken glass and rubble everywhere... I may never be ready to re-live that horror... Sure I did the right thing firing off those shots, but no, the timing wasn't yet right. I took one shot of the ward, then switched to video mode and did a panorama sweep, just to make sure everything was still in working order, then tucked it back in its case again.

Just the car then, I thought to myself, making a mental note to check the next day. I hoped fate hadn't dealt me aces and eights yet again, the way it had in nineteen eighty-seven, the year of the 'hurricane' that wasn't. The Clio iMusic was my first new car since the Yugo I bought in September that year. Yes... I know! But it was new, and it was mine OK? Plus, it was good enough for Bruce Willis in one of the Die Hard series. That made it good enough for me... One month later, my first ever brand-new car was buried under a tree! I honestly think if I'd gone back to St Matilda's Bay and found my Clio under a tree, I would have cried for the second time in two days, something I hadn't done since I went to the cinema to see Jon Voight in The Champ.

I cried that night. But it didn't stop me going back again the next night and watching it again. And crying again. I toyed with the idea of calling the local police to check on the state of my car, but decided they may well have more important things to be dealing with at that particular time. Instead, I walked along the corridor, found a vending machine selling a brown liquid that actually resembled coffee, even though it tasted nothing like it, took it outside, found a free bench and smoked two more cigarettes. I know they're almost certainly bad for me, but all the time my doctor tells me I'm in good health, I see no point giving up one of life's pleasures...

Contrary to popular opinion, I take my health very seriously. As a condition of my return to Brannigan's, I was given private health cover, which meant what amounted to an annual M.O.T. on my body. Consequently, ever year around my birthday in February, I go to the Gatwick Park hospital and have every inch of me pinched and probed... Blood tests are done and as an asthmatic, stringent breath tests also. As a smoker my doctor despairs of my habit, especially when he has to admit my lungs are in a better condition than many people half my age, even the non-smokers. I'm afraid until the day comes when she tells me curries, pizzas, lager, wine and cigarettes (or any one of the

35

above) are showing genuine signs of wear and tear on my body, I shall continue to enjoy life's little special moments… I counteract all my badness, with regular exercise, walking three to five miles on work days, and ten or twelve during my days off. It seems to be working. I strongly suspect that one day, all this will come crashing down around me, but for now…

The following two weeks are pretty much a blur in my memory. I have vague recollections of what I did, where I went, who I spoke to, etc., but little more than that I'm afraid. Maybe it was the delayed shock the hospital doctor had warned me of… Or it could have been the excitement of how I anticipated my life panning out over the future weeks, months and years. On at least three occasions, I thought I saw Kathy at the end of my bed, but each time I blinked my eyes or came to my senses, I realised it was an illusion, or maybe just a combination of shock and drugs. The main thing I can assure you of is that the weeks following my discharge from hospital were all good.

Most importantly, Minnie had made a full recovery—although obviously missing her mother—and we had become firm friends. This was made a whole lot easier by Tom's kindness in letting me stay in his spare room for some considerable time. While realising I was never going to be the new 'daddy' she had hoped for, she gladly accepted me as a second grandfather, in lieu of her father's father, who I learned she had also never met. Well, every little girl deserves two grand-fathers, correct? And true to form, despite every attempt by her *real* grandparents and the police, the absent father never materialised.

To this day, he still hasn't, but it no longer bothers Minnie. She has Tom and I to take care of her, plus Tom's wife Alice, although virtually house-bound with arthritis, does what she can. It transpires she has some wonderful stories from her childhood days and Minnie is enthralled to hear them whenever possible. You may have gathered by the present tense in that last sentence that yes, I *did* remain in St Matilda's Bay after the flood. In fact, it could not have turned out better. Talk about every cloud, etc. But there is more, much more to my story than 'happy ever after'…

Firstly, I should point out that my Clio was in perfect condition protected, no doubt by the size of the Mariners. That in itself was a blessing, considering all the running about I had to endure at the time. Not only did Minnie need regular check-ups for the first four weeks—Tom had his own car of course, but was reluctant to leave Alice for any length of time—but I found myself driving into Hobart town centre two or three times a week, visiting banks and estate agents. I had learned the cottage closest to the beach had been put up for sale a few weeks before the flood. Had I had more than ten seconds to spare as I guided the six of us to those railings, I may have noticed the 'FOR SALE' sign in the garden.

By the time I returned to the area, three days later, it was nowhere to be seen. I only found out by chance, when one of the other neighbours spotted me walking past and pointed it out. Sadly, it was not just the sign that was missing. The garage, half of the kitchen, the corner of the spare room upstairs and a large chunk of the front room had also vanished. Someone... I assume the authorities or the estate agent, had boarded it up and covered the damage with tarpaulin, but the devastation was still clear to see. However, this worked in my favour. Due to the damage, and the fact that old Mr Taylor had cancelled his property insurance when he moved into his 'granny' flat in his daughter's back garden in Leeds, the asking price had dipped drastically. While I felt sorry for his loss, there was nothing I could do to change that.

Indeed, once we agreed a price, I even added a bonus for him by way of compensation. All of this meant that, given the sale of my home in Surrey, plus my pension fund, ISA's and savings, I could afford to move, re-build Windy Cottage—I assure you it was named after the weather and not, as several of my friends suggested, because they saw me coming!—and still have a few bob in my savings account for emergencies. In addition, Brannigan's had agreed to keep me on for the next three years, working from Tilda's, so I had a regular salary top-up to keep things ticking over. That just left Ellie, Stevie J and the family to pacify...

Ellie and Stevie, my karaoke partners, though sad to see me go, allegedly, wished me the best of luck and promised to visit whenever possible. I completed three more shows with them, all emotionally charged from my point of view, saying endless 'goodbyes' to people I would quite possibly never see again. I had made many friends over the eighteen years of presenting karaoke shows, but as in any other working environment, many of those were more acquaintances than true friends... The family were even *more* agreeable! In truth, I think they probably saw it as a possible cheap holiday destination from time to time, and I was happy with that. I saw little enough of them as it was, so they would be more than welcome.

When I mentioned Minnie to my little grand-daughter, Cheryl, she quickly found a new 'best friend', asking me for Minnie's mobile number and Skype (whatever that was). I managed to put her off for a few weeks but eventually gave in. The two of them were so keen on the idea that Cheryl's mother, Tom and I had to give in. We considered it only fair. They were both pre-teens, my grand-daughter being the older by three months, plus Minnie was the only young girl living in St Matilda's Bay so we all agreed it would be good for both of them. Cheryl of course wanted to come down immediately so I had to explain, without the full horror story, that I would have nowhere for her to stay for a few months, but promised as soon as I had a spare room, she would be the first person invited to my new home. This, along with the swapping of the afore-mentioned phone numbers (and Skype?) seemed to pacify the little ladies. For now...

I then had the job of saying goodbye to my neighbours in Smallfield. That was almost as hard as the karaoke people. Some of the residents of Laburnum Court I had known since I moved there, twenty-five years earlier. They were good enough to throw a farewell party for me and I felt the tear ducts welling up once more. The same has to be said for my former local pub, The Plough and Furrow. Though never a regular drinker, I was in there most Wednesdays for Gary's pub quiz, plus karma had put on a few shows there also, so it was still quite a sad moment as I walked away from there for the last time. If nothing else, I would miss their delicious Cumberland sausage and mash in onion gravy. I hoped the menu in either The Beachcomber or the Mariners would come close...

7

And so to work…

I had kept in touch with my child-hood friend Erik from Tristan Da Cunha down the years. I even had his people do my loft conversion back in the nineteen-eighties. I knew he hired no-one but the best, so I made the call. Being of a similar age, but having his own business, I guessed one of two things. Either he would be nearing his own retirement, or he would hang on to the bitter end like me. I took a chance and it paid off. Erik had indeed been thinking about packing it in. And having heard of my plight, cheerfully offered to spend the next few months helping an old friend to re-build his dream home. He even offered to bring a couple of trusted colleagues down with him to speed things up.

All of this, once he supplied his quote, saved me in the region of ten thousand pounds, not to mention considerable time and the anxiousness of having strangers in and out of my precious new property for the next year or so. As it turned out, the weather was particularly good to St Matilda's Bay that autumn and the following winter and the entire job was completed shortly before Easter the next year. Erik's team were magnificent. I have to say every single one of them was reliable, hard-working and significantly, Eastern European. Erik and I had agreed terms for all four to stay in the Mariners. It was out of season so we had a good deal on that score. In all, the additional work-force had stayed in Tilda's for a total of four months.

Although the cottage was structurally sound, there had been an awful amount of cosmetic work to be done. Erik's team each seemed to be proficient in plumbing, roofing, electrics, plastering and of course the basics… Painting and decorating. Erik himself stayed on with me through the winter to add the finishing touches. I wanted it much as it had been in Steve Taylor's day, in keeping with the village tradition, but with a few added extras, experienced only by those with permission to enter. Our progress was hindered slightly by the weather in January and February, not to mention my giving Erik the guided tour of my new home land.

It was his first ever trip to Cornwall and he wanted him to sample it all first hand. Consequently, the final touches took two or three months rather than the estimated two or three weeks. I wasn't complaining though. It was always a pleasure showing friends around the area, and great to have Erik's company...

By that time—soon after Christmas—I had moved into Windy Cottage, had Minnie sleep over a few times to give Tom and Alice a break, been back up to Crawley to present a very tearful final karaoke show in the pub where it all started for me, The Downsman—all had been invited down any time and most had said they would—and even arranged for Cheryl to come and stay for a few days during the February half-term break. As expected, she and Minnie got on like the proverbial house on fire, spending most of the days on the beach, despite near freezing temperatures, and the evenings enjoying supper in front of the first log fire my little 'Smiler' had ever seen. This had been one of the extras I mentioned.

I had always wanted an open fire but the former owner had chosen to block the fireplace. No doubt it had become too much to cope with at his age. I'd even resumed my 'friendship' with Kathy, who had been amazed to find I was now living just a few miles away from her. She jokingly accused me of stalking her. Our conversations had been so few over the past months that the poor girl was starting to think I was losing interest. Not possible! Kathy had been the best thing that happened to me for some considerable time and, even though much of what had kept us apart had been beyond my control, I still felt guilty, promising to make it up to her one day soon...

I managed to talk Erik into staying for the Easter holidays so that I could organise a grand re-opening of the cottage, now completely restored to its' former glory with re-claimed bricks and timber. Thanks to Colin, the landlord of the Mariners kind offer to use his car park, I decided a garage was no longer a priority. I still had the garden to sort out but I had plenty of time on my hands for that little project, sticking to my Brannigan's shift of 'one week on / one week off'. Despite my earlier comments, I was actually looking forward to working on the garden, which surprised many people, myself included, who were convinced it would be one large patio by the summer. Who knows? Maybe I'll take up golf and fishing as well...

No, seriously, that was never going to happen! A wise man once told me that cricket was the only sensible ball game. If you played golf, you had to hit a ball, walk a few yards and hit it again ad infinitum. If you played football, you kicked the ball and sooner or later you would get it back and have to do it all over again. The same could be said for hockey and rugby. But in cricket, when you hit the ball, some other mug has to fetch it!

I had got to know several more of my neighbours by then and planned to invite them all to the grand re-opening of Windy Cottage. My immediate 'next doors' were a couple in their late forties or early fifties, the Bonnell's, Sarah and Adam, who had moved down to Tilda's when their children left home. He was something in finance, working from home most of the time, with occasional trips to London, while she played house and did endless work with the local Women's Institute and various charitable organisations. They seemed like a lovely couple, if a little above my class... Middle as opposed to my 'working'... The one thing that surprised both Tom and myself—it came up several times during late night whisky-sampling sessions—was that, to the best of our knowledge, neither of their children had ever visited.

There again, I have to say, Adam gave me some excellent advice in the early days of the planned purchase of my new home so who am I to judge or criticise. As I've said on many occasions, I had hardly been the best father in the world... It was strange how many of the locals simply accepted me, a former council flat kid, into their lives. Maybe the vast publicity my 'hero' stunt had generated had something to do with it. Right up until the completion of Windy Cottage, the local newspaper had run monthly updates, including dozens of photographs, of our progress.

I can't say I was over-joyed at this but as I've said before, they have a job to do and I couldn't deny I was news. Next to the Bonnell's, was a young recluse called Debbie aged, at a guess, around thirty. Little was known about her other than the fact she had moved down from London 'a few years ago' and kept herself to herself and was rarely seen in the village. As far as Tom was aware, she never visited either of the pubs and had all her groceries delivered by one of those 'You Shop—We Drop' vans. Every so often she would be spotted driving off to who-knows-where in her almost new Fiat 500, the recently re-vamped model that apparently drives under water, according to the advertisement campaign on television. If seen she would always smile and wave. Most of us guessed she was mending a broken heart or something of that ilk. Having said that, Debbie was very kind to me when I first started on the re-build.

Many a time we ran out of coffee or sugar and she always lent me some with a cheery smile... At this time, the residents of St Matilda's Bay had no shopping facilities at all. Before its virtual demolishment by the tidal wave, in addition to the usual seaside souvenirs, postcards and ice creams, Connie's had sold the odd essential, but for now we had to drive into Harwick for even the simplest of things like bread or milk. When you took into account the lane's one-way system, that was something like a twelve-mile journey to 'shop local'... One good thing though, I'd heard Rachel—which *was* her real name—had somehow managed to escape the flood through the back door of the shop and come out of it with little more than cuts and bruises, much like myself...

On the other side of Debbie lived a former teacher, Barry Marlow. Very chatty, always working in his garden, which I had to admit was magnificent. Now I know absolutely nothing at all about flowers but the colours all complimented each other and it was clearly head and shoulders above the others in Tilda's, and that was saying something. If they ever held a 'Prettiest Village' competition in Cornwall, our little bay would win hands down. And not just for the gardens either. From the two thatched cottages along the lane towards Harwick to the many brightly coloured doors and window frames in the bay itself, it was, and still is what can only be described as picture postcard. From the first day I saw Barry's garden, I knew I had a challenge on my hands if I was to get even *close* to it.

Oh... He was also my one and only drinking buddy in the re-opened Mariners and a mine of (mostly) useless information. When I say drinking buddy, I'm not suggesting Barry was an alcoholic or even close to it. Truth be told, he probably only went to the pub once or twice a week, but if we met there, he would always be willing to join me for a chat. I suppose, considering his former life as a primary school teacher, his head was bound to be full of all kinds of random, though sometimes useful information. Apart from the beer, we had one other thing in common, both being supporters of Manchester United.

Before everybody starts with the usual choruses of "typical southerner" and "glory hunter" I would just like to say, in my defence, that on my first trip to see them, an eighth birthday present from my mother, they lost 3-1 to Chelsea. I had no idea at the time about Munich, or the fact they were that close to being the first English club to win the European Cup... Having watched them lose, I felt sorry for them, and it just stuck with me, from that day to this. Barry, although quite a few years younger than me—I venture to offer mid-fifties as my estimate—and I spent many a happy evening at the bar discussing the heroes of our respective years following their progress and occasional down-fall.

Names such as Best, Law, Pearson, Coppell, Hughes, etc. easily sprang to mind, as did the blatantly obvious Cantona and Ronaldo... But it was the unsung legends that we talked about the most: The likes of Billy Foulkes, Carlo Sartori, Martin Buchan and my own personal favourite, Brian McClair to name but a few. The one thing neither of us touched upon was our past. I don't believe my early life as a milkman or off licence manager ever came up, and as far as I can recall, Barry never once spoke of his teaching career. Robin van Persie's name cropped up on more than one occasion though...

It would be fair to say that, despite the fact we were all on smiling and waving terms, I had very little to do with the other residents of the lane leading out of St Matilda's Bay. I tended to stick to those in the immediately vicinity, our own little cul-de-sac of five cottages, two pubs and Connie's. We did sometimes bump into each other on the beach, or in the pub, but it was rarely more than a quick 'hello' and, from their side, to check how Windy Cottage was coming along. It mattered not to me. I was never that social a person, happier in the company of my close friends, most of whom I hoped would be descending on me for the afore-mentioned house-warming party.

The plan was to add 'Bring your own tent' to the invitations. The back garden, by then cleared of its' rubble and broken fences, was large enough to hold seven or eight family sized tents, and in the event of rain, or anyone not *owning* a tent, Tom and Alice had kindly offered their spare room to anyone who cared to bring a sleeping bag. Sarah and Adam had also offered garden space for half a dozen people—preferably not children and hopefully not in the habit of throwing up after a good party.

Not trusting the British weather for one moment, I happily accepted their kind offers. Barry seemed a little reluctant, but eventually said he didn't mind one or two camping in his garden if we ran out of space. At the time of making my decision to throw a party, I hadn't set eyes on Debbie for several weeks, which was not unusual. In any event, even though I planned to invite her, something told me she would probably politely refuse. I didn't even consider asking her about spare rooms or camping... And then there was Colin of course. Colin Hughes, whose name was hanging over the front door of the Mariners

Arms, proudly claiming him to be the licensee. Now there *is* a character! It would be fair to say that he is something of an enigma.

A Surrey man like myself, he had moved to Cornwall after the collapse of his marriage, followed within weeks by a monetary wind-fall due to the death of an aged aunt in Canada, whom he had never even heard of, let alone met. During one particularly late-night chat at the bar, he revealed it had always been his dream to own his own public house, so when the opportunity arose, back in 1998, he jumped at it. But what can I say about him? He's one of the loveliest guys you could wish to meet, but like the rest of us, he has his good points and his bad points. He's the perfect host, always cheerful and chatty to the locals and holiday-makers alike. But at the same time, he can be really stubborn. He's always right, even when you prove him wrong. Black could often be white in Colin's world.

And on top of that, he's probably the most sexist man I've ever met. Colin was born about fifty years too late. Had he been married in the nineteen-fifties or sixties, he would have been in his element, out at work Monday to Friday, faithful hard-working 'wifey' staying at home washing and ironing, cooking and cleaning, sending him off to work with his bread and dripping. Consequently, now in his late fifties, Colin had never re-married. But for all that, he runs the best village pub in the area, albeit the only village pub in the area for most of the year. The Beachcomber only opens in the summer season, St Matilda's being too small to sustain two public houses, and the only other one, the Station Hotel in Harwick, closed, along with most of the local shops, soon after the tin mines suffered a similar fate. I was intrigued by the name of the Harwick pub though.

Colin explained that St Matilda's Bay used to have its own station too, though it was a three-quarter mile trek to get there. It was one of several branch lines that snaked their way across the Cornish countryside until Dr Beeching's axe fell fifty years earlier. In fact, the St Ives branch I mentioned earlier is one of the few to survive, but then the difference between St Ives and St Matilda's is between fifteen hundred and two thousand. That's the number of visitors St Ives can house in any given week during the summer season, with its many Bed & Breakfast houses, several pubs and at least four nearby caravan parks that I'm aware of. Tilda's has no B&B's and room for just ten overnighters in Colin's pub…

Which is where I came in. Having looked after my workmen the previous winter, Colin very kindly offered to accommodate ten of my friends for the upcoming Easter get-together if needs be, free of charge if he had no paying customers. As I said, he's a good lad. I was fairly sure if any of the Redhill and Crawley crowd *did* turn up, they would more than pay their way in bar takings… Everything was now in place. I had been offered beds for about twenty people, plus garden space, for tents, which would 'house' a further twenty or thirty if necessary. As I was only expecting in the region of thirty to forty, I envisaged no problems, especially if the current fine weather held…

The most extra-ordinary thing about Colin—and I only discovered this after a long conversation regarding the pros and cons of living in the rural countryside of Surrey—is that he was born and raised about one mile from my own birth-place, either side of Earlswood Common on the outskirts of Redhill. We never met. Quite remarkable, as someone once said… We even shared one naughty fact from our past. Earlswood had its own eighteen-hole golf course on the common.

Both of us used to wait in the bushes and ferns of the common for 'lost' golf balls. Most golfers could not be bothered to search for lost balls for more than a few minutes, so the likes of Colin and I would collect them and sell them back to the club house at the week-end. Some of the balls had not actually been lost of course. They were just moved slightly, making it almost impossible for their owners to find them. Most week-ends, you could make enough money for a few bottles of Corona and packets of Spangles…

As I left the Mariners that evening, I couldn't help wondering how many customers Colin would have on day one of my Easter party, or indeed if it would be worth him even opening… I began planning the invitations, resolving to put Kathy at the top of the list…

8

I simply adore waking up by the coast... The sound of the seagulls in the morning, the rolling waves of the ocean... The salty air drifting in the through the windows... I even keep one of the bedroom windows open during the winter purely for those simple pleasures. Having spent much of my adult life living just outside the town of Redhill, with the main London to Brighton railway at the bottom of my garden, then a further twenty-odd years living just three miles from Gatwick Airport, the relative silence of my new home was almost eerie. But in a good way.

It reminded me very much of my childhood when, due to my mother's illness, I had spent many months growing up in Brighton on the South Coast. Now better known as the gay capital of Europe, in my childhood days, it was a simple yet lively town... A town where children could safely wander down to the beach—about fifteen minutes from my Great Aunt May's house in Waldegrave Road—and back with no fear at all. It's the same feeling here. I'm sure if ever she chose to do so, young Debbie would have no qualms about walking to Harwick and back after dark. For *my* part, I tend to spend my early evenings taking a casual stroll along the cliffs towards Cork Bay, some seven miles or so along the northern coast.

There's a footpath leading off of our lane, just a few yards past Tom's cottage. Only the locals seem to be aware of it, though even they seem not to use it that often, if ever. There is no sign-post, possibly removed by one of the said locals in order to keep the cliffs 'ours', so I found it purely by chance. Even Colin didn't know about it and Colin knows everything. On the Wednesday before that Easter, I took myself up onto the cliffs. It was the perfect evening. With just two days to go before the world descended upon me—OK, so maybe about forty friends and family to be more precise—I needed some 'me' time to clear my head and make sure I had left nothing unprepared. Accommodation was sorted. I had enough food and drink to feed the five thousand, or it seemed like it by the state of my two freezers and the shed which was currently doubling as a wine cellar-cum-brewery.

With the help of Lisa, better known as Lala for no good reason, one of Colin's two barmaids—both of whom would be joining us after the pub closed—I had about ten hours of non-stop music to feed through iPods and stereo speakers. The garden was as clear as it could possibly be, again in the hope that the weather behaved itself.

I'd prepared a temporary brick-built barbecue—from spare bricks that had been in abundance over the previous year, for obvious reasons. The hard standing which used to house Steve Taylor's garage would make the perfect dance floor should anyone choose to shake a leg or two. I had a 'definite' guest list numbering thirty-two, but had allowed for up to fifty…

As I walked along the cliffs in the moon-light, contemplating the next few days, it occurred to me I had to be one of the luckiest men in the world. I'd had a wonderful life so far, albeit with the odd hic-cup along the way. But now I found myself living in a village very few people were aware of, with some lovely new friends, an 'adopted' grand-daughter, not to mention a new love interest… I walked for a good hour before turning back. As the sun began to set, I looked out over the sea to the twinkling lights of the South Wales coast and thought again of Kathy… So close and yet so far…

Good Friday—16.00: So far, I had forty-seven guests in the house and garden with, I was certain, at least another twenty still to arrive, not to mention Colin and the barmaids, Lala and Rara, real name Rachel but she adopted Rara to avoid confusion with the young lady in Connie's. Sadly, Kathy was unable to be there as her mother was not at all well at the time, but promised we would catch up very soon… I had seriously under-estimated my popularity, or maybe the popularity of the Cornish coast as opposed to a town centre.

Cheryl had arrived just before lunch, along with my son Richard and daughter-in-law, Clare. I had the pleasure of her company for all of ten minutes before she asked where Minnie lived. Reminding Richard's wife, just how safe it was living here, I took Cheryl the few minutes' walk up to Tom's cottage, asking her to be sure to come back to Windy Cottage when Tom and Alice were ready to join the party. She promised she would as she ran into the arms of her new best friend, the two pre-teens finally meeting one another. That was four hours earlier. I hadn't seen her since. To ease Clare's concerns—Richard was fine about it, the vodka helped—I took her along and introduced her to Tom and Alice.

The girls were happily playing in the back garden, but they would all be along shortly. Alice assured me she would make the effort 'even if it's just for an hour or so'. The up side of Alice not staying too long was that if the girls started to get tired or over-excited, they could go back there any time they liked. This they did, around eleven o'clock, though I heard later from Alice, she could still hear them laughing and giggling well into the early hours…

The party was a reasonably sedate affair for the early part of the evening. The music subdued, more in the back-ground rather than tunes to dance to. I'd held similar parties back in Surrey for the previous eight years. I always found a mix of old and new went down well with most people, although there would always be someone asking 'What's this shit?' or words to that effect. OK, fair point, so I admit not everybody is a fan of the Bay City Rollers… The barbecue was still going well after the sun sank below the westerly cliffs, an old work colleague, Lindon keeping everyone topped up with the usual burgers, hot dogs, etc., plus the odd ribs and a few steaks for those with a real appetite.

A huge pot of baked beans was sitting on a hot plate for those who felt the need. Whenever Lindon fancied a break, usually for a cigarette while his girl-friend wasn't looking, Lala and Colin took over for a few minutes. It had been as I expected. Dead as a door-nail, the Mariners had closed at eight and Colin brought the girls over. Rara was in her element, mixing some special cocktails she had concocted especially for the occasion: Blokie's Banger (Blokie being my nick-name for as long as I cared to remember), Rara's Rough One (loosely based on an old cider recipe) and the Easter Explosion (God only knows what went into that one, but the spirits store was seriously depleted by the time she finished serving them)…

All went down exceedingly well, especially with the older generation. Many had never tasted a cocktail, but Rara assured them it wouldn't kill them and that it would 'do wonders for your libido!' The least said the better. Suffice to say the calm of the late afternoon and early evening was gradually turning into a cross between a rave and a good old Cockney knees-up, the likes of which had rarely been witnessed in St Matilda's Bay. Had it not been for several glasses of vodka and Red Bull, I might have cared what the neighbours thought. Needless to say, by nine o'clock it was becoming pretty lively in the living room and garden of Windy Cottage. The music had mysteriously grown louder.

Matt Munro and The Eagles had become Pussycat Dolls, the Sex Pistols and the Rolling Stones. Strangely, I heard something that sounded like that little Canadian, Justin What-not, but I know for a fact he's not in my collection. From what I know of the girls' taste in music, I thought it unlikely to be theirs either, but one never knows, does one? People were dancing everywhere. I'd had the brain wave of putting one of the four speakers on top of the shed, aiming it at the beach. Consequently, several people were down there singing at the top of their voices and dancing in the moonlight.

On refection, there was no chance of any complaints from the neighbours... They were all in my garden... Except for Debbie. She had promised to try and come but admitted to not being a big fan of crowds or loud music. Having said that, she also added that I wasn't to let her spoil my fun and that I should party all week-end if I chose to do so. Which was exactly what I planned to do if the body could handle it. Just when I thought it couldn't possibly get any rowdier, the Karaoke Krew, plus what seemed like the entire clientele of my favourite pub, The Downsman, arrived at my front gate...

I was completely over-whelmed. Even though I knew several old friends from Crawley and its surrounding area were coming down, I was not prepared for what came next! Forty-eight of them had hired a coach and made the trip from my old home town and it left me speechless for several minutes...

"Don't they know how to build a proper road down here Blokie?" Stevie asked... "We just had to walk the last bloody mile! Get me a beer, will ya?" All of that as he was giving me the biggest man-hug ever. I watched over his shoulder as the familiar faces, faces I hadn't seen for three or four months, trooped up my front garden path: Linda, Barry, Jojo, Leia, Lisa P, Anne, Tim, G-Man, Kimmy, another Rachel—I was starting to think there were more Rachel's in this world than Daves!—Leo, Fat Bloke, Neil and the twins, Anna and Wendy... The list was endless. So many happy, smiling faces... Until that moment, I hadn't realised how much I missed them all.

It didn't change my opinion of Tilda's or Windy Cottage though. It was still the right decision, but I vowed to invite each and every one of them down on a regular basis... But only one or two at a time in future. I didn't even *think* about where they were all going to sleep that week-end. It only occurred to me the next day. I found more than a dozen tents down on the beach. Strictly speaking, I was told (by Tom I think but not certain) it was illegal to camp over-night on that beach, but who was going to know? Certainly, the villagers weren't about to report it, and nobody had seen a police car in the village since the days of the flood and its' aftermath.

I found myself involved in so many really deep conversations about the advantages of living by the coast, the local pubs, the weather—yes, that old chestnut never fails to rear its ugly head... I don't recall if we resolved anything that night, due to the large amount of alcohol consumed by one and all, but I do remember something about world peace and all of us living on the moon... Weird!

The night went really well. I was strangely sober, despite sinking numerous beers, plus a variety of Rara's cocktails, one of which was thrust in my hand every time I ventured into the kitchen. Cue Jonah Lewie... As far as I could tell, everyone had a great time. Cheryl and Minnie danced their socks off until they could dance no more, then walked back to Tom and Alice's to talk the night away. Jojo showed everyone some amazing dance moves. Kirsty, as always, danced on the table and by some weird stroke of luck, didn't fall off. My ex, Ellie, arrived with her new man—decent fella if you forgot he was a Spurs fan—but couldn't stay the whole week-end as her work insisted, she came in on Monday and the coach wasn't booked to return until the Monday morning.

A few people found a spare table in the back room and, thanks to Linda bringing the special 'group holiday' playing cards, began a very loud game of 'wank'. It's not what you think, but even so, I was grateful they waited until the children had departed. It's based on a famous card game called Uno, but thanks to someone known to all as Blondie, it gained a new name one of our group holidays, somewhere in the Mediterranean. Like many of the stupid things we do in life, it seems a lot funnier after a few glasses of vino collapso. Thanks Blondie.

Stevie had brought his laptop with him and managed to wire it up to my television so that we could have a nostalgic karaoke session. Just when I thought I'd never have to hear Robbie's Angels again, there it bloody was! I once said, and I meant it, that I would be happy if I never again heard that song, along with Bohemian Rhapsody and virtually everything by Adele. Between them, and I suppose I have to take some of the blame for this, radio stations and karaoke shows have ruined some of our favourite songs for me.

Talk about over-played! I'm told some of the villagers in Harwick heard our impromptu show two miles away. To be absolutely precise, I think it fair to say a good time was had by all. Colin made his excuses and left soon after midnight, offering the next day's opening time as his excuse for an early departure, but not before grabbing one of Stevie's microphones and advertising "Full English in the Mariners any time after ten, only a fiver!" It was a decision he would live to regret...

9

I always remember my dear old mum telling me breakfast was the most important meal of the day. Back in the days before practically everything became bad for you, be it milk, eggs, white bread, meat, sugar, salt, etc., my mother would not let me leave the house in the morning before I'd polished off a good fry-up. It's something I've lived by ever since. While the rest of the world was trying to survive on muesli, fruit or low-fat yoghurts, I was—still am—tucking into sausage, bacon, eggs, beans and fried bread. It hasn't killed me yet, and as I've said many times, if I go tomorrow at least I'll die happy. I would hate my last thoughts to be 'Why didn't I have that bacon sarnie and just one more cigarette?'

So, there we all were, about thirty of us—the rest had yet to surface—banging on the pub door just a few minutes after ten o'clock that Easter Saturday morning. Despite most of us only having two- or three-hours sleep… and not exactly the most comfortable sleep… Barry remembered Colin's kind offer during the previous night's festivities and suggested we all pop over the road. Four or five of the revellers lifted coffee mugs a few inches off the table and muttered something that sounded like "Uuurgh", which we took to mean 'No thanks, I'm happy with this.' But the rest of us, notably Barry, Stevie and myself were just about ready for sausage, bacon, eggs, hash browns, baked beans and anything else the landlord was willing to throw on the griddle… No answer.

I tried around the back of the pub, where the kitchen was located, over-looking the car park. 'Maybe he's already got some on the go.' I offered, optimistically. No sign of him. Nothing. All doors and windows still securely locked. I almost screamed…

"Go and grab Lala," I said to anyone willing to listen. Blank faces stared back at me. "The redhead doing the Barbie last night." At this, one of the Crawley crowd—I think it was Wavey—sauntered off in search of the barmaid,

52

who I was sure would have a key to the pub. Last seen downing Alka Seltzer, at least I knew she was awake, if not yet resembling a human being. Five minutes later, she turned up, big silly grin on her face, holding the key aloft and muttering something about men not being able to hold their drink… Half an hour later, we were all sitting in the saloon bar with self-service mugs of coffee, while Lala cooked a mountain of eggs and bacon. No sign of any sausages, baked beans, hash browns, mushrooms, toast or Colin, but it didn't matter. All that *did* matter at that precise moment was getting hot food in our bellies and soaking up copious amounts of alcohol.

I looked out over the bay, spotting a few more of my guests crawling out of tents on the beach. One or two were glancing around as if to say 'where the fuck are we?' It had truly been one of those nights. As far as I was concerned, it could not have gone any better. The guests, the food, the drinks, the singing… Probably the best party I had ever thrown, and there's been a fair few I can tell you… I was woken from my day-dream by the sight of Cheryl and Minnie skipping down the lane. I opened up one of the windows and called them inside. It seemed they both had a wonderful time at the party and they both swore blind they were tucked up in bed by mid-night, which I discovered later was a little white lie.

That didn't worry me in the slightest. I was just happy that my grand-daughter would clearly be delighted to come and stay more often, with or without her parents, but more importantly, that Minnie was smiling a real smile for the first time in nearly a year, since that awful day when so many innocent people, including her beloved mother, had lost their lives in an instant, because of an untameable animal called the sea. I cuddled them both tightly as they entered the bar and came across to where I was sitting…

By the time eleven o'clock came, Lala had satisfied us all with her excellent, though limited supplies of food. Still no sign of Colin and the pub was due to open. As luck would have it, Rara was on duty that lunch-time and came in to deal with the few customers who had made the effort to visit our pretty bay, while Lala joined us for coffee.

Someone said we should get her something for all her hard work and it was agreed the one thing Lala liked more than anything was a night on the ale… If there could be any complaints about St Matilda's Bay and the surrounding area, it would have to be the lack of things to do and places to go if you were under the age of thirty. Back 'home' in Crawley, there were pubs that stayed open most of the night, plus two- or three-night clubs only a short taxi ride away, where you could dance your socks off until six in the morning.

Not to mention London or Brighton, both of which were less than an hour away on a train. No such luxury in my new home though. Hobart town was as close as we had to the night life of West Sussex and that was a good twenty miles or so away… And so, it was agreed. While I had invited everyone for the entire Easter week-end, I hadn't actually planned any further than the Good Friday night party. Therefore, we all agreed we would take Lala out for the night later that Saturday. As it turned out, there were only fifteen of 'us'. Ellie and Steve had decided to drive home so that the lady wasn't too shattered for work on Easter Monday.

A few people took the opportunity of hiring cars and checking the local area. I couldn't believe how many of my friends had never even been to Cornwall. Others elected to have a quiet night in—I had already said people were to treat Windy Cottage as their own and come and go as they pleased. Linda and Barry found they had a common interest with Alice and Tom— Bridge. So that was *their* plan for Saturday evening… Pretty much everyone had their own ideas as to how the night would pan out.

Whatever happened, the cottages, the beach and the Mariners were all within a few minutes' walking distance of each other, so nobody would be too far away from the others should they change their minds… As we left the Mariners, we all left the agreed fiver on Colin's till, complete with a note, written and signed by Stevie—the two of them really hit it off the previous night—saying 'Cheers for brekkie ya lazy git lol'. Just as we were crossing the road, back to Windy Cottage, Debbie came flying out of her house, looking horrified, slammed the door and ran to the back of the pub.

Moments later, her Fiat 500 came screaming out onto the lane, wheels spinning, kicking up dust and gravel and sped up the hill at a ridiculous rate of knots. "Who was *that*?" Stevie asked, always an eye for a pretty girl… I gave him what little I knew and left it at that. We all headed back across the road. I spotted a few of my previous night's guests walking on the beach, enjoying the mid-morning sunshine. It was a very pleasant day. Not yet warm enough to venture into the ocean but definitely t-shirt and shorts weather…

"Morning…" came a quiet voice. We turned to see a bedraggled Colin hanging out of an upstairs window of the Mariners Arms. We all smiled, some laughed and said a few 'hellos' back at him. He looked confused but it would all come back to him later. I don't believe Colin was ever much of a drinker.

I once managed to talk him into a 'down-in-one' but it was a feat I never succeeded in repeating. He reminds me of an ex-girlfriend of mine, Susan Lister. As a teenager, it was fair to say she had a few extra pounds. Nothing to worry about but you know what girls are. If they reach size eight, they're fat! So, it surprised me when she gave me the news that she was starting a new job on the Pick 'n' Mix counter at Woolies. As it turned out, the constant smell of sweets actually put her off the taste and within six months she had lost three stone. Maybe the same could be said for Colin and alcohol. Perhaps you really can have too much of a good thing…

The garden was a mess, but nothing that couldn't be put right in an hour or two. In fact, a couple of the girls were already working on the back. It had been a mad night and I suspected it was going to be a quiet day, at least until Lala's session in the evening. Linda and Barry were back up at Tom and Alice's, no doubt discussing grand-children and the good old days. They were of a similar age group and had much in common. Ricky Moore, one of the Crawley group, was sitting on a sun lounger—not sure where *that* came from but it certainly wasn't mine—slowly sipping a Stella Artois. His drinking exploits were something of a legend in West Sussex.

Gary, Jojo's husband was sitting next to him, but with just a coffee mug in his hand. Jojo herself was in the kitchen with Kirsty, ploughing through the washing-up. Colin would have loved the sight of the girls doing housework while the men were drinking outside. I passed the living room where last night's karaoke screen had reverted to its original form of being my television. Half a dozen people, drinking coffee, watching the BBC rolling news: North Korea threatening to declare war on the South complete with archive video.

A prostitute and a police-woman murdered in Kings Cross complete with the customary grainy photographs of course. Andy Murray failing to win a Grand Slam tournament, complete with monotonous interview… Nothing good. Nothing changed. That was the main reason I rarely watched the TV news or bought a newspaper. There was rarely anything uplifting in the news. More often than not, it was one long round of crime and recession, doom and gloom. I smiled to myself, again content that I'd made the right move. So maybe nothing ever happened in St Matilda's Bay, but the sun came up and went down again.

The pub opened on time, usually. Day-trippers came and went, mostly leaving the beach as clean and tidy as they had found it...

At least no-one ever declared war on us, or murdered our prostitutes or policemen. Not that we had any prostitutes, to the best of my knowledge, unless Sarah next door was turning tricks for the holiday-makers while Adam earned his crust in town. And as for the police, any self-respecting murderer would have to search high and low to find one anywhere near *my* sleepy village. In the back of my mind, the previous night, I had half expected one to turn up and pull the plug on us at some stage. It had been that loud. To be honest, I wouldn't have minded going down in history as having that in common with Springsteen and McCartney.

But no, it never happened. I wandered upstairs. I could hear the shower pumping steaming hot water down on someone's weary body. I could hear snoring from one of the bedrooms and through a crack in the door, I could see Margaret and Derek still fast asleep. Returning to the kitchen, I offered to help the girls and was told to grab myself a coffee and 'get out of here'. I obeyed the command. Golden rule. Never argue with girls suffering hangovers. Just let them do what they have to do, and if that means tidying my house, so be it. I happen to be one of those really annoying people who never get a hangover.

It doesn't matter how much alcohol I consume, or how much I mix my drinks, I'm still up at the crack of dawn, happy as Larry and full of the joys of spring. Many of my friends hate me for that... Briefly. I remember one night when I was visiting my adopted daughter Lucy (long story that I shall not bore you with). We had both been through some tough times and agreed we needed a bloody good night out. I arrived at her house in Kettering about six in the evening. We finished two bottles of wine before hitting the town about eight. Three or four pints over a few games of pool were washed down with vodka shots, then we were off to a cocktail bar in the classier part of town.

Two of those—no idea what they were—and we were off to the karaoke bar for more pints and Sambuka shots. I don't actually remember leaving that particular bar, but apparently, about three in the morning we ended up in a bar that had its own dance floor. We bumped into some more of her friends and more drinking was partaken, plus dancing. I don't believe I danced at all. I sincerely hope not at any rate—think dad dancing at weddings and that's me—but Lucy did. She remembers looking across at me at some point and I had fallen asleep on a chair in the corner, shot glass in hand. It was then she decided it was time to get a taxi. I have no recollection of any of this.

Nevertheless, I was up at seven, making coffee for us both. I couldn't help noticing the living room table as I passed through to the kitchen. There stood an almost empty bottle of wine. We had obviously had more when we came home, but even *Lucy* couldn't remember that. The poor girl had a three-day hangover and vowed, as people always do at such times, never to drink again. I was fine. She hated me. We've done it again since…

The rest of that Saturday in Windy Cottage passed peacefully enough. I had pizzas delivered in the afternoon for those who hadn't managed Lala's pub breakfast or ventured over to the Mariners for lunch. Considering they had a fifteen-mile journey, they were surprisingly warm… The house was once again clean and tidy, mainly thanks to the efforts of Kirsty and Jojo, with a little help from Sarah, Leia and Clare. Much of the previous night's fun and games was discussed in various groups in the house, the garden and down on the beach. Someone had bet Ricky that he wouldn't go for a swim in the sea about three in the morning. This was Ricky Moore. You don't bet him or dare him to do *any*thing, because he will. And he did. Ricky has been known to drink washing-up liquid for a bet. Don't try this at home!

Others were discussing how good someone was at singing, even when drunk. That was followed by how bad someone else was for the same reason, although in this particular case, nobody could remember the singer's name. Many of the conversations were on the merits of living in St Matilda's Bay as opposed to Redhill or Crawley. I think it fair to say that apart from my former home being close to the airport and within easy reach of London and Brighton, most agreed they would choose my current home every time. I have to admit the locale was one of the few 'cons' I considered before purchasing Windy Cottage, but then, how often had I been to London in my life? I could count them on the fingers of two hands. I was fairly sure I could live without that.

However, being in the close vicinity of Gatwick, gateway to the world, was a very different kettle of fish. I was well known for loving my holidays, taking at least two or three trips to sunnier climes every year. Ellie and I even had five holidays within a twelve-month period back in the good old days, where money was no object and sunshine were an essential part of our lives. Virtually always to the sun, just for the record. Cold weather simply disagrees with me. My only concession to that was our Christmas break in New York. Freezing cold, snow covering Central Park... But we loved it.

Other than that, I can honestly state I have never had a cold holiday, and never will do. Yes, that one I thought long and hard about when deciding to move to Cornwall. In the end I decided that even though Gatwick was a good three- or four-hour drive away, it would give me the ideal opportunity to re-visit old friends and stay a couple of nights before flying out to Corfu, or Crete, or wherever I fancied. Problem solved.

Cheryl and Minnie were playing Frisbee on the beach as the last of the stragglers came down-stairs and we adjourned to Colin's pub to plan Lala's night out. As much as I loved the Mariners, and my guests were growing to like it also, it was agreed by all that a trip into town was called for. Someone said they knew a good club in Truro and Colin pointed out there was an excellent Indian restaurant there too. Quite a few of us were fans of Indian food so that was agreed in a flash. Colin also knew someone who hired out mini-buses and owed him a favour. So, for the princely sum of fifty pounds, we had two mini-buses, plus drivers, willing to take up to twenty-four people for a good night out.

I chose not to go. Not because I felt too old to go clubbing, and I would have loved the meal, not having had a sit-down Indian since my move, but more because I felt it my duty to stay at home and entertain the rest of my guests. Despite much attempted arm-twisting, they eventually conceded and the chosen twenty-four were agreed upon. Judging by the tales Sunday morning, I gather a very good time was had by all. Five people didn't remember coming home. Kirsty failed to fall off any tables yet again. The food was delicious, and the whole night cost Lala absolutely nothing.

Perfect. As for the rest of us, many of the lads, including me, were crowded round the television to watch Match of The Day. Easter is traditionally a Premiership-deciding week-end. With two or three games crammed into little more than a week, more often than not, you had a pretty good idea who would, or wouldn't be in with a chance after the Easter football programme was completed. Being fifteen points ahead of our nearest rivals, my beloved Manchester United had it virtually sewn up. Nothing short of a total collapse, or major injuries to Rooney, Welbeck and van Persie, was likely to stop them.

A narrow win over Sunderland, thanks to an own goal kept us well clear of our 'noisy neighbours' for another week. Sadly, a 1-0 defeat by Chelsea on

Easter Monday put us out of the FA Cup, killing off any chance of another 'double' but you can't have everything. Having said that, I had to hand it to Demba Ba for the winning goal, a stunning volley!

Most of the girls were over in the pub, some back on the alcohol, others on fruit juice or Coke, echoing Lucy's words. It wouldn't last, it never did. Tom and Alice were in my back room, yet another game of bridge with their new friends. Minnie and Cheryl were upstairs Skypeing their friends (?) and chatting endlessly about mutual future visits to Northampton and Tilda's. They would go back to Tom's later in the evening once the card tournament ended. Cheryl's parents, Clare and Richard, had seen very little of their daughter over the week-end, and were able to relax for once, knowing she was in safe hands. Where they lived, it was not considered safe to let children out on their own.

A sad but true reflection of much of our once-great country. But down here, no problem. It was probably the most relaxed I had ever seen the two of them and I enjoyed that. I was even looking forward to future visits for simple family week-ends. Even Richard surprised me. A renowned clubber in his youth, he had turned into a devoted husband and parent almost over-night. As for the rest of my Easter guests, I believe they all had their own agenda's. It resembled a larger version of our famous group holidays just a few years earlier. Singles and couples would converge on a hired villa, somewhere in the Med, and spend the entire week just doing whatever they wanted, whenever they wanted, and with whoever they wanted. It was the perfect scenario.

In normal daily life, quite often someone would do what their chosen partner wanted to do, simply because they had no choice. It is just something people do for the person they chose as life partner. Whereas in a group, there is nearly always someone else who wants to go for a walk, or pop into town, or hire a car and go in search of an undiscovered sandy beach... You had choice, and nobody had to do anything they didn't want to do. My week-end party was just like that. Many new friendships were formed, and they would last, without any threat to current relationships. I've said it before and I'll say it again, it was a perfect week-end, and one that I will never forget. Strange that it was born out of tragedy...

10

Easter Sunday was a day of reflection. Not in a religious way, although five of our group chose to walk the two miles to the nearest church in Harwick, but more a reflection of who we were, where we were going, whether we would ever all meet up again like that… Of course, we all said we would, but in truth, we knew deep down it was highly unlikely. The chances of a group of people living so far apart—from Northampton, Canterbury, Crawley, Kettering, etc.— ever getting together in one place again were extremely remote. I could think of only one possibility, but hopefully that day was still a long way off. I just thanked 'whoever' that I was able to bring us all together in one place this one time.

I have a wonderful photographic record of that week-end. I must have in the region of four hundred shots of so many of my friends and family just having a great time. Admittedly, many of them would never make it onto Facebook, but I'm sure it seemed like a good idea at the time. Isn't alcohol marvellous? As things turned out, many of us over the following years, not always including me for various reasons, managed quite a few similar 'get together' such as this, albeit with not everyone being able to make it, but at the same time, new friends were also introduced to the Easter group.

Apart from the main event, the Good Friday house-warming party, the only other arrangement I had made prior to the Easter week-end, was the farewell dinner in the Mariners on the Sunday night. Virtually everybody who had accepted the invitation said they were planning to stay for the whole week-end, returning home on the Monday in preparation for work on Tuesday morning. That was even before the coach turned up, also booked to go back to Crawley on the Monday. Therefore, I was expecting around thirty or so—which later became nearer to sixty—for dinner that Sunday night. I fore-warned Colin. As it was still very early in the season, he would normally cater for about twenty or thirty locals, plus maybe a few out-of-season tourists, on a Sunday evening.

Most of these were from nearby Harwick, who by then considered the Colin's hostelry their 'local'. Normally they would have three or four designated drivers, although some would risk the two-mile drive home after three or four pints. Risky, bearing in mind the one-way system, but to date none of the villagers had yet been stopped by the police, let alone charged for drunk-driving. So, it was only fair that Colin was aware of what to expect. He ordered in extra standard 'pub grub', the usual steaks, fish, gammon, pies, lasagne, etc., plus a couple of extra barrels of the local cider. I was amazed at how many of my guests actually took to the cider. It seemed like a case of 'when in Rome' to me.

Apart from those who *had* to leave early for various personal reasons, the entire guest list was sitting around eight separate tables in the saloon bar. Six at one, ten at another and so on. Even Cheryl and Minnie were there, a first for both of them. I couldn't speak for Minnie's past experiences of public houses, but Cheryl's only previous visits had been to the Wacky Warehouse in the Air Balloon, close to my former home in Horley. Naturally there was no such thing as a Wacky Warehouse in St Matilda's Bay, or anywhere within a fifty-mile radius as far as Tom was aware. Consequently, Clare and Richard faithfully promised to take her to one when she visited Cheryl in Northampton.

For Minnie, who I was almost certain had never set foot in a pub before, that Sunday evening, and the thought of future outings to my son's family home made her think all her Christmases had come at once. It has always amazed me how resilient children are. Less than a year earlier, the poor child had lost her beloved mother under the most horrific circumstances, yet here she was getting excited at the thought of an hour playing around in a room full of slides, rope ladders and thousands of brightly-coloured plastic balls. We had to remind both the girls that this could well be the one and only chance they had to enjoy such fun, as there was an age limit for those activities and they were both very close to it.

It reminded me of a family fun day they held at one of my local pubs, The Black Horse, way back in the nineteen nineties. A bouncy castle had been hired especially for the afternoon. The children loved it and played until the sun went down. But the real fun started after they had gone home, when the so-called 'grown-ups' had the chance to play! If you've never seen a bunch of drunken men and women on a bouncy castle, watch out for it at a pub near you...

I could not remember a time in my life when I felt so chilled. Surrounded by all my family and most of my friends, enjoying a really good pint of the local brew, the dubiously named Willie's Waif rough cider, and putting away an enormous plate of my favourite pub food, Cumberland sausage and mash in onion gravy, followed by Steamed Treacle Pudding. I'm afraid that's another thing some of my friends occasionally 'hate' me for. The ability to eat like a pig and drink like a fish, not to mention two or three sugars in every cup of coffee, without putting on any weight. By the time I left school, I had reached six feet tall and weighed ten and a half stone.

Apart from a brief period while I was living with my ex, when I ballooned up to eleven stone for no apparent reason other than good living, I had never varied more than a few pounds either side of that ten and a half stone, with a thirty-inch waist to go with it. To coin a cliché, most people I knew only had to look at a cream cake and they would put on ten pounds. Shame… Breaks my heart! The talk was relaxed and easy, as it generally is with old friends when they get together on evenings such as that. Talk of what a lovely week-end, which I thanked them all for later in a very short speech.

The odd mention of my coming back 'home' at some stage, which I promised to do, but only to visit. And the promise of regular visits by them, to me, although as I stated earlier, preferably 'just a few at a time please'. Clare and Richard took the little ones back to Tom and Alice's cottage about ten. The beach, the sea air and the constant running around in their joyous excitement for most of the week-end, not to mention the very late-night chats in bed, had finally caught up with them. They needed their beds. We all said our good-nights to the girls, promising a proper good-bye the next morning.

Tom and Alice stayed with us, happy to let the fruit of my loins wander in and out of their cottage as though it was their own. I don't believe either of our homes were locked even once the entire week-end. My speech was short, mainly thanks to several people moaning and groaning about it, and simple. A big thank you to them all for coming and the hope that we could do it all again someday. Nobody drank too much, apart from Stevie who, for some inexplicable reason, decided that Cornish Guinness was even better than his local brew, though not quite up to the standard of Dublin's own fine original of course. Strange, as all English Guinness is brewed in the same place, and he'd never crossed the Irish Sea. But that was Stevie. He downed six pints before taking his leave, returning to the tent he was sharing with Ricky and Wavey in my back garden.

Linda and Barry were next to leave. They had practically made their home in Tom and Alice's cottage and, not surprisingly, Tom and Alice would be equally sad to see them go. I suspected a rubber or two of bridge before bed-time. By mid-night, officially closing time, though nobody seemed to be rushing to kick us out and lock the doors... Indeed, I spotted Rara setting up another round... there were just twelve of us remaining in the bar. Rara brought the drinks over and joined us for the last hour. The talk was of old friends, happier days, future holidays—I still planned on joining eleven of them for the group holiday to Gran Canaria later that year—and, yet again, what a bloody great week-end it had been. The coach was due at eleven the next day. By two in the morning, we were all tucked up on sofas, in beds or in tents. It had been one Hell of a house-warming party.

At lunch-time the next day, Easter Monday, I was chatting lazily, about nothing in particular to Colin and Lala over the bar of the Mariners. There was very little talk of the week-end, it had all been said the night before. Apart from Colin telling me what fabulous friends I had, 'although that Ricky Moore was a bit odd to say the least... What on earth were he and Hev drinking?' I should just give Heather—Hev—a special mention as the one person I have met with the drinking capacity of... I don't know... A camel maybe? When I first met that young lady, she was a barmaid in The Downsman. Her reputation went before her and she did her level best to live up to it. While drinking on duty was strictly forbidden, the moment the 'time' bell rang, the gloves were off!

Someone who had only heard of Hev but never met her, stupidly asked her if all he had heard was true. Hev's reply was: 'Probably.' Having indulged a few pints himself, he challenged her to a bet. Rather than pouring away the dregs from the beer pump trays, he bet her she would drink it, all mixed up in a pint glass. Now I can think of only one thing worse than warm lager. That's warm *stale* lager, mixed with Best Bitter, Real Ale, cider and Guinness! The poor man really did not know Hev at all. Either that or he assumed her reputation had just been a local legend. Wrong! The girl *is* a legend! And she won the bet...

However, back in St Matilda's Bay, life should now get back to some form of normality, I assumed. There were about ten or twelve other customers, but I didn't recognise any of them. To be honest, I was happy to have the lack of genial conversation at last. Meaning no dis-respect to any of my wonderful friends and family, all of whom I loved dearly, I was so looking forward to the peace and quiet of my own home, where I could shut the door, draw the blinds, switch on and old Inspector Morse and retreat into my own little world once again.

Tomorrow, I planned to start on the design for my garden, but that Easter Monday night was to be *my* time. I even contemplated switching off the phone, but I knew some of my former guests would want to let me know they were safely home in Northampton, or Redhill, or wherever, which indeed was the case. I left the pub around three, went home and made myself a toasted cheese and onion sandwich and settled down for an afternoon nap. The telephone woke me at about four. The first of them, Leia and (the other) Rachel had just arrived safe and sound in Horsham.

There were five other calls, the last one being Lucy about seven, who had made it back to Kettering, more than three hundred miles away. And that was that. All done. The party week-end was officially over. Feet up. Television on. Pre-recorded Endeavour Morse on the screen, the one about the murdered Oxford Master, found in the Charwell... Cup of hot strong coffee in one hand, with three sugars of course, and a JPS SuperKing in the other... Whether or not there was a God, this was truly Heaven.

Annoyingly, I have one of those brains that only switches off when I'm drinking. Then, I assume it doesn't actually switch off, it probably just gives up talking to the rest of my body and lets me get on with the serious work of bringing glass to lips... Despite the intricate tale of gruesome murders in Oxford—surely the most dangerous place to live after Midsomer—my brain decided it was time to mentally plan decking, and water features, and all those other things Alan Titchmarsh taught us all back in the nineties. In addition to an over-active brain, I also possess an extremely vivid imagination. Night times are the worst. Or the best, depending which way you choose to view it.

All my life I've had it. During that period between going to bed and finally drifting off to sleep, my imagination springs into life. I go into fantasies, like a twenty-first century Walter Mitty. I become invincible. I can do anything. I can make myself invisible. That's one of my favourites. It's fantastic what you can do with the power of invisibility. Depending on my mood at bed-time, I've been known to push people down flights of concrete steps—that would be people who have done me wrong in my life-time—then watch as witnesses swear blind there was nobody near that person and they must have simply slipped, while the victim knows for a fact that he, or she, felt a hand in the small of his, or her, back. Another favourite is to step onto a football pitch, in my invisibility cloak obviously, and deflect a Carlos Tevez shot away from the opponent's goal, or similarly, deflect a Rio Ferdinand header *into* an opponent's goal.

You would be amazed at how many Premierships have been won and lost thanks to my night-time fantasies. However, I digress. While watching Sergeant Lewis near-missing a Triumph Roadster heading in the opposite direction on a narrow country lane, and thinking how much actor Kevin Whatley had aged over the past ten years, my brain was planning rock pools and gravel paths. I gave up on Morse and went for my favourite walk along the secret footpath up onto the cliffs. The moon was no longer with us, so I took extra care not to venture too close to the edge as I watched the waves roll in through the night sky.

It was a warm night, I had only a thin jumper over a t-shirt and jeans. I hadn't planned to walk too far, but you know how it is. When things are on your mind, time just seems to fly by. Before I knew it, it was turned half past eleven and I was a good three or four miles from home. As usual, I had seen nobody along the cliff-tops. I sat and enjoyed a cigarette as I watched the lights flickering along the coast of South Wales, wondering if anyone was sitting on a beach over there, thinking the same thoughts as me.

"Hello…" I jumped as I heard her voice. In all my time at St Matilda's Bay, by then close to a year, I must have walked those cliffs a hundred times or more, and never once see a single soul. As far as I could ascertain, there was no other way up there other than my secret footpath. I called it *my* secret as I hadn't even mentioned it to the neighbours. Clearly Tom and Alice would not have managed the steep climb, and I guessed Sarah and Adam would be too busy for such leisurely activities… But that still left the rest of the villagers, plus those from Harwick. No, as far as I was concerned, this was my secret part of Cornwall… Of England in fact… And I have to confess I was not best pleased to find I was no longer the only one of about sixty million Brits to be acquainted with it.

Unfair of me maybe, but it was just one of those little bonuses that helped convince me that I had made the right move coming down to this quaint part of my home-land. As soon as I turned to look at her, waves of long blonde hair cascading down over a flowing black dress, or possibly even a night-gown, my momentary displeasure evaporated. Was this still my wild imagination delving into my being? Was I about to be swept away in a wave of erotic passion? Not a hope in Hell...!

Without even looking at me, she pointed out across the ocean, "That big cluster of lights over there is Swansea," then with a slight move, "and that's Cardiff. I've got friends in Cardiff, I used to work there for a while. Your party sounded like fun." This sudden change of subject set my mind racing. One second, she's talking about her life in South Wales, the next she's exchanging pleasantries about my week-end. I couldn't help wondering why I'd never seen her up here before. As if she had read my mind, she continued, "I don't mix with people very much I'm afraid and on Friday an old friend of mine died. I usually only come up here after mid-night so I know I'll be alone. It gives me a chance to assess my life. The rights and wrongs. The past and the future. I found this place quite by accident soon after I first came here. Why did she have to die like that? She was a lovely girl, despite everything..."

Her jumbled sentences were confusing me, but at least I now knew why we had never met on the cliffs before. She only came up here after midnight, for whatever reasons were in her muddled but very pretty head, and I had never been up here even *this* late before. Normally it would be early evening. I loved to watch the sun go down over the sea, but if it became too dark, the over-grown path back down could be difficult to navigate. "I'm sorry to hear about your friend Debbie," I offered, trying to keep some semblance of a conversation going, "but you should have popped round. It might have cheered you up after the bad news..."

We both sat on the grass, a few safe feet away from the sheer drop. Not a word was spoken for several minutes. She accepted the cigarette I offered her and we sat and smoked in silence, that comfortable silence of old friends, or lovers, even though we were relative strangers. "I have to go," she suddenly said, flicking what was left of her half-smoked cigarette over the edge of the cliff... "It was really nice talking to you. We must do it again sometime."

Though surprised and a little disappointed at her sudden departure, I managed to say, "You know where to find me... Any time..." before she almost vanished into the darkness. I'm not a heavy smoker, rarely more than ten a day, often less, but in those last thirty minutes I'd got through three in very quick succession. In the bad old days, I used to smoke twenty or maybe thirty a day, simply because everybody else did. If someone in the pub, usually one of my locals, either The Plough or The Causeway, handed round the packet, you automatically took one.

Then sometime later, somebody else would do the same, so you took another one. Then it was your turn, and so it went on. Plus, if Bazza was with you, it was a cast iron certainty one of you would go home minus a lighter! In those days it truly was just a very bad, but sociable habit. Nowadays, I generally only indulge my 'filthy habit' when I really want one, and I have to say I still enjoy a smoke. I try not to do it in front of children or non-smokers, but if I'm on my own I see no harm in it, apart from what it may be doing to my lungs and bank balance.

I actually infuriated my doctor, and the practice nurse at my old surgery. Since joining a private health scheme, operated and paid for by my employers, Brannigan's, I have to have an annual fitness and health check, part of which involves blowing into something that resembles the cardboard tube at the centre of a toilet roll. I gather it monitors your lung capacity. Anyone who suffers from asthma will know what I'm describing. It seems my lung capacity is on a par with that of a non-smoker forty years my junior. So, there's one good reason for not giving up something I still enjoy very much. As for the financial side of smoking, I confess I once worked out approximately how much I'd spent on cigarettes during me forty-plus years as a smoker and it scared me. Mainly because it was the equivalent of somewhere close to one hundred bloody good holidays... And you know how much I enjoy my holidays. Still, it was too late now, for me at least.

If you're a smoker, and you haven't yet reached, say forty years of age, work it out for yourself and do the right thing. Give it up right now and spend the next forty years exploring this wonderful world of ours. I watched Debbie walking away until she completely disappeared along the cliff-tops. I made no attempt to follow her. She clearly wanted to be alone again, having had her fifteen-minute chat with the neighbour she barely knew. I wasn't about to spoil that moment for her, or myself. I liked her and hoped we would talk again someday soon. I even felt a little guilty at having such a great life when hers was clearly troubled.

I felt a further twinge of guilt as I reached for my fourth cigarette, going against everything I spoke of just now, then waited a good twenty minutes before making my own way down the winding footpath. As I walked past Debbie's cottage, I noticed a light on in the window above her front door, no doubt her bedroom. I looked away, fearful that she might glance out and see me looking up. Yes, I really liked her. Not in a sexual way, or even a loving way, but… I didn't know quite how to describe my feelings, but she was someone I felt I could sit up all night talking to without getting bored for a single second.

There again, if that night's conversation had been anything to go by, it was doubtful I would have understood a single word. A bit like smoking in the sixties to Pink Floyd, although JPS did not exist then so we had to make do with rolling our own… I climbed into bed at ten minutes past one in the morning, all thoughts of pot plants and trellises far from my mind… Up on the cliffs, although I'd been concentrating on Debbie and her problems, I couldn't help glancing over at the South Glamorgan coast, wondering if Kathy was looking over at Cornwall. Damn, I missed that girl. It was all well and good chatting on the phone, but nothing compares to sharing real time with someone you care about.

Not so long ago, we'd been regular visitors to each other's homes, mostly for the fun and games of being with a new partner—although we wouldn't really describe ourselves as such—and our mutual love of drinking until we were rat-arsed. Throughout 2012, we'd barely been apart, but then she had to move to South Wales shortly after Christmas and our meetings slipped to monthly. Somehow though, it still worked. But circumstances had kept us apart recently and we had reverted to e-mails and phone calls. But it kept the 'relationship' alive. I made up my mind to get over for a week-end soon… By a quarter past one, shortly after helping goal-keeper David De Gea save the penalty that won Manchester United yet another Champions League trophy, I was in a deep sleep.

11

The next morning, I decided it was time to stop spending money on pub food and takeaways and start preparing and cooking my own meals. There were two very good reasons for this. Firstly, the nearest Indian restaurant that offered home delivery was nearly nine miles away, and however good those tin-foil cartons were, my chicken Madras was inevitably almost cold following a twenty-minute drive. Luckily, I had a micro-wave for such eventualities. Let's be honest here, it was practically the only time I used it… That and warming up mugs of coffee I'd left so long they were almost cold. I have certainly never cooked in it.

The second reason for doing my own cooking was that, despite Colin and Lala's best efforts, slaving over a hot barbecue for more than three hours, I still had more than a week's supply of burgers, sausages and pizzas stacked in the freezer. Now I have to admit, on many occasions, I have told friends, usually over quite a few pints of Carling Darling, that I could cheerfully live on curry and pizza, but even *I* had my limits. As soon as the freezer was back down to a manageable level, which was in point of fact, nearly two weeks later, I would fill it with 'proper' food for a change: Chicken Kievs, Chilli Con Carne, Steak Pies, plus anything else Iceland had on offer. Oh, and a couple of bags of chips of course. But that was for the future. Today was garden planning day one.

I already had quite a few ideas of my own. I'd even managed to down-load a programme on my laptop that let you draw your own garden on screen and, magically, turn it into a very realistic set of 'photos', plus a panoramic video so that you could do a virtual walk around your planned garden, moving a pot here, or an ornament there, as you wished. I even knew it would work as it was almost identical to the one B&Q had used when Ellie and I were planning our kitchen back in Smallfield ten years earlier. I was surprised to find just how accurate it was.

We kept the print-outs they gave us and when the kitchen was completed some six months later—we fitted it ourselves, which took about five months and three weeks longer than the experts would have taken, but saved us two thousand pounds—I took five or six photographs from the same angles and apart from the fact that there's were computer generated, you couldn't tell the difference. We were most impressed. Which was why I was happy to design my own garden on the PC, but with a little help from Barry Marlow, the former teacher and now full-time home garden expert. He would later advise me what plants should go where, and what time of year to plant them for the best growth results, and 'certainly not there' as they would either get too much sun, or not enough.

Following my breakfast of sausages—there were now only about twenty left—baked beans and toast, I checked the weather and donned my trusty old leather jacket that had stood me in good stead for several years and through all kinds of weather. It had even survived 'that' day. Not bothering to lock up, as I now felt a part of the village and considered it safe to leave the door on the latch, I wandered the few yards past Sarah and Mark's, then Debbie's and along Barry's garden path. Colin shouted something rude across from the pub which I chose to ignore. He knew I'd heard him and in return I could hear him laughing at his own crudity.

Sarah had waved through the down-stairs window as I walked by. I waved back, smiling. There was no sign of Debbie, although I have to admit I deliberately didn't look as I past her cottage. I'm not sure why. Maybe it was because of her news. I didn't know if a cheerful smile would be appropriate when someone's just lost a friend. I remember the bizarre, but also understandable attitude of friends I'd known for years, each time I bumped into them during the weeks following my mother's sudden death. Instead of the usual 'Hi, you old bastard' or something even worse, I'd get a subdued 'Hello mate, how *are* you?' or 'Hey Paul, let me know when you're OK for a pint. I know it's not a good time, but…' and then the conversation would dry up, the sentence left unfinished…

So, I walked straight past Debbie's place and into Barry's magnificent garden. His was one of just two cottages in the village with a traditional thatched roof. The other belonged to a property developer who rented it out at exorbitant rates to business colleagues and their families through-out the summer season. It was, at that time, empty and had been since the previous

September, or so Colin told me. Those last visitors were, in his own words, stinking rich and a complete pain in the arse, demanding things such as lobster and caviar, and insisting he order in a case of Chateau Neuf Du Pape. When told he only served lager, cider, house wines and the standard spirits, they left in a huff and never came back. Colin didn't care about the loss of their money and assumed they'd spent the rest of the week hiring taxis to take them 'somewhere more civilised'…

Good riddance, thought Colin, who, like me, came down to Cornwall to get away from such pretentious garbage, not to expect it all on tap. I looked up and noticed the ivy that adorned most of the front of Barry's cottage was edging dangerously close to his thatching and remembered him telling me that as lovely as it looked, it was a nightmare keeping the creeping, clinging plant at bay. You didn't dare let it get to your thatching or it would 'eat' it. I assumed that wasn't to be taken literally, but as a former townie, I couldn't be certain.

I knocked on his front door, remembering him telling me the bell wasn't working… 'Might get it fixed one day, there again might not', he had told me enigmatically. Barry would sometimes come out with the strangest things, but you couldn't help but like him, and admire his green fingers… The door opened, "Come in my boy, come in, good of you to pop round."

As I said, strange. For one thing, calling me 'my boy' seemed a trifle odd—shades of Marie, back at work calling me young man—as he was at least five years my junior, maybe more. I guessed the expression might have stemmed from his days as a school teacher, but as he never talked about it, I would probably never know. Then there was the 'nice of you to pop round'… Not only had we already made the arrangements over one of Rara's cocktails the other night, but *he* was doing *me* the favour, so in fact it was nice of him to *have* me round… We sat and talked about nothing in particular for half an hour or so, enjoying two cups of very strong filter coffee, just how I liked it. I was keen to get him onto the subject of my garden but didn't want to push him on it. Indeed, there was no rush, I had all the time in the world, especially with summer just around the corner, a time even a non-gardener like me knew was the best time of year for re-designing your entire acreage.

Admittedly, I was unsure of what to plant and when, but that could wait. While I was quite prepared to do all the ground-work, deck-laying and gravel dispersal, I needed Barry to tell me which parts of the garden I needed to keep free to plant 'whatever' he thought best, and when. We had to agree on just how

71

many flowers and plants I should have, not only to have the desired effect, but also for easy maintenance. I had no intention of spending all my waking hours weeding and seeding, pruning, plucking and dead-heading or whatever it was genuine devotees got up to.

All I wanted was somewhere I could sit of an evening, in my own little world of peace and tranquillity, enjoying the fruits of my labours, so to speak... After the second cup of delicious coffee and a cigarette—Barry was one of the few people I knew that had no objections to people smoking in his house— 'Gave it up twenty years ago but still miss it'—I showed him my print-out 'photos'. He was impressed. The computer age had pretty much passed him by.

Nowadays, a PC was one of the first things four and five-year-olds starting school were introduced to, even though most of them had already dabbled at home. In his day, Barry explained, they were still getting by with the three R's. Bearing in mind computers were already widely in use at my son's school in the nineteen-nineties, I couldn't help but wonder just when Barry's teaching career had ended. Was he a local man? Was Cornwall really twenty years behind the rest of the UK as many us of had been led to believe? I may never find out. There was much more to Barry Marlow than met the eye...

Taking my photos, and after checking that I had copies, Barry began drawing over them. His artistry would never bother followers of Constable, but they did just what was required and showed me how my garden could look with just a little artistic effort. Over yet another cup of coffee, this time from a freshly brewed pot, he offered me cuttings from a few of his own favourites. I'm not going to pretend I had a clue what they were, as every name was in Latin and my own knowledge of that language was Amo, Amas, Amat, Amamis, Amatis, Amant, which was all I remember from my Grammar school days apart from the fact that my Latin master was a brilliant shot with a board rubber.

This was the nineteen-sixties remember. I did however recognise Begonia, although I may have spelt it wrongly. I also asked about a personal favourite, the clematis, which happily grew back every summer in my back garden in Surrey. While I was happy to leave that episode of my life behind me, I really liked that plant with its lilac, almost purple flowers. 'Oh, that'll grow practically anywhere' I was reliably informed. Having received the promise of a complete list of what I needed to create my perfect garden, and with the offer of his company to the garden centre when the time came, I prepared to take my leave of Barry's company, thanking him as I did.

He replied that it was a pleasure to talk about his favourite subject to someone who was genuinely interested, even if I *didn't* possess the famous green fingers. I thanked him once again and headed for the front door. As I passed the entrance to his lounge, I was surprised to spot what looked like the very latest model of Dell PC on a side table. Curious thought I...

Amended photos in hand, I found myself whistling as I ambled back down to my new home. Life was good, at least in *my* world it was. Having saved a fortune on the re-build of Windy Cottage, thanks to my old friend Erik, I found myself in the enviable position of being able to afford to splash out a little on superficial things such as the garden. I already had plenty of ideas of my own. Now all I had to do was build those ideas around my prospective flowers and plants. Despite the Latin names, Barry had also pointed out the window at each specific bloom the name related to. Of those he suggested, only one I found disagreeable to my eye.

Luckily, I knew which one it was now, and would strike it from my list as soon as he brought it round. If questions were asked, I would simply say that I didn't want to look like a copy-cat gardener, emulating all of his fine work. Not only would I get to lose the unwanted product, it should also boost his ego to receive such a compliment from someone several rungs below even a novice on the ladder of horticulture. Again, despite the temptation, I resisted glancing into Debbie's garden in case she spotted me. It might embarrass the poor girl, or worse still, she might fear the intentions of a man old enough to be her father. I'd already been down that particular romantic road once in my life and, as enjoyable as the experience was, I was not yet ready to try it again...

I decided to waste no time and set to work straight away. I switched on my PC and while it was warming up, pondered my neighbours. On the face of it, from day one I had considered St Matilda's Bay a typical village with the added bonus of having the Atlantic Ocean on its door-step. But the more I thought about them, the more I thought many of them were not exactly what they appeared to be. With the exception of Tom and Alice, every one of them seemed to have skeletons in their cute little Cornish cottage cupboards...

Why, for example, had Colin never re-married, or even entered into any form of casual relationship, if local gossip was to be believed. It was now more than twenty years since his separation and subsequent divorce. And he certainly had a thing for the ladies, if his flirtations with any that came into the Mariners Arms was anything to go by. I'd seen him in action. If he put his mind to it, I swear he could charm the knickers of a nun. But as I also spotted, many a time, if any of the ladies made any attempt to reciprocate, he would hurriedly make a joke of it, or change the subject. So, what was Colin's story? Had his ex-wife really turned him off women for life? Was he a closet gay? I'm sure in Brighton, nobody would have given it a second thought if he was, but as I mentioned earlier, this was Cornwall. And much of Cornwall always seems to be at least twenty years behind the rest of the country. And it's more remote spots, such as Tilda's, possibly even further back in time…

Then there was Sarah and Adam, my immediate neighbours. As I said, a very nice couple, always ready for a smile and a chat, sometimes even a good session in the pub. I'm sure Adam worked hard for what I assumed was a very large salary. Anyone in finance *always* seemed to be in the money and Adam was clearly no exception. He drove a top-of-the-range Mercedes and Sarah had her own BMW, and last year's model at that. Their cottage was the largest of our group at the bottom of the hill. Due to the structure of the cliffs, it actually stood about ten feet higher than Windy Cottage, giving them practically the same views as I had, but without the wind factor of being the one that over-looked the beach.

Even its garden was larger and longer than mine, again because of the way the cliffs dipped behind our row of cottages. If I was an estate agent, despite outwardly looking quite similar, I would estimate theirs to be worth at least fifty-thou more than mine, quite likely more. And what of Sarah herself? The fact that she was best known for her work with the W.I., plus her involvement with some of the local charities, suggested the Bonnell family weren't in need of money. I would also stake my life savings on them both having a good pension fund for what, about ten- or fifteen-years' time, I guessed.

So again, on the face of it, the perfect married couple… So why did their grown-up children never visit them? Adopted and moved on maybe? Abused? I thought that highly unlikely, but then what *does* a child abuser look like? Who knew…? Not every child-abuser has long white hair, smokes big cigars and presents television programmes, or stars in soap operas for that matter… Then of course there was the elusive Debbie, who was rarely seen in day-light, rarely went to the pub, even though she kept her car parked behind it, with the landlord's permission I should add, and wandered the cliffs after mid-night.

Now that *was* strange. Most young girls—OK, so she was in her thirties, but with me having turned sixty, she's a young girl—would never go wandering about, miles from anywhere, in the dark.

True, along with the rest of the community, I considered Tilda's to be one of the safest places in the world, but still... As for her reclusive life-style, that threw up still more questions. Did she work from home? Possibly a journalist for one of the better class glossy's, like Vogue. Maybe even a former model for such magazines, then forced to retire because she hit thirty, or ballooned to a size eight. She certainly had the look of a model. I didn't think she looked familiar, but then most of the models I would recognise made their name on page three of The Sun.

Was she a lady of independent means? Lottery winner maybe, escaping the money-grabbing relatives and begging letters. Whatever Debbie's story was, one thing was certain in my mind, she definitely *had* a story. But would it ever come out? That was anyone's guess... My over-active imagination went into over-drive once more. Rarely seen in day-light, walks the cliffs at night... Wasn't it somewhere in the West Country that the first 'official' sighting of a vampire was recorded? Which brought me back to Barry. Ah, Barry Marlow. Now there *was* an enigma. With apologies to Jeff Hardy and any TNA fans, I would go as far as to say a charismatic enigma. Nobody knew where he came from, though his accent had a vaguely Midlands lilt to it. He used to be a school teacher, but of which age group? And how long ago?

Most of the evidence suggested at least twenty years ago, but having said that, he didn't seem old enough. And what had he done since? On the other hand, on his occasional jaunts to the pub, he was the life and soul of the party, not a care in the world. But was it all a charade? My mind started running along the same lines as it had when considering Debbie's story, though this was now my conscious mind, so no thoughts of the living dead... Both single, it seemed. Neither obviously working, unless from home. Neither apparently short of cash, judging by cars and clothes, etc... And what was a techno-phobe like Barry doing with a PC? I suddenly realised I was turning into Tom Barnaby. Or should I say John these days?—Am I the only person who thought it strange that a former Midsomer gardener, who once tried to get into Joyce Barnaby's knickers, should return seven years later as Tom's cousin, now a detective?—I was starting to suspect all of my lovely new friends and neighbours of having committed some heinous crime all of a sudden... Just three days ago, these people were in and out of my house, enjoying my old friends' company, sharing food and drinks with us all… And now, here I was wondering if one, or all of them was a mass murderer or something.

Maybe they were all part of some outrageous swingers group, or perhaps sado-masochism was the thing people did to amuse themselves in this part of our glorious country! I once knew a sadist who met and began dating a masochist. You would think a match made in Heaven, but no. he offered to tie her up, which she gladly accepted. He donned a black leather mask with just the tiniest slits to peep through at her naked body. This thrilled her. She feigned an attempt to struggle free from the bonds that held her to the bed.

He went to the wardrobe and retrieved a whip. It resembled the medieval cat of nine tails. By now, she could barely contain her excitement. "Mmmmm…" she purred. "Are you going to whip me now, Master? Mmm, beat me to within an inch of my life!"

He looked down at her pure white body, the ropes holding her down, securely tied to each of the four bed-posts, gave an evil laugh and replied, "No…"

So, were all my neighbours hiding a dark secret? With the obvious exceptions of Tom and Alice, who were clearly innocent of any crime you could possibly imagine. They were just who they were, the loving grand-parents of my grand-daughter's new best friend. Which, if they lived in Oxford, or Denton, or Midsomer, would put them right at the top of my list of suspects… It was about then that I realised that my night-time fantasies were beginning to take over my waking hours. This wasn't right. I had to get back to my garden planning and face the fact that I was now living in my favourite part of Great Britain, with some lovely new friends, a glorious view of the beach and one of the best pubs I knew, complete with a top bloke for a landlord. It was stupid of me to think anyone in St Matilda's Bay might be hiding a dark secret… Wasn't it? I needed Kathy, and I needed her now!

12

Despite accepting the fact that I was being a complete idiot, thinking such dark thoughts about my new neighbours, it still kept me awake for half the night. And when I finally drifted into slumber, I was rudely awakened by Debbie, in a long white nightgown that was dripping with blood, shaking my shoulder and screaming, "HELP ME... HELP ME!" As I looked up, there was Barry, standing in the doorway, axe in hand, with an evil grin that said 'You can't escape me this time bitch...' To my shock and horror, in the corner of my room Adam and Sarah were making love... No, make that screwing, there was no love in the way he was brutalising his wife anally... I couldn't believe what was happening in my own house, my own bedroom... With all my neighbours...

As Debbie clung tightly to me, blood stains now seeping through to my bed-clothes, I heard Lala cheerfully calling 'last orders at the bar...' I woke up in a cold sweat. Even though I *knew* it had only been a dream, a very *bad* dream, I couldn't help but switch on the bed-side table lamp... Just to be sure. I was alone. No blood-soaked bed linen. No axe-wielding former teacher. No blood-soaked white dresses. No anal sex. Nothing. Yet it had been so real. And then a chill ran down my spine. I felt the dampness... But it wasn't Debbie's blood. For the first time in fifty-odd years, I'd wet myself...

I awoke late the next morning, having slept in the back bedroom, the one the sun *didn't* burst through at the crack of dawn. I picked up my mobile from the chest of drawers to the side of the bed and was shocked to see it was nearly ten o'clock. I hadn't slept that late in years, not even after Friday night's party or the drunken session with Lucy. I simply don't do lay-ins. Many years earlier, I had calculated the average person loses about twenty-five years of their life by sleeping an average seven or eight hours a night.

Personally, I can think of much better things to do with my time, so even if I have a day off, I'm always up and about by seven or half past at the latest... I decided there and then to put all thoughts of my neighbours harbouring evil secrets out of my mind, and go back to thinking of them exactly the way they really were. Adam was a highly successful financier, whose wife didn't need to work.

They simply needed to escape the hustle and bustle of the big city. And no, Sarah did *not* have a secret life as a high-class prostitute. Barry was also just what he said he was, a former teacher who had decided he could no longer cope with children of any age. He now stayed at home, tending his garden, and earning his keep lecturing on-line for the Open University, hence the PC he preferred people not to know about. He was just too modest to mention his Cambridge degrees. He enjoyed the simple life and just wanted to keep it that way. Or maybe I had simply been mistaken. It could just as easily have been a portable flat screen television, I spied.

Colin, of course, was enjoying a steamy affair with one of his barmaids, probably Rara, who had made no secret of her passion for older men... And wasn't she always the one who offered to stay behind and tidy up, telling Lala to get herself home to bed? No wonder the two of them always seemed so cheerful, yet tired. And poor Debbie? No *way* had she been kicked off the modelling circuit for dabbling with cocaine!

She had simply earned enough money that, at thirty years of age, she decided to quit before the wrinkles came. Moving down to Cornwall was the best way to escape the temptation of one last shoot. It didn't matter to Debbie *how* much Elle were offering for her to make a come-back. She was finished with it and that was that. Come to think of it, maybe that face *did* look vaguely familiar. There... Neighbours sorted and back to normal. Admittedly, the fantasies were still there in my head, but only in a good way... Time to start working on the garden.

I hadn't expected Barry's list quite so soon, but as I made my way downstairs, I spotted a note on the welcome mat. 'Sorry if I'm too early but I thought you might be up...' it read. Stapled to it was a list of Latin names I didn't recognise, but was sure the garden centre just the other side of Harwick would employ just the man to translate for me, or point me in the right direction. In any event, didn't garden centres tend to put both English and Latin names on those little pegs? Much in the same way the Welsh use both languages on their road signs... No rush, though.

First, I needed to find a good builder's yard. One that not only stocked sand, cement, paving slabs and gravel, but was also willing to deliver down a hill that an expert coach driver wouldn't risk. At the time, I was only planning on the front garden. I wanted to have it ready for the onslaught of summer visitors, which gave me about two months. The rear, which could not be seen from the road, could wait. That was a project *for* the summer months. I planned decking, a rock pool complete with waterfall, some clever lighting, plus the obligatory garden furniture.

I would also be on the look-out for one of those hammock-swing kind of things... I wasn't sure what it was called but it would be perfect for when Cheryl came to stay, but without looking 'childish'. After all, she wasn't far short of becoming a teenager. But all that could wait. I would check with the garden centre and builder's yard when I went there, if only to get a cost estimate, but no purchases until the front was completely finished to my total satisfaction. Call it vanity if you wish, but I had no desire for a hundred or more day-trippers to see my front garden doing a passable impersonation of a war zone! I turned on my trusty laptop.

As luck would have it, I found a builder's—Webster's—not too far from the garden centre. A glance at the web-site proudly announced it was a family business started by, and still partly owned by a local man, Robert Webster. I couldn't help smiling and wondering how he felt fifteen years earlier when Bob the Builder burst onto the scene. Embarrassed? Maybe. Alternatively, 'Robert' might have found it good publicity. I pictured him in his office and instead of answering with his full name, as many people do, perhaps he would simply say 'Bob the Builder' and test the reaction of the caller.

Silly idea, but still a damned site better than some that had run through my over-active mind the past twenty-four hours. I dialled the number... A sweet voice answered the phone, "Webster's Builders, Sarah Hall speaking, how can I help you?" That killed off all my previous wild imaginings. I gave the lady my name and address and asked if they delivered and whether or not there was a minimum value charge for deliveries.

Without even stopping to take a breath she replied that yes, they could certainly deliver and that delivery was free for any orders over two hundred pounds, or there was a thirty-pound charge if the total cost of my materials was less than, etc. It was all too quick and rehearsed for my liking, as though she was reading from a card... And probably filing her nails at the same time. I was tempted to ask if they sold left-handed screwdrivers but thought better of it. After all, I might need several deliveries before my work was complete, so instead I politely asked her to double-check my address as I lived in... "That's fine sir, I know it well. My cousin Lisa works in the pub down there. Our drivers know it well."

Sarah had interrupted my flow and at the same time told me all I needed to know. Silly me. I should have recognised the name. Webster's had practically re-built St Matilda's Bay the previous year, out of the goodness of their hearts, and gaining some excellent publicity at the same time. I thanked Miss Hall and promised to pop over later in the day to view the merchandise and place my order, which I assured her would easily exceed the delivery limit. We hung up... Going back to the web-site, I ran through the items I needed to complete all but the flower beds. As it was, Windy Cottage had a red brick path running in a straight line from the gate to the porch. That pleased me as I wanted a slightly winding path and had it presently been concrete, it would have meant hiring one of those noisy road drill things and I didn't fancy operating one of those at my age. I can turn my hand to most things, but I was fairly sure one of those would get my bones rattling.

Either side of the winding gravel path, I planned uniform rows of something Latin. Brightly coloured, but not growing or spreading too much. I'd finally lost the metal railing that ran along one side of the path, almost reluctantly as it had saved my life... Then there would be two small patches of lawn, so not too much mowing. The outside edges of my garden were going to be the hardest part. I rather fancied something I'd seen on holiday one year, not too far from here, in Torquay. It was a kind of palm-tree look-alike thing, surrounded by something resembling large blades of grass. It all combined to look similar to a cross between an Oriental garden and Hawaii. That might sound a bit crazy, but if you'd ever been to Devon, you would know what I mean, and with the right lighting—something I was *very* good at—it had a fairy tale appeal. It wasn't just for the benefit of passers-by or Cheryl and Minnie; the simple fact is that I'm a big kid at heart and the idea appealed to me.

I mentioned this to Barry but he poo-pooed the idea, saying you could only get away with such things on the South coast as the weather was totally different. He went on to tell me about micro-climates, horse-shoe bays and the Gulf Stream... 'Why, they even have *real* palm trees down there, none of that look-alike stuff', he pointed out. All of this meant nothing to me, but I was sure he was right.

Clearly the Northern coast, the Atlantic coast, with its mile upon mile of rocks and cliffs wasn't designed for palm trees and the like. Never-the-less, I was going to prove him wrong. I wasn't sure quite how just then, but I would. Thoughts of thermal lighting and under-soil heating were running through my mind. One way of another, I was going to have something in my garden that Mr Marlow didn't... A palm tree.

I will skip over most of the following week, due to the fact that I was working at my proper job, moving helicopter spares around the world. It was a job I still loved doing, even after twenty-five years, hence my agreement to stay on for an extra three. It was the only employment I'd ever known where every day was different, always a new challenge. One day I might be moving half a dozen nuts from Aberdeen to Norwich, a simple over-night courier would suffice.

The next day, I might have to transfer an engine from Trinidad to Malaysia and that *could* be a challenge. There were even times when a hand-carry would be called for. This was when and aircraft was "grounded" and could not fly until the defective part was replaced. Bearing in mind some of our oil and gas contracts earn up two or three thousand dollars an hour per helicopter, you can understand how it was imperative to move that spare part, regardless of cost, from "A" to "B" as quickly as possible. In certain parts of the world, notably West Africa, Australia and South America, freight is not treated with the same urgency as it would be in the USA or Europe for example. Due to its vast size, it can take three days just to move something from a remote part of Australia— and some of our bases were in extremely remote parts—to a major city with an international airport. Using road and air-freight alone, to move something from Barrow Island, Australia to Kharg Island in Nigeria, could take close to a week, which could mean losing thousands of dollars in revenue, while that particular aircraft was sat on the ground unable to operate.

Hence the need for the occasional hand-carry. This involved a volunteer, normally a Brannigan's employee, literally picking up the item from his local stores, putting it in his hand luggage and walking it through to his flight and jetting off to some far-reaching part of the world. Thanks to this necessity, I was lucky enough to visit such places as Stavanger in Norway, the island of Tobago, Budapest—the River Danube really *is* as beautiful as it is portrayed in film and song, plus the hotels show free porn channels for those interested in such erotic delights—and my favourite trip of all, to Macao, a two hour drive up the coast from Rio De Janeiro in Brazil. Rio was, to me, in equal parts, the most beautiful city, the most dangerous city, and the saddest city I had ever visited. It was the middle of February in the late nineteen nineties... Carnival fortnight.

When you hear someone say 'everything stops for carnival' you don't realise how close to the truth that is. About the only people who work in Brazil during the carnival season are those in bars, shops, restaurants... In fact, just about anyone who can make a living out of carnival. Plus, the authorities, of course. Freight sheds do not come under any of those categories, so if Brannigan's shipped a Fuel Pump to Rio arriving on February 17th, it would be sitting there until carnival ended, possibly a week or ten days later. Then there would be the backlog to work through, so our Fuel Pump could effectively take anything up to three weeks to get from "A" to "B", and in our world that was unacceptable. Which was why yours truly was on a thirteen-hour flight out of Heathrow in the early hours of the morning, somewhere around the middle of February that year.

Now if you're a smoker like me, you can imagine how that felt. Due to the lack of sleep the previous night, plus the time zone change, not to mention the boredom factor, I drifted in and out of sleep most of the way to Sao Paulo, my arrival city in Brazil before the short internal hop to Rio. Possibly the most bizarre thing about the flight was that they were showing a selection of Clint Eastwood films, five in all. At one point I can vividly recall Harry Callaghan being chased by two bogus motor-cycle cops suddenly finding himself in a deserted South America-looking town, playing 'keepy uppy' with a cowboy hat, Lee Van Cleef and two six-shooters... Right turn Clyde! It made *my* day. Back to sleep... I think it's true to say almost everything about that trip either surprised, shocked or amazed me.

On arrival, I couldn't believe airport workers—I could see them out of my window as we were taxiing—were wandering across the tarmac smoking. As were the officials checking my passport, and the lady behind the coffee bar counter. For myself, I'd had two by then. I imagined the chef, tossing the pancakes around the back of the café with a cigarette dangling from his lips and decided not to eat. Following the one hour hop to Rio, I was met be a chap called Mike, one of our overseas engineers, shortly after three in the morning. Nice chap Mike, for several reasons. A fellow Manchester United supporter, which gave us plenty to talk about on the drive up the coast to Macao, plus he was married to a local Brazilian girl called Cora, some thirty years his junior, drop-dead gorgeous and a fabulous cook.

Macao is not to be confused with the similarly named Macae, which is a thriving city in a completely separate part of Brazil. Over the following three days—one condition I made when accepting the trip was that I had a day sight-seeing—I discovered Brazil was exactly what I expected it to be. The girls were all stunningly beautiful and most liked older men, preferably European and white. The sun was unbelievably hot, the hottest I'd ever known. The rich live within spitting distance of the poor, and the bars stay open all night.

It was about four in the morning when Mike said, "Fancy a beer?" I'd been flying for close to fifteen hours with nothing but caffeine to keep me alive so, despite the time, and you have to remember *my* body clock was telling me it was about ten o'clock at night, I happily said yes. Anyone who's had the dubious pleasure of flying through five or six time zones will know how I felt. Whichever we you chose to look at it, it was definitely beer o'clock... We pulled over to the side of the road, by what looked like an all-night garage.

I was surprised to see three young children standing by the road-side, holding cans of Coca Cola. It was the middle of the night for God's sake... Once inside, the beers and glasses were taken from the freezer and placed on the table in front of us. Within minutes they were ready to drink. I remembered glancing at Mike's dashboard and noticing that, even at this time of night the temperature was still in the thirties. Ridiculous. A couple of hours later, he dropped me at my hotel and vanished into the night, heading for the nearby oil refinery to deliver our pump. "A" to "B" in nineteen hours.

Pretty good going and easily worth the just under one thousand pounds it cost the company to send me. My knowledge of Brazil was limited. Pele, gorgeous girls in yellow and green football shirts, that statue on a mountain and Barry Manilow's Copacabana. That was about it. Before leaving me, Mike promised to pick me up in the morning—I had no idea when that was... two hours away? Ten?—but as he headed for the hotel door, he turned and said, "If you go out, make sure you stick to the lit roads. And if you fancy another beer, go to Charlie's Bar along the beach. It's run by an American fella and very popular with all the white guys out here."

I didn't go out. I decided to do my sight-seeing in day-light. I went to my room and without even looking at the book I'd brought, went straight to sleep. You will have to forgive me if some of the times do not make sense. Much of my three days in that country are still a blur, and I never *did* get used to the time difference. It didn't help having bars that stayed open all night either... The following day, Mike picked me up and took me to his house, just a five-minute walk from Macao beach.

I had the most incredible breakfast of pancakes, scrambled eggs, bacon and some fruit I'd never even heard of let alone tasted before. It was all washed down with the strongest black coffee, possibly the best I'd tasted since a holiday in Turkey some years earlier. Fabulous. After that, we strolled down to the seafront to admire the white sand and blue sea in all its glory. From Mike and Cora's house, I'd already heard the music, but to see it first-hand was a wonderful sight. Even that early in the morning—I gather it was around ten a.m. so I'd slept for no more than about five hours—I counted seven different bands, some playing on the beach, others walking up and down the promenade. Girls in minute bikinis dancing. Men in shorts louder than the music, leaning up against trees just watching the world go by. To Mike and Cora, this was a regular event.

Apart from the annual carnival, each of the coastal towns had at least two or three private ones of their own. I suppose, to the locals it was no different from our village fetes back home, but to me it was something special. No hoop-la for example. Macao itself was not much bigger than St Matilda's Bay, with a local population of around two hundred, but it had been boosted immensely since the late nineteen-eighties by the arrival of the oil and gas community who were housed about two or three miles further up the coast in its own portacabin village. It was on Macao beach that I first saw the darker side of Brazil.

As we strolled along in the hot sunshine—I had sensibly packed my wide-brimmed hat and factor fifty—we were joined by a young girl, possibly about eighteen at a guess, who quickly fell in step with us. She was pushing a buggy with a screaming baby in it, no more than about eighteen months old. Holding her hand was another child of about three or four. She was also heavily pregnant with a further child and babbling away in Portuguese, occasionally glancing up at me.

Cora said, "Keep walking, take no notice." I did, and gradually we lost her. Once we were well clear of the young mother, Mike's wife explained she was offering to sell me her un-born baby for ten English pounds. I learned this was a regular thing between young Brazilian girls and any white male, be it American, British or main-land European, many of whom worked locally in oil and gas exploration. I tried to put it out of my mind and enjoy the atmosphere, but the experience stayed with me most of the day. I was learning just how poor some of the natives really were and it was staggering to find that so many Brazilians were rich beyond our wildest dreams, while things like that young girl were going on practically on their door-steps.

The remainder of the day was spent admiring views, having a beer or two, returning to their house for a late lunch and even a little dancing on the beach. Cora nearly collapsed at the sight of my two left feet, while she of course had that natural rhythm that seemed to be born into every South American. Mike just sat back and had another beer, smiling all the while. I couldn't help wondering what hours he worked, if any. For most of my three days he was never far away. That evening, we'd agreed to meet for a farewell drink in Charlie's. The morning after, he was to drive me back into Rio so that I could spend a few hours exploring the famous city with that statue and the best-known beach in the world, before taking a taxi back to the airport. I arrived at the bar around eight in the evening, I think. It was hot, sticky, smoky and full of loud Americans and even louder music, also mostly American.

There were two ceiling fans that didn't appear to do anything to alleviate the heat or disperse the smoke. For the second part, I was not complaining. Hopefully, I would inhale enough of the stuff to see me through the flight home. The beers, yet again, came straight from the freezer. With the aid of my ever-vivid imagination, I was half expecting Humphrey Bogart to walk in. It didn't feel real to me, more like a movie scene, something out of Key Largo maybe, or Casablanca. Mid-way through my second beer, a gorgeous girl strolled up to my table and crouched down in front of me. She was wearing a pure white shift dress which only complimented her olive skin. Stunning! She was muttering something I didn't understand, but I wasn't about to complain. What normal red-blooded male would? She had to be about nineteen or twenty and clearly wore nothing under that dress. Her erect nipples and the fact that her knees were slightly apart being somewhat more than a clue.

And no, I wasn't dreaming this time, it really did happen exactly the way I'm describing it. Distracted by this young lady, I almost failed to notice another one behind me, as her hands gently massaged my shoulders, then slowly moved down to my chest, fingers circling my nipples. Rather than stating, or doing the obvious, I glanced around the bar and realised nobody else was taking the slightest notice of this double seduction. I took a large swallow of cold beer. Just as the first girls' hands began to caress my groin, I heard Mike's voice, although I couldn't understand the language. All in a matter of seconds, the girls had gone and Mike was at the bar ordering two beers.

On his return to the table he apologised, saying he should have warned me. It was always the same when a new white man came to town. The girls would automatically assume he was an oil worker, no doubt with plenty of money in his pocket, far from home, wife, girl-friend... I guessed the idea was for one of them to distract you—that had certainly worked—while the other one deftly picks your pocket, relieving you of your wallet, cash and credit cards, then they both vanish into the dark streets where no white man dares to go alone. I had already been partially warned but still almost fell for it. I said as much to Mike as I thanked him and started on my third beer. But I was wrong. They were both prostitutes. I could have had them both, all night in my hotel, for about thirty pounds. Worse still, they were no more than fourteen years old. I learned a lot from Mike those three days and not all of it good. For example, the kids outside the bar at four in the morning? They had almost certainly stolen the Cokes from the back of the bar and were now selling them, cut price, to anyone passing with a raging thirst. It was probably the only income their families had.

On the way back to the airport, I noticed the rich/poor divide that Cora had told me about. On one side of the road were shining white villas, mansions almost. Yet on the other side, no more than fifty yards away, were the shanty towns, with literally thousands of huts made from corrugated iron sheets—no windows—where entire families would live, if that's the right word for how they survived. The huts were deliberately built no more than four feet apart so the police couldn't drive between them, or to them if a thief or rapist made his escape into the hills. Crime was rife. Rape, murder, all sorts. Not a place to visit on my one and only trip to Brazil.

Again, I had to put it out of my mind and try to enjoy the good things about that beautiful but sad country. The last things I remember about Brazil are nearly burning my feet on Copacabana beach. I was busy looking up at the statue of Christ the Redeemer staring down at me—yes, I had finally learned its name—staring down at me from the Corcovado Mountain, and not as I'd always thought from Sugar Loaf Mountain. The joys of world travel. You really did learn something new every day. Not all of it good...

No such exotic excursions for me the week after Easter in St Matilda's Bay however, for which I was very thankful. As much as I enjoyed my travels, I had just two short months to have my garden to a standard that would elicit words of praise from the summer visitors to our little village. As much as I loved my work, that week I found extremely frustrating. Not because I had three different operational Chief Engineers screaming down the phone at me… I knew the pressure they were under from the oil companies and they would all be satisfied and full of gratitude by the end of the day.

No, it was more the fact that I wanted to move forward with my garden, and my next week off was still five days away. I suppose I could have simply ordered on-line, but I like the personal touch. While I'm happy to order Janet Devlin's latest offering on iTunes, or the new Nicci French from Amazon to down-load onto my Kindle Fire—after all, you can't go wrong with something mass produced like music and books—but I have never entirely trusted on-line photographs. I'm not just talking about the woman on a dating web-site who describes herself as blonde, but turns out to be grey, or the man who claims to be thirty—which he may well have been when that picture was taken—but in reality, will not see forty again… For evidence, I offer you the menu signs you see outside Spanish bars, or any other European tourist-trap restaurant come to that.

The food that arrives on your table never looks quite as good as it did in the photograph. It may well *taste* as good, which I suppose is most important, but that fact remains it doesn't *look* the same. Which all leads me back to gravel and paving stones. Sure, they would still feel the same under-foot, but would they be the right colour? I'm very fussy about colours and they had to be just right, especially when they were going to be on show to the general public that coming summer. No, for me, it called for a personal visit to Webster's, and for that, I had to wait another five bloody days! Hence my frustration. I'm sure anyone who's ever bought a dress or suit from an on-line catalogue will understand exactly how I felt that morning. I shall say no more. On the 'up' side, I did receive an unexpected visitor on the Friday morning.

It was ten a.m. and I'd already had my eggs and bacon, and two cups of strong black coffee, plus successfully talked one of our French suppliers into air-freighting a Spar Tube to Karratha, Australia, by the Air France flight out of Paris that same afternoon. I was flavour of the month with my Supply Chain manager once again. At least for a few hours. The door-bell rang, and bearing in mind I had a solid front door with no glass panes, I was unable to have an advanced warning of how gorgeous my near neighbour looked, even at that early hour in the day… And without make-up. It was odd to see her in pyjamas, covered by a black and red silk dressing gown. It *shouldn't* have seemed odd, as most of the village, myself included, had often ventured outside in such attire, normally to pop over to the recently re-opened Connie's, which was now much more than an ice cream parlour and souvenir shop.

It was now a mini-market also, which meant no more panic buying from Tesco's on-line Shop and Drop service when you ran out of milk. Even Rachel was back where she belonged, behind the counter in a brand-new uniform, but with the same name-tag. That's the other Rachel, not to be confused with Colin's barmaid, better known as Rara... For some reason, that particular Friday morning, I'd actually got myself dressed, rather than lounging around in my own PJ's. I often didn't bother until it was time for my lunch-time pint over the road, as I rarely had visitors that time of day. The residents of Tilda's only seemed to come to life in the afternoons for some reason. I let Debbie in and showed her into the kitchen. The kitchen has always been the hub of family life in my world.

Prior to being re-housed in a draughty first floor council flat, I grew up in two different houses, both of which had very similar oak tables, large enough to seat about eight people, even though there was hardly ever more than three or four of us. British families in the nineteen fifties and sixties tended to have strict rules about what was done where in the family home. Much of the time was spent in the kitchen. The back room was for relaxing in the evening after the children had gone to bed. The front room was only ever used for special occasions, such as the vicar popping round... I understand much of rural France is *still* like that. When I married, we moved into a Victorian house which again had a huge kitchen. Because of my history, I re-designed it to include a breakfast bar. When I moved to Smallfield, where Ellie and I lived for nearly thirteen years, it already *had* a breakfast bar. Perfect. As Debbie and I walked the short distance from front door to kitchen, I couldn't help wondering what had prompted her first ever visit to my humble home. Despite her promise to try, she never *did* call round for a drink the previous Friday.

"I feel I owe you an apology and an explanation," she began, accepting my offer of coffee, not too strong, white with no sugar. Totally incompatible. Thirty years age difference and we didn't even share the same taste in coffee. Still, a man can dream, can't he? I could think of no good reason for either apology or explanation. So, she'd failed to turn up for my house-warming party, interrupted my solitary walk on the cliffs one night, nearly run me over Saturday afternoon outside the Mariners and barely spoken two words to me in the year I'd lived just two doors down... Hell, I didn't even know her surname! Perfectly normal. No apology or explanation required, I thought, though maybe I was biased by the fact that she was so God-damned pretty and I couldn't stop thinking about dragging her upstairs, ripping off that silk dressing gown and cute PJ's and making mad passionate love to her for the rest of the day... Sorry Kathy, but I'm only human after all. Her words broke my reverie and brought me back down to Earth... She spoke, uninterrupted by me for a full five minutes:

"I'm afraid I'm not a very social person. Or should that be sociable? I'm not sure. English never was a strong subject. I've always got by with my looks and personality, though I suppose you'd find that hard to believe considering we've barely spoken and I didn't come to your party. It's just that I don't mix with people very much. I moved down here to get away from crowds but now I realise that you can be much more alone in a crowd than in a village where everyone wants to chat to you. In big towns and cities, everyone ignores you, or they're talking on their mobile phones and don't even know you exist until they bump into you, mutter 'sorry' and move on. You can be anonymous in a big town.

"I'm surrounded by lovely people down here but don't even know them, don't really *want* to know them, and I don't mean that to sound rude but I don't think they'd want to know *me* so I lock myself away indoors and let their world get along perfectly well without me being a part of it. I watch television but couldn't tell you what was on, I'm in a day-dream most of the time. I didn't even *see* you last week when I nearly ran you over and that was so rude of me, and dangerous, and even then, when I came home, I just shut myself away again when I should have come around and apologised but I couldn't, you see. There were too many people... And the children. I just couldn't. The only time I feel really at peace is on the cliffs.

"I sometimes think about jumping off just to see what it feels like to fly, but I'm not suicidal despite everything, it's just the freedom I want to feel. The freedom to come and go as I please without feeling they're watching me all of the time. If only things had been different, I might never have come here. I should have gone to New Zealand when I had the chance but that would have been wrong. Mummy would never have forgiven me if I had. Oh, *why* did she have to die?

"It should have been me, not her. Then there's the dog of course. But it was still wrong of me to spoil your night up there, you looked so peaceful. I should have just turned and walked away and you would never have known I'd seen you. Thank you for the cigarette, you're a very kind man, inviting me to your party even though you don't really know me. Life could have been so different if I'd just turned away more often. Do you see what I mean?"

On the point of saying those last words, she had looked up at me, tears streaming down her face. I hadn't noticed before as her head was resting on her hands through the entire speech, eyes looking down into her half-finished cup of coffee, as if afraid or ashamed to make eye contact. In answer to her question, I wanted to say 'I don't have the faintest clue what you're talking about Debbie', but all I could manage was 'I'm sure everything will work itself out, you really mustn't worry so much, life's too short', as I put my arms around her and held her close to me. Her arms shot around my waist and clung so tight I nearly lost my breath. She was sobbing uncontrollably by then.

There was no point trying to hold a conversation with her in her current state, so I just stoked her hair and thought back over some of the things she said. Most of it was garbled, even more so than that night on the cliffs, but one or two things stood out. In those few brief seconds, she was in my arms, I tried unsuccessfully to make some sense of it all. She hated crowds, didn't feel safe around people, could have gone to New Zealand but didn't, someone had died, but shouldn't have... And then there was the dog of course. Of course? What dog? Who died? Why should Debbie have died in her place? And why hadn't she emigrated to New Zealand? For a miniscule moment, I wondered if she was on some kind of drug, prescription or otherwise... For whatever reason, she was one very mixed up, quite possibly very frightened young girl. I wanted to help if I could.

Did she have family? Parents? A doctor? Why wasn't anybody doing anything to help her? It was at that point I knew I had not one, but two missions over the following weeks: Finding a way for palm trees to flourish on the rocky Atlantic coast, and getting to the bottom of Debbie's problem. Then, hopefully, resolving it. This was no fantasy; this was real life in all its ugliness. I was awakened from these thoughts by the sound of a 'ping', my company Blackberry ringing. Someone needed a Main Rotor Blade moving to Scatsta in the Shetland Islands and they wanted it yesterday. How I wished I had a TARDIS sometimes. Life would be so much simpler. But then I'm a person who thrives on the adrenalin rush, so I headed into the front room to activate my laptop. I called out to my visitor, "Sorry about this Debbie, I have to work. Help yourself to another coff…" but I heard the front door softly closing. She was already gone.

13

I'm sad to report I saw nothing of Debbie over the next few days. This came as no great surprise as it had already taken her a year to even *talk* to me, let alone allow me a glimpse into her psyche, bizarre though it was. However, I was sure the day would come when we would once again speak of dogs and death and New Zealand. In the mean-time, I had work to deal with over the following days, plus my planned visit to Webster's the following Tuesday, just as soon as I had handed over my work-load to Dave, my partner-in-crime, who worked out of Norwich in East Anglia.

Although, strictly speaking, we were expected to stay on-line all day for the hand-over, we inevitably completed what was in fact usually a fairly simple task, by mid-morning and it was rare for either of us to be on-line after about ten or eleven the morning of day eight. Therefore, by mid-day, I was wandering around Bob's yard, not only checking the colours of various local stone slabs, but also picking up hints for the future. I fell in love with some of his garden furniture. I found the perfect swing, hand-made locally from re-claimed railway sleepers. Considering eighty-five per cent of Cornwall's railway network had been raped fifty years earlier, there had to be thousands of them just waiting to be turned into door-steps, benches and, for the more adventurous craftsmen, garden swings. That was noted for the future.

As was a rock pool made from real Cornish rock, not the artificial moulded type you found in Surrey garden centres, one of which I confess I used to own. This particular one was designed by Bob's son Gerald I was told. Of course, I would have to design my own, but this certainly gave me a very good idea of what *could* be achieved with just a smidgen of imagination. And as you know, I have that in abundance. Having found exactly the right colour slabs and gravel, I made my way into Bob's office to place my order and ask to speak to Gerald, if he was free for a few minutes. He was, and happy to talk. Gerald Webster could only be described as the train-spotter of gardening. If asked, he could probably tell you the exact spot the sleeper was lifted from that was used to create that garden swing. If pushed, no doubt he would know the last train to pass over it back in nineteen sixty-four or whenever… And its loco number… And the number of passengers it was carrying that day… And… I chose not to push him.

What I *did* want to know was how to grow palm trees on the North Cornwall coast, with its sometimes-freezing winds and lashing rain. As it turned out, due to the cliff formation that almost surrounded St Matilda's Bay, and the peculiar South-West facing beach, one of only two on the Atlantic coast apparently, it might just be possible. Was this the horse-shoe effect Barry Marlow had touched upon? The afore-mentioned cliffs formed a barrier against the worst of the weather that might have hit the bay had they been a few feet lower, whereas those North winds only ever hit the outer reaches of our village, about half-way up the hill en route to Harwick. This was encouraging.

So, was it possible? Had anyone actually tried it before? I knew from my wanderings that none of the seven buildings at the bottom of the hill had palm trees, unless they were tucked around the back… He assured me it *was* possible, even without my outrageous suggestion—according to Gerald—of under-soil heating, though he did consider it rather inventive. I think he appreciated meeting a like mind for a change, instead of his regular customers. For 'like' read 'ever so slightly strange.' I made a mental note to try and think of other outlandish ideas for my forthcoming gardens. I would certainly bring them to his attention if I did. He also mentioned he had a cousin, Merv, who worked part-time in the Harwick Garden Centre, whom he assured me would be very helpful in my quest for the unusual, "The Webster's are famous for it in these parts, sir. If it's out of the ordinary, we've either got it or we'll get it."

It was a proud boast, but I believed him and promised to speak to Merv when the time came to start my planting. Did they stock palm trees? No, but Merv would get me one, or two if I asked him. Quite cheap too. Never having bought anything more than a pot plant for Mother's Day, I had no idea how cheap a cheap palm tree might be. Was fifty pounds cheap? Five hundred? In hindsight, I suppose I should have asked… I drove out of Webster's in a very good frame of mind and with Bob's promise that my delivery would be with me the very next day. That gave me just the rest of Tuesday to clear a space in the front so that I didn't cause too much of an eye-sore, or worse still block the narrow lane.

I smiled and waved at Sarah as I left the office, not even bothering to double-check the lorry could navigate our lane. She was sat behind a very tidy desk, complete with her own name-plate, busy on her laptop. She was not filing her nails.

Due to the narrowness of the lane, and its one way system that reached all the way to the B3285, the journey that took me to Webster's had taken me less than ten minutes, but the drive back took nearly twenty-five, passing through Harwick village itself, the same route I had taken when I first arrived. I took more notice this time, it being the first time I'd driven down the lane in day-light since the day of the flood, and at that time I was only interested in finding the beach, a drink and something to eat. Many of the houses in Harwick, though pretty, were in need of a lick of paint, and some of the gardens were in urgent need of some tender loving care. A full-time job for my friend Barry perhaps.

But this was a dying community. It had been dying for twenty years and there was very little the locals could do to stem the flow towards a lingering death. The boarded-up Station Hotel was additional proof of that. I wouldn't even have known its name if I hadn't been told. It had the look of a public house, but no name displayed above the door. No brightly coloured Great Western Railway locomotive on a swinging sign, though the frame still stood there, alone on the edge of the deserted weed-strewn car park.

That is deserted other than the rusted, possibly burnt out remains of what was once someone's brand new Vauxhall Astra. I pulled into the car park. It didn't seem right just to drive through without stopping to pay homage to the village that helped put money in Colin's bar till. A village that would probably never again have its own pub, or Post Office, or railway station... Just a lonely Co-operative Store serving the once thriving community. I walked the few yards to the railway bridge and looked down to where the single track used to be. The track that only last century, before virtually everyone became part of a two-car family. The track that used to take villagers for a day at the sea-side. I crossed the road and looked down again at what was now a cycle path cum bridle way.

A few yards away, I could see the remains of what was once Harwick Station. The platform remained intact, though completely over-grown with weeds and brambles, cut back just far enough not to endanger riders of either horse or bicycle. I'm sure both must have loved the freedom of riding without the fear of cars and lorries... But I'm equally sure the children who used to ride the train to St Matilda's Bay to build sand-castles, paddle in the sea and eat ice cream loved it so much more all those years ago.

To the side of the co-op ran a narrow lane called Station Approach. I wandered down it to find what was left of the old station building. It wasn't boarded up like many of Harwick's closed businesses. All the windows and doors had been either smashed or removed. From what I assumed had once been a busy commuter car park, I could see right through to the track bed. As I walked though, I noticed there were still a few posters stuck to the walls of the ticket office, advertising day trips to St Ives, among other long-gone delights.

Plus, the most recent time-table, dated 1994. All of which was barely readable thanks to twenty years of un-checked graffiti. Cigarette ends, lager cans and used condoms told me how often British Rail actually checked on their dis-used property, if indeed it *was* still their property. Many of the thousands of stations, closed by either Dr Beeching or in Harwick's case, lack of local prosperity or need, had been purchased privately and turned into luxury homes, normally by railway lovers, or steam fanatics, deep in nostalgia… But not this one. Not Harwick.

It was simply a rubbish tip and occasional playground for the local vandals and teenagers… At the far end of what remained of its platform, I stood and imagined how it must have been twenty or thirty years ago. Commuters heading into Hobart or Truro departing from Platform One. Others off to the bay for the day waiting patiently on the opposite side of the tracks… I suppose what surprised me most of all was how they ever thought the extended branch from Harwick to St Matilda's could ever make a profit. The former track bed couldn't have been much more than two miles at the outside. It would almost have been quicker to walk. Heading back up Station Approach, just beyond what used to be the village pub, I spotted the main reason for Harwick's dilapidation. The remains of a closed-down tin mine.

A feeling of guilt swept over me. Along with almost every other tourist who had taken the trek to one of the most stunning parts of the UK, I had only ever seen deserted tin mines as a photo opportunity. Something you often saw on Cornish postcards or calendars. Or on the opening credits of Wycliffe, the Cornish Detective. Well at least *some*body was still making money out of them. Unfortunately, it was probably a combination of photographers and publishers from London, rather than the locals, the ones that really needed the money. I walked as close as I could get to this particular one, just for a look, a glance into

Harwick's history, to a time when the Station Hotel was probably bursting with customers, pockets full of locally-earned cash... A time that would never return to Harwick...

As I walked back to the Clio, a friendly face called across the road and waved at me. I didn't know his name, but I recognised him as one of Colin's regulars. He looked cheerful enough, but made no attempt to cross the road to talk so neither did I. The mood I was in, I didn't imagine he would want to listen to my thoughts on the demise of his village, as sympathetic as they were. I climbed back into my car and headed home. Ten minutes further along the lane, I passed what I supposed was probably St Matilda's own station. I couldn't be sure as it was buried within the trees, but it seemed to be of a similar build to that which I had seen in Harwick, and the lane shortly after it bore a remarkable resemblance to the cycle track, ending as it did, at the top of the hill leading down to the bay. I vowed to take a stroll back up the hill one day to see if I was right.

If I was to be a true resident, it was only right that I should know something of its illustrious history. I vowed to not only inspect the remains of the station, but also to speak to Tom, fountain of all local knowledge and brush up. Having seen the differences between Harwick and Tilda's, just two short miles apart, I couldn't help think *our* station, though presumably closed at the same time, would still have all its doors and windows intact, frames painted the regulation GWR green... Possibly now a museum... I even half-expected to see smoke coming from its chimney and a classic 0-6-0 Pannier Tank engine stood at the platform...

14

The following weeks didn't go exactly to plan, although Bob was as good as his word and had my slabs, building sand, gravel, plus various other bits and bobs, too numerous to mention, delivered the very next day, and I had cleared the front garden of all unwanted items such as the red-brick path, several large ornamental rocks—I planned to make use of those in the back, or maybe a rock garden—and a rather ugly gargoyle, which Minnie thought looked 'rather cute' and helped me to move. Thus achieved, and with a front garden that resembled many I had witnessed in Harwick, I had five days, Thursday to Monday, to make a start in converting a building site into something similar to Barry's effort.

While I was well aware it would take more than just those five days to even get the slabs bedded in and the pointing done, I did at least hope to have the ground-work done and ready for the *real* work to start. I hadn't counted on the unpredictability of the Great British weather. The past three weeks had been wonderful, even better than I had hoped for, considering much of my Easter party was planned for the back garden. It had been mild, almost warm most of the time.

I hadn't lit a single fire, despite having logs piled high either side of the fireplace just in case. It hadn't rained for at least five weeks. Well, not what you could *call* rain anyway. We'd had the odd shower, but nothing lasting more than a few minutes... Then bang on cue, the sky darkened, the black clouds stared angrily down over the bay, and the Heaven's opened. OK, so I was prepared. I had a tarpaulin ready to cover the sand if we had a shower, so ten minutes earlier, around the time I thought night had come early, I rushed outside, covering the huge sack and anchored it down on all four sides with paving slabs. As the first drops fell, you just *knew* it was going to be a heavy one. I don't know what it is about British rain, but I instinctively knew, without even looking at the sky, that this was not going to be a five-minute shower. When I *did* look up, the sky was just one solid wall of dark grey.

The waves were rolling in six or seven feet high, thankfully nothing like the previous year though. These stopped as they hit the foot of the cliffs. They wouldn't even damage the re-built red, blue and yellow beach huts. The dozen or so people on the beach, mostly locals walking dogs or just taking some exercise, had long gone. They left when the sky turned light grey and you could still see a break in the clouds. If we had been a larger community, the surfing brigade would be hurriedly changing into their rubber suits by now. I imagined hundreds of them on the beaches of Newquay and Perranporth, just ten or fifteen miles further down the coast.... Despite the glorious white horses we often experienced in Tilda's, we never have to suffer the onslaught of Beach Boy fans, due to the size of our beach. Even on a normal wave the sea reaches more than half way to the cliffs.

On a day like this, any surfer risking the ride would do far worse than wipe out. He'd be smashed to pieces against the rocks... No, this was no short sharp shower. This was going to last a good hour or two, which would kill off any chance of my getting started on the garden today. It was already three o'clock and the daylight would be dwindling in three or four hours, or sooner if those clouds didn't clear pretty soon... It was still raining, though not quite the torrential down-pour we had seen earlier in the day, as I turned off the bed-side lamp just before mid-night. I'm one of those people that sleep with the curtains open more often than not. I like to see the sun rise in the morning. Even the front room curtains down-stairs are hardly ever closed, unless I'm entertaining.

That Thursday evening, I couldn't help noticing the lights of the Mariners Arms were switched off just after nine. I could only assume no-one had ventured out during the storm and Colin gave up waiting, saved a few over-heads and went upstairs to his own living quarters. No wonder The Beachcomber didn't even bother opening at all until the end of April or early May. Even the customers from Harwick were loath to attempt our hilly lane in such weather. Tom had told me once it turned into a river during such storms, which were quite regular so it seemed, though this was my first one, so I'm not entirely sure of Tom's definition of the word 'regular'.

Neither of Colin's barmaids worked regular evenings during the week at this time of year. They simply weren't needed. Rara and Lala shared the lunch-times and Sundays, with both working the Friday and Saturday evenings.

During the summer, one or the other would quite often be asked to do mid-week evenings if the weather was fine, though the pub next door also took its share of the summer load, which suited Colin. He made a comfortable living and preferred not to have a crowded pub. On one of his quieter nights, I had casually suggested he tried holding a quiz night.

He wasn't too keen until I offered to host it for him. I suggested maybe we should try it after the summer season ended, just for the locals I said, like a community night out. He saw pound coins in front of his eyes and agreed to give it a try come September... As I lay there listening to the rain rattling on the roof of Windy Cottage, various thoughts ran through my head: How long would this rain last? When would I have the pleasure of talking to the delightful Debbie again? Soon I hoped... Would the quiz night work? Would my palm tree survive weather like this? The answer to that would have to wait until I actually *had* a palm tree. And putting aside my ridiculous thoughts of steam engines at St Matilda's station... Would it really be in better condition than Harwick? I honestly thought so.

Apart from anything else, there were no teenagers in our village, and if Crawley teenagers were anything to go by, Harwick's variety were highly unlikely to walk two miles, unless there was the promise of a few beers, a pack of cigarettes and the chance of a sexual encounter at the other end. It was just then, as I was drifting away into dream-land, that I realised two things: Firstly, that I hadn't been the Invisible Man for as long as I could remember, and secondly, that I hadn't had a cigarette myself since just after Minnie and I had moved the gargoyle from front to back. I couldn't say why, but maybe it was the realisation that I had finally come home. That was the last thing that crossed my mind before I was dead to the world...

I awoke around six-thirty on the Friday morning, just as the sun came up. Although there was no sign of it through my bedroom window, just the vague brightness of the Earth's life source trying to force its way, unsuccessfully I might add, through the clouds. At least one of last night's questions had been answered. It was still raining! Had it rained all night? There was no way of telling thanks to the deep, but restful sleep I'd just enjoyed. But either way, there it was, the familiar pitter-patter of rain-drops on my roof yet again.

Tempting though it was to pull the covers over my head and have an extra hour, I resisted it and went down-stairs to put the kettle on. Having done my ablutions, I could wait no longer... I had to check. Yes, there it was. One ready-made water feature had magically appeared in my front garden. Or to be more precise, it *was* my front garden! And I wasn't alone. In the dead of night, just as the Tooth Fairy was putting a pound coin under hundreds of children's pillows, the Landscape Garden Fairy had given us *all* a brand new water feature. How nice of him. Or her… It was clear that no progress would be made today.

Any chance of yesterday's rain seeping into the soil, allowing me to start laying sand for my winding path, was neutralised by *today's* shower, albeit far less heavy than it had been. It simply topped it up. A tiny part of me hoped it would be gone later in the day, or maybe tomorrow, but the larger percentage of me knew damned well it wouldn't. I was also resigning myself to the fact that I was now going to get no further on my front garden until at least a week next Tuesday, which would not only take us into May, but it also meant that any day-trippers would see Tom's garden, then Barry's, even Debbie's and Adam's, think how pretty they looked… And last but not least… "Oh, it's such a shame. You'd think they'd make an effort, wouldn't you? It spoils the whole look of the area!"

I could hear the comments now and there was not a single thing I could do about it. Even Colin would make a few quid out of it. He was a great one for story-telling was Colin. I knew for a fact that the first person to mention that 'mess over the way' would get him spinning some yarn which, God only knows why, the tourists always fall for. "That's where Buster Edwards, you know, the Great Train Robber hid from the police while he was on the run for three years. Not on the run at all, he wasn't, just tucked away down here. Course they caught him eventually. His son owns it now but only comes down in the summer to get away from the papers. Press and TV always after him for a new angle to the story, you know what they're like…" I bet you think I'm making that up but I swear it's the truth.

I heard him with my own two ears that week-end, relating his tale to a couple from just outside Tunbridge Wells. I was sitting there at the bar as he told it. He even had the nerve to nod in my direction and say, "Paul here, will tell you it's so if you don't believe me, int that right Paul?" What could I do? I could hardly turn round and say "No! That's a pile of bull-shit! It's *my* house and I'm in the process of renovating it, and the garden, after seventy-nine poor bastards drowned in a tidal wave last year!"

Could I? After a few seconds silence, during which time I hoped Colin would be shaking inside, scared I might spoil the story which would be all over

Kent within the next few days, I looked up and without actually making eye contact with either customers or landlord, just said, "Arr…" trying to sound like a local. The Kentish couple bought another round, plus one for Colin and myself, proving my point. Another twenty-pound note soundly deposited in the Mariners' till. It's an ill wind… God only knows what imaginative story Colin would invent if we ever had a coach load of American tourists dropped by. Not that I'm saying the Americans are gullible you understand.

Even so, once the Kentish couple had left the pub, having chosen to stay for a meal and two more drinks, I had to take Colin to task over it… "I really wish you wouldn't do that mate! It's not fair to me when I'm doing my best to get the place back to normal," I began, "and one of these days, someone's going to check one of your yarns and when they find out it's a load of bollocks, they might come back and have a right go at you. Had you thought about that?" His answer was to smile and say, "But I bet they'll buy another few drinks…" I gave up. Infuriating, but you couldn't help but love the man.

The last few days of my time off weren't a complete wash-out if you'll pardon the pun… Not being a gardener, I couldn't be sure if it was the climate, the soil or whatever, but by mid-day Saturday, all the water had drained either from or into my front garden. By three that afternoon, despite the odd spot of rain, which I chose to ignore, I had virtually levelled the entire area and was ready to mark out the designated areas I planned to put the path, rock gardens and flower beds. Armed with more than a hundred wooden pegs and a ball of twine, I began from the gate and made a very loose "S" shape along to the front porch. Carefully checking the distances with my trusty measuring stick—a sawn-off broom handle—I did exactly the same on the opposite side, giving me the desired windy path, exactly three feet wide.

I'm sure Barry 'Capability' Marlow would have told me there's a tool that does precisely that, but I've made do with what I had all my life and I wasn't about to change now. Old dogs and new tricks do not mix… I then did the same again, using the sawn-off part of the broom handle, to give my path a six-inch border on either side. I'd thought long and hard about the planned gravel path, my original design, and in the end, decided it would require constant maintenance, i.e., raking over every time someone used it. The final design was winding Cornish stone slabs, to walk on, interspersed and bordered with the gravel, thus making it not only attractive, but also functional and low maintenance. The six-inch borders were to house various heathers, a tried and trusted breed of plant that could live through *any* weather.

Plus, if the right colours were chosen, heathers were also highly decorative and brightened up any garden. Again, apart from the odd trim if they grew too wild, they took very little looking after. Carefully measuring from the path outwards, equidistant from gate and porch, I marked out two rough circles that would eventually become matching—I hoped—rock gardens. It would mean bringing back all the rocks I'd taken to the rear of the house but hey, nothing wrong with a bit of exercise. Just to be sure I'd made no mistakes, I re-measured everything and it all checked out. I even crossed the road to see how it looked from another view-point. After all, not every day-tripper was going to pass on *my* side of the road. To the un-trained eye, it looked perfect. There was one other check I needed to do, just to be absolutely certain... I looked across the lane and yes, the angle should be about right.

I smiled as I noticed a CCTV camera just above one of the upstairs windows. Like St Matilda's Bay was a hot bed of crime! I could just see Colin chasing an elderly man up the lane for not paying for his half of Guinness and bag of Cheese and Onion crisps. I went to the back of the pub and knocked on the door. The Mariners Arms wasn't an all-day pub that early in the year, but I knew Colin wouldn't be too far away. Once inside, and having cleared it with the 'boss', I went upstairs and into his bedroom which, for a single man, was remarkably clean and tidy. Bed made. No socks and pants lying on the floor. I made a mental note to compliment him. I went to the window and looked down on my garden, some twenty feet or more below. Yes, that was as good as it was going to get.

The path looked to swerve gently from one end to the other, just enough to make the walk interesting rather than a tour of the garden. The circles either side also looked as though they were positioned correctly. I went back a very happy man, feeling as though things were really moving along now. I checked the time, and realising I still had at least two hours of day-light left, grabbed my decorative fencing. It was those semi-circular blocks of wood, held together with rust-proof wire that you see rolled up in garden centres. I know I wasn't the first to use it, but I also thought it was an unusual way to finish off a rock garden and path-way. Half an hour later I had two almost perfect circles of nine-inch-high wooden flexible fencing either side of what would be my new path.

The plan was to virtually fill these man-made troughs with top soil, then build up the rock-pile on top of it.

Lastly, I would filter more soil into all the gaps and plant as much heather as it took to cover it all. As long as I spaced the plants out wide enough, they wouldn't cover all the rocks. The last thing I wanted was what would appear to be one giant pile of heather. I'm sure plenty of gardeners would tell me there's a much easier way to perform this trick, but I wanted to do it *my* way, so that in the unlikely but possible event of anyone passing and making complimentary remarks, I could genuinely claim it as all my own work. Indeed, I even prayed Barry wouldn't stroll down my way and watch what I was doing. There's nothing worse than somebody watching you work, especially if that someone happens to a person who actually knows what he's talking about.

I even decided to leave that part until Monday, when I knew Barry usually went to visit an old friend in Bude. If all went well, it would be done and dusted by the time he returned. If nothing else, I had stolen Colin's thunder. This week-end, he wouldn't be able to spin his Buster Edwards yarn to any visitors. That would be a pint I owed him I'd be willing to bet... Checking the time once more, I estimated I might just have time to lay my red-brick borders. These would hold the other heathers and also stem the over-flow of gravel from the path. Luckily, these I'd stacked up against the side wall rather than taking round the back, so having laid a bed of sand, I carefully put them end to end the full length of the path, then again, the second row, six inches away from the path forming the required border. Shortly after seven, as the light was starting to fade, I stepped back to admire my handiwork. Most satisfactory, even if I *did* say so myself.

Tidying all my tools away in the shed—good boy—I came back around the front, sat on the door-step and had my third cigarette of the day, while contemplating a pint. Don't ask me why, but all of a sudden, I had this over-whelming urge to invite Debbie for a drink. The moment I thought of it, I looked across at the unusually busy bar and thought better of it. She didn't like crowds so the Mariners was out of the question, and as I really fancied a few, driving into town was also a non-starter. Then it struck me. What about Sunday evening? Sundays are notoriously quiet in pubs across the country, unless you ever visited The Castle in Reigate, Surrey in the late nineties.

But Tilda's was pretty much par for the course. With the exception of our farewell party at Easter, I don't believe I'd seen more than half a dozen people in there on a Sunday. I made a deal with myself. As long as I'd completed the path and borders tomorrow, I would drag up the courage to call round and ask her over there.

Sunday morning, I was up with the larks, or should that be seagulls now? Either way, I'd had breakfast and two cups of coffee, donned my tattiest jeans and sweat-shirt and by ten o'clock was practically banging on the door of the Harwick Garden Centre. By ten-thirty I'd purchased a huge selection of heathers that I was assured wouldn't spread too far and would last me 'forever'. I remembered my mother buying a selection of twelve dwarf pines to line the border between our garden and the public footpath when we were living in Hitchings Way, Woodhatch. They were guaranteed to last 'forever' but only three of them survived the first winter.

My mother was never backward in coming forward and sometime in early March, returned to the site of her purchase, only to find the premises closed down. Not a happy lady... I thought maybe this last part of my salesman's promise was more than a slight exaggeration but let it go. I didn't even stop to discuss palm trees with Gerald's cousin Merv. That would have to be postponed to a later date... No rush. I knew I had more than enough plants to do the borders, but they wouldn't go to waste, they would form a starting point for the rock gardens, which I was still hopeful of getting done on the Monday.

Upon my return, I brought my shovel out from the shed... I was eternally grateful to old Mr. Taylor for selling me the house as seen. In his time, I'm sure he would have rivalled Barry in the gardening stakes. There were tools in his shed I didn't even recognise! The down-side was of course the flood damage, but the most of the equipment was serviceable again after a really good clean. The next hour was spent carefully shovelling sand into the wide space that later in the day would be my path. I left it fairly loose, much easier to bed paving slabs into. I may not know much about gardening, but paths and patios I can do with my eyes shut.

That's what comes of never having lawns or flowers or in fact anything that grows. By two o'clock, my path was laid, with only the gravel remaining. I hadn't rushed it. I wasn't about to make any mistakes just because I planned a pleasant evening with a gorgeous young lady. Even as I worked, my opening lines were being rehearsed in my head, "Hi, look, I'm really sorry to disturb you. I know you don't really do the social thing, but I so enjoyed our little chat the other day—little white lies come in handy at times—and I just wondered if I could tempt you over the road for a glass of wine or something. Just as a friendly, neighbourly gesture, nothing more. I mean I know we're both single but I don't want you to think I'm trying get into your knickers or..."

OK, so maybe that last part needed a re-think, but after several attempts at rehearsing my chat-up lines, I was fairly sure I'd got just about the right words to say that would make it almost impossible for her to refuse... Now for the gravel. Again, it was a delicate job, although any spillage could soon be brushed off of the slabs, and any that fell into the red-brick troughs would soon be buried under top-soil, so it wasn't a major issue... I know it's one of my many annoying habits, and I do have quite a lot of them, but whenever I'm working on a complicated task, I do have to take a step back and check how things are progressing. Therefore, once the path was completed, I was over the road again, only outside the pub this time, not all the way up to Colin's immaculate bedroom.

So far, so good, I thought, smiling both inwardly and outwardly... Satisfied with phase one of Operation Front Garden, I then proceeded to fill the border troughs with top-soil and began to plant my heathers, being careful to space them out evenly, and also that they colour-matched in parallel... A purple one nearest to the gate, then a light blue, then a lilac shaded plant and so on, all the way up to the front doorstep, which was also made of the same red bricks that formed the original path, so I had a perfect match. And only four heathers left over which I would say was pretty good judgement on my part. I tucked the odd ones out the back for tomorrow.

To be honest, it had been a perfect day. Admittedly, I still had patches of mud either side of my new path, but other than that, it was looking good, beginning to take shape. The weather had been kind to me, just the odd shower that I had managed to work through. Only five cigarettes all day and I even heard the occasional compliment from people strolling down to the beach, or coming out of the pub. As a non-gardener, I was feeling pretty damn proud of myself. As I said, a perfect day. Now all I had to hope for was the perfect evening to round off a highly successful week-end.

Knowing Colin didn't normally do food on a Sunday evening, I sat down to a quick snack from the freezer, a simple steak pie and chips, washed down with a glass of chilled white wine. I'm not that much of a drinker, but I do sometimes like a glass with my dinner. However, I'm no expert, not a connoisseur... I know the difference between a graves and a sauterne, but I'm just as happy with a supermarket wine box, which is why I always keep one in the refrigerator—I've always wondered why there's a "D" in the abbreviation 'fridge'—for times like this... I showered and changed into smart casual, had cigarette number six and wine number two—yes, I was just a little nervous—then remembering my earlier thoughts, brushed my teeth for the second time since dinner, gargled with Listerine Ultra and made my way downstairs.

One last check in the mirror to ensure I didn't look like I'd just walked off a building site, then off up the road the few yards to Debbie's front door. I rang the bell but heard no sound, probably not working, maybe I should offer to fix it... Then I knocked on the door... No answer. I tried again, a little louder, but not so loud it would scare her. Still no answer. I stepped back a little. I could see no light on anywhere. Had there been one on as I approached? Has she switched it off to pretend there was nobody home? Was it too early to have the lights on? No way of telling, but the house was in silence, which suggested there really *wasn't* anyone at home. Or was I just kidding myself? Possibly she had seen it was me and deliberately not come to the door.

I walked over to the pub alone, grabbed a pint of Carling and took a seat by the window, ignoring Colin's 'smart tart tonight' comment. I wasn't in talkative mood. At least not with Colin. Not tonight... Four more pints followed that one, then another of my favourites, large vodka and Red Bull. Followed by another of the same. Did I say something about not being much of a drinker? Well, we all have our moments. By closing time, I wasn't drunk, but I was certainly pleasantly merry. I'd even shared a few jokes with Colin and a couple of guys I'd never seen before... As I left the pub, I took a quick look in the almost empty car park. Almost empty except for a bright red Fiat 500... I went to sleep that night trying to convince myself she'd been relaxing on the sofa in the dark, enjoying Pink Floyd's Dark Side of The Moon on her iPod... With head-phones on... And a joint.

15

I can't begin to explain why, but I've always been fairly successful with women. I've never considered myself particularly attractive. Sometimes described as 'nice'. More recently 'too nice', whatever that means. It would probably surprise many people that have known me down the years, but I'm quite shy, until I have a microphone in my hand... On reflection, I suspect my varied part-time musical career had much to do with it. In much the same way as my peers assumed I was smoking at fourteen—If offered a cigarette, I would take it, say I'd only just put one out and pop it behind my ear for later, not actually having my first cigarette until I was eighteen—by the general conversation during school breaks or in the Sovereign Youth Club, I would claim my conquests of the opposite sex to be somewhere between that of Mike Jarvis, allegedly three or four new girls every week—and we believed it!—and Jim Murray at a meagre one or two a month.

In truth, at fourteen I was only interested in music—The Kinks, The Who and the Rolling Stones mostly—or football, nineteen sixty-five being one of the golden eras, that of Best, Law and Charlton. I was an average looking teenager... Nice hair, good teeth, polite manners, etc. Nothing special. I was no Adonis, but no Frankenstein's monster either... Just average. That all changed at age seventeen, when I bluffed my way into DJing for a mobile disco outfit.

Suddenly, all hell broke loose. Almost over-night, I was living Mike Jarvis' life, only mine was genuine. Five years of that and I probably had more notches on my head-board than Rod Stewart! Certainly, more than Sir Cliff Richard... I finally walked out of that life when my dream of performing in a live band coincided with the arrival of teeny-boppers. One of our regular gigs was a youth club in Merstham on a Friday evening. By the time the seventh thirteen-year-old girl had asked me to play Donny Osmond's Puppy Love, I realised that at the ripe old age of twenty-two, I was 'too old for this business'.

Due to it being a youth club, the gig would finish at ten, and we 'grown-ups' would nip down the road to The Feathers for a couple of pints before heading off home. It was there that I bumped into an old school friend, Jerry Willmer. We'd formed a band at school and at thirteen, we *knew* we were going to be the next Beatles. We weren't. While *I* walked away, Jerry never gave up on his dream and by then was touring Surrey and Sussex with a covers band, doing old Merseybeats and Herman's Hermits numbers to pub crowds who, like myself were sick of the Partridge Family and longed for the return of guitar bands.

It transpired that Jerry had been trying to track me down for months. You have to remember these were the days before mobile phones and the internet. If you lost touch with someone, or they moved, as I had, it could be a nightmare to find them again. So, it was pure chance that we met in the pub and Jerry told me Barley, his group, were looking for a new drummer, who could also harmonise a little.

It took me all of ten seconds to make the decision to walk away from mobile disco's and enter the world of live music, *real* music. If I thought the female attention was high as a DJ, it went through the roof as soon as I began drumming around the pubs. Those seven years were one long party, especially after Jerry's sister Carol left Barley to get married and I took over the lead singing. We were the only group on the pub circuit with a singing drummer. It didn't occur to me at the time, but thinking about it now, once you get past Phil Collins, you struggle to think of even a *famous* one. I don't honestly believe Ringo counts... Which reminds me of a famous quote.

When asked by a journalist if he considered Ringo Starr the best drummer in the world, John Lennon laughed and replied, "He's not even the best drummer in the Beatles!" I make no apologies for repeating that one... Looking back, it's not something I'm proud of, but I honestly lost count of my encounters, for want of a better word, around nineteen eighty-five, as it passed forty.

I was a single man during the late eighties and for most of the nineties... Add to that, the onslaught of presenting karaoke shows, you can imagine the temptations that came my way. The combination of alcohol and music is a heady mix, and I threw myself at it head-long. I have to skip over the period between May seventh nineteen ninety-nine through to December twenty-eleven, as my score rose by just one, mainly because for the first in my life I fell in love and discovered the true meaning of commitment. I even felt a twinge of guilt at my former lothario life-style. During that period, the temptations were still there, though God only knows why, as by then I was well into my fifties.

I resisted every single one of them. I would like to play the nice guy and say I'd grown up during those thirteen years and that for following eighteen months, I became a born-again virgin, but I'd be lying. There have been a further five since then, six if fellatio counts. As I say, I'm not proud of it, but mention it purely as a statement of fact… And also, because I was trying to think of a good reason for Debbie ignoring my call the night before. Had she had bad experiences with men in her life?

If so, she needed re-assurance, needed to know we aren't all like that, whatever 'that' had been. Was there a violent ex-boyfriend lurking in the background somewhere, trying to track her down while she hid behind a women's refuge charity that find's safe homes for such victims. At around thirty, I assumed she hadn't run away from abusive parents. I even began to think on the dark side. Blame it on my vivid imagination if you like, but it crossed my mind that maybe she'd worked in a bank or some other financial institution and found a way to relieve them of—let's give it a nice round figure—five million pounds. That would explain why she was so far from home—I still couldn't quite place the accent—and didn't appear to be gainfully employed.

St Matilda's Bay would certainly be a tough place to find if the police were searching for her. After all, I only found it by accident. But then if she *had* run off with a substantial sum of money, if she really *had* been that clever, then surely, she would have thought it through and make sure the cash was safely tucked away in a numbered account somewhere… Like the Bahamas, for instance. In which case, she would have been out there with it, laying on a beach with a Mojito in her hand. And surely Adam would have recognised her. Didn't all these people in high finance know each other? Didn't they all drink in the same wine bars in the city? Didn't they all swap one company for another on a regular basis, moving their skills to the highest bidder?

No, Debbie couldn't possibly be a white-collar criminal, it just didn't add up. So, what else then? The slaughter of those school children in West London a few years back? The police never *had* arrested anyone for that. The sniper had vanished without trace. Maybe Debbie had been working in an office block over-looking the roof-top where they'd discovered the empty shell cases. Were the police, at that very moment, searching under cover for the man who resembled that photo-fit of an approximately thirty-seven-year-old unshaven dark-haired man while they kept her safely ensconced in the peace and quiet of Tilda's Bay?

Too ridiculous to be true, I thought to myself, but then these things did happen... No, I finally decided, it was definitely a 'man' problem of some kind. Maybe I would never know. Either way, I would love to know the true story of why a young lady, who looked so full of life, would hide herself away in our sleepy little village. I was woken from these thoughts by a knock at the door. A glance at the kitchen clock told me it was just after eight. I'd been up since six-thirty, originally planning out my day, then realising I could do nothing until Barry drove off, normally about nine.

Having worked out my timing for the rock garden construction, my mind had naturally drifted back to the previous night and Debbie's apparent refusal to open her door to me... I put my second cup of coffee down on the kitchen table and ambled out to the front door, making a note to self to add even a small pane of glass to my front door sometime in the near future. I've never been one for surprises. While I can be quite spontaneous under certain conditions—I once packed my bags and flew to Tenerife within five hours of waking up one February morning, simply because I was thoroughly sick of the British winter— I nearly always like to know how my day is going to pan out. In the few short seconds, it took me to walk from the kitchen to the front door, I pondered all the possibilities.

Colin had done his back in and needed some beer barrels moved in his cellar—highly unlikely. Barry calling round to see if I needed any help re-building my front garden—definitely not. Sarah calling to say she was worried about Adam, who hadn't come home last night—Complete nonsense as his car was over the road, just inside the Mariners Arms car park. Tom asking if I'd have Minnie for the day as he had to take Alice into Truro for urgent medical attention—hopefully not. Debbie, highly apologetic for missing me last night and 'would I care to call round this evening for a proper home-cooked meal and maybe a few glasses of wine to make up for it...?'—Not a hope!

"I can see you've been busy and as I'm off into town in a bit, just wondered if there was anything I can pick up for you..." So, Barry *had* been monitoring my progress after all. I'd been thinking he would have no idea how it was going, as he rarely called round, and never went to the beach, but somehow, he'd spotted my progress. Without making any comment about my new path—

it occurred to me he was now the first neighbour to have used it—he continued, "Hope you don't mind my asking, but you *did* say you bought most of your groceries on line. Thought you might like some proper food for a change..." For the life of me, I couldn't remember ever saying that, not to Barry Marlow or anyone else for that matter. Did he have an ulterior motive for calling round that morning? He had that look of a man who had *never* shopped on line himself.

It took me back to the days of the corner shop, where there was always a chair in the corner for little old ladies to rest their weary bones while someone in a stained apron, resembling Arkwright, deliberately took about twenty minutes to make up her order, so that she wasn't rushed back out of the door. I'm not being sexist when I say 'little old lady'. That's just the way things were back in the day. Ask Colin... I could imagine Barry in just such a shop and thanked him for his kind thought, adding 'nothing I can think off right now, ta.' Curiosity grabbed me and I had to ask if that was his only reason to visit... "Well, I didn't think Webster's truck was here to add an extra ton of sand to the beach," he replied as he walked back along my new path.

Without turning around, I heard him mutter something that sounded like 'coming along nicely...' Did I also catch the words 'palm' and 'tree' in there also? I smiled. Quite a compliment from someone who could rival Charlie Dimmock in garden design... But why *did* Barry Marlow have a computer, yet deny it? Was he a closet Spice Girls fan, downloading iTunes onto his iPod under cover of the night? Or was it something more sinister? Despite the warm sunshine, I felt chilly as I wondered just why he gave up teaching all those years ago...

Enjoying my third cup of coffee of the day, plus my first cigarette, I watched out of the front window as Barry's car pulled away, heading up the hill. There was a brewery truck outside the pub and, spookily, Colin was standing next to it doing that thing where you push your hand into the small of your back as if to relieve some ache or pain... Back trouble? Needs a hand with the heavy lifting? I really *must* stop this fantasising. I was half expecting to see a tearful Sarah running out the front door and an ambulance outside Tom and Alice's. Thankfully, neither happened that Monday morning.

I glanced up at the clear blue sky. Not a cloud in sight. It was going to be a beautiful spring day in Tilda's. I had no idea how many bunches of heather I would need that day, so decided to complete the rest of the operation before my next trip to the garden centre. Two hours later, nearly mid-day, I had two rockeries, as symmetrical as I could possibly make them. I crouched down for an eye-level view… To the naked eye, they were even the same height. Now I know this sounds a little sad, but I even brought my measuring stick out to be sure. It might not have satisfied the exacting mind of Hercules Poirot, but within an inch or two it was near enough for me. By half past twelve, I was in deep conversation with Merv, the resident palm tree expert of Harwick.

"Seriously," he began, "I don't think I've ever had anyone this far North ask me for palm trees before sir." The way he said 'North' made me feel like I was in the Outer Hebrides or some such far off place, when after all, the South coast of Cornwall, with its miles of sandy beaches and naturally thriving palm trees were less than an hour's drive away. Never-the-less he agreed with Barry about the shape of the bay and its' climate but unlike my neighbour saw no reason why they *shouldn't* survive and grow quite happily in my part of the county.

Merv checked a few on-line catalogues and made a few telephone calls to confirm availability, prices, etc. and I promised to return when the time came for planting. Having selected another large batch of heathers, plus ordering the required amount of top-class turf, which Merv promised me delivery of 'in a few days', I made my way home. "Shit!"

In my tangled mind, too busy making up wondrous stories about my landlord and neighbours, I'd completely forgotten something I'd briefly thought of a few days earlier. So much had happened since that day, it had slipped my mind that the gate and its adjoining fence needed a lick of paint. That was something Barry could have picked up for me, or possibly, almost certainly the garden centre would have stocked a simple tin of outdoor gloss white. Could I be bothered with another half-hour one-way tour of the Cornish country-side for a tin of paint? I decided not. Apart from anything else, I'd even considered trying a different colour, one that wouldn't distract passers-by from what was going to be—if all went to plan—the second-best front garden in the bay.

The paint could wait for another day… As I parked my Clio next to Debbie's Fiat, I spotted a happy smiling Sarah waving to me from the garden of her own cottage next to mine. The sun always brought out the very best in people, wherever you lived, and St Matilda's was no exception. The lady and I passed a very pleasant ten minutes or so discussing the merits of gardening, me complimenting hers, especially the fine rose bushes she was currently pruning, and she praising my efforts at replacing the combination of Steve Taylor's 'somewhat uninteresting' choice of colours, plus the obvious flood damage. I hoped I didn't make it *too* obvious that as much as I enjoyed the company of this rather attractive middle-aged woman, I was at the same time keen to return to my *own* quest. That of getting my heathers planted before the return of Barry, normally around mid-afternoon.

This, I believe, I succeeded in doing by stepping over my little fence—that white definitely had to go—and continuing our conversation from beside the rock garden nearest to our dividing wall. With a brief 'back in a moment', I managed to grab my trowel from the shed and concentrate on planting my recent purchases as Sarah continued her tale of her former neighbours' complete lack of imagination. If only she'd known about mine, I doubt she would still be talking to me… "And as for that little fence," she gasped, "whatever possessed him to paint it white I'll never know."

I replied in agreement, adding that it was on my 'to do' list. Decision made. Lucky, I *hadn't* gone back for that tin of white. One does like to keep in with one's neighbours, doesn't one?

By three-thirty, I was sitting on one of the benches outside The Mariner's Arms, dressed only in shorts and t-shirt for the first time that year, slowly enjoying a cold pint of Carling and a cigarette, looking across at my semi-completed garden with pride. My chest swelled further each time someone stopped to look at it and I heard words like 'pretty' or 'love that pathway' drift across the lane. I put all bad thoughts about Debbie, Adam and Barry out of my mind. The sun was shining. It was a glorious day. I had only the turf to lay before I could start thinking about palm trees again. It would all be ready for the summer invasion. To put it crudely, I was as happy as a pig in shit. Life was great.

What could possibly go wrong in such a beautiful spot such as this? It had had its moment of tragedy and had moved on. I had fabulous neighbours, as friendly as you could wish for, with the possible exception of the enigma that was Debbie—but still very easy on the eye when spotted—regular visits from Minnie, whom I had now taught to play chess and I felt would actually beat me in the not-too-distant future, a great pub with good food, a normally cheerful landlord and two flirty barmaids… After sixty years of towns, all-night trains, aeroplanes, hyper-markets, screaming children and the rest, I had found my little piece of Heaven right here in the West Country, the first place I ever fell in love with, way back in the late nineteen-sixties… Unable to move any further forward until my next week off—tomorrow being Tuesday, I'd be back on the

Blackberry and laptop keeping my helicopters in the air—I finished my pint, crossed the lane and tucked my rolls of turf around the back, under the kitchen window, reminding myself to keep them moist as per Merv's instructions 'if I didn't have it laid within three days'.

Finally, I had an evening off with nothing planned. Minnie never came around on a school day. Barry *might* just call in if he thought to wander down after tea. I had seen him come back while sitting outside the pub, but he only waved, didn't come across to check on my progress, so I wasn't expecting him. Sarah and Adam were hardly ever seen of an evening, unless I spotted their car heading up the hill, possibly to their favourite Italian restaurant, a little place they'd discovered some time ago, just off the Truro Road.

The great thing about Cornwall is that virtually everywhere else in Cornwall was less than an hour's drive away. So, the big cities were just as accessible as St Ives, or St Michael's Mount.... Tom and Alice would of course be taking care of Minnie, and as for Debbie, I knew *one* day she'd be back. She would just appear out of nowhere, apologise for no apparent reason and start rambling on about friend's dying, or dogs, or something else I wouldn't have a clue about. Then she would leave and I wouldn't see her for another few weeks. I was beginning to accept we would never be friends, let alone anything more. I'd even made a point of taking my cliff walks early in the evenings to be sure of returning well before mid-night. As stupid as it sounds, I actually didn't *want* to bump into her. What I *really* wanted was for her to come to *me* again…

Knowing I had the evening to myself, and with the daylight hours lasting longer each week, I now had at least two hours before darkness descended. It was still warm at six o'clock, but I decided to change into jeans and put on long-sleeved shirt over my 't'. It didn't matter where you lived, the temperature nearly always dipped near the coast, especially as it was still only May. Having polished off a nice hot spicy chilli, I started up the hill. I was going to check the state of our railway station, hoping beyond hope that it didn't reflect that of Harwick.

I genuinely didn't believe it could be as bad as that, and I wasn't disappointed. As I walked down the approach lane, two cyclists passed me with a cheery 'good evening'. The lane this end was considerably wider than at Harwick. A few yards along the lane I had spotted a sign warning cyclists, and indeed horse-riders to Beware of Cars. I had assumed this was to slow them down when approaching our lane. The station itself was a good quarter mile along the un-named lane. Maybe it had been called Station Lane or some such twenty years earlier, and for most of the twentieth century, when mum and dad packed the buckets and spades and took the ten- or twenty-minute branch line for a day out at Tilda's, but if so, that day was long gone.

I was sure it hadn't appeared this far away when I spotted it from the road the other day, but sure enough, there it was. A magnificent example of Great Western architecture inspired by, as were most structures in the industrial West Country world, by Isambard Kingdom Brunel, the man best known for his design for the Clifton Suspension Bridge, various steam-ships and of course his work on the Great Western Railway. His motto seemed to have been 'Why build a house when you can have a mansion?' One glance at the Clifton, or indeed the Royal Albert Bridge over the Tamar near Saltash, and you will see how Brunel's constructions could easily have been completed at half the cost, had they not been so extravagant... It was a point not lost on the authorities he had to convince to put up the finance for such projects.

My first sight of St Matilda's Bay station—a good twenty minutes from the bay itself, due to its position more than fifty feet above sea level—struck two chords with me. Firstly, as per my earlier thoughts in Harwick, it reminded me of the branch line near where I spent much of my child-hood, Kemp Town Race Track, on the outskirts of Brighton. Again, due to the contours of the South Downs, the branch from the main-line station was partly uphill, covered three or four miles, and took nearly half an hour to travel. I should point out I learned this information from my Great Aunt May who was old enough to remember it closing, not that many years after its grand opening at huge expense.

Apparently, it was only built for the benefit of Queen Victoria, who had a particular love of Brighton—hence Prince Albert's magnificent Oriental-influenced Pavilion in the heart of the city—and horse racing. The Kemp Town branch enabled her to travel from London to the race track without ever leaving the royal coach. The reason it was so short-lived? The simple truth is that it was actually quicker to walk than to take the train, such was its diverse route, so nobody else, certainly not the average man on the street ever used it. Add to that the fact that by the early part of the twentieth century, the royal family had their own fleet of that brand new invention, motor cars... The second thing I noticed about our station was that it would not have looked out of place as the grand entrance to one of London's main termini. Picture a miniature version of Hampton Court and you've got St Matilda's Bay station. It was huge.

Thanks again to Brunel, virtually every station on the GWR, sometimes known as God's Wonderful Railway, however busy or important, looked just like this. To this day, there are several examples of them, far too many to list and many of them purchased by private owners following their closure. Something had told me this wasn't just another dis-used station from a time gone by. Lost in my thoughts of child-hood memories, I'd completely failed to notice a man of around sixty years of age, tending to his vegetable garden.

I would like to think nobody would ever accuse me of being a train-spotter. Certainly, I loved the smell of a steam train, and if ever I'm near a preserved steam railway, such as Dart Valley, then I will always take a ride. I call it nostalgia. It takes me back to my child-hood, when travelling by train was the norm.

It brings back many happy memories for me, and probably many other people of a similar age. But I can say, hand on heart, I have never sat on the end of a platform, Ladybird note-book in hand, jotting down every engine that stopped or passed through. I just didn't see the point. And as much as I appreciate the hard work put in by volunteers to re-open these pieces of British history, I've certainly never been tempted to involve myself in such activities. Bearing in mind I used to live just ten miles from the Bluebell Railway, one of the best-known preserved lines in the country, I could count my number of visits on one hand, and that would normally be to take first my two boys, and later my grand-children. I thought of it as an important part of their education, on a par with visiting a museum or art gallery, but much more fun.

I certainly never entertained the idea of spending every spare week-end clearing land-fill from cuttings, or re-pointing the Imberhorne viaduct in an attempt to extend the line to East Grinstead, though I know of people who did. No, for me it's just the sheer beauty of seeing such machines in action... As I say, pure nostalgia, not an obsession. And I feel no guilt at my total lack of assistance in bringing these lines back to life. My train fares do that... But as soon as I set eyes on the exquisite building before me, my thoughts came flooding back. I'd even seriously toyed with buying my own station, back in the nineteen seventies when property was reasonably inexpensive and so many of them were up for sale at ridiculously low prices. I'd gone as far as to view Mayfield Station, situated on top of a hill, just off the local by-pass.

For all I know, it may still be there, and still up for grabs. At the time I recall thinking how easy it would be to develop. Most station buildings were on a single level, like a bungalow, so no stairs to worry about in your old age. Virtually all had lavatories, one Ladies and one Gents, easy enough to convert one of them into a shower and utility room. Ticket offices and Waiting Rooms could be easily, and cheaply converted into kitchens, living rooms and bedrooms. Many had gardens like this one, perfect for children, and there was never a shortage of parking space, as the one I was currently standing in testified to.

You could have fitted fifty cars in the overgrown piece of wasteland, though the thought of St Matilda's station car park ever being full made the mind boggle. We didn't even have fifty residents… I chose not to disturb the man in the station garden. From others I'd seen in the past, some had been happy to talk for hours on why exactly they'd chosen such a residence, but on the other hand, there were those who simply wanted to be left alone like any other private resident.

Let's face it, you wouldn't normally walk up to somebody's front door and ask for the guided tour, just because you liked the mock Tudor look of the place, would you? So why would you expect anything different from someone living in a former railway station, or a windmill or lighthouse for that matter? Yet people did… I'd managed a glimpse of his face and thought it vaguely familiar. Possibly an occasional drinker in the Mariners. If so, I would maybe someday strike up a conversation with him and discuss the merits of his chosen abode. As I turned to walk away, I noticed something quite ingenious. He had blocked off the open end of the double platform and turned it into a swimming pool.

Back in the village, I bumped into Barry, quite literally. He came straight out of the privet archway that covered the entrance to his cottage, without looking. By coincidence, I was glancing over my shoulder to check what the sound was that was attacking my ears. It was nothing more than a basic Ford Focus with a dodgy exhaust, but it was enough to distract me long enough not to be aware of Barry's exit. We both made our apologies, which was fair enough as we were both equally to blame for the collision, and in any case no harm was done. We both laughed. "I was just coming down to see you," he said. "For someone who's only ever had a paved garden before, I reckon you're doing a fine job their old son."

Coming from the master, this was a compliment indeed. I invited him along for a coffee and to pick his brain. I wasn't going to mention palm trees though… What I wanted was advice on the best plants to put on the outside edges and also something for under the bay window, to break up the wall. Once settled into my living room with two cups of steaming coffee, I stopped him spouting Latin at me yet again and switched on my laptop. He visibly shrank back into his chair. 'One day I'll get to the bottom of this' I thought to myself.

He quickly overcame whatever was bothering him and I brought some ideas up on the screen. I'd already saved some examples into my favourites and told Barry exactly where I wanted them. He pointed out why one of my choices would not work under the adjoining wall, lack of sunshine, but agreed with most of the others and genuinely seemed quite impressed. Having finally agreed what should go where—that would be a few of my days taken up the following week—we fell into relaxed conversation over another coffee, this time complete with a personal favourite of mine, chocolate Hob-Nobs. I learned that, by a strange coincidence, the chap I'd seen at the station was its former station master.

Having spent most of his working life there, he couldn't bear to let go when it closed… We chatted amicably for a good hour or more, without computers cropping up again, until he tactfully remembered I was back at work the next day and bade me good-night. I thanked him and saw him to the door. Tomorrow was indeed a working day for me so I chose to have an early night. The old fall-back of toasted cheese and onion sandwich made up for the lack of a proper dinner and saw me wrapped up in bed by eleven.

16

The following week *flew* by. Not only was it the busiest shift I'd had all year, but I also had to combine it with on-the-job training via video-link, for two new members of staff. My manager had originally asked me to go to Aberdeen for the Tuesday to Friday, but when I pointed out how much cheaper it would be by video, he readily agreed. I'd always found managers tend to jump at the chance of money-saving ideas and this only went to prove my point. I couldn't be happier to escape that one. Working from home had two major advantages for me.

Not only could I pick and choose when to eat, drink and smoke—assuming I had time—but it also meant during quite periods, I could continue planning the rest of my garden on-line as well as in my mind. I even found it helped to keep my brain active and I'm one of those people who can easily switch from one job to another in the blink of an eye. My concentration never wavered, as shown by my success rate in the quickest and most accurate movement of aircraft spares. One of my former directors, Stuart Barry, once told me it would make him a very happy man to come into my office and see me with my feet up, reading a book, because if *I* wasn't working, it meant all of his helicopters *were*.

I cannot truly say my current management team would feel the same but to date, it has never happened. Sorry Stuart... I did, however, have the odd few minutes here and there to revert to garden planning, but on day three, the Thursday of that week, I had another problem to contend with. I'd got to the point where I was unsure whether or not I could handle another interview with the lovely Debbie, but I was given no choice. Shortly after lunch, there was a knock at the door. As I opened it, she brushed straight past me and into the kitchen, turning to face me as she leaned up against the worktop, "Paul, I am *so* sorry to interrupt whatever you're doing," she glanced around as if checking to see if I had visitors, "but I really don't know anyone else down here and I need some help urgently."

She was shaking her head from side to side and wringing her hands together as though some major catastrophe had come into her life. Perhaps it had, but she seemed to take an age to reveal it. This was so different to the last time she came round, when I couldn't get a word in edgeways as she continued with her diatribe. This time she just stood there, clasping her hands together and staring around my kitchen as though looking for inspiration as to where she should start. Was this the moment she would break down and reveal all? Was I finally going to find out about the dog? Despite my earlier indifference, I confess I was *bursting* to hear what she had to say. I wasn't about to push her this time, nor would I take her in my arms and assure her everything would be fine, because I was no longer certain that it would be. It took all my self-control not to ask any of the questions that were screaming inside my head.

We both stood there in silence for at least two minutes. I heard the familiar 'ping' of an e-mail coming in. Then another, and another, until I could no longer ignore them. It was more than my job was worth, to coin a phrase. I said, "Sorry Debbie, but I'm working at the moment and I really must check that…" as the fourth 'ping' came from the living room.

"Please stay right there," I begged her, holding my hand up like a policeman on point duty, forbidding her to 'go'. "This should only take a few minutes. Put the kettle on or something, or," I remembered an un-opened bottle of wine left over from Easter, not to mention the cheapie box I always kept on hand for emergencies, "help yourself to a glass of wine if you like, steady the nerves. You'll find a bottle of dry white in the fridge."

I raced into the front room to check the four e-mails. 'Ping', five e-mails… "Why now?" I almost screamed at the machine. Out of the corner of my eye, I caught her running past the gap in the door-way, followed shortly by the slamming of my front door. Out of the window, I could see her rushing along the path, hands rubbing at her eyes. The poor girl was in tears again and all I could say was 'hang on there, I've got work to do…' What a total pratt! Just as she was about to reveal her deepest fears to me—maybe—I'd picked the same moment to put my work first, which of course is the correct sequence of events, but it didn't make me feel any better about the whole scenario.

To make matters worse, three of the e-mails were simple 'thanks' in response to something I'd sent earlier, one was a reminder that the coffee machine on the third floor would be out of action for the remainder of the day due to maintenance… This was in the Redhill building, three hundred miles away… And the last one was asking me if I'd thought about claiming back my PPI… "No, I fucking haven't!" I literally screamed at the laptop. Then as an after-thought, "Bollocks!" I lit a cigarette…

That was it. I couldn't take any more of this. I *wouldn't* take any more of it! I was going to get to the bottom of this if it killed me! The terms of my contract demand that I stay on line from 07.30 until 18.30, then after that, I only need to react if someone calls the emergency line, which is automatically transferred to my Blackberry. In reality, both Dave and I tend to stay on line to keep the work-load down, otherwise it would be almost impossible to manage the first few hours of the following day. But tonight, I was going to stick to the letter of the law and shut down dead on half past six. By twenty-nine minutes to seven, I would be banging at Debbie's door, and this time I *wouldn't* give up and leave it for another day.

The final two hours of that shift seemed to take forever. Certainly, there had been work to do, parts to move, and I moved them… On auto-pilot. I'd been doing the same thing for so long, many parts of the job I could do with my eyes shut and my hands tied behind my back, metaphorically speaking. That was how those two hours passed. In between moving gear boxes to Norway and Radar Indicators to Nigeria, I went over and over what I was going to say to that young lady. I shan't bore you with the details because you've heard it all before. Plus, at precisely twenty past six, I saw the Fiat 500 pull out of the car park. Was that woman psychic or what?

Ten minutes later, I was in the Mariners, a chilled pint of Carling already cooling me down. "What's up with you then lover?" No, Lala and I weren't in the throes of a passionate affair, it was just something she called all her close friends, male *and* female, and right at that moment I was proud to be counted as one of them. It was her I'd actually hoped to see. I had taken a chance on her working as the evenings were now becoming busier, and as luck would have it, Colin had chosen this very week to ask the girls to cover the odd evening…

"So, what do women want, La?" I started. "I mean I've seen Mel Gibson in the film where he gets a bang on the head and all of a sudden, he's able to hear what they're thinking, but that's only a comedy and even *then,* it's confusing…"

"Well, it depends what exactly you mean mate. If you're talking romantically, most women like to be wined and dined, have doors held open for them—not me personally mind…"

"That's precisely what I mean! You've hit the nail right on the head. If I held a door open for you, you'd turn round and tell me how perfectly capable you are of opening your *own* doors, and anyway, I *didn't* mean romantically..."

"Aha," a twinkle appeared in the corner of her eye as she pulled me another pint, "so it's sexual, is it? Well personally I'm all for it being a bit rou..."

"No!" I interrupted her, before she went into tales of biting, hair-pulling and 'bum fun'. Bum fun? Where the Hell did *that* come from? Fun? Not in *my* book it isn't! "I'm just talking generally, hun. Like, without meaning to sound sexist, which I suppose this is, but in a good way for girls, well *most* girls that is... I don't necessarily include *you* in this, although it might do... What I'm trying say is that 'in general' we men are shallow right?"

She nodded, so I presume I hadn't given any offence yet. "We see a girl with a short skirt, or a nice bum, big boobs, whatever, and we think 'I would'. But most girls normally go for brains over brawn, yeah?"

Her eyes glazed over as she did her best impersonation of a ladette, a geezer-bird, "Well I *do* enjoy watching the rugby with the sound down, especially when they go down," she paused for crude effect, "in a scrum I mean."

"Yeah, but you *know* what I mean, La, stop trying to wind me up! Take the classic 'Does my bum look big in this?' There is just no correct answer to that!" I swallowed the dregs of pint two, and while my favourite barmaid re-filled the glass, I carried on with my rant, "Then there's the red dress / black dress thing yeah?"

Lala looked slightly blank at that one. I took another mouthful of lager... I was beginning to get right into this by now, "Girl's going out somewhere special. Comes downstairs with two practically identical dresses, one red, one black. Says to her husband 'Which do you think?' No La, don't interrupt because again, there is no right answer... If you choose the red one, she says 'So what's wrong with the black one?' and vikky verky right? Or if you make the mistake of paying them a compliment, like 'Whichever one you wear will look perfect on you darling...' you get something like 'Can't you *ever* make a decision? Go on. For once in your life...' And so, it goes on!"

A large vodka and Red Bull with three chunks of ice magically appeared on the bar in front of me. She leaned across the bar and whispered—I respected her for the whisper, "This is about Debbie, isn't it?" Before I had a chance of making some pathetic, half-hearted denial, she added, "Don't deny it, Paul, it's blatantly obvious."

She smiled and walked along to the other end of the bar to serve one of the few other customers. I contemplated downing the drink in one and walking out, not giving her the pleasure of hearing me admit she was right... But she was a bloody good mate, and I'd been bending her ear for the past hour. She deserved better than that. I still downed the drink in one, but waited for her to return to *my* end. This, she did two minutes later, complete with a refill. "Yes, it is, as a matter of fact, but not in the way *you're* thinking so you can take that filthy grin off your face Miss Bagshaw!"

"I do apologise Mr Evans," she replied, complete with mock courtesy.

"Seriously La, I don't know how to put it... We've had a few chats lately and... Well as some of it, probably *all* of it was quite personal, and almost certainly told in confidence. I wouldn't want the poor girl to think I was talking about her behind her back."

"But you are..." She could see I was about to snap back at her and quickly added, "I'm sorry lover, I'm just teasing you. This really is serious, isn't it?"

"Yes, I believe it might be, but not in a romantic way, or a sexual way..." I emptied the red and silver can onto the vodka, took a large gulp and added, just to show her I hadn't completely last my sense of humour, "And not in a *bum* fun way either! Yuk!"

Despite the odd flirty joke—you could *never* get through an entire conversation with Lala without it—I was actually quite serious. Although I had this really good thing going with Kathy, and I definitely had no intentions of spoiling that, I really wanted to break through Debbie's tough exterior and try to discover what was going on in here pretty little head.

"Oh, I don't know Paul, I once..." I held up my hand yet again to stop her. I'd heard her getting quite explicit with Stevie only a few weeks earlier and at this particular moment I really did not want to know. The intimate details of Lala's sex life could wait for another day. "Enough already."

"So OK, you can't tell me what it's all about but can you give me a clue, without disclosing the lady's nasty little secrets?" She was still making light of it, for which I couldn't blame her. After all, what did I really know about Debbie? For that matter, what did *anyone* in the bay know about her? Judging by what little gossip there was, absolutely nothing. "So, she's actually spoken to you then? I don't think she and I have exchanged more than a few hellos."

"That's just what I mean, hun. All I can say is she's very scared of something, but I don't know what. She goes for late night walks so that nobody sees her. She never goes down to the beach, presumably in case someone should try to start up a conversation..."

At that point the vodka and Red Bull fairy waved her magic wand one more time. I took a sip... "She's rarely seen out in daylight and no, I *don't* believe in vampires to save you asking. Over the past three weeks, we've had three conversations, two of them in my house, and when I say 'conversations' I mean she's made three statements because I barely got a word in, and very little of it made any sense. She goes on about people dying and a 'poor dog' and no, I don't believe she's on drugs... Oh, and apparently a friend of hers seems to have died in mysterious circumstances last week-end... A female friend... She definitely said *she* died, or why did *she* have to die, something like that... And as I said, that was only last week-end, yet she's seemed a bit weird every time I saw her, even before that. Am I making any sense?"

"No, but it's certainly made my evening shift go faster..." I looked up at the clock. How the fuck did it get to nearly closing time? Had I really been rambling on for over three hours?

"I am so sorry La. I didn't realise the time..." I felt really bad, but she insisted it wasn't a problem and even offered me another drink. "Oh, go on then. One for the road. Or should that be lane? Or even one for a few short steps?"

I reached into my pocket and pulled out... A ten-pound note. I placed it apologetically on the bar. "I honestly didn't expect..." My voice drifted off; sentence unfinished. Lala laughed and told me to put it away...

"You can sort it out tomorrow babes, I'll be in here lunch-time..." I promised I would, but I had one more question for her before I left the bar.

"Will you do me a huge favour La? If you bump into Debbie, will you check for me, just to see if she's OK, like? I really do think there's something going on with her. I think it's something she has no control over, but it's scaring the shit out of her... I think she's trying to tell me but hardly knows me so I suppose she doesn't know if she can trust me or not. I thought maybe with you being a girl..."

"Yeah, course I will babes, no problem," came the reply. Then came the Lala sense of humour. Staring at an invisible creature next to me, "Oh, hi Debbie, how *are* you? Killed anyone I know lately?" Then she turned back to me, "...and how exactly am I supposed to do that? I barely *know* the girl and I've only clapped eyes on her four or five times. Look, I'm really sorry mate, I'm happy to listen to you, it really *has* been a fascinating evening, but what *do* you expect me to say, *if* I ever see her again?"

I pondered the problem—I understood what she meant... "All I ask is, if you *do* see her, just something casual, kind of matter of fact, the sort of thing you might say to anybody with that haunted look of hers. I don't know, how about 'Debbie, are you OK, you look like you've got the weight of the whole world on your shoulders this morning' or afternoon of course, depending when you see her... *If* you see her..." Lala looked genuinely concerned. As I finished my third, or was it the fourth vodka, she rested her hand on mine and whispered softly, "Of course, I will, babes, but no promises yeah?" It was all I could hope for...

17

"Any trace on Martin yet?"

"Nothing we can really act upon boss. That new mobile's only been used once, and even then, only for a few seconds so we had no chance to triangulate it. All we know for sure is its somewhere in the South West."

"So, you're saying it could be anywhere in Devon, Somerset or Cornwall then, doesn't really help us a lot, does it?"

"I'm afraid it's worse than that guv. Martin could even be as close as Dorset, or if we're being honest, possibly even South Wales at a push... Sorry, but unless that phone's used again... We're doing what we can but it's a lot of ground to cover."

"...and the holiday season just kicking off, great! What about the spotters? Nothing there?"

"Not yet boss, but like I said there's so much ground to cover. Plus, Martin could be holed up somewhere, hardly going out at all, what with all these home deliveries now-a-days."

"Get some more men down there. Concentrate on the big towns and the popular holiday resorts, it's easier to hide in a crowd..."

"OK boss, will do."

"We have to find Martin or we're in deep shit, do you understand?" He slammed the desk for extra effect. "And we've only got three months, four if we're lucky..."

18

Cheryl and Minnie's new found friendship was proving expensive. While all involved, Alice, Tom, my son and daughter-in-law, and myself of course were happy with it, none of us were enamoured at the thought of either girl making the journey between Cornwall and Northamptonshire, more than four hours on three separate trains, on their own. They were only twelve after all… I couldn't help thinking back to my childhood days in Brighton, when two or three years younger than that, I would make the twenty-minute walk home from the sea front, or the cinema, on my own, often after dark during the winter. But those were more innocent days. If anything bad was happening to children back then, it was behind closed doors.

Fast forward to the twenty-first century and it seemed no-one was safe on the streets, or indeed on a train… Old or young, male or female. Without letting Tom or Alice know, so as not to hurt their feelings, or make them feel guilty for being pensioners, when the time came for Minnie's visit to the East Midlands, I arranged, and paid for Clare's 'few days with an old school friend in Exeter' which meant Tom only had to make a short drive at minimal cost, for his grand-daughter to accept Cheryl's invitation to spend the half-term holidays with her…

I couldn't believe it was nearly June. While my work was loaded with good points, notably the complete lack of the Monday Morning Blues, suffered by many Monday to Friday workers, the one draw-back was that you often lost track of time…. Mondays to me were either 'Yay, another day off work' or 'Yeah, last day of the week!' Don't misunderstand me, I still loved my job, but not as much as my time off… The first clue I had that summer was nearly upon us—June was just seven days away—was seeing all the doors and windows of The Beachcomber thrown wide open, no doubt airing the pub after the long winter closure.

It was landlord Brian Issom's first summer opening since *that* day, as most of the previous summer had been spent re-building his hobby. Yes, hobby. That's what Brian called it. He had always wanted a pub, but didn't fancy the daily grind of daily opening all year round, hence his three- or four-month season, depending on the September weather. It was an arrangement both he and Colin were in agreement over. Brian enjoyed his hobby, meeting all the holiday-makers, while Colin was in his element running a year-round pub and earning a good living from it. Brian was a likeable guy, from Warlingham in South London.

For the benefit of visitors and locals alike, he would exaggerate his accent to such an extent, he could have been a true Cockney. Combined with the Chas and Dave songs that were often heard blasting from his juke box, made him and his pub quite a novelty. It had proved to be very good for business in the past, and would no doubt do so again that year. I promised myself a visit one day…

Clare's imminent arrival in Exeter, and subsequent phone call came through that Friday morning. I rushed round to Tom's to give Minnie the good news. She'd been so excited and talked of nothing else all week. Tom was to meet Clare in the car park at two that afternoon. I just *knew* Minnie would have a million questions, so Clare and I had a little white lie prepared. No harm in that, and we'd tell her the truth, complete with a perfectly valid explanation, as she grew into a young woman. Living in the relative safety of a Cornish village had sheltered the girl from much of our cruel world. There was no need for her to know the harsh reality just yet.

Let her enjoy the innocence of childhood a little longer… I was to go Northampton myself the following week for a few drinks with Lucy, and a day or two with the family, eventually driving Minnie home the Friday evening… With all this intricate planning, plus my on-going renovation of the garden, not to mention the fact that I still had three more days on Brannigan's duty, I had put Debbie completely out of my mind. There simply wasn't enough room in my tiny brain to hold any more than three things at any one time. It's a 'bloke' thing, or so the ladies in my life have always told me. And anyway, Lala was going to have a word for me, wasn't she? Though I didn't hold out a lot of hope on that score.

Even if she *did* succeed in 'bumping' into her, I had serious doubts that she would gain information of any value. Something told me if Debbie was going to open up to anyone at all, it would be me. I can't explain why, it was just a feeling I had… I gave Minnie a big cuddle, wished her a wonderful time and promised to see her 'next week'. On the way back, I called in to see Lala and pay last night's bar bill… An hour later, the clouds came over and we had what can only be described as a short, sharp shower. Or as *I* called it, a 'that'll save me hosing down the turf' shower…

That evening, I had a surprise visitor—no I *still* hadn't put a pane of glass in the front door. I hadn't been expecting anyone and if I'd chosen to hazard a guess, which I didn't, my first would have been Tom, possibly to let me know Minnie had arrived safely. Although the words had never actually been spoken, I strongly suspected Alice and he were secretly glad of a week off. Naturally, both grand-parents doted on the little girl, and who wouldn't, she was a joy… But it couldn't have been easy for them. They were no spring chickens, had had to cope with losing their only daughter at the same time as doing their level best to replace her in Minnie's eyes.

Add to that Alice's incapacity, Tom's energy levels must have been stretched to the limit. It didn't help that there was no-one else under the age of thirty within easy and safe walking distance for a twelve-year-old girl. Like Minnie herself, all her school friends went to Harwick, and most lived there also… Even *I* rarely chose to walk around the local lanes. There was always the possibility of some boy racer using the one-way lane as his own personal race track. We never actually saw them, due to living in the short cul-de-sac that ran from the lane to the bay, but you often heard them… I imagined Alice and Tom, with time to themselves for a change, with their cups of tea, later cocoa maybe, curling up on the sofa pretending to be love-sick teenagers again…

Except their choice of television viewing had no doubt matured. I was pretty certain they were loving their seven days of freedom, and missing Minnie like Hell in equal measures. My second guess as to my caller would probably have been Barry. Since our first casual chat about gardens, he seemed to have taken a genuine interest in my progress. So much so that I even felt a tad guilty keeping my plans of palm trees from him. I suppose it was only natural he would be interested. After all, there was very little going on in the gardens between us. All the Bonnell's had was lawn, which to be fair, Mark kept neat and tidy. He also appeared to have some kind of arrangement with Debbie, as he kept hers trimmed as well.

I don't believe I'd ever seen Debbie in the garden… Front *or* back. Sarah seemed quite content pottering with her rose bushes…. I don't think Barry saw me as a threat to his own efforts—I certainly had no intention of being so—but it did intrigue me a little as to just why he took *such* a keen interest. Hopefully, he just wanted our village to look 'nice' for visitors—mine was indeed the first and last garden people saw, depending from which direction they came—and not because I might accidentally un-earth the body he'd secretly buried there, under cover of darkness, while Windy Cottage stood empty for several months.

Don't panic! I wasn't *seriously* thinking that... It was just my imagination running away with me, yet again... I doubted very much if my evening visitor would be either of my immediate neighbours. While always polite if we met, neither Sarah nor Adam tended to mix with the rest of the village, join in any gossip or drink that often in the Mariners. I was sure beyond any doubt they had never darkened Brian's doorstep for a pint of his best Mild. Heaven forbid! In my mind I tried to picture them two of them having a 'right old Cockney knees up'. No... I would say their brief visit to my house-warming—they had stayed about an hour—had probably been the only local social evening that had ever enjoyed their company. And fair play to them. If you chose to move out of town to get away from it all, the last thing you would want is to become a part of it all, all over again.

I respected that in the same way that I respected all the villagers for leaving me alone during my working week... The very last person I suspected to be at my door—in the few short seconds it takes me to move myself from living room to hall-way, Brian, Colin, Rara or Lala never so much as crossed my mind—was Debbie. I wasn't wrong, although I *was* surprised to see Adam Bonnell on my door-step... "Come in." I gave my best welcoming smile. "What brings you round to my humble abode this fine evening?"

"It's a little bit awkward to be honest Paul... I know Sarah and I haven't exactly been the most neighbourly of neighbours, but I need a favour." Now that *did* come as a shock! Mr and Mrs Independent needed a favour from *me*? What could I possibly have that they didn't? Or couldn't get from a simple telephone call? He followed me through to the living room. I offered him coffee 'or maybe a beer? Glass of wine?' He said coffee would be fine, as I reminded him, I was on call all week-end and doubted there was much I could do to help.

With the new Connie's open and by then well established, he obviously wasn't looking for a cup of sugar... "Yes, I knew this was a working week-end for you, which is why I'm afraid I assumed you would be on site for most of it."

"All of it means, sadly, I'm a virtual prisoner in my own home until Tuesday morning." I tried to make light of it, though Adam seemed to have lost his sense of humour. Without further comment regarding my work, he continued, "You see, the thing is, I have to go to Switzerland for a few days, big money deal I'm setting up and they need me 'sit loco' as it were and, well, to put it bluntly, Sarah's not too keen on being left on her own down here, miles from anywhere in a lonely cottage…" Sit loco? What was he, a bloody engine driver or something?

I barely managed to stifle the smile. I still couldn't see where this was leading. Did she want to move in with me for the week-end or something? "I know I often stay the night in the town flat, but it's only ever been the one night at a time, and we spend hours on the phone whenever I'm away. She feels as though… Well, as though I'm right there beside her. We talk until she goes to sleep." He was wringing his hands as though he was really worried for her, scared even… I tried to remember where I'd seen that hand-wringing thing before… Probably on television sometime… "You see this Swiss thing, well it's likely to go on into the early hours so I'm not going to be able to call her that often, so I just wondered… If it's not too much to ask…"

If he ever got around to actually asking me, I'd probably say 'yes' but he was taking forever… "The thing is, if you didn't mind, and as long as you don't have plans or visitors or anything, I was hoping you wouldn't mind her coming round *here* for the evenings. She gets very nervous on her own you understand. And it wouldn't be a problem during the day, she's got a million and one things to keep her busy, her charities and everything… Just the evenings I worry about. And it would only be the three nights, I'll be back on Tuesday, Wednesday at the very latest…"

How could I refuse? The poor man was clearly desperate, and despite my earlier thoughts, wondering why they never saw their grown-up children, they were obviously still very much in love for him to be this concerned… "No problem, mate. It will make a pleasant change to have some company of an evening. She can keep me in coffee while I'm working." I smiled. He looked so relieved, I thought for a minute he was going to hug me, and that would have been *so* out of character. Instead, he stood up and shook my hand, very firmly, a real man's hand-shake, very business-like.

I could easily picture him surrounded by foreign financial delegates, sitting round a huge polished oak boardroom table, making decisions that would affect all of our lives… Agreeing the price of a barrel of crude oil for the next three months for example, or the changing fortunes of overseas commodities (whatever that meant) … Having reached an agreement—with me escorting her back next door as soon as I was ready for bed—he shook my hand again.

The look on his face really was that of genuine relief. You would have thought I'd just saved Sarah's life, rather than agreeing to 'put up with' someone to have an adult conversation with and bringing me endless cups of coffee. I could visibly see the colour flowing back to the man's cheeks… I *know* this was probably my imagination running riot yet again, but at that precise moment, I would have bet Windy Cottage on him not going to Switzerland that week-end. Instinct was also screaming that Adam Bonnell had nothing what-so-ever to do with finance either… Apart from the vast sums of money some invisible benefactor was paying him for what he was *really* getting up to that long week-end… I put it to the back of my mind and concentrated on talk of roses and gallons of hot, strong, black coffee—with the statutory three sugars of course—as I went to answer the two 'pings' I'd heard as I saw my next-door neighbour out the door.

As luck would have it, the entire week-end was relatively quiet on the Brannigan's front, especially after the madness of my previous shift. With the exception of asking a close colleague, Lindon, to hand carry an Alternator from Aberdeen to Bergen for me—Norwegian baggage handlers and freight shed operatives had chosen to stage a forty-eight-hour strike—it was very much 'run of the mill'. As I hadn't had a Tesco delivery for nearly a week, I checked the kitchen cupboards and fridge for anything I might need while Sarah was around: Coffee, tea, milk, sugar, ham, cheese, just the usual… I seemed to be low on cheese so I popped over to Connie's for a pack of Canadian Extra Mature—Rachel kept some in especially for me. I didn't have the heart to tell her I'd only bought it that once because I'd run out. Tesco's own was more than a pound cheaper.

Therefore, I stopped putting it on my on-line list and continued buying it from Connie's. I saw it as doing my bit for local shops. I made the short trip over the road. Rachel, as always, was in the mood for a chat. She could talk the hind legs off a donkey, that one. She made a point of reading two or three of the morning papers every day before opening, so she always had something to give her opinion on: 'Did you see that about David Cameron?' or 'Can you believe the price of petrol going up again? I don't know how people can afford to drive any more... Of course, as you know, *I* don't drive, but if I did, I think I'd have to give it up!' Etc., etc., etc... The really clever thing about Rachel is that she knows her customers.

Not the day-trippers of course, even though she seems to have an instinct in that direction too. But for the locals, she makes an effort to know what they like, not just their taste in cheese or fruit 'n' veg, but the kind of television shows they watch, the films they might make the effort to go and see... It means she can hold a conversation with any one of us without reverting to the weather, as many shop-keepers tend to. The girl was, still is, an absolute delight, the whole village love her to death, Harwick villagers too.

Many of her customers come from Harwick, as does she, so she's always got some gossip to spread, bless her. I wondered... No, I daren't ask just now or I'd never get back to work. But one day maybe... In the mean-time, I paid for my cheese, gave the little lady a cheerful 'see you soon' and wandered back across the lane, still wondering who Connie was and how she managed to keep that shop going... No, I daren't or that vivid imagination of mine would kick in again...

Sarah arrived shortly after seven on the Saturday evening. During the day, it had been quiet enough for me to take the Blackberry outside and get one half of the turf laid. The one thing I hadn't thought about was how difficult it was going to be, laying strips of rolled up mud onto a patch of ground that had only one straight edge. What with the winding path, the space allotted for 'whatever' under the window, the borders down either side and the rock gardens, under the fence—yes it was still white, but I hadn't forgotten—was literally the only straight line. Simple answer then.

Lay the first roll parallel to the fence and work my way back to the cottage. Not as simple as it first sounds though, as the very first roll I laid fell about three inches short of the pathway. I stood there contemplating the answer. I wasn't sure a tiny piece of turf added on to the end of the first 'run' would actually take... But I seemed to have no choice. Using a narrow-bladed spade—at this point millions of gardeners would be screaming at me: 'It's not a narrow-bladed spade you idiot, it's a...' but how was I to know?

I wasn't a gardener, was I? So, using my narrow-bladed spade, meaning the bit that goes into the ground was considerably less wide than a standard spade—I'm not a complete idiot!—I was just trying to trim the first part of the next roll to fit the little gap. OK, I admit it, I must have looked a total novice kneeling there with my roll of prime-cut turf, a spade and a tape measure close by—when I heard a voice I didn't recognise, coming from behind me, "Ye cannae dae it like that, yon fella…"

I turned to see the owner of the voice, a complete stranger to me, watching me and scratching his chin, while the woman next to him tried to stifle a giggle… "What we want tae be daein' is cuttin' a wee length off ye next roll tae giv' ye plenty tae wuk with." I was never too sure how to spell 'work' when spoken by a Glaswegian, but 'wuk' was how it sounded, so 'wuk' would have to do… At least I understood what he was advising me to do, and of course it made perfect sense. Why I didn't think of it myself I have no idea. Basically, it wasn't a lot different to laying laminate flooring, which I'd done several times before, and without fail, *always* cut it into easily workable lengths.

I thanked him and proceeded to do just that, as he and his wife walked on down to the beach, shaking their heads and still laughing at the wee Cornishman who couldn't lay a simple lawn… And it worked. Then I thanked my lucky stars it had been a man I would most likely never again set eyes upon and not Barry Marlow. He would never have let me live it down. I don't know why I looked up… Call it second sense or whatever you choose, but I did… And there was Colin, hanging out of one of the upstairs windows. He winked and me and said just one simple sentence, "Och aye the noo, canny lad."

Roughly translated, that meant 'I'm going to get a lot of mileage out of *that* one for the next few weeks.' I cringed, but bravely continued, making sure to trim each roll well back from the pathway… As I said, I succeeded in laying the whole of one side before the 'pings' became so regular, I just had to go back in and do some more 'proper' work. As the Blackberry hadn't actually rung, I knew the 'pings' were something that could wait an hour or two without costing the company a small fortune. Sarah arrived just as I'd signed off for the day. As I let her in, I couldn't resist another peek at my afternoon's work in the garden. I have to say I'd done a pretty good job, eventually.

Even *she* agreed with me, suggesting I might want to sort *her* garden out when I'd finished. Her cheeky grin told me she was only teasing me thank the Lord. If I had my way, this was the one and only time I would ever involve myself with anything of a horticultural nature. If I'm honest, I had even considered astro-turf, but decided against it purely because I knew exactly what Barry's reaction would have been. I would probably have been banished from the bay for life! As Sarah stepped into the hall-way, I spotted a familiar face heading up to the lane… As much as I appreciated his earlier advice, I really did *not* need another lesson in the art of turf laying from Jocky Wilson!

19

My long week-end with Sarah was not only highly enjoyable, but also entertaining, and at times even educational. Most surprising of all, was to find that despite our different backgrounds—Sarah was decidedly middle class at the very least—we had something in common. A love of good food. I took her thin summer jacket, hung it in the hall and led her through to my living room. As she sat down, she started to say, "I really *must* say…" "Before you go any further," I interjected.

I know it's rude to interrupt someone when they're speaking, especially a lady, but I wanted to make sure we set off on the right foot, "I don't need any explanations or thanks or anything like that. As I said to Adam, it'll make a nice change for me to have someone to talk to of an evening. As much as I adore little Minnie, and she is getting so close to beating me at chess these days… Well, as you can imagine, a twelve-year-olds conversation can be somewhat limited. Plus, if you're happy to keep me in coffee, I'll take that as a bonus." Speech over, I sat back in my own favourite arm-chair, safe in the knowledge my guest could now relax without a single pang of guilt, or debt of gratitude…

"I was just going to say, how well I thought your garden was coming along…" The expression 'shot down in flames' sprung to mind. I could feel the colour rising in my cheeks and I didn't know how to respond. I was so embarrassed. For the second time that day I'd made a total pratt of myself. I simply held my head low and replied, "Thank you, you're very kind."

"Not at all," she came back, "It's *you* that's being kind, letting me…"

"OK, let's stop this and start again." If one of us hadn't said it, we would have been thanking each other, or apologising all evening. She smiled. I laughed. We both laughed. "Coffee?" I asked… "I do believe that's *my* job." Sarah's reply had a smile to it, if indeed it's possible verbally, as she made her way to the kitchen. Ice broken, I asked if she needed a hand, to which she simply said 'I think I can find my way around a man's kitchen.' Then we both laughed again. I left her to it, right after my request for strong, black with three sugars.

I learned a lot about Sarah and Adam that first evening, though little of it relevant, just chit-chat. She loved talking about him though, almost in a way a teenage girl talks about the new man in her life. Whatever the chosen topic, and there were many, her answer would always be, something along the lines of 'Oh, yes, that's exactly what Adam says,' or 'You could be right, but Adam's always thought…'

I was beginning to wonder if Sarah had a life of her own, or if she needed Adam's permission to walk and talk, or even to breathe. If I had a pound for every time, I heard his name that first evening we spent together, I think I could have bought Windy Cottage all over again. Either she loved her husband almost more than life itself—as they say in the movies—even after more than twenty years together, or she was completely under his control, like some kind of financial Svengali. To be brutally honest, I neither knew nor cared. I was simply enjoying her company. In between her constant 'Adam this' and 'Adam that' I learned much of her charity work involved cancer relief—I didn't have a single cigarette while she was in my home—and was shocked to find some charities were government funded far less than others, even the 'killers', which seemed ludicrous to a layman like myself and 'surely something should be done to change it'.

Apparently, that was how much of her time was spent, lobbying our local MP, the hospitals and even the Prime Minister, but like everything involving politics 'These things take time, and time is something these people have very little of.' I could sense the conversation taking a turn towards the deep and serious.

Time to lighten things up, I decided… "Would you mind if I asked you a favour Sarah?" Judging by the look on her face, she had no fear of her host asking 'Why do we never see your kids down here?' or 'Has Adam *really* gone to Switzerland, nudge nudge, wink wink?' Of course, as tempting as it was, that was the last thing I intended to ask… "I know the deal was for evenings only, but I just wondered if you were free tomorrow lunch-time?"

The simple fact was, in my haste at putting my Tesco order in the previous week, I'd completely forgotten Minnie would be away that week-end. Tom and I had got into the habit of having each other round for Sunday lunch over recent months and like an idiot, I'd ordered a chicken to go with the half empty bags of roast potatoes, parsnips, Yorkshires, etc. that were nestling in my freezer. I have to say I'm a huge fan of roast dinners, but living on my own, I rarely bothered until I grew close to Alice and Tom… "It's only Aunt Bessie's but I'd be happy to share it with you if you fancy a roast." Her little eyes lit up like a child's in a sweet shop.

It seemed her beloved Adam had at least one fault in his repertoire. He virtually lived on fry-ups and takeaways. His entire life was an endless round of fish and chips, sausage, egg and chips, chips and chips, with the odd Chicken Chou Mein thrown in… Apart from their monthly trip to the Italian restaurant for 'some of the most amazing pasta dishes ever!' Sarah and Adam hardly ever ate anything else, and she couldn't even *remember* her last roast dinner….

"Aunt Bessie is fine by me," she beamed. "What time?" Having agreed a late lunch was best, just in case work dragged on after my contracted one o'clock finish, she said she'd be round about two. "Then lunch will be served at three, madam." Said I, trying to sound like a posh waiter. Further laughter ensued… By the time I walked her home, I had no idea where four hours had gone. She was very easy to talk to and seemed more than happy to join me for lunch, even offering to keep me in coffee during the afternoon if the weather held 'so you can get the other side done', she motioned at my garden.

With a final 'good-night' and the assurance that should she need me for anything, she only had to call me. I pressed the post-it note into her hand that bore my number. I walked the few short steps back to Windy Cottage with a spring in my step. Despite the complete lack of anything remotely romantic, and I was sure there never would be between Sarah and I, it had in fact been the first evening I'd spent 'one-on-one' with a lady for several months… Oh Kathy, where are you when I need you?

Sunday on the computer was every bit as easy as the day before, so having everything cleared up by one was never a problem. I'd checked the timing of the chicken and made sure the oven was on early enough… It's fair to say my faithful Auntie did us proud. She 'cooked' everything to perfection. Even the gravy was hot and devoid of lumps— 'thank you granules'. All was tastefully washed down with bottle of Blue Nun, and old favourite of mine from my Redhill days, but on this occasion supplied by my guest, the lovely Mrs Bonnell.

I have to say the morning's telephone call from Adam had set her in the right spirits for the day, which was a good thing…. Finishing my last glass of wine, and hoping there wouldn't be too much laptop activity, I thanked her for accepting my invitation, and for bringing the wine... "I used to be a big fan," she explained. "I'm no expert, but as the art critics say, 'I know what I like'."

I complimented her taste. She had a wistful look about her today. I was tempted to probe but thought better of it. There had been no need though. Picking up her almost empty glass, she smiled and said, "Brings back happy memories." I let the silence hang there, knowing there was more to come... "I remember my dad taking me to the Thieve's Kitchen, where he worked as a chef. I used to help with the washing-up as a child. Then as I grew older, he'd bring home a couple of bottles of wine for the family dinner, and this was one I really loved, but you can't buy it *any*where down this way..."

She stopped talking and looked at me. I suppose I must have looked as if I was in my own little world, which I suppose I was in a way. Either that or ignoring her, which I wasn't... "Paul..." she patted the back of my hand. "Are you alright?" I snapped out of it, drifting back into the real world once again... "Did you say the Thieve's Kitchen? Not the one in Worthing, owned by the Roberts' Off Licence group by any chance?"

"Oh my God! You're kidding me! That's unbelievable! *Nobody's* ever heard of Roberts'... There was only about fifteen off licences in Sussex, and one restau..."

"Plus, two more off licences in Surrey... Reigate and Dorking," I added, "and I was Relief Manager in both..." We both collapsed in fits of laughter at this ridiculous coincidence. Following on from learning Colin was born just a few streets away from me, this was starting to get out of hand. Next, she was going to tell me Adam used to be the barman at The Island in Hove where Copa Karaoke played many a time... But no, she didn't. The rest of the afternoon was spent discussing my many and various places of gainful employment—eighteen in all—before landing at Brannigan's. I'd been a guard on British Rail, a Unigate milkman, and yes, it is true what they say, a furniture removal man, window frame delivery driver, part-time postman, electrical wireman, including an unfinished apprenticeship, making hearing aids...

There wasn't much I hadn't turned my hand to by nineteen seventy-five. Sarah sat there smiling through it all, possibly happy to hear subjects unrelated to finance for a change. She even chuckled at my admission to a vandalism charge on my criminal record. I imagine the only criminal record *she* would have had would be something like Joe Dolce's Shuddup Yo Face...

I never *did* lay the rest of the turf that afternoon. Again, the time flew by and before we knew it, it was time to take the lady home again. Not to worry. My shift finished on Tuesday and I had the rest of that day, plus most of Wednesday to lay the other half. It wouldn't take more than a couple of hours if the success of the first side was any guide. The Monday evening came and went with similar pleasantries. I had still learned nothing more about her family, other than her father having been a chef. I assumed there was a mother somewhere, and possibly brothers and/or sisters, as she'd mentioned her 'family' in Worthing.

Yet in all that time together, something like eighteen hours, not a single mention of their children. On the *good* side, apart from a casual comment about him returning 'tomorrow', I didn't recall Adam's name being spoken even once after that first evening…

20

My two days in Northampton passed without incident. I made the journey in just under four hours, armed with the customary flask of coffee and a couple of packs of cigarettes from the two-hundred carton of Superking Blacks, kindly supplied by Adam upon his return. I detest motorway driving, but I simply did not have time to take the pretty route. Ken Bruce kept me company for most of the drive—only fifteen points on Pop Master, hardly my finest hour—followed by a little help from Jeremy Vine and a discussion on the recent changes in the benefits system... Cheryl was over-joyed to see me, which gave me a warm glow.

I watched over her and Minnie on the Wednesday evening so that Clare and Richard could have a rare night out. His mother lived no more than a ten-minute drive away but rarely made the offer. On the Thursday, I made the thirty-minute drive to Kettering to catch up with Lucy and the boys. As I turned into their cul-de-sac, I spotted Robbie, her eldest, chatting to some friends. He was sat on his bike, with the rear wheel just hanging off of the kerb.

Deliberately screeching the tyres, I put my foot down and aimed straight at him, making him nearly jump out of his skin, swerving out of harm's way at the last second. I continued up the road, with him chasing me like a mad man, and parked outside number ten. Despite my unsuccessful attempt to turn him into road-kill, Robbie threw his arms around me as I stepped from the Clio. That's just the way we are, and it's the same with his younger brother Josh. From the moment I re-acquainted myself with Lucy—I hadn't seen her for about ten years until twenty-ten—her boys and I were more like mates, irrespective of the fifty-year age gap.

When Lucy was seventeen, I had unofficially adopted her after some trouble at home and she ended up sleeping on my sofa for a year or so, before meeting and marrying the boys' father. When they moved 'up North', money had been tight and she was unable to keep her mobile phone active and we lost touch, sadly. She had always been good friends with many of the same people I knew, in and around Crawley, mostly on the karaoke scene. Many of them would ask me for regular updates, and thanks to my son Richard being married to her sister, I used to get all the gossip... Some of it good, some of it not so good.

Of course, to protect her reputation, I only passed on the good. But over the past couple of years, I haven't had to, as she pops down and stays for the odd week-end for a few drinks and a catch up with old friends. We even managed to drag her out to Majorca with us on one of our group holidays... Her first ever trip abroad as a single girl and how she loved it! Although I have to admit she really missed the boys, even phoning them two or three times a day, but that's what being a mother is all about I suppose... Of course, my move to Cornwall had put a stop to her visits, but I'd assured her there would always be a free holiday for her and the boys as soon as I had Windy Cottage habitable once more.

And for all the problems Lucy has had to endure in her young life, homeless at seventeen, married with two children by twenty and divorced three years later, she is *still* a lovely girl and a brilliant mother. Although many people disapprove, she was far and away the best drinking buddy I've had. I say 'was' because there is now a new one on the horizon of course... Unfortunately, due to the lack of available child minders, Lucy and I were unable to repeat our earlier session, crawling home in the early hours for 'just one more glass of wine'. On reflection, it was probably not a bad thing, bearing in mind yours truly was in sole charge of driving Minnie back home to St Matilda's the next morning.

Even though I never suffer from hangovers, I do still get that fuzzy feeling when you're not too sure what's going on around you... Hardly conducive to a four-hour drive, mostly on the motorway. I planned to leave fairly early and try to beat the rush on the M5. It was now the beginning of June and believe me, you do *not* want to be travelling South-West on that motorway any time after lunch on a Friday. Picture the M25 in the rush hour, and then treble it. The world, his wife and several thousand caravans will be heading in exactly the same direction if you do... All off for their annual week in what they hope will be sunshine.

Some to the surf around Newquay, while the older generation and many of the families would be heading for one of the thousands of caravan sites and holiday camps around the coast. Possibly some of them would be drinking in the Mariners that coming week. Maybe even the odd one or two doing the same as I had many years earlier… Simply turning up in a spot you could easily fall in love with and stay for a few nights, before moving on and having an illicit affair with Looe, or Polperro, or any one of the hundreds of delightful spots down that way… So instead of hitting the pubs and clubs of Kettering—which I swear has more watering holes than Ibiza town—we settled down for an evening of pop quiz on a DVD. When I say 'evening', does three a.m. count or is that officially morning? Naturally she asked after Ellie and I was able to answer quite honestly that I hadn't thought of her for several weeks…

Having woken at seven, intent on preparing breakfast for the others before I left, I discovered we had no milk. Typical of Lucy's untidy mind, but I remembered a convenience store only a few minutes' walk away… Problem solved. The other three were just coming alive as I returned and prepared coffee, juice and cereal for them. Between grunts and groans and yawns, Lucy broke the news to the boys, "We're all invited down to Paul's for a week in the summer holidays."

I was sure Robbie and Josh would be pleased, but nothing had prepared me for the reaction I got. In his haste to rush over and thank me, Josh managed to send his bowl of Rice Krispies, complete with half a pint of milk all over the kitchen floor. It didn't stop him though.

With a quick look over his shoulder, and a 'sorry mum' he was in my arms like a shot, holding me even tighter than Robbie had the day before, if that were possible… Having said my good-byes, and promising them all I would see them in a few weeks, I drove back to Richard's house, picked up Minnie, watched her say her *very* tearful thanks and farewells to all, especially Cheryl—who I learned later would be an absolute nightmare for the next two days—and made my way to the A45, just a short hop to the M1 on the first stage of our journey home. We were armed with two Tupperware cartons of sandwiches, courtesy of Clare, two bottles of orange juice and a flask of coffee. The intention was to drive straight through, call of nature breaks excepted. Assuming all went well— I looked across at the dashboard clock, it read '10.15'—we should be back in St Matilda's Bay by mid-afternoon. Things *didn't* go well and we were very lucky to even get there the same day!

The journey had begun smoothly enough. As we hit the M1, we'd missed the morning rush hour traffic en route to Birmingham. I'd toyed with the idea of cutting across country, via Stratford and joining the M5 near Cheltenham, but eventually decided that allowing for traffic lights, town by-passes, etc. it would probably be just as quick to head North, take the M45 South of Birmingham and pick up the M5 near Bromsgrove. The plan worked. By half past twelve, we were already approaching Bristol, at a steady 70 mph and with only one toilet stop... Already well over half way.

By a quarter to one, we were in a car park near Avonmouth. By car park, I mean the traffic on the south-bound carriageway had come to a complete stand-still. To make matters worse, there seemed to be no obvious reason for the delay... I've been involved in many curious incidents while driving over forty-odd years. For example, hitting a horse 'side on' while driving down a country lane, rolling a friend's Morris Minor while trying to avoid a fox that ran straight out in front of me on the delightfully named Sewage Hill, just South of Redhill, was narrowly missed on the M3 by a bouncing wheel that had escaped from a speeding Ford Escort, and probably the scariest of all, falling asleep at the wheel on the M1 near Luton.

While the other incidents were all firmly blamed on outside influences, beyond my control, this one was totally my own stupid fault. At around nine o'clock one Sunday evening, the manager of the trucking company I was working for, called and asked if I could be in Newcastle by eight the next morning, pick up some window frames and deliver them to a warehouse in Leeds later in the day, then head home as he had another urgent job for me on the Tuesday. Bearing in mind I had been awake since seven that morning—I was at the time also managing a Sunday League youth football team—and was clearly not going to see a bed *that* night, I turned it down.

He then offered my silly money and by eleven o'clock that same evening, I was already the other side of London. Cutting a long story short, and believe me there is nothing more boring than motorway driving—I would rather sit through a Westlife concert—by six o'clock the following evening, I was back on the M1, just passing the junction for Milton Keynes, then recently having gained the status of 'new town' complete with its own tourist attraction, concrete cows (?), when tiredness finally caught up with me. I felt my eyes closing, and genuinely believing I wouldn't make the next driver's rest area—I had only just passed Newport Pagnell—I did what I considered the only sensible thing... I pulled over onto the hard shoulder, checked to make sure the near-side lane was clear behind me, stepped out of the cab and walked onto the grass verge to stretch my legs and take in some fresh air.

Now before everyone starts screaming 'That's illegal', I was well aware of that, but as I explained to the traffic cop five minutes later, "Surely being off the main carriageway in my current state is a damned site better than risking other drivers' safety trying to reach Toddington, or whatever the next stop is...?" I couldn't believe it when he apologised but added that it was *still* illegal and insisted, I climb back into the cab and drive on. So, I did just that. Later, I had been very tempted to test him legally through the courts, balancing the law against safety, but thought better of it as they already had me on record for driving on bald tyres and would probably think I was just looking for some kind of revenge on the police in general. I opened the window as I drove off, then I closed it again.

Then I opened it once more... Switched the radio on, and off, and on again... Anything to keep my concentration levels alert for what I thought was about thirty miles until I could 'legally' stop for a rest and some strong, *very* strong black coffee. I remember seeing the signs for Luton Airport... Then after that, nothing... I was awoken by the sound of a fellow trucker's air horn, just seconds before I would have I hit the central reservation at around sixty mph... As I say, I have *never* enjoyed motorway driving. Not before that, and *certainly* not since... As you will now be aware, the previous year's flood of St Matilda's Bay was far from being my first near death experience. I hoped it would be my last...

On the subject of 'illegal', I'm sure everyone is aware that it is also illegal to leave your car parked in the middle lane and go for a stroll around on a motorway, having a cigarette and chatting to other drivers while sitting on the rails of the central reservation... Which is precisely what I was doing by a quarter past one that Friday lunch-time as Minnie finished off the last of the cheeses and pickle sandwiches. At least she'd stopped asking if we were there yet. Nobody had a clue what was going on. Traffic on our side of the M5 had simply stopped moving.

After ten minutes or so, one by one, various drivers were stepping out of their vehicles to see if they could see what was causing the delay by being a few feet higher off of the ground. Then someone climbed up onto the railings, and another scaled the nearby embankment, but still nothing. Due to a bend in the road in front of us, we could only actually see about a quarter of a mile ahead, which didn't exactly improve matters... Then suddenly the strangest thing occurred to some of us at almost exactly the same moment. The steady flow of traffic on the north-bound carriageway had not just dwindled... It had completely ceased to exist.

Not a single car, lorry or coach had passed our way for ten or maybe fifteen minutes. I even saw two men step over to the other side and take several photographs of this bizarre situation. It was around that time that the word started buzzing around that there had been a major accident about two miles further south. We all returned to our vehicles and turned on the radios. Mine was still tuned to Radio Two but there was no word coming through on the Steve Wright programme. I took that moment to call Tom to explain why we might be a little late and ensuring him that his grand-daughter and I were perfectly safe. I didn't want him, or Alice to hear a news-flash regarding whatever accident there may have been. They would only fear the worst. People just do.

Making sure Minnie stayed tightly buckled into the passenger seat, and by no account was she to leave the car, I stepped back out to hear someone say the air ambulance was on its way. At almost the same time, two police cars, sirens blaring, blue lights flashing, sped past us on the other carriageway, heading in the wrong direction... It was a further fifteen minutes before we heard, and then saw two helicopters approaching. They were no more than a mile away and I realised just how close we'd been to becoming yet another statistic of motorway madness. I'm in total agreement with the police service's hard-line attitude that there are no such things as accidents. They are always someone's fault, whether it be accredited to bad driving, bad vehicle maintenance, jay-walkers or idiot cyclists—especially in London—who think they have the right to jump red traffic lights, or mount the pavement to avoid them...

As we passed the scene of the accident some forty minutes later, it was clear by the various twisted piles of metal and glass that had once been someone's Toyota, to name just one of the vehicle's, this had been a very serious incident. A large truck was parked at the side of the motorway surrounded by wooden poles. The whole area had been cordoned off with bollards and that part of the M5 was reduced to just one lane for more than a mile...

Minnie and I finally arrived home just after five, following a two-hour delay at the 'incident'. Alice welcomed her grand-daughter into her arms as though she hadn't seen her for months, rather than just one week. I imagine the thought of us being that close to being involved also made the welcome home that much warmer. Tom offered me a Scotch, which I gladly accepted, and needed, as we

146

left the 'girls' to it and adjourned to the kitchen so that I could relate the full details, not that there was much to tell.

Indeed, Tom himself seemed to know more than I did. According to the local news, a lorry had shed its load of timber and seven cars had either ploughed into it, or into each other trying to steer clear of the horror in front of them. Miraculously, no one was killed, but there were nine people taken to hospital, two of them in Intensive Care Units with a fifty-fifty chance of pulling through. As the police would say, and I agree whole-heartedly, 'there are no road traffic accidents, only incidents that could have been avoided'... I would *not* want to be the man, or woman who had 'secured' that load...

21

Motorway delays apart, it had been a good week all in all. I'd had some quality time with my family, fun with Lucy and the boys, seen how close Cheryl and Minnie had become—both looking forward to my grand-daughter's planned week-long visit in August and best of all, if my friends and family will forgive me for saying it, not one single thought of super-spy Adam, Debbie the former Page Three girl turned heroin addict, or Barry's dark secrets hidden in the depths of a computer he doesn't admit to owning. I'm ashamed to admit, at one stage, I even combined his former life as a teacher with the computer he didn't want anyone to know he had, and came up with the word 'paedophile'…

But now I was back. Back to my dream home, where nothing bad ever happens, the sun always shines and all my neighbours are angels who wouldn't hurt a fly. Instinctively I looked up to see if I could spot any flying pigs and saw the ominous dark grey clouds moving in from the Atlantic. God bless America I thought, wishing Cornwall could get its weather blowing in from Cuba, or Mexico… Anywhere rather than the USA's Eastern Seaboard…

An hour later the storm hit St Matilda's Bay and it rained solidly for three hours. Two or three of us even stepped outside under awnings and porches to see just how bad it was and how long it might last. As usual, the Harwick lane leading down-hill into our dead-end street transformed into a mini river, flowing down to its final resting place on the already rain-soaked sand. While aware that lightning rarely strikes twice in the same place, I doubt anyone in our village will ever be able to look up at a dark angry sky without wondering…

I've mentioned before about 'every cloud' and this one was no exception. Thanks to the over-night rain, the earth beneath my front window and along the outside borders was beautifully soft and easy to turn over in preparation for planting the *Rhododendron obtusum* and *vitalba*, which I was collecting from Harwick that Saturday morning.

Thanks to Mr Marlow, and with a little help from gardening web sites, vitalba I learned was my favourite clematis, a little bit of Surrey I wanted recreated in my new home, and the rhodo obtuse thingy was blatantly obvious... Until Barry pointed out, "Aha, so you *don't* know it all just yet then. It may well be part of the same family, but what you're actually getting is Azalea."

OK, so I still had much to learn, especially as I hadn't even *thought* about the back garden yet, and that was three times the size of the front! But at least I knew what a *Cordyline autralis* was, and Merv said he could get me one in less than five days that would grow to around five metres and cost me less than one hundred and forty pounds, which apparently was a bargain compared to some of the bigger garden centres. "Thanks Merv, so you're saying it's a hundred and thirty-nine, ninety-nine, right?" He hesitated and responded in the affirmative. Why do we not do away with this ninety-nine pence business? Nobody in their right mind is fooled by it!

The 'Pound Shop' has the right idea. I opted for a slightly smaller sized palm, supposedly only growing to about four metres—I didn't want to be accused of being showy—at 'less than one hundred and twenty pounds'. Figuring I should have the remainder of the front completed over the week-end, I arranged for delivery the following Wednesday, just after my next shift finished. I confess that, in my excitement, had Merv said he could get me one 'tomorrow' I would have asked for Monday. With Barry presumably out for the day, I would have *loved* to have seen his face when he came home, parked behind the pub and turned to face Windy Cottage. But I'm a patient man, that pleasure could wait another week or so...

It brought to mind another of my mother's favourite sayings—she seemed to one for every occasion. 'If something's worth having, it's worth waiting for.' My time would come soon enough...

Call me fickle if you like... Call me gullible if you prefer... You can even call me Val Doonican if it pleases you, but however you care to look at the way I choose to lead my life, I make my own decisions and live or die by them, with nobody else to blame when things go wrong, or indeed to take the credit when I get it right. I felt I'd succeeded in most of what I'd attempted to do in my first year in my new home, the place I intended to spend the rest of my life in, however long that may be... I had a very good relationship with all my neighbours, albeit low key in one or two cases... I was welcome any time at

Colin's pub, and got on well with both the barmaids... I considered Rachel a good friend, and superb purveyor of gossip, when I was in the mood and had time to spare... I was even a surrogate parent and teacher to a wonderful twelve-year old girl... Everything in the garden was rosy, with no pun intended I assure you... The job was going well, Windy Cottage was looking better every week and I saw myself almost as a children's story-book character, living happily ever after... So why wasn't I? Happy I mean, as in one hundred per cent happy rather than ninety-nine point nine... I was convinced it was no longer my imagination playing tricks on me.

There was something just not quite right about our peaceful little bay. More and more I felt that at least one of my neighbours, the people I'd come to call my good friends over the past year, the people who appeared to like and trust me, the people who had happily eaten my food and drank my alcohol all Good Friday night, was not quite what he, or she seemed... I wasn't suggesting that any of them were bank robbers or murderers in hiding or anything as serious as that. In fact, I don't know *what* I was thinking, I couldn't quite put my finger on it.

Maybe one of them was a victim of abuse or blackmail rather than being the guilty party... Maybe it was the dark thoughts I always tended to have after turning the lights out at night, unable to sleep... Possibly I'd just spent too much time watching television detectives discover that sleepy villages and picturesque towns were never quite what they appeared to be... But then again, maybe there was something in the old saying 'If something seems too good to be true—as St Matilda's Bay did to me when I first found it—then it quite possibly is...' It would not be much longer before I found out...

22

I had always thought myself something of an amateur sleuth, mainly thanks to my afore-mentioned choice in television viewing, plus my love of the novels of Nicci French, Agatha Christie and the like. I was amazed to hear a rare interview with Miss Christie, where she described Monsieur Poirot as 'an insufferable little creep', then proceeded to write a further nine novels centred around the Belgian detective. She was quite right of course, but you don't expect to hear it from the character's own creator. My favourite stories were always about violent crime—I also love film series' such as Die Hard, Lethal Weapon and Dirty Harry—I'm told this is a common trait amongst peace loving individuals like myself.

Apparently, we inadvertently release all of our innate aggression within our imaginations, often including violent dreams, or through the tales of others. Certainly, this was true of myself, never having been involved in a single fight throughout my sixty years on this often incredibly violent planet. And that, despite following my beloved football team, home, away and in Europe, right through the nineteen seventies at the height of virtual gang wars between rival supporters.

Somehow, often by talk alone, I had avoided as much as a bloody nose… I relished the challenge of a new story, even the more recent offerings of Martina Cole excited me, with the many turf wars of modern gangster life, in and around London, even though I'm sure like many other authors, the storylines were vastly exaggerated. But my heart still lies firmly within the murder mystery with all its carefully plotted twists and turns. I have been known to 'switch off' during a good Rebus—I recently down-loaded the entire collection of Ian Rankin, surely the modern king of crime thriller writers—and try to see past the smoke and mirrors, ignore the red herrings and solve the problem before the final chapter. I even solved the mystery of The Mousetrap, just half an hour into that famous record-breaking stage play.

There is a blatantly obvious but cleverly disguised clue quite early in act one. My love of such stories had encouraged my mother to take me to see it—my first ever trip to London's theatre land—as my seventeenth birthday present. On the off-chance, I had in my pocket a pen. At the given moment, I scribbled a name on my programme, and quietly asked mum to pop it in her handbag for safe keeping. As we left the New Ambassadors theatre—it would later move around the corner to St Martin's—I asked her to take a look at my programme. She turned to me in amazement asking 'How…?'

I replied by supplying the clue which she, and I suspect most of the audience, had completely missed. I shall reveal neither the clue, which I imagine remains in the play to this day, nor the murderer for the benefit of those who have yet to see it. I will however suggest that should you choose to go; you believe nothing that you see. The eyes and ears can very easily be deceived. I understand that, while the basic story has never changed in more than sixty years—The Mousetrap was born one year after yours truly—the author agreed to allow the production staff to add their own red herrings, which vary from time to time. On our particular visit, shortly before 'curtain up' an obviously drunk young man leapt from the front row yelling 'It was Ralston. Giles Ralston done it!'

This was closely followed by insane laughter and his hasty removal by two burly theatre staff members. Before the play began, another member of staff stepped onto the stage, apologised for the unfortunate incident and hoped it would not spoil our enjoyment of what was still an excellent play. By the interval, it was clear to most of the audience, if not all of them, that Giles Ralston could not *possibly* have committed the murder, but then as my mother pointed out, "You never know what goes on in the mind of a crime writer." How right she was. I shall say no more…

The Saturday morning went pretty much as planned. I collected my azalea and clematis, plus two six feet by eighteen-inch trellises to attach to the wall of Windy Cottage, one either side of the window. It was my intention to train the clematis to surround said window. I had turned over the soaking wet earth and dug the necessary holes for each plant, bedded them in, and covered each with a few inches of top soil which included what Merv called a miracle ingredient 'guaranteed to enhance the growth of my blooms'. I had left a gap at the road-side end of the border nearest the beach.

I hoped Barry would not spot it any time within the following days and ask the obvious question. I already had an answer ready if he did. It was to house one of those quaint old letter boxes you used to see in many villages to save the postman what was often a considerable walk to the owner's front door. 'I just haven't found the exact model yet,' I would say. I didn't like the thought of deceiving my friend and sometime mentor, but I would if needs be. Thankfully, the need never arose. Though he did call round on the Sunday to compliment my progress—which was in point of fact my completion of the front garden, save for the palm—he either didn't spot the gap, or simply chose not to mention it.

We actually spent a rare hour together, enjoying a pint on one of the rustic benches outside the Mariners, mainly so that I could admire my handiwork, in particular its symmetry—a nod to Poirot there—from a comfortable distance. It also gave me the chance to probe carefully into Mr Marlow's private life a little. I had already formulated a plan of action, to delve into the lives of my neighbours without actually appearing to do so.

In Barry's case, I would at some point in the near future, have need to borrow his computer as 'I was just checking out some garden furniture for the back and the damned laptop just crashed on me. The shop in Bodmin told me to take it in on Monday but it might take up to a week to repair, etc.... Would you mind terribly, if I borrowed yours for half an hour or so? I really want to get this sorted while I'm off duty.' It all sounded plausible enough. If he asked why I hadn't asked Adam, or Debbie, or Colin, I would simply explain that as I was looking for garden equipment and should I need it, his input would be very much appreciated.

How could it fail? Surely, he wouldn't refuse a desperate neighbour in need of urgent assistance... It was easy enough to point the conversation in that direction. To the best of my knowledge, Barry's only interests were horticulture—obviously—and due to his Monday outings, cribbage. I'm sure there must have been more to the man's world, but if so, he never mentioned anything. Inevitably, that Saturday lunch-time in early June, over our second pint, the conversation turned to our respective gardens. Due to the lie of the rocks behind our cottages, his garden was actually several feet shorter than mine, though about the same width... "My main concern," I began, "is how to fill so much space without more grass. You know me and lawn-mowers..."

His response was to suggest, as I often had young children around, and sometimes staying with me, I should try building a tree house in the old yew that hung over the far end of the garden, "I don't mean one of those red and yellow monstrosities you see in garden centres, but something you could design and build yourself... You have the imagination, and you're bloody good with your hands..." He had once admired the oak wall units I had built around the fireplace to hold the usual ornaments, photos and nick-nacks.

He continued, "Then you could turn that entire corner into some kind of magical secret garden for the little ones... A windy gravel path, or maybe crushed slate, a few Oriental plants and grasses, Gramineae and bamboo would look good and they'd grow high enough for the kids not to be able to see over. Add a few Bonsai trees for effect and Bob's your uncle..." He took another sip of his second pint as I wondered what on Earth a Gramineae was. The man was a genius. In a few short minutes, and with very little prompting, or indeed input from myself, he had already designed about forty per cent of my back garden. Unwittingly, he had also laid the foundations for my investigation into his background and whatever secrets it held...

"I wouldn't have a clue where to start looking for such exotic plants." I eventually explained. "Mind you, I'm sure Google will have the answer. It's never let me down yet." There... My plan had already been activated. It was now only a matter of time. A few weeks later, possibly right in the middle of erecting the tree house—yes, I really *was* going ahead with his excellent ideas—my computer would conveniently be hit by a mysterious virus... Barry's response to my Google comment was to move on and suggest 'maybe a patio outside the French windows, with built-in barbecue, just in case you ever decide to throw another party...' He hadn't bitten. Not yet. But one day he would.

One day soon. And on that day, I would pounce... Any further discussions were curtailed by the arrival of Colin, eager to give us both the details of his summer season plans, commencing that very evening. I had already spotted the colourful, chalk-laden sandwich board, proudly announcing to all who passed The Mariner's Arms that the Cockney Wurzels were making their 'grand return to Tilda's' and appearing 'live here tonight'. They had been suggested to him by Brian from The Beachcomber.

Brian had spotted them some years earlier and brought them to his own pub, where they performed a monthly gig right through the summer season for six years, bringing in huge crowds... Brian's words. I imagined 'huge crowds' to be about fifty people, compared to his usual twenty or thirty the rest of the week… But Colin was quick to point out there had been more than two hundred at their farewell show in 2009, when Brian 'couldn't be arsed with the extra work any longer'.

Apparently, their unique brand of music was a legend all over the West Country and people would travel miles for two hours of their clever re-writes of famous songs, strange accents, and general fun. Colin had managed to obtain the phone number of one of the band and offered them a one-off special, that might turn into a regular booking if all went well. Being of a musical back-ground, I had to admit I was tempted. It was Saturday night after all, and what better way to spend it than in the pub? After all, the Cockney Wurzels may well be as entertaining as both the bay's landlords seemed to think they were. Having said that, and already having been witness to Colin's sense of humour, I had my doubts.

Colin left us both with a cheery 'Hope to see you later gents'. As soon as he was out of ear-shot, Barry muttered, "Well he won't be seeing *me* later, *I* can tell you! Bloody racket!" I guess I just don't age in the same way as some people. While Barry, I'm sure, would happily spend his Saturday nights with a good book and his radio tuned to something classical, 'growing old disgracefully' was an expression that could have been invented especially for me. Without comment, I smiled at my friend's words and inwardly made up my mind to pop across later that day. After all, if it really was just a 'bloody racket' I didn't have far to go home, did I?

In my younger days, I had enjoyed many and various encounters with live audiences. In most cases, putting the Osmond-loving teeny-boppers of Surrey to one side, they were enjoyable. In the liberated days of the nineteen sixties and seventies, working as a DJ for Cyclops Mobile Disco, I even had my own little band of groupies, as did my partner at that time, Dave Richardson. We would turn up at each gig in an old Austin A4 fan, loaded with equipment and vinyl— it was vinyl or nothing in those days…

Even the cassette tape had yet to be invented—and we would share the spotlight for about three hours, whipping the crowds of teenagers into a frenzy with songs like Dance to The Music by Sly and The Family Stone, and Groovin' with Mr Bloe. As the mainly female audience grew more and more excited, the empty van had other advantages… My life on the road with Barley had been similar. For some reason, the singer always receives more female attention than the rest of the group, and despite also being the drummer, and usually at the back of the stage, the late seventies and early eighties were no different.

As I've recounted many times before, my sexual encounters down the years are not something I'm particularly proud of, but at the same time, neither am I ashamed of them. They were days of sexual freedom, the days before AIDS took a firm grip on the sexually active in the UK. I can say without any fear of contradiction that I never once took advantage of any of the girls during that period, and I can also say with absolute certainty, that all were of legal age. Neither did I ever indulge the disgraceful habit of discussing those encounters the following night in the pub with 'the lads', as many did. On the other hand, I know for a fact that some of my then partners did.

As the word spread around the pubs and clubs of Surrey and Sussex, on more than one occasion, I would be handed a note saying words to the effect of 'My mate Trish reckons you're a fucking good shag Paul. Call me any time.' This would be followed by the girl's telephone number. I admit I called some of them, if things were quiet on the sexual front. Nothing much has changed, only the name.

These days we call them fuck buddies and the girls are just as guilty of it, if guilty is the word, as we men. I even heard that my number was displayed on the back of a Ladies lavatory door in Westerham's Grasshopper at one stage, but for obvious reasons, that has never been confirmed... Despite being, by then, well into my forties, the early days of Copa Karaoke weren't a lot different. Beyond my belief, and that of my partners, I was *still* the subject of quite a number of female desires. Being once again a single man, I did not always refuse, though I admit to being a little more fussy in my choices. I would say my favourite memory of my Copa days would have to be a tiny blonde girl, with a stunning figure which she was more than happy to show off, who was a regular singer at the Sunday Service, our show in The Castle, Reigate. Every time she came up to sing, I would be standing just off stage, not wishing to share the spotlight, as she sang some powerful love ballad... Vanessa's songs were *always* about romance.

Each time she reached a particularly intimate line, she would look me straight in the eye and sing those words not just *to* me, but deep inside me. I would melt. Over the weeks I became almost obsessive about Vanessa. Other people would tell me it was just her stage presence, her showmanship, teasing me… One or two even hinted she was gay. It was true she always arrived with a group of girls, never with a boy-friend, but that was true of many girls. It didn't by necessity make her a lesbian. Mind you, those one or two advisors proved to be correct. A chance meeting with Vanessa one lunch-time led me to actually being in the position to partake in a one-to-one conversation with her.

Throughout my part-time musical career, it had always irked me that I never had the chance to really get to know many of the people I called my friends. They would come and say their hello's as we were setting up, then three hours later, and usually slightly drunk, they'd come back with 'great show tonight' or 'see you guys next week' and vanish without trace until the next time. Many of them, I only got to know by their first names, or in some cases their nick-names, such as Cabbage, or Wavey, or Cakey… God knows where *that* one came from!

I'm sure some of the residents of Uckfield would be able to explain it though. So, it was always a pleasure to bump into one of our devout followers purely by chance… I barely recognised the little blonde at the bar, the subject of many late-night fantasies over recent months. In ripped jeans and loose rugby shirt, she looked a world apart from the girl I knew on Sunday nights. I imagine the same could be said for most performers, famous or otherwise. I hardly think Shirley Bassey pops down to Waitrose for a pint of milk in full-length sequinned gowns…

"I was hoping I'd see you in here sometime." She opened the conversation. "Lee told me you usually called in on the last day of each month." Lee was the landlord, bloody nice bloke to quote Tim Nice-But-Dim, and the latter was perfectly true. I always popped in to drop off the next month's karaoke posters around that time. Working as I was, just a couple of miles away on Redhill Aerodrome, it was a pleasant break from the daily toil and a chance to catch up with Lee, discuss the future and maybe even negotiate a pay-rise. "Can I ask you a slightly embarrassing question?"

Those eyes were burning into my soul yet again. I could ignore her choice of clothes… An old sack would not have abated my thoughts. I noticed the very large gin on the bar in front of her and imagined her waiting there for me, religiously all week, just for this chance meeting, building up the courage to ask this 'embarrassing question'… Her gorgeous deep blue eyes never lost contact with mine as she asked, "Have you ever made love to a lesbian?" Heaven knows how many gins Lee had wound down her neck the past hour or so, or however long she'd waited for this moment in her young life—I guessed her age to be about eighteen, possibly a year or two older but no more... Lee passed me a pint of Fosters, my usual tipple in his hostelry.

I took one very large swallow from the glass as my dream girl went on to explain how she'd known from a very young age, 'about ten I think', that she preferred girls... "No, that's not true." She corrected herself. "Not just *preferred* girls, but had no feelings for boys at all, not so much as the slightest tingle... You know." Her eyes lowered to clarify the point. She then went into great, or maybe I should say lurid details of her experiences with other young ladies. As she came to a convenient pause in the titillating tale, she finished the remainder of her gin and tonic, which Lee immediately replaced with another of the same. I hasten to add her entire story so far had been 'sota voce' and I was the only person privy to it.

Taking another large gulp of my lager, I wondered where this was leading... Why had she chosen yours truly, a humble karaoke presenter to be her what? Confessor? Did she see me as some kind of priest? After a large sip of her newly-refreshed glass, she resumed her eye contact with me and explained that she had never, she repeated the word to accentuate it... *Never* even considered having sex with a boy, or *man* until she clapped her eyes on me. I could have fallen off the bar stool at that moment of stark revelation. Until that very second, I had considered the possibility that she saw me as some kind of father figure. Maybe her own father had rejected her 'coming out', refusing to accept any daughter of his may never give him the grand-children he yearned for. I'm sure many other thoughts had run through my mind during her 'confession', or whatever you choose to call it, but *that* had not been one of them.

To conclude that part of my life, and surprisingly it does have a happy ending, I can confirm we spent a very enjoyable evening at my flat, a few days later, and Vanessa and I remain friends to this day, staying in contact via e-mails and the odd exchange of photographs—Oh, the joys of Facebook—updating each other's lives. I can also reveal that our evening together, as enjoyable as it was for both of us, has never been repeated. While admitting it was 'fun' and educational—in her own words, she didn't want to go to her grave never having had a cock—it didn't change her attitude to men, or girls, and she has been living happily with a girl called Zoe for the past seventeen years... True to my belief in refusing to 'kiss and tell' that episode remains our little secret. Vanessa therefore is not the lady's real name...

23

At this point, I have to offer my thanks to Brian Issom and Colin Hughes... Saturday night with the Cockney Wurzels was the best fun night out I'd had in ages. The combination of musical expertise and West Country humour had me in stitches for most of the evening. If you ever get the chance to see them 'live', don't throw it away. It will be well worth it. Hearing Combine Harvester sung by 'Chas and Dave' was a high-light, but I think my favourite had to be 'The Wurzels' version of Rabbit, with its clever re-write to include the legendary 'Beast of Bodmin'.

Possibly the cleverest of the evening's songs was their own version of Sideboard Song. It was hard enough to fit all the words into one line in the original, without substituting cider for beer and somehow replacing the actual sideboard with 'me grandma's effing larder'. The lead singer assured us that 'effing' was short for 'flipping'. I'm not entirely sure any of us believed him. Due to the lateness of the hour, and the fact that after the first minute we all got the hang of the chorus, the singer dropped the last two 'effing's' and let the audience fill in the blanks. It wasn't rocket science... I don't know how they squeezed all those words in, but they managed it.

A fabulous evening was had by all and Colin was well impressed with the turn out... I estimated eighty or ninety people, most of whom I'd not seen in St Matilda's Bay before, fairly certain that most of the crowd were a selection of their own fan club and quite possibly some of the visitors who had now started cramming our pretty little beach and swelling the coffers of both pubs and Connie's Mini-Mart. I say 'most' I didn't recognise, but I was surprised to spot Sarah and Adam over the far side of the bar.

This hadn't struck me as their style of entertainment, but like the rest of us, they were joining in all the famous choruses and even the required 'ooo-aars'. Though we didn't speak, we exchanged nods of greeting early on, and the odd smile during the show... Shortly after eleven-thirty, and three encores, Colin took to the make-shift stage—the raised area under the saloon bar window—and thanked everyone for coming, asked for one more big cheer for the boys—which he got—and promised they would return in July, reminding them to 'check the web-site for details'... Colin had his own web-site? Wonders will never cease.... My next thought: Does *Barry* have his own web-site? Yes, even after five pints of Carling Darling and the obligatory vodkas and Red Bull, the amateur detective's brain was still active...

Being a very warm and pleasant early summer night in St Matilda's Bay, there seemed to be no rush for anyone to leave the Mariners. I'd managed to escape before the vast majority and positioned myself on the only remaining free bench outside the pub. I glanced across the road at the cottages, most of which had their upstairs windows open to allow the cool air in. There was a shimmer of light coming from the Bonnell's living room, no doubt part of a timed security system.

Despite the almost total lack of crime in the bay, you could never be sure, especially in the summer with all its strangers. I made a mental note to install something similar. No lights at all in Alice and Tom's. I assumed, along with Minnie, they had turned in for the night. I could see a side window open upstairs, but the front window, that of their own bedroom was closed to keep the noise down I suspected. Barry's windows were all closed of course. No chance of that 'bloody racket' creeping in. There was a light on in what I guessed might be Debbie's bedroom, though I couldn't be sure... I was still trying to work out how best to strike up a conversation—preferably two-sided—with her, in an effort to probe her past and indeed her present.

Glancing down the lane to the sea, I could see The Beachcomber was still doing good business, even though the best show in town had been just a short walk away. Brian had re-opened the previous night, making no big effort to publicise it. 'If people want a drink, they'll see the doors open in the day and the lights on at night' he offered as an explanation. A little further down the lane, where it widened enough for drivers to do a full circle had they missed the 'No Through Road' signs, or hoped they might find a car park, there were about twelve cars blocking each other in.

Presumably their owners had tried behind both pubs and found them full. Most were probably customers of either Colin or Brian's, and with both public houses closing at the agreed time of twelve mid-night, hopefully there wouldn't be too many arguments as people made their way back home, or to a caravan park five miles away, or wherever... I turned back to see Brian and a couple of people I didn't recognise had taken their place at the opposite end of the bench. "They've still got it then." It was Brian who had spoken. The Beachcomber had been quiet enough for his wife, Patricia, and Rachel, who in the summer helped out behind the bar once Connie's closed at seven, to cope with while he strolled down to check on his recommendation. I readily agreed with him.

Nobody in the bay knew of my history in the music business and I had no intention of turning into one of those people who take a morbid delight in criticising or finding fault with every little thing. So, the bass could have been turned down a tad for my liking, and their lead guitarist hit a couple of bum notes but hey, nobody's perfect. I'd broken enough drum sticks in my time to know these things happen. And the least said about my vocals the better! It had been a great show and who was I to tell someone who's been doing pretty much the same show, with enormous success for more than twenty years, how to adjust their sound system? It was at that precise moment in time that I realised in one respect, I was no different to any of my neighbours.

I too had a secret past I had no desire to share with anyone. Maybe a little further down the line, but certainly not just then. Why, therefore, should they share theirs? For all I knew, Adam really *was* a financial whizz-kid. Having made his pile in the days of the 'yuppie', he simply married one of his assistants, Sarah, and 'emigrated' to the peace and quiet of the West Country to escape the madness and the rat race that was London's famous square mile. And of *course,* their children never visited. How many university students could afford the odd commute to Cornwall? And what the Hell would they do if they *did* come down? St Matilda's Bay was hardly the den of iniquity that university life offered them. Within hours they would be texting their friend's, asking them to call with some emergency or other that 'couldn't possibly be resolved over the phone. You simply must get the next train back to Edinburgh!'

My brain reminded me that quite often over the past year, I had gone several days, weeks even, without seeing hide nor hair of my immediate neighbours. No doubt *they* were the one's doing the visiting. I smiled to myself as I pictured—I had no idea of their names—Sarah and Adam's children hurriedly dumping dozens of beer cans and bottles in the communal waste bin, driving to the Recycling Centre to dump countless old pizza boxes, and hiding the bread and baked been tins 'somewhere my parents would never dream of looking', so they never learned their loved ones lived on nothing but beer, pizza and beans on toast. Lastly, a reward would be offered to anyone who could locate the vacuum cleaner, last seen at Christmas… Did it never occur to the Bonnell offspring that their parents had done exactly the same thing about twenty years earlier, just like every other student had? Of course not…

My thoughts then turned to Barry. Rather than being a child molester, it was more than likely the opposite had been the case. Inner city schools had been a war zone back in the late twentieth century, when he finally threw in the towel. The more likely scenario was that he, himself had been the victim of violent attacks, possibly by teenaged boys twice his size. With the change in the law that said you could no longer give them the proverbial 'clip round the ear' without them searching out Esther Rantzen's phone number, even children as young as seven or eight were no longer as innocent as they'd been just ten or twenty years earlier.

No wonder he got out when he did. That kind of atmosphere would have tested the patience of even a mild-mannered anti-violence person such as myself… As for Tom and Alice… Well, they were just Tom and Alice, one of the loveliest couples you could wish to meet. No secret past, dark or otherwise… Just exactly what they appeared to be. Once devoted parents and now equally devoted grand-parents and designated guardian of the delightful Minnie. And Debbie?

As I sat there in the warm night air, I could see her as a young girl, breaking into the sometimes-sordid world of glamour modelling, often riddled with drugs and the constant offer of more money for going just that little bit further: 'Go on Debbie, take the rest off, just this once. All the girls are doing it these days, it's almost respectable. Why, you can see them in your local newsagents. It's all just an act. A show they put on for the public. Glamour model one minute, devoted wife and mother the next. Here, why don't I bring my buddy Craig in… Have another glass of wine Debbie… Maybe you and Craig could do some work together… Boy-girl sets are very popular with our customers…'

While Debbie may be blonde, she was definitely not dumb. Of course, she would have walked away from a sleaze-ball like that. While Page Three was the acceptable side of glamour modelling, the under-belly was never too far away for girls who wanted to earn a little extra cash, but Debbie had more respect for herself than that and as they used to say in the popular Sunday tabloids, made her excuses and left. Debbie one, Degradation nil… Having convinced myself that Colin had given up on women and relationships after one disastrous marriage that had ended acrimoniously, I finished my pint, said good-night to Brian and walked back across the road.

One thing I have to say about the effects of drinking alcohol is that my thoughts tend to go much deeper than when I'm sober. As I tucked myself into bed that night, gradually listening to the last of the cars leaving St Matilda's, I had yet another profound thought, brought on by my own secret past: 'The human race... While we are all different, we are all the same...'

If I'd thought for one moment that the Cockney Wurzels were to be my only surprise that week-end, I should have known better. Firstly, Tom and his family called round on the Sunday morning to admire the almost completed front garden, with Tom admitting that he 'didn't do as much as I should with mine, but what with one thing and another...' He had no need to finish the sentence. I knew what an effort Alice had made just making the few yards from their cottage to mine. We spent a very pleasant morning, drinking coffee, eating biscuits and Minnie very nearly beating me at chess—the closest she'd ever got!

Her grand-parents were rightly proud of her. We touched briefly on last night's music, with Alice pointing out 'it sounded like everyone was having a good time', then going into great details of how she'd met her husband at a dance... Her voice became wistful as she described how much they both used to enjoy dancing... 'But we mustn't dwell on the past, must we? It's the future that matters.'

She patted Minnie's head to drive the point home... I couldn't fail to notice Alice's eyes had become watery. Was that the pride she held for her adored granddaughter, or the memories of dance hall days with a young Tom? My second, and even more unexpected pleasant surprise that Sunday, was a visit from Debbie. It was shortly after nine. I'd enjoyed a particularly good chicken casserole, even if I say so myself, and was just settling down to a film on one of the many 'freeview' channels, an adaptation of a John Grisham novel I'd enjoyed on long dark winter while living in Smallfield, the title of which escapes me just now. Believe me, there is precious little else to do if Smallfield's winters are long and dark, as most of them were... I hit the record button and walked to the door.

Of course, I had no idea that it was Debbie, but I had at least made enquiries of a local carpenter, who promised to come and have a look at my door and offer a competitive quote. 'As compared to whom?' I was tempted to ask. I'd checked all the local newspapers, and double-checked with my trusty old friend

Google. To the best of my knowledge, Michael Felgate was the only registered carpenter within a thirty-mile radius.

As for those outside that limit, I guessed they would want a call-out fee, plus travelling expenses and for all I knew, over-night accommodation. Mr Felgate would be round this coming Thursday. Why not before Thursday? I didn't ask. I was just obliged to him that he was willing to come at all, since it was probably no more than an hours' work… As I opened the door, I tried my hardest to stop the beaming smile spread across my face. 'Keep it casual.' I told myself. 'No dragging her in and grabbing the first available bottle of wine and insisting she stay the night.' I gave her a gentle smile and a 'Hi', as though we dropped in on each other all the time. I made no attempt to invite her in…

"I'm sorry, are you busy? I wondered if I could come in and talk to you for a few minutes…" The voice inside my head was yelling: 'Yes, of course you can, really good to see you again, very welcome, stay as long as you like!'

"Yeah sure," was what I *actually* said, "come in and sit down. Can I get you anything? Coffee? Wine?" I stepped back to let her through. The bottle appeared from behind her, "I thought perhaps I owed you this, to go along with an apology that I *know* I owe you…"

As she took the far end of the sofa that I'd offered her, I switched off the television, reminding myself to stop the recording later of I'd have seven hours of the Shopping Channel that seemed to take over every station after about two in the morning. I wouldn't mind so much if most of them weren't selling tat in dollars and only available in the USA by 'dialling the free -800 number right now'. I retired to the kitchen in search of a corkscrew. Trust her to bring round a proper bottle. Every bottle I'd had since moving into Windy Cottage had come with a simple screw top.

Other than that, it was the Tesco box I always kept in the fridge. I knew it was there somewhere. As I opened and shut every drawer in the kitchen, I tried to remember where I'd last seen it. For Christ's sake, I couldn't even remember what it looked like! Then I spotted it, in that most obvious place, resting on top of the mug tree that the Bonnell's had given me as a house-warming present back at Easter. To date I hadn't used it, but I had to keep it on show just in case. With a 'pop', I managed to remove the cork undamaged, so no nasty bits floating in the wine, and poured us each a glass. The bottle was chilled, presumably only out of Debbie's own fridge for about five minutes, so I placed it carefully in the door of mine, ready for the inevitable top up…

Ignoring my protestations, she insisted on apologising for a) being possibly my most inhospitable neighbour, b) for interrupting me that night on the cliffs, c) for babbling on at me last time she came round, then walking out without even saying goodbye, and most importantly d) 'because you deserve an explanation, you deserve the truth...' "And the truth is," she began, "that I wasn't being entirely honest with you Paul. I *was* running away from my past. I'm *still* running away."

Although in my head, I had criticised her one-way conversations before, there was no way I was going to interrupt, even with the slightest 'go on'... I didn't want her to lose the thread and revert to her ramblings of her last visit. I sat in silence, sipping her wine as she told me the whole sad story... "I'm married Paul, or at least I was, technically still am. I'd known Len for about two years before we got together. He was always one of the lads, a man's man I think they call it. One for the ladies you know? He was a good deal older than me—I was twenty-two at the time—and he showed no sign of settling down. I was just a waitress in Oliver's, one of the Plymouth bars he and his mates used to drink in."

I was very tempted to say there's no such thing as 'just a waitress'. That's like some women who say they're 'just a housewife'. Without the waitresses, labourers, road-sweepers and all the rest of the Great British work force, those marvellous people who tend to think of themselves as unimportant, our wonderful country would grind to a halt. But I said nothing... He would always flirt with me, but then so did most of the male customers. It was nothing more than that. He didn't try to grab my bum or anything like that, the way some men do when they've had a few too many. Just a laugh and a joke. I took no notice and got on with my job. Then one night, he told me later he'd been planning it for months but struggled to work up the courage, he stayed behind after his mates had gone, and asked me out. We chatted for a while, then I thought to myself 'why not? So, he's a bit older than me'—fifteen years as it turned out— 'but reasonably attractive, in a rugged sort of way.'

Obviously not short of money as he was in Oliver's most nights. Not married as far as I could tell, certainly not wearing a ring...' so eventually I said yes. So as not to bore you with all the details,"—I found out later that year exactly why she didn't— "the long and the short of it was that we were married six months later. Within weeks of the wedding, he told me to give up my job. He wasn't having any wife of his being leered at by drunks. Then he'd start staying out late, much later than a quick drink after work, and when he came home, he expected dinner on the table followed by what can only be described as his own personal gratification. I don't rightly know how to describe it. It certainly wasn't love-making. Some nights it was closer to rape." She was clearly getting very emotional.

I know I said I wouldn't interrupt, but I asked her if she wanted a break, offering her another glass of wine. She followed me out to the kitchen and continued her story as I re-filled both our glasses… "After about three months, I couldn't take any more. He'd started to hit me by then. Nothing that would show, no broken bones or anything. One morning, I just waited until he'd gone to work, packed as much as I could cram into our three suitcases and left him, to come down here. Old Mr Taylor, the one who used to own your cottage, this cottage, was a friend of my dad's and he mentioned the empty place two doors up, thought it was up for rent.

"My dad realised I had to get away from Len and offered to help with the rent. I'm ashamed to say he's still paying it, and now I can't work because I'm scared to go out in case…" At this point, she completely broke down and fell into my arms. I'd finally got the truth out of her but there still seemed little I could do to help, other than hold her and stroke her hair as before.

"This time I didn't say anything shallow like 'It'll all work out Debbie', because I was no longer sure it would do. I felt the day when she could safely walk the streets again was a very long way off… If ever."

Having calmed down a little and seeing how late it had become, she said she really ought to leave, but hoped I understood why it was hard for her to talk about such things. I answered in the affirmative, followed by the question I should have asked five minutes into her horror story, "Why didn't you go to the police, take out a restraining order or whatever it is they do?"

"Because he *was* the police!" So, if she reported it, who would they most likely believe? An honest hard-working copper without a stain on his record, not a blemish in his career after more than twelve years' service… Or a blonde waitress who'd been saved from a life of drudgery, serving chicken and chips to drunken lechers, who had nothing better to do with their lives? I could see why she made the choice to come to Cornwall. So maybe it wasn't that far from Devon, but it must have seemed like a million miles away from a cruel and dominant drunk of a husband. Afraid for her father's safety, they'd even agreed a plan.

Before Len even had a chance to go to her dad's, her dad went to him, demanding where his daughter was and 'what have you done to her?' He had made such a row that some of Len's neighbours had come out to see what all the fuss was about. After that, Debbie and her father knew he wouldn't *dare* cause problems… And so, it seemed, life would continue in the same vein for my neighbour for the foreseeable future. I wished there was something I could do to ease the situation, but I could see no possible way.

The best I could do was offer her the invitation to come round to my humble home any time she pleased, "No pressure, just feel free to drop in any time, for whatever reason…" After she'd gone, I thought of a million questions that maybe I should have asked her, but realised I probably already knew the answers, like was her husband still living in the marital home? I would imagine so. Had he officially reported her as missing? I considered that highly unlikely. Why didn't she simply divorce him, citing—if she preferred not to reveal the violence she suffered—an irreconcilable breakdown of the marriage? Presumably because to start any form of legal motion would mean her having to reveal her address, which she clearly had no desire to do. With her former husband being in the service for twelve years, he no doubt had friends who could 'legally' make life very difficult for her.

The odd stopping of her car because 'you were swerving all over the road madam', or waking up in the middle of the night because 'we had reports of a prowler in the vicinity so we're checking you're OK madam.' The list goes on. There had to be some way out of her situation. She couldn't possibly live the rest of her loveless life pretending she enjoyed her own company and had no wish to share it with anybody else. If she didn't do something to force the change, I could see her ending her days here as a very lonely spinster. Debbie deserved better! One of my many mottos is 'There are no problems, only solutions.' For once in my life, I couldn't see one.

24

On the Wednesday, Merv's van arrived with my palm tree. I'd already checked with the garden centre and was advised to 'get it in the ground as soon as possible, mate'. As I was back on duty by then, I stood it up against the side wall, out of the view of all but the very keen observer, promising myself I would take my allotted lunch break—I often didn't take one at all, opting to work straight through—in about an hours' time. Luck was on my side as the time approached one o clock. A silent Blackberry and very little action on e-mail, or my parts chart gave me all the excuse I required. The hole had been dug first thing, in preparation for its arrival.

It seemed I'd overdone it on the size of the hole, but better too much than not enough and I assumed, rightly as I later learned, the deeper the roots, the stronger the tree. Having pressed down the soil and added some of Merv's own personal miracle-grow, I stood back to admire it. And I wasn't alone. Colin had spotted me and by then was standing by his main entrance nodding and smiling. I had no idea if he was aware that 'palms don't grow on the north coast old son', but not being from this part of the country, probably not. I have to say it looked magnificent, like a giant pineapple bursting into life. Now all I hoped for was a long and happy life for my new pride and joy, plus the approval of a certain Mr Marlow of course.

My prospective carpenter, Michael— 'call me Mickey, everybody does'— Felgate arrived on the Thursday morning as promised, and he was only half an hour late. Apparently, he completely missed our cul-de-sac the first time around and consequently had to do the complete one-way system a second time. I thanked my lucky stars I hadn't booked one of the longer distance workmen or there would have been extra mileage to pay. He came armed with a pad, tape measure, and a pencil behind his ear.

"Simple job," said Mickey, as I offered him a cup of coffee, "only take an hour or so, milk and one sugar please, trying to lose a bit of weight, right in the middle you say? Cost you a hundred and twenty including the glass." I was just about following the conversation and pointed out I would like that mottled type you normally use in bathrooms... I wanted to be able to tell if my visitor was male or female, blonde or brunette, one or two of them, or if unseen, I could assume it was Minnie. I did *not* however, want them to be able to see me.

"Make that a hundred and thirty den, sir." And how about one of those little security things you can look through that make people look like they're standing in a gold-fish bowl? The kind of thing you see in hotel doors... "Make it two hundred for cash and you've got a deal." We shook on it and he took some precise measurements as he drank his coffee. He had been in my house no more than twenty minutes before he was back out the door, saying he'd do the job on the following Thursday. As I closed the door, I thought to myself 'perhaps he only *works* on Thursday's.' Cornwall and its residents have it, or should that be *their* odd moments...

During my eight-day working shift, I'd got into the habit of popping over the road for a pint soon after six-thirty, as I shut down the PC and put the dinner on. I wouldn't like to say if it was a good or a bad habit, but it was certainly becoming a regular thing so I guess it would have to be called a habit. In the old days, both in Redhill and in Smallfield, I had never done that, always electing to go straight home, sometimes to a wife, other times to a partner.

Either way, it just never happened, possibly because the nearest pub in both locations was a good ten- or fifteen-minutes' walk away and I certainly wasn't going to take the car there. It only had to be someone's birthday or I'd bump into a neighbour I hadn't seen for months and before I knew it, three or four pints would have gone down. And the one thing I will *never* do is drink more than two pints then drive. I know I'm safe on two because about ten or twelve years ago I was stopped and breathalysed after *three* pints, and passed... Just. The policeman warned me how close I'd been and since then, never more than two. On reflection, considering my job, plus on-line shopping, it probably wouldn't matter as much if I was banned from driving now, but back then, without a car, I would have been out of a job. And I can't imagine the reaction from the respective other halves... No longer a problem though, with two pubs within walking distance... Happy days.

25

"We might've had a stroke of luck, guv..."

"Well spit it out, Smithy!"

"Our contact picked up another call, see, only about a minute but enough to pin-point it on the map..." His guv'nor was all ears, hoping for good news at last... 'We certainly deserve some.' His underling went on, "It was about half a mile up a hill, leading out of a little place on the North Cornish coast called St Matilda's Bay, and..."

"Shit! It fuckin' would be by the sea!" The guv was obviously not as pleased and they'd hoped he'd be.

"But you said to check the towns and coast, coz it was busy, guv. Easier to..."

"I know what I said you fucking idiot! That doesn't mean I wanted it to be though! There must be thousands of people coming and going every day!"

"Not here there isn't. It's barely on the map. Not even a "B" road guv. In fact, our man down there nearly missed it, thought he'd shed an eye-lash." He laughed at the thought, but his superior wasn't smiling. "Anyway, not only is it miles from anywhere, the sign-post off the main road is over-grown by the greenery and there's only about a dozen or so people living there."

"Go on..." He wasn't actually smiling, but his mood had certainly improved. He'd stopped thumping his desk and most of the red in his face had vanished. The boss no longer looked like he was nearing a heart attack.

"He reckons there's only about eight birds and six blokes living there. OK," he did his best to stop his boss interrupting him... "I know what you're thinking. It could still be a tourist, but it's one hell of a coincidence that it's in the same general area as the last call we picked up yeah? Not only that... But how many tourists leave an out-of-the-way place like that at four in the morning?"

"You've got a point there, old son, so what do we know about these people?"

"I've got one of our men checking it as we speak guv," Smithy replied. "We should have more details in a day or two…"

"Good, come back and see me when you have something more concrete."

26

Friday morning saw me at my laptop by half past six in the morning, following an emergency call from Norway. They were extremely apologetic, forgetting the time difference and thinking it was actually an hour later, my normal starting time... Had I not had the rude awakening, I may never have noticed Barry Marlow standing on the lane outside Windy Cottage, looking at my palm tree and slowly shaking his head in dis-belief. He hadn't spotted me through the crack in the curtains, so I chose to ignore it for the moment. I was sure our time would come. Whatever either of us might say, the proof would eventually be 'in the pudding' as the saying goes. If it was still standing and heading for its proposed five-metre height, I may just get the last laugh.

That week-end turned out to be one of the best I'd had in my first year in St Matilda's Bay. That same Friday afternoon—I was staying indoors and doing my level best not to bump into Barry—there was a knock at the door. As my new window and peep-hole were still six days away, I approached the front door with more than a little trepidation. To my surprise, Kathy stood there, bearing gifts (i.e., One bottle of wine and another of vodka). One of the great things about my casual relationship with the little lady from near Swansea, formerly Eltham, was that we both enjoyed pleasant surprises.

All the time she was living in South London, just fifteen miles away from my own former home, we would often call each other out of the blue and arrange a meeting that same evening, or maybe for a week-end away. However, since both she and I had headed west, we agreed that it would probably be just week-ends from that point on. This wasn't a problem as we both had busy working lives. Strangely enough, as the crow flies, the mileage is not much further than it had previously been. Sadly, we're kept apart by a large expanse of water known as the Bristol Channel. By road, it's now about a three-hour trip.

Hence our agreement that should either of us feel the sudden urge for a long week-end of alcohol with the other, we would just 'turn up' on each other's doorstep. Given the length of the journey we each decided to give the other advance notice if we were *not* going to be free for whatever reason. It wasn't convenient, from my point of view, if Cheryl was staying with me for example. I'm not entirely sure she would appreciate granddad crawling home at two in the morning, in the arms of a woman younger than her own dear mother. Other than that, we did try to meet up at least once or twice a month, a habit which had become sadly lacking over recent months, mainly due to the re-build of my new home. Truth be told, apart from the odd chat to Rara and Lala over the bar, my love life was somewhat of a mystery to my neighbours.

In fairness, none of them had ever asked. Had I been a younger man, no doubt one or two might have expressed an interest, but when a man reached sixty, people tend to think he's either lost a wife or simply no longer feels the need for female company. On my previous week-ends away, I imagine they assumed I was just visiting family or old friends back in Surrey or Sussex. Surprisingly, for a village, they all tended to keep themselves to themselves most of the time, and very few questions were asked. That probably explains my own personal thoughts from time to time with regards to *their* private lives. Having said that, they were soon to discover there was life in the old dog yet, especially when they noticed the age difference… The unmistakable age difference. Being nearly thirty years younger than me doesn't bother Kathy in the slightest. It's not as though we were planning a future together, or marriage.

We were, and still are, a couple of people who enjoy the same things in life. A good Indian meal, a few drinks, travel, sunshine and yes, the passion is still there as well. She actually said at one stage that she couldn't understand why Ellie had chosen to leave me, bearing in mind everyone claims I'm the same man I was when we met, just thirteen years older. I found myself defending my ex, though I'm not sure why. "People change," I said. "Just because she enjoyed Cornwall, Cyprus, food and drink, and me when we first got together, doesn't mean it should last forever." Kathy still couldn't understand it. "Well, if *I'd* been one of your friends, or hers for that matter, I'd have told her how bloody daft she was being and no mistake!"

In fact, many of our mutual friends had said the same thing, though I doubt many were brave enough to say it to her face. Never-the-less, Kathy and I agreed it was no longer important. It was all in the past, forgotten. What *was*

173

important was how the neighbours, Colin and the rest were going to react... Kathy's a petite blonde with a great shape, no extra flabby bits or the famous 'big bum'. The only exercise she gets is walking and when she's with me.

For the first time in my life, I was enjoying the company of a young woman not obsessed by her weight, or shape, or how she looked. I was fairly sure people would like her. Those of my friends in Crawley who had met her fell in love with her in an instant. She's one of those people you just cannot help liking. While never having been to any form of higher education, she has an amazing knowledge of many subjects, but without sounding like a know-it-all. She will happily join in any conversation and has this happy knack of making the other participant feel that he or she is the clever one. Even my *female* friends like her, which is not always the case. I often find a single man's female friends become surrogate mothers in the absence of the real thing. They seem to know better than me, who or what is good enough for me, or not as the case may be. I'd got to know the little lady pretty well by now, although the start of our relationship, if you can call it that, had been somewhat unusual...

Katherine (Kathy to you), South-East area, 33 candles on my last cake, drinker, smoker, looking for male with same taste for fun nights out. Recently single but getting on with stuff. Proud to be gay but looking for a fella to bounce ideas off. Age is just a number. Not looking for sex, so no girls please— for now lol.

I have to say I was quite naïve about dating sites. It never occurred to me that people who sounded so sincere could tell so many lies. Things such as Match.com hadn't existed before I met Jo, or if they had, I was not aware of them. Consequently, when I put my details on Just-For-Fun.com every word was the truth, the whole truth and nothing but the truth, 'warts and all' which would explain why I was happy to chat to Katherine—Kathy—on line for hours on end. Neither of us spoke about our past failed romances until much later. We both agreed the past should stay in the past. My age was no concern to her, neither was her chosen sexual preference off-putting to me in any way. I'd been brought up in Brighton so it was far from a new experience. Many of my friends were gay and proud of it, male and female...

We met for the first time about six weeks after I hit the 'Accept' button, following her friend request. It was then we both admitted to telling just one lie each.

Kathy and I agreed to meet in hotel bar approximately mid-way between Smallfield and Eltham, about five miles North of Reigate on the A217. I think both of our initial reactions were the fact that we actually looked exactly like our photographs. No lies there then. We had steak for dinner and chatted freely about our varied taste in music, places we had visited at home and abroad. All of this over two bottles of wine followed by Tia Maria on ice. It was only as we returned to the main bar area and ordered another drink each that we both realised a slight hitch to our plan.

I swear it had not been the intention of either of us, but we both suddenly knew we were going to be unable to drive home at the end of the evening. Having said that, it didn't seem to bother us. The evening had been going so well, we probably could have sat up drinking and talking all night, but the bar was closing at midnight. I tentatively asked if it would be in order to check the adjoining hotel for available rooms. Without any hesitation at all Kathy agreed it was a great idea and that we could grab a couple of bottles from the bar and *still* drink and chat all night.

"I'm so sorry," I began, as I returned to the bar, "but they didn't have any twin rooms mate, I had to get a double… But it's got a sofa and I'm quite happy to have that once we've polished off the wine."

"Its fine Paul, don't worry," she smiled. "I don't mind sharing. Cuddles are always good and we could always keep our knickers on." I have no idea what our fellow drinkers thought as we both laughed out loud for the very first time… Three hours, two pints of lager and a few vodkas later, we bought not two but three bottles of house rose and headed for the room. It was nothing special but it had all we needed for a night of alcoholic fun. The only drawback was the total smoking ban throughout the building. We both found that we smoked a lot more when drinking than we would normally do, so it was a pain in the proverbial to have to put shoes back on and go outside every half an hour.

Maybe it was the drink, or possibly just that we were having such a good time that we no longer cared, but Kathy spotted a sign on the bathroom door that read: 'Please keep this door shut when having a hot shower or bath as the steam can set off the smoke alarm'.

"Shall we?" She suggested. So, we did. We discovered that as long as you kept the bathroom door firmly closed, and opened and closed it very quickly when leaving, we could quite happily smoke to our hearts content in the smallest room. It is a practice I'm ashamed to admit we repeated in several other hotels during the following weeks. Again, this does have its drawback. It means you have to use half a can of deodorant in the morning to clear the odour of stale cigarettes. However, it's so much better than having to go outside every time, especially if it's raining or freezing cold...

I have no idea what time it was when we finally agreed we could take no more alcohol. All but the last couple of inches of the third bottle had been consumed and I for one was absolutely shattered. Kathy called me a lightweight but never-the-less made no attempt to finish the bottle herself. Time for bed... I can vaguely remember some really daft comments as we began to undress. "Nice bum!" Kathy observed as my jeans fell to the floor. I gave it a silly wiggle which made her laugh again. God only knows what the people in the next room must have thought. I responded with "Nice tits!" as her bra came off. She struck a glamour pose, pouting as she squeezed them together.

"And keep them on!" I reminded her, pointing at her underwear. To this comment, she turned her back to me, copied my wiggle and pretended to pull them down... Then gave that silly girlie giggle that only comes out when she's drunk and jumped into bed, covering herself up to the neck. I practically fell over trying to remove my socks. In the end I gave up and sat on the edge of the bed to take them off, still managing to over-balance twice. More giggles.

Eventually I succeeded in removing all but my black boxers and slid in beside her... "Bollocks!" I sat up again. "Teeth!" I'm terrible like that. However drunk I get; I still have to brush my teeth before going to sleep. There is nothing worse than the taste of last night's alcohol and cigarettes in the morning. "Oh, leave it Paul, we both stink to fuck anyway so who's gonna give a shit?" She grabbed me and pulled me closer until her head was resting on my chest. That was to become our favourite sleep position in later weeks. OK, so for once I broke the hygiene rule and left the ablutions that night. I lay there in the dark, stroking her hair and thinking how lucky I'd been to find such a good mate, when she suddenly said, "I lied to you Paul, I'm sorry."

I waited as she kept me in suspense for several seconds. Had this all been a joke? Maybe she'd done it for a bet. Worse still, she could have been married with three little kids at home wondering where their mother was... As her hand crept down over my stomach and onto the front of my shorts, she revealed, "I'm not a lesbian." We lay there in silence for a few more seconds as my body reacted to her touch.

"I lied as well," I admitted. "I actually *asked* for a double room…" The rest, as they say, is history.

Consequently, it did not surprise me at all that, by nine o'clock that evening Kathy was not only the main topic of conversation in the Mariners, but also the centre of attention. On more than one occasion, I was taken to one side and told I was a 'dark horse' or a 'lucky bastard', to which I simply smiled sweetly and took another mouthful from my pint of Carling Darling. We even had the pleasure of an invite to the Bonnell's for Sunday dinner, an offer we politely declined with a hopeful 'next time' as we had a prior engagement. Due to Kathy's love of animals, I had already promised to take her to the donkey sanctuary that day. She even surprised Adam with her knowledge of the finance world, albeit limited and far less than his own. She went on to explain her brother was a city banker.

Unfortunately, this comment was made within Colin's ear-shot and he took great delight in explaining, loud enough for all to hear, that 'where he came from, that's rhyming slang', followed by howls of laughter. To her credit, she also saw the funny side and immediately came back with 'So you know my brother then', which brought still more laughter. Yes, they soon took to Kathy. So much so that Colin completely lost track of time and failed to call last orders until well after midnight. Then after the Harwick crowd had made their way home, he locked the doors and invited us both to stay for afters with the girls and himself. No prizes for guessing our response… 'Only one rule with my lock-ins,' our host explained, 'no beer, just shorts. I can't be arsed to go changing barrels this time of night!' Almost as one, Kathy and I high-fived and yelled, "Vodka!"

The others gave us that 'we can see why you two get on' look, and weren't about to argue with them. As more and more vodka was consumed, mine diluted with Red Bull, hers with Coke, tongues started to loosen. Questions were asked that would never have been asked of a total stranger if the inquisitor had been sober, which is why the whole story came out. We had both recently come out of fairly long relationships. By coincidence it emerged that Kathy's ex had been to the same drunken motor biker's week-ends as my own ex. That had given us yet another thing in common. We also had disrupted child-hoods, mine because of my mother's illness, leading me to be raised in part by Aunt May in Brighton, hers due to being made a virtual prisoner in her home as a four-year old. Kathy came from Eltham and it was not a good place to be in the early nineties, following the murder of black teenager Stephen Lawrence.

On a lighter note, some mutual friends had suggested we join one of the many 'Find Your Perfect Partner' web sites. In March 2012, shortly after my return from Cape Verde, I had settled into the same way of life I'd followed between separating from my ex-wife and meeting Ellie. During those years I was perfectly happy. I had everything I wanted: good job, great friends, karaoke... It was only when I met Ellie that I realised what I'd been missing. Following my week with Marie in Cape Verde and Mauritania, I found I *did* like the idea of being close to one special girl again. My problem was a matter of trust. I wasn't sure if I could ever believe in or trust another girl again, which is quite ironic when you consider I spent the first six months of my time with Jo earning *her* trust. With Kathy it was different.

Neither of us was looking for anything serious. By the same token, neither of us was looking for a quick grope and the odd quickie. Within days we had become cyber-inseparable, spending hours chatting on line about anything and everything. It soon became obvious that we cared not an iota about each other's past. There was instant trust and total honesty between us, or so we both thought until that first night in the hotel. Genuine ages exchanged, plus some of the worst photographs we could find. We agreed if *that* didn't put us off, nothing would. And it didn't. Within weeks we'd met up, had a few drinks, told each the whole truth and were already planning our first week-end away...

As usual, it was Colin who dragged the conversation down to sewer level. Where most of us aspire to reach for the stars, *his* only goal is to climb high enough get up to the gutter. In a rare quiet moment, he leaned across the bar, looked Kathy straight in the eye, nodded in my direction and asked, "Come on then pretty girl, how often... You know?" The winks and nods continued for two or three seconds, during which time, Rara managed to slap his arm and tell him in no uncertain terms that you 'don't ask a lady questions like that.'

Undeterred, Kathy met his leery gaze with her own and having taken a large swig from her tumbler replied, "Normally twice, but on Red Bull," she stroked my arm and kissed me, "probably three." The girls all laughed and cheered at someone who could finally match Colin in a war of words. However, he wasn't beaten yet and came straight back with, "Do *you* ever join in?"

At that point, we *all* collapsed into fits of drunken laughter... Colin gave Kathy a huge genuine smile and said, "You, my lovely, are more than welcome in the Mariners any time... Girls, drinks all round."

On my way back from my third visit to the Gents—or was it the fourth?—I almost bumped into Lala... "Did you still want me to have a quiet word with the lovely Debbie?" She winked and walked on, not requiring my answer.

"Oh, and Rara," Kathy pointed out shortly before we staggered home, "trust me, I am no lady!"

Just one more large one each and we headed home. On the way over earlier in the evening, or maybe that should be yesterday, she had stopped and admired all that surrounded her... "You've really landed on your feet here Paul. I mean, putting last year aside, this is close to fucking Heaven mate! The cliffs, the sea, no traffic, the sound of the waves at night, two pubs just over the road..." She paused, "and best of all, with a really powerful telescope, I reckon you could see right into my bedroom window." I patted her bum and laughed.

"Remind me to leave the curtains open in future," she added... We were just at the front gate of Windy Cottage when, presumably spurred on by her own naughty thoughts, she suddenly grabbed my hand and exclaimed, "Let's go up on the cliffs."

It has to be said that right from the start of our friendship, or relationship, whatever we choose to call our coming together, we found we shared a love of the great outdoors, in more ways than one. When I say I once made love in the middle of a crowded park in Dorking, on a sunny Sunday afternoon, you will understand what I mean. Trust me, it can be done. Girl in long flowing skirt and no undies. Bloke in shorts. Girl on top pretending to tickle and play-fight... Nobody takes a blind bit of notice. On this occasion though, for once I had to put my foot down and tell her no. Although she knew virtually all there was to know about my dubious encounters with Debbie, I didn't want to risk bumping into her in our drunken state. Without going into details, I truthfully pointed out how dangerous it could be up there at night, 'especially when you're pissed'.

With my promise to take her up there Saturday evening, we left it like that and headed inside. Now here's another thing we have in common. It doesn't matter how much we have to drink, we *never* go to bed without a coffee. Slight difference though, Kathy takes it white. I grabbed the small bottle out of the fridge as she loaded up the mugs... "Wow! You must've known I was coming!"

So shocked was she at seeing me with half a pint of liquid poison in my hand, she spilt most of the sugar on the worktop. I just winked at her. OK, so a man is entitled to some secrets. The fact is, I only have milk in the house if I know friends or family are calling round, or even staying for a few nights. Milk, tea bags, cereal, the kind of things normal people like. Of course, being a working week-end, she knew I wasn't expecting visitors so was quite impressed. The answer of course was very simple. Everybody knows workmen drink gallons of tea, normally with milk. So, on Thursday morning, knowing Michael 'Mickey' Felgate was coming to measure up the door, I was prepared. We chatted like old mates over the late-night coffee until, holding up three fingers, she said, "Fancy proving me right?" I reserve comment...

27

Saturday morning began in much the same way as our previous Saturdays had. I think by then, I had lost count of our full week-ends together. In the early days, it had been three or four evenings a month. One of us would drive to the other's house, pop down to the pub—The Plough if she came to me, and The Grapes if vice versa—then stagger home for the usual bout of hanky-panky, followed by a mad dash home in the morning, for one of us, in time for work. I'm not too sure how it grew into week-ends. It may have been my inviting her down to Rye for the week-end, as I had friends there, plus there are some great pubs. Putting all that aside, it's just a lovely seaside town, within easy driving distance of what I used to call home.

I had discovered Rye several years earlier and felt the peace and tranquillity of the place reminded me of what I *now* call home, the West Country. We had four week-ends there in all, then one thing led to another and before we knew it, it had become a regular monthly thing. This didn't deter us from the odd over-nighter in between, you understand. We saw our week-ends away as a bonus. I would have to say my two favourites were Kathy taking me up The Shard on its opening day, followed by a fabulous meal in Covent Garden, then a short stroll into the West End to see We Will Rock You. I kept thinking 'this day has got to end sooner or later' but at the same time hoping it never would. In fact, it ended with a night in the Regency Hotel, just off Park Lane. As we lay in bed, about two in the morning, she had a confession to make, "I'm afraid we'll have to find a café in the morning. As much as I wanted to make your birthday something to remember, I'm fucked if I'm going to pay twenty-five quid each for breakfast!"

We both laughed and fell asleep in each other's arms. No, it wasn't love, not yet and probably never would be, but it was special. *She* was special! And for the record, the café just off Westminster Bridge does a fantastic breakfast for less than a fiver each. The rest of the day was spent being 'tourists', trekking around the parks, St Paul's, the Tower, Big Ben, all the things we'd both done as kids but never really appreciated until then.

Three months later, I reciprocated by taking her to Paris. It was something I'd always wanted to do. I'd been before, but only with a group of friends. I'd even been to Paris once with my son as part of a Euro-Disney package... But never with a lady. And as Paris is known to be one of the most romantic cities in the world, I had to give it a try. We took the EuroStar through the tunnel direct into the city, settled into the pre-booked hotel, then as we did in London, became proper tourists again. I know it's clichéd, but there is nothing quite like sailing down the Seine, past the illuminated Notre Dame to the sound of an accordion.

Call me an old softie if you like, but despite my earlier way of life, deep down I really am a romantic. Again, as we had done in London, the next day we strolled around Montmatre watching the artists, down to the Eiffel Tower, past the Pompidou Centre with all its brightly coloured maintenance pipes on the exterior... We both thanked God her birthday was in May. Paris in springtime really is at its most beautiful. As much as I had loved everything about *my* birthday, it had been in February and London was freezing! I've often wished my mother had enjoyed her 'naughties' in October rather than May so I could have been a summer baby.

Having checked my Blackberry and smiled to myself as I noticed I had nothing I needed to rush into, I gave Kathy a nudge and started our usual early morning badinage, "Oral?" I asked.

"Breakfast," the lady replied... It was just one of those silly things couples say or do in the early days. Depending whose house we were in at the time, the owner would ask the question and the guest would respond with the need for food. It had actually started with quite a long drawn-out conversation all those months ago, but over a period, had minimalised to just those two words. As we made our way down the stairs, I uttered a few more, "Me kitchen, you Connie's." She didn't understand.

I had to explain that while I was clearly aware of her arrival, hence the milk in the fridge, I had no idea it was turning into an over-night stop. So, as I only had eggs in the fridge, she would have to pop over to Connie's and grab some basic essentials. From day one, we had always enjoyed a bloody good fry-up in the mornings. Leading her to the door and pointing her across the road, I gave her a twenty-pound note and said I'd get the coffee on... As Connie's is only a matter of seconds further away than the Mariners, I was concerned that she had not returned after ten minutes.

'How long does it take to buy sausages and bacon?' I thought to myself. Then it struck me. Kathy hadn't had the pleasure of Rachel the night before. It was now nearly ten o'clock Saturday morning and I rightly supposed her arrival was the talk of the village. I poured myself a second cup of the strong black stuff, poured her milky one down the sink and waited...

"God, this place is just like being at home, only worse," she laughed as she finally returned, armed with the breakfast requirements. As I started to prepare the most important meal of the day—don't let anyone tell you otherwise— Kathy told me how she'd been accosted by Raechel, who wanted to know every little detail about my week-end visitor, although at the same time stating she already knew a fair bit, after a chat with some of the people who had been in the Mariners the night before. Having satisfied our beloved shop assistant, she had then been stopped by a cheerful 'Good morning young lady, you must be Kathy...' It had been Barry, eager to tell her what a fine catch she'd made in me, though my gardening skills left something to be desired, ending with 'that palm I'll never take'.

It had been a fine Saturday morning. After our meal, I showed her what seemed to be Tilda's private footpath up to the cliffs. She was well aware I was unable to venture too far from my laptop and accepted it as a part of my working life. 'Next time I'll come down when you're *not* on call'. This was followed by a question regarding how well I knew my neighbours. "That's where I saw him," she pointed across the back of Tom's garden and into Debbie's.

Over breakfast she had mentioned getting up in the early hours and, glancing out of one of my rear windows, had spotted what she assumed to be a man, dressed in black— 'maybe a dark suit, or could've been joggers'—coming out of someone's back door, climbing over the next fence and vanishing into the undergrowth... 'Just about here', she indicated where we were standing. I made a casual comment about her dreaming or sleep-walking and carried on up the rough uneven steps that led to St Matilda's cliffs. We spoke very little, saving our breath for the climb, but inside, I vowed to tell her all I knew about my neighbours, and why, right then, I was very concerned for one of them in particular.

As we sat on the grass, over-looking the bay, Kathy was amazed we were the only two people up there. I lit two cigarettes, passed one to her and explained my thoughts about the hidden footpath we had just ascended. Below us to the right, we could just about make out the roofs of the four cottages, and the front of Connie's and the two pubs. Swarms of people were already making their way down the lane to our little beach, preparing to enjoy a day in the Cornish sunshine, maybe a pint or two, or an ice cream. Surely all of them were aware of the tragedy the previous year. Maybe that's why they came. Maybe some of them had even been here on that fateful day. I'm certain not one of them even considered the possibility of it happening again, not today, not this beautiful summer's day.

I shivered as I remembered the horror of being slammed almost into oblivion by that huge wall of water. A part of my brain thought what an amazing sight it would have been for anyone standing up here on the cliffs. Like watching a movie that you weren't really a part of. Like walking in the rain and splashing in a puddle of water, not knowing how many creatures were being crushed under foot… I quickly shut down that part of my mind. Although it would always remain in my memory, and that of all my new friends and neighbours, it was never openly spoken of… About a mile or so behind us, I pointed out our closed station, now Jim Murray's private home, complete with swimming pool.

Alongside it, some thirty or forty cars were now parked. Almost as though someone had read my mind, I heard that Jim had sold the land that had come with his home to the local council and turned it into a visitor's car park—£5 for a full day. Whether or not it would boost tourism in our bay remained to be seen, but at least it reduced the number of cars endlessly parked outside our cottages. Before my arrival, the residents of the bay had vehemently fought the council's plan to paint double yellow lines along the length of our cul-de-sac, preferring to trust visitors to respect our privacy and use the car parks behind the Mariners or The Beachcomber.

'There's even a good local bus service comes down from the main road', they had argued. And they'd won the battle. The council gave in but warned them that not everyone was as trustworthy as they might have hoped. Of course, the council were correct. Many a time you would find a car parked half on the road and half on the small grass verge outside your home, but it caused little problem to them—us—and it was normally only for a few months in the summer, or on a Saturday night when the Cockney Wurzels came to town. We were happy to live with it, for the sake of the other nine months of the year without unsightly bright yellow lines everywhere.

Almost without realising it, Kathy's hand had crept into mine. As if reading my mind, she turned to me and said, "It must have been awful... That day." She understood why I preferred not to discuss it and instead pointed across the water at what resembled a model village. "I can see the pub from her,' referring to the White Lion in her home town of Ystalyfera, at the same time emulating an old Fosters beer advert.

I smiled and said something about buying that telescope 'to help me through the cold lonely winter nights'. I decided now was the time to tell her the whole truth about my neighbours. Everything I knew, or suspected, even fantasised about. Over two or three more cigarettes, and remembering to keep a check on my Blackberry, I told her all about Barry's former life as a teacher, his claim to be a cyber-phobe yet still owning a computer, which he denied... Even my darkest thoughts about him being a paedophile in hiding.

Kathy laughed at that ridiculous idea, as did I in the cold light of day, but adding 'They have to live somewhere...' Then I explained all I knew about 'born too late' Colin, how he had been born just a few streets away from me, his lack of female partners, my suspicions that he might be gay, 'but afraid to come out', and his sexist attitude, 'but for all that, he's a really nice fella'. She already knew why I was so close to Tom and Alice and little Minnie, 'my new family', so I skipped over most of those thoughts as it brought back too many bad memories of that day.

Next, she learned my unfounded ideas on my immediate neighbours, Sarah and Adam Bonnell, the ones she'd met in the pub the previous night. 'They seemed really nice,' Kathy had said at the time, but it still didn't stop me telling her of my thoughts and doubts about them. How I'd considered Adam to be a spy, or a financial criminal... Why they never saw their children...

"You should write a book with that imagination of yours!" She said, as I approached the story of Debbie.

"Oh, you haven't heard the best of it yet," I responded. "Let's walk." We lit another cigarette and proceeded to stroll along the cliffs, still not another soul in sight as the clock turned twelve and the sun grew stronger. I was in t-shirt and faded jeans while Kathy had on a cotton summer dress, reminiscent of that afternoon from my dim and distant past in that park behind Dorking shops. The one by the football ground with the railway line running past it…

As we walked, holding hands like young lovers, we alternated between the cliff edge, staring down at the sea, gently lapping the rocks below—some people had wandered along from the beach and found a secluded spot in the sun—and the next minute we would be on the Southern side, looking out over green fields, trees waving in the light breeze and the village of Harwick in the middle distance.

I pointed out that despite my many walks along the cliffs, I was still yet to find another way up here, which explained why I'd never seen anyone else up there in my year living here. Kathy's hand slipped suggestively into my back pocket and squeezed… Yes, I knew that time would come, but not just then. "The next village you come to along here is Morwenstow, but I haven't been that far yet. Compared to Tilda's it's a city! Maybe there's a way up here from there, I don't know, but if so, the locals certainly don't walk *this* far."

We found another quiet spot to sit and admire the view across the sea, as I decided now was the time to tell her all I knew, or suspected about Debbie… I told her all my early thoughts, suspicions and fantasies. How she'd come to see me once or twice and babbled on about nothing in particular. How we'd met 'up here' in the middle of the night and why she only came onto the cliffs at that time. How she'd always disappeared without explanation. How I'd imagined her as a high-class prostitute… That brought a smile to Kathy's face.

How I'd tried to get Lala to find out more about her, and finally all about her violent and abusive husband, a policeman of all things and how her father was trying to protect his daughter as well as himself by making her disappearance official. "To the best of my knowledge, her father and I are the only people who know she's here." I ended.

"You fancy her, don't you?" was Kathy's response. It wasn't said in a jealous way, it was a simple and honest question. Neither of us did jealousy. We were both free agents to come and go as we pleased, and see whoever we wanted to without fear of reprisals or guilt. It worked and we were both happy with that, although as far as I knew, neither of us had been intimate with another partner since we met. I almost told her not to be ridiculous as Debbie was thirty years younger than me, but immediately realised that would be *me* being ridiculous. Instead, I replied truthfully that I felt protective of her, almost like a father would be. Kathy knew me well enough to know I was speaking the truth.

She squeezed my hand again, which spoke volumes about our trust in each other...

"That makes me wonder about her visitor at the crack of dawn..." She looked me straight in the eye. "That could have been her father, not wishing to be seen down here in case her husband suspects where she is but hasn't been able to pin-point her exact location... Or maybe it *was* her husband and he found her and... God knows what he might have done during the night! We should check when we get back..." So, it wasn't just me wanting to play Sherlock Holmes then. Almost as a spur to send us back to the cottage, at that precise moment my phone rang.

No, it wasn't the police informing me of the violent death at 4 a.m. of one of my neighbours. I had work to do. As much as Kathy and I were enjoying the view, the warm sunshine and each other's company, we were both relieved at having a reason to return. I was equally keen to check on Debbie to ensure she was safe and well. Having explained to my caller that I would check on the whereabouts of his shipment of urgent Tail Rotor Blades and call him back within the hour, we headed back to the bay.

En route, we devised a plan. I was to go home and resolve the shipping problem, while Kathy would call round to Debbie's cottage with a really flimsy tale of how we'd run out of filter coffee and 'you know what Paul's like... so fussy and he tells me you use the same brand and Rachel's run out and...' It sounded convincing enough the way Kathy put it to me and after all, all we needed was for Debbie to open the door and show she was fine, fit and well, so the story itself was secondary. She was so trusting of me, following her revelations about her husband, we thought it highly unlikely she would either go over to Connie's to verify our story, or consider the fact that we'd never shared our love of the same coffee...

As we arrived home, Colin was putting up the brightly coloured Stella Artois parasols over the benches outside the Mariners. It was going to be a busy week-end for both him and Brian in The Beachcomber. Colin waved a happy 'good day' to us both, asking if we'd be joining them that night. The sign outside advertised the Night Crawlers—Live Music here tonight. I had never heard of the band, presumably local, but called back 'Quite possibly' before we entered Windy Cottage. My palm looked mighty fine blowing in the summer breeze. I couldn't wait to see Barry Marlow's face as it not only survived, but thrived and flourished over the coming years... I hoped. Kathy and I also shared an eclectic taste in music. Both of us liking several current bands as well as many of the 'oldies'.

We were both huge fans of Muse, a fairly local band from Devon. Kathy had even been to see them twice, that was twice more than myself, sadly. We also shared a love of The Kinks, The Who and best of all, the late great Dusty Springfield, surely the 'blackest' white girl ever to come out of British musical history. "Being gay," Kathy laughed, "of course I liked Dusty!" Her gayness had become a standing joke with us by then. Kathy's that is, not Dusty's.

In addition, we were always open to new suggestions, so would almost certainly try the Night Crawlers later. Not surprisingly, we also had singers and bands that one of us liked, but not the other. I have always been a huge fan of Take That, past and present, with or without Robbie... Kathy could never see the appeal, stating they were for eight-year-old girls, not sixty-year-old men. But then, almost hypercritically claiming a life-long passion for Westlife.

Go figure, as our cousins across the pond would say. We agreed to differ on that one although I will confess to singing along to What About Now on more than one occasion. As usual, I blamed the alcohol... As much as I loved the girl, in my own way, I still failed to understand the minds of the female species... It brought to mind a drunken conversation I'd had many years earlier in the Parson's Pig, a very pleasant hostelry not far from my former home in Smallfield.

A group of us lads would meet there on a Thursday night, mainly because it was a favourite watering hole of many air hostesses from nearby Gatwick Airport in the nineteen eighties. That was a time when they were still air hostesses, or trolley dollies, before they became politically correct and called themselves cabin crew. However, I digress. The topic of conversation turned to religion. Now anyone who's known me down the years will know there are two things I positively refuse to discuss. Not in private or public, neither with friends, lovers nor strangers. They are religion and politics. Those two subjects have caused more arguments, fights, relationship breakdowns, even wars down through the centuries than any other topic known to man... Having satisfied my caller with DHL tracking details, I related this story to Kathy over coffee as we finalised our plan to approach Debbie...

There had been about six of us in the Pig that night, drinking quite heavily, chatting up the girls and generally having a bloody good night out. I've no idea how the subject got around to religion, but it did. The conversation became more and more heated with comments such as 'if there is going to be a second coming, why hasn't he come yet?' and, bearing a striking resemblance to my own private thoughts, 'so how come God lets so many of his so-called acts happen, killing thousands of people?'

' As time went on, various members of the group noticed I hadn't uttered a single word… "Come on then Paul," one of them said, and they all looked at me… "What do *you* think?" Our area of the bar went quiet. Some of the people knew exactly what I thought, that it wasn't worth discussing, but others who didn't know me as well, were keen to learn how I felt on the subject. I briefly explained my reasoning for not joining the debate, but, "I will say one thing. I will ask you one question. Do you believe in Heaven and Hell? And if so, how do you perceive it?" This was a little too profound for some of them who simply spluttered nonsensically and ordered another pint.

Others predictably mentioned fire and brimstone, angels and harps… "In my opinion," I began, "Heaven and Hell, if indeed they *do* exist, would be one and the same place."

Now, I couldn't say for sure if a lack of intelligence had stunned them, or simply an overdose of lager, but not one of them said a word for some considerable time. Eventually, one of the air hostesses asked me to explain. My answer brought on yet another prolonged silence, and explains the parallel with Kathy's love of the Irish boy-band Westlife… Knowing one of the other girls' taste in music at that time, and comparing it to that of my own, I looked her square in the eyes and explained, "If you died tomorrow—and we all hope you don't—and you arrived in a pretty pink paradise where Donny Osmond and David Cassidy songs played all day long, you would think you'd arrived in Heaven, correct?" I left it there…

Shortly after a late light lunch of omelette and salad, Kathy left me to my laptop—I had one or two things that required my immediate attention—and departed Windy Cottage in search of a hopefully safe Debbie, and maybe a cupful of Douwe Egberts Special Turkish. Once my work was completed, I contemplated my life with, or without Kathy. With her, life was one long round of laughter, music and alcohol, which seemed to make us both very happy.

It took away all thoughts of ex's, various levels of distrust on both sides, the flood, the fact that if my grand-mother was to be believed, I had only just over twenty years left on this Earth, and how much of that time I wanted to spend with my current love interest. True, we had agreed to take each day as it came, and it is also a well-known fact that people in their thirties live for the future as well as the present, but people in their sixties have to accept there is not that much of a future to live for, so tend to enjoy the present while they still have one. I was sure Kathy had her private thoughts about me, ones she was not prepared to say aloud, and rightly so. I was the same.

For all my independence—I was, as always very satisfied in my private life as a single man—there were, quite naturally, times when I wished there was someone else's head on the pillow next to mine when I awoke in the mornings. Not for the first time, I wished irrationally that Kathy was twenty years older, or that I was twenty years younger. The thought would pass. It always did. Once she had returned to South Wales and my life returned to something like normal, those thoughts wouldn't enter my head again for at least a week or two. Having said that, when I first moved to St Matilda's Bay, those same thoughts had been about a month or more apart. I had to accept they were becoming more regular. Maybe I was falling in love again. I hoped not, for both our sakes... Half an hour later, Kathy returned with the news that my neighbour was indeed perfectly safe and well, and shockingly had agreed to go for a drink with her the following night. I couldn't believe what I was hearing... Kathy explained:

"I'm afraid I told a few little white lies, so please don't take offence at anything I say, because it's not true, OK?" I agreed, intrigued. The moment she opened the door, I could see she was fine. I'd been so wrapped up in my thoughts of what to do if there was no answer, all our carefully laid plans of coffee went completely out of my head. Seeing she was of a similar age—and you never said how fucking gorgeous she looked you bugger!—I explained who I was, with you like, and without meaning to sound rude, wondered if she fancied some female company, someone of the same age group if you know what I mean.

At that point, I may have winked in a way that said as much as we enjoyed each other's company, you and I were thirty years apart and didn't always think or feel the same way about things. Oh my God, Paul, I do hope I haven't hurt your feelings, I mean I didn't mean it but..." I smiled and took her hand, kissed her lightly, telling her everything was fine and I *knew* she didn't mean anything by it. In fact, I thought her ingenious to come up with a story like that at a moment's notice... She looked relieved and continued, "Well anyway, she invited me in and explained how you'd only spoken a few times—you have a huge fan there by the way, *I* can tell you. I might have to keep careful tabs on you once I've gone! Where was I?

Oh yes… She seemed really pleased to have someone her own age to talk to. It was the first time in ages apparently. I didn't mention the man, or woman I thought I saw this morning… On reflection, he or she, was definitely about thirty or maybe a little older. I didn't see the face but you could tell the way 'it' moved, 'it' was quite young… Not a teenager or anything but certainly around my age… So anyway, that seemed a bit odd, her saying she didn't know anyone else down here the same age, but I let it go. In any case, it could have been a would-be burglar who changed his mind for some reason. I couldn't be *sure* he'd actually come out of her house; he might have just been casing the joint or whatever it is would-be burglars do… She certainly didn't look like someone who'd had a disturbed night, for good reasons or bad…"

The smile Kathy gave me at the point of saying 'good reasons' reminded me we hadn't made love once since her arrival. Despite Colin's lurid comments, we had gone straight to sleep after coffee, and even though the thought had been there, up on the cliffs, we hadn't actually followed it through. 'Maybe tomorrow', I decided. As I believe I may have mentioned before, my life with Kathy was all about having fun of one sort or another. Should sex rear its' pretty little head from time to time, it was always a welcome bonus. We were good together for any number of reasons and sex was far from being at the top of the list.

OK, so maybe not that far… I found myself noticing I nearly always called our occasional coming together and exchanging bodily fluids, love-making. It wasn't sex, or shagging or screwing or 'at it like rabbits'…It was lovemaking. Maybe that was telling me something. Maybe it told *both* of us something. It was true to say that in our many drunken moments, one of us would say 'let's fuck', and we would, but even then, it would be soft and gentle for the most part… Always assuming we over-looked the odd teeth marks I would wake up with…

As I poured another coffee, and lit us both a cigarette, Kathy explained how she and Debbie had agreed to have a drink together on Sunday night, "I don't know why, but it just seemed the right thing to say at the time. I suggested she joined us over the road tonight for the Crawlers gig, but she doesn't like crowds. I guessed from what you told me that she might be afraid of being spotted by her ex or one of his cronies, but before I could suggest another time, she did so herself.

"'I'm free tomorrow night though' she said. Now what, with us playing Holmes and Watson, should I read into that statement. She would be 'free tomorrow night'… Did that mean it wasn't so much the crowd in the Mariners keeping her away tonight, or that she was busy? Busy with the man in black maybe… Or woman, as the case may be… Anyway, I hope you don't mind but I accepted the invitation and we agreed to go to the other pub for an hour or two of girlie chat. She specifically said The Beachcomber, almost as though she didn't want to be seen in Colin's pub, but I can't think why…?"

I could think of several reasons, and told her so. Colin's nosey attitude for one, wanting to know everything about everyone, right down to their inside leg measurement. The fact that Sarah and Adam sometimes drank in there, but rarely in Brian's pub for some unknown reason, and meaning nothing against any of them, Debbie was not the most neighbourly of neighbours. "With good reason of course," I added to clarify.

Then there was her own quite legitimate fear of being seen by one of her husband's mates or colleagues, plus the possibility of me being there. While the whole village knew by then that Debbie and I 'got on', this was clearly designed to be a girl's night out. I thought it only fair to point out that Rachel, from Connie's, also worked behind the bar, suggesting they chose a table as far out of ear-shot as possible, adding "Don't get me wrong, but when it comes to gossip, Rachel's worse than Dot Cotton and Hilda Ogden combined!" Never-the-less, I was impressed by Kathy's improvisation and told her so. In return, she promised to pass on any information gleaned, however much Debbie begged her not to.

28

In an effort to impress the boss, Smithy had taken it upon himself to go in search of the elusive Martin himself. It wasn't just about the money, but he felt his loyalty had been brought into question and made up his mind to resolve the situation. In his line of work, failure wasn't an option. He could only imagine the repercussions. He pulled up at the agreed meeting place, an old car park by a deserted railway station in the village of Harwick. As he stepped out of the car, his informant was leaning up against a blue Toyota, the only other vehicle there, if you ignored the burnt-out shell of an old Ford Fiesta. Spotting Smithy, the other man dropped his cigarette to the ground and crunched it into the weed-strewn gravel with his right foot.

"What is this fucking shit hole? It's full of chavs and the houses are even worse than the Isle of Dogs where I grew up!" Images of steel girder bridges spanning canals and railway tracks came into his head. Dark, dangerous streets he'd walked with his dad, down to Cold Blow Lane—never had there been a more appropriate name for a football ground—the former home of his father's beloved Millwall football club, prior to its move to the new den in the early nineteen nineties. The supporters chant of 'No-one likes us, we don't care' has struck fear into many a visiting rival fan down the years.

"Not important," said Smithy. "All that matters is finding Martin. What have you got for me?"

"Let's walk," the other man said, heading in the direction of St Matilda's Bay, and ignoring Smithy's protestations of 'not walking anywhere since I was ten'. En route, he explained it was only about a mile—fifteen minutes—to where Martin's mobile phone signal had been picked up the other day. Looking down at Smithy's paunch, he added, "And the exercise will do you good."

Smithy ignored this, lit a cigarette of his own and walked alongside the other man, who he now knew as Mitch. "Just Mitch, I never use my full name on *jobs like this. So, what's the deal? What's this man Martin done to piss your boss off?"*

"Need to know basis mate," was Smithy's reply, "and all you need to know is that there's five grand to whoever finds Martin, and another five to whoever gets the job done." This seemed to satisfy Mitch and they walked in silence until they were half-way down the hill leading to the bay.

Mitch grabbed Smithy's arm and said, "This is it. So how do we play it?"

Smithy looked around. The place was virtually deserted apart from what looked like a driveway, leading to a new car park. The drive had no name, but there was a sign saying 'Beware of Cars'. Beyond that he could just see the edge of an old red-brick building and what looked like a busy car park. Ignoring Mitch's question, he asked, "Who lives there?"

Mitch replied that it was 'just an old man, about seventy I reckon, who used to run the railway station there. When the line closed, he bought the building, retired and called it home for the past twenty years... The car park's new, built for the day visitors.'

"Too old," said Smithy, "so what now?" Mitch explained the cycle track that led back to where they had left their cars, then pointed back to the lane and both men headed down the hill into St Matilda's Bay. Smithy had deliberately chosen a Saturday for this visit, feeling quite rightly that it would be easier to blend in with the crowd. He had put on a light open-necked summer shirt and slacks. He carried a camera, looking every bit the tourist. Mitch had also been advised to do the same and was dressed casually in t-shirt and faded, ripped jeans. Smithy thought he looked like a member of Bros, but said nothing. He would have to do...

"All we do is stroll around, keeping our eyes and ears open right? We take a few photos of the beach and the pubs... Two was it you said? We don't speak to anyone unless they speak to us first, got that?" Mitch replied 'you're the boss Smithy' as they turned the corner and into the cul-de-sac that was the bay itself. "And we don't use names. We're old mates so if we speak to each other at all, no names! Remember, we have no idea what this fucking Martin looks like... Could be twenty-something or fifty-something... Maybe somewhere in between. So, we don't ask questions, we just wander about the street, the beach, the pubs, keeping our eyes and ears open all the time. See what we pick up."

"Look, it's none of my business, but wouldn't this've been easier mid-week? There are hundreds of people here today..." Mitch offered.

"You're absolutely right my friend," replied Smithy, halting their progress to put a hand on his companion's shoulder in what seemed like a reassuring way... "It's none of your business!" To himself, he wondered where the boss found these people. Of course, it would've been easier on a Wednesday, but then even in their summer clothes they'd be bound to stand out like the proverbial sore thumb. And they had to remember, even though they had no idea what Martin looked like, or even if he was here in this God forsaken part of the world, there was more than a 50/50 chance that Martin would recognise them! Or at least Smithy...

29

The remainder of Saturday passed without significant event. Still no visit from Barry to berate me for going ahead with the palm tree. All was quiet next door... Possibly Sarah and Adam had ventured out for the week-end. Minnie had called round and asked if we'd both like to have tea with her grand-parents. "You may as well get to know *all* my new friends," I said to Kathy, and she readily agreed. Tea was a pleasant relaxing affair, with Alice telling Kathy what a lucky girl she was, and me butting in to tell everyone that in fact *I* was the lucky one. The two girls chatted happily about their respective tastes in music. I believe I heard that favourite swear word of mine, Westlife, mentioned about seven times.

I told myself she would grow out of it and discover real music one day, then remembered even Kathy enjoyed some of what they loosely class as 'music'. Alice, Tom and I talked aimlessly about the weather, village life and such, until Alice reminded me that my granddaughter Cheryl was coming to stay in a few weeks. Minnie over-heard Cheryl's name being mentioned and immediately dropped all talk of Beyonce and Jay-Z... "Can she come and stay here one night gran?" Clearly aimed at Alice, to which the reply of 'Certainly she can my love' came resounding back.

Kathy and I shared a secret smile, both of us enjoying this spell of family life. She was well aware of my unspoken history with the little girl, and latterly my fondness for her grand-parents. Although totally aware of my grandfather status, and completely undeterred I should add, she had yet to meet Cheryl. Maybe one day. I wasn't sure exactly when. Cheryl had become very attached to Ellie as she grew up and still missed her terribly. They spoke on Facebook from time to time, and had even met up once on Cheryl's last visit to Smallfield before my move. I was unsure how she would react to a new lady in her grandfather's life... I was reassured by the fact that children are resilient. And how could anyone fail to love someone like Kathy?

The evening was great! Once again, I had to congratulate Colin on his choice of live band. The Night Crawlers were a 'covers' group and their rendition of Dire Straits classics brought back many happy memories of my days with Barley. They also did some fabulous versions of Fleetwood Mac songs, and a lot of new material by the Kaiser Chiefs and the Stereophonics. All well-known songs to music lovers like Kathy and myself. As the evening grew later, and the music louder, we found ourselves singing along, quite loudly and perfectly in tune I might add, to practically every song. The shock of the night came when the lead singer asked me to join him on stage. I had no idea why. I'd never seen the group in my life, never even heard of them... They were from Falmouth and this was their first ever gig in the Mariners.

I stood in stunned silence for a few seconds as other people in the bar started cheering at the thought of a total stranger being asked on stage... I glanced at Kathy, who simply smiled. I looked over at Colin who seemed to be in on the joke... A joke that only I was not privy to it seemed... Never being one to refuse a challenge, I made my way to the stage and stepped into the spotlight. Everyone was cheering. I could hear Kathy's shrill whistle as the opening bars of a familiar tune began... Within seconds I heard the falsetto tones of a Sting impersonator sing the words 'I want my MTV'. I had no idea how exactly I'd got myself into this position, but the audience seemed to be enjoying it. One glance at Kathy—she winked at me—told me she'd had a quiet word, either with Colin or with the band, possibly while I was in the loo... Money for Nothing was always a favourite of mine back in the day, and I was soon into it on my cue.

If I say so myself, and yes, I know self-praise is no recommendation, but the seventy-odd people in the bar seemed to agree... I think I was pretty bloody good, and more importantly, from a singer's point of view, word perfect. I left the stage feeing really good about myself. I waved and mouthed my thanks to everyone, ignoring the temptation to answers their cries of 'more', and headed back to where the conspirator was clapping and cheering louder than anyone. I could easily have gone back up and done Sultans of Swing, or Romeo and Juliet—a firm favourite for the slow song near the end of a Barley gig—but I'm a firm believer in going out on a high, leaving them wanting more, so no. I put my head down, trying my damnedest to look shy and embarrassed, as the Night Crawlers moved into The Office theme tune, Handbags and Gladrags.

Maybe another time... We enjoyed a couple more drinks—both free as a thank you from Colin—and a few more songs before the band finally quit at nearly ten minutes to twelve. One of the band even came over to shake my hand and offer me another slot if ever they returned here. I thanked him for giving me the opportunity, and told them I thought Colin would have them back any time. Whether or not he would, was not my concern but it seemed like the correct thing to say at the time, and I made up my mind there and then to drag out my old Dire Straits CD's, just in case... By the time Kathy and I were safely back indoors, I was genuinely buzzing from my experience. Apart from a few warm-up songs on karaoke, it had been the first time I'd sung on stage since 1989.

The buzz took me right through the following couple of hours. Both Kathy and I will be eternally grateful to Colin and the boys in the band for that. I hadn't been on such a high since the first time she and I had spent the night together. Even *she* seemed excited by the whole thing. It was one of those moments you experience from time to time, where you feel so proud of what somebody else has done, rather than celebrating your own successes. Whatever we may have thought privately, about this just being 'a bit of fun', we were definitely becoming closer by the day. I still wasn't sure if that was a good thing or not. Only time would tell. There was no rush, we had the rest of our lives to make decisions like that, didn't we?

The next morning, we woke up in each other's arms, with Kathy sprawled across my chest with her hand dangerously close to my arm-pit. Even though I was sure we'd see the funny side, I had no desire to start the day with a tickling session and raucous laughter. It was Sunday morning and I just wanted to enjoy the moment. I grabbed the Blackberry from the bedside table without disturbing her. She had that deep breathing that only comes from a satisfied life and peaceful sleep.

Nothing on the work front so all was looking good for the day's agenda: Breakfast at ten, then off to the donkey sanctuary for a few hours. We'd left the window open as it was such a warm night. I could just about hear the bells of St Mary's church wafting over from nearby Harwick. I couldn't help wondering how many of the community actually made the effort to go. Certainly, none of *our* merry band of villagers would have been counted as a part of their congregation. I'm not saying they were all atheists, or agnostics, but I knew for a fact none of them made the effort... I've never investigated the theory, but Tom assured me that several centuries ago Tilda's, along with many villages in that part of the world were largely Pagan. The story goes that when the Church of England made plans to religiously educate the residents of St Matilda's Bay, the lanes were barricaded and the churchmen were fought off in much the same way that they had more recently fought the local council over the yellow line situation. The only difference being that nobody died during the 'yellow line' fight, as opposed to the 'alleged' thirty-plus, way back in the fifteenth century.

Consequently, we remain one of the few villages in England not to have at least one church. Strictly speaking, this makes St Matilda's Bay a hamlet rather than a village, but everyone called it a village so who why as to argue? From what little I'd learned of our local history, I couldn't help wondering why they would have bothered in the first place, bearing in mind the largest population we had ever had was thirty-one. I've always thought it odd the way different parts of the country treat religion in different ways. Back in my former Surrey village, there are three churches and one chapel within easy walking distance...

Breakfast over, we began our hour-long drive to the Perrancroft, home for more than forty animals rescued at great expense to the local charity, from all four corners of the world. For no apparent reason, it had always been a charity close to my heart. Jo and I had visited this particular sanctuary many times, always buying ridiculous souvenirs purely to boost their funds. Apart from the change of female company, this day would be very much the same....

There were the odd 'pings' from my Blackberry but nothing I couldn't deal with there and then. Two jobs would require my urgent attention once the USA woke up, but that wouldn't be for another three or four hours... We spent more than three of those hours at Perrancroft, fussing over the donkeys, feeding them, walking them, even chatting to them. Kathy said one of them reminded her of her ex—something to do with bushy eyebrows—so she called it 'arsehole'.

It was said in a friendly voice so the poor creature didn't take offence. It was done in the same way as I'd once done to an old mongrel I had as a teenager. As long as you say it with a smile in your voice, animals still think you're being nice to them. But just to be on the safe side, she gave 'arsehole' special love and attention. 'Well, you never know...' she explained.

We stopped for a coffee in the souvenir shop on the way out, picking up two fridge magnets and a cuddly toy while we were there... I had two surprises that day. Firstly, I was amazed to see Kathy stuff not one, but two twenty-pound notes into the donation's box on the way out—as far as I can recall, I'd only ever put ten in, it made me feel a little guilty. Then as we approached the counter, I recognised the lady taking the coffee orders. It was Sarah, my next-door neighbour.

She beamed at me as Kathy ordered our drinks, "Oh it's *so* good of you to come," then glancing at my companion, "and you must be Kathy. Thank you so much for coming today." I suppose I shouldn't have been surprised to see her. After all, Adam had said that his wife worked tirelessly for various charities, but the look on Kathy's face was a picture. She turned to me with a kind of 'Who *is* this woman?' expression. Before I had a chance to explain, Sarah did it for me. Reaching out a hand in greeting she said, "I'm sorry, I'm Sarah, Paul's next-door neighbour. Rachel told me you were down here for a few days…"

Why was I not surprised? I imagine the entire bay knew all there was to know about my week-end visitor two minutes after she purchased yesterday's breakfast. I'd be amazed if there wasn't a piece in the local paper the following week, complete with Kathy's life history, bust measurement and the name of her next-door neighbour's dog! You have to love village life. Thanks Rachel. Still, it saved me a job… "I'm due a break," Sarah added. "Mind if I join you?"

Of course, we didn't. The three of us spent the next twenty minutes discussing the plight of not just donkeys, but all the mistreated animals in our cruel world. I confessed to my feelings that the overkill of television advertisements did little or nothing to help the situation. Over the previous Christmas, I had sat through so many 'save the donkeys', 'polar bears are dying', 'this child in Africa survives on filthy water that's slowly killing him, but he has no choice, but just three pounds a month could save him. What will *you* be drinking this Christmas?' and many, many more, that instead of reaching for the phone to donate, I found myself working out how much it would cost me if I answered *all* of their heart-felt pleas.

As I spoke, both girls were nodding their agreement. In the end, I had to admit to giving to none of them. I couldn't afford to donate close to fifty pounds every month, so in the end, I did nothing… "And I'm afraid I blame television for that!" I took a sip from my coffee. Not bad but could do with being a little stronger, but I said nothing. No doubt in a bid to keep overheads down, they didn't exactly splash out on the best grounds.

My honesty has got me into trouble many times in my life, but I was pleased to see both of the girls agreeing with me, Kathy pointing out that 'and in the end, you don't like to give to just one or you'd feel bad about the others.' Damn! That girl knows me too well. In fairness to Sarah, even she didn't try to sway me towards her own chosen preference. Instead, she changed the subject completely…

"Adam's away this week-end, so why don't you both come round for dinner later, or tomorrow if you have plans? I'd be glad of the company and it would be nice to get to know you better." This last was aimed more at Kathy than me. After our previous week-end, I don't think there was much Sarah and I didn't know about each other. Of course, I couldn't swear to the fact that everything she had said had been gospel, but she was certainly very open, and seemed sincere. How I'd ever had those crazy thoughts about her and Adam I'll never know. She was just a good woman, with a loving husband, doing great works for charity, wasn't she?

"I'd love to," said Kathy, "but I'm afraid I've already got plans for this evening, and I go home tomorrow. But next time I'm down…" She left the sentence unfinished in such a way as to make it clear we would happily accept, should Sarah ever extend the invitation again. I was sure she would. I found myself wondering where the week-end had gone. Sure, we'd crammed a lot in but going home tomorrow? How did that happen so fast? And I wasn't even going to see her that evening…

On the drive back, Kathy asked if it was OK for her to come back to Tilda's in a couple of weeks, rather than me going up to South Glamorgan. "You know I don't have a lot of friends up there, and this place is stunning. I really love it here." Her hand rested on my left thigh, not too far up, more a gesture of affection that a suggestion that we pulled into the next lay-by. "I love spending time with you Paul, and this is just so much better than my place."

I had to agree with her. As much as I enjoyed my time spent in Ystalyfera, it was only because I was with Kathy and some of her crazy friends. The beach, just a few miles away, was nothing special. The only pub in the village, the White Horse, left much to be desired. I supposed having no easy access competition gave the landlord licence to do very little and add several pennies to the price of a pint. The Grapes, a good half hour walk away did however have a wonderful menu, including a Corned Beef and Potato Pie that was the best I had tasted since my mother's. Plus, we both enjoy a good walk, so it enjoyed our custom on more than one occasion… No, on balance, Kathy was right.

Tilda's *was* a much better place for us. I wondered how long it would be before one of us hinted at the obvious. I was still in two minds. We *were* good with each other, and for each other. Both of us had very similar tastes, similar tolerance to alcohol, similar ideas on cigarettes, friends, pubs, neighbours, how often to enjoy sex, where and when, even a love of chess and much the same television programme preferences… Although I really should try to wean her off of EastEnders, far more addictive than any drug known to man.

On the other hand, should things become more serious and settled between us, how long would it be before the age gap reared its ugly head again? I'd been down that road and had no intention of travelling it again, only to reach a dead in in ten years' time. I didn't have the answer. *We* didn't have the answer! Despite the sunshine blazing through the windows of my little red Clio, I felt a shiver run down my spine and felt glad of the warmth of Kathy's hand on my leg… "Penny for them?" She asked.

I realised I'd been deep in thought for about five miles. "Sorry, miles away, just thinking of those poor animals." I lied, then immediately realised it was pretty much the first time I'd ever lied to her, if you ignored the twin room thing. She squeezed my thigh as if in understanding. Did that mean 'that' conversation was becoming ever closer? Who knew? Another thought occurred to me en route. If Adam had been so keen to ask me to watch out for his wife the last time he was away for a few days, why was it he had been happy to leave her alone *this* week-end?

30

It was nearly four o'clock as we pulled into the bay. I didn't even try to park behind the pub. I could see at a glance it was packed. Packed with cars whose owners were hopefully in the Mariners, but a percentage were almost certainly using it for a day's free parking while they went to the beach. That time of year, both pubs were usually crammed and as Colin pointed out, it was cheaper to let them park there than to hire security to monitor them all. He had a point. Through the windows I could see it was even busier than last night. The local campers and day trippers were certainly out in force. Plus, the benches outside the pub were over-flowing and there were even a few sitting on the low wall to the beach side of my cottage.

It was as though the whole bay area was Colin's extended garden. I had no objections. For the most part, they were clean and tidy. I had never found empty Coke cans or ice cream wrappers in my garden. Even the cigarette ends were stubbed out on the road or the nearby rocks. I often wondered how many were dropped between the cracks in the rocks. The rocks that had been a part of the beach until *that* day, but were now stacked up like huge bowling balls under the cliffs, looking like a natural barrier between the cliffs and the beach, to all who were unaware of our recent history. I broke my own cardinal rule and parked right outside Windy Cottage, leaving just enough room for Kathy to climb out without having to step over the fence at the same time. I would move it to its rightful place behind the pub once the holiday-makers had made their departure.

Most of them, especially those with children, were usually gone by about six or seven, as soon as the sun began to lose its warmth. Across the road, we spotted Rachel, refreshing a stack of oranges and bananas outside Connie's. Kathy called across and she waved back, smiling. I wagged a finger at her, suggesting she was in 'big trouble young lady'. Rachel put on her best innocent face and went back inside, no doubt wondering which particular indiscretion she was being berated for this time. Could she have known we'd just bumped into

Sarah? No doubt Kathy had mentioned our proposed excursion the day before and Rachel, bright as a button, had put two and two together. It bothered neither Kathy nor I, and Rachel knew I was only kidding her. After all, Kathy and I had no secrets from each other, did we?

With all of this going on, plus the many people walking to and from the beach with drinks and ice creams and those silly little plastic windmills that last about five minutes in anything stronger than a mild breeze, I'd completely failed to notice a man standing at the far edge of my garden, the beach end of my fence, under my swaying palm leaves of which one day I would be so proud. It was Barry Marlow. Dressed in light brown slacks and a yellow t-shirt that would have looked so much better on a teenager—not that I was in any position to give advice on dress sense—he turned to me and almost accusingly said, "So you did it then."

He turned his gaze to Kathy and added, "I suppose this was *your* doing!"

In fairness to Kathy, she didn't know Barry the way I did. His brash comments had upset many people in his time and she looked as though she had just joined that illustrious list. In truth, I had mentioned the palm tree once or twice on the telephone, even pointing out Barry's objections and his reasons why I shouldn't even entertain such a 'ludicrous idea' on the North coast. But what with everything else going on that week-end, added to the fact her visit had been out of the blue so to speak, I hadn't had time to prepare her fully for the likes of Rachel, or Colin, or indeed Barry. In those few brief seconds, I scanned my memory banks and couldn't recall the subject of the palm tree being spoken of since Kathy's unexpected arrival two days earlier.

However, she always has been the mistress of the amazing. In those same brief seconds, she had recognised his comments and before I'd had time to think of my own response, she held out her hand and extended an invitation on behalf of us both.

"You must be Mr Marlow. I'm *so* pleased to meet you. Paul told me so much about you… Most of it good I should add. Won't you come inside for a drink? Coffee maybe? Or perhaps a beer?" I have to give Barry his due. I couldn't say whether or not he was taken aback by Kathy's greeting, but if he was, he kept his composure and showed no sign of surprise. He smiled in acceptance of her offer, and we all went inside. He couldn't resist a little dig though. "And I'm right about that tree. You'll see if I'm not young man." I smiled. That 'young man' line never failed to amuse me.

So much for our thoughts of revisiting the cliffs in daylight for a little outdoor fun. I knew once Barry had settled in for a beer, it wouldn't stop there. Kathy would offer him another. He would think it rude to refuse and before we knew it, it would be time for Kathy to meet Debbie for their girlie evening in The Beachcomber. I quietly said as much as she opened the fridge to take out two tins of Fosters, while I put the kettle on.

She playfully grabbed me in a very private place, smiled and said, "We've got years of naughty fun on the cliffs to come honey. This is my chance to meet the neighbours. It would be rude of me not to make the most of it."

As she headed off to the front room, where Barry had made himself comfortable in *my* favourite armchair, I couldn't help but smile again. She was of course absolutely right as always. And I did like the part about having years. That at least made us sound semi-permanent. Once more Kathy amazed me with her ability to 'get on' with everyone she met, old or young, male or female. They were all the same to her. It reminded me of a sign outside my local pub back in Surrey: 'There are no strangers in this world, only friends you have yet to meet'. That summed her up.

The whole world was her friend, and the whole world seemed to love her for it. It would be an enormous loss to anyone who failed to meet that lady sometime in their lives. It gave me a very warm feeling deep inside. I had no idea what her ex had done to piss her off, we rarely if ever spoke about our past lives, but one thing I knew for certain… It had been his loss rather than hers. I remembered back to our early days of cyber-chats. She sounded more like a child of the sixties rather than the nineties, a hippie almost, with comments like learning far more from life than she ever learned in school.

One thing Kathy had said stood out more than any other, and I think it explained why she got on so well with everybody she met. I can't remember the exact words, but it was something along the lines of: 'I always speak my mind quietly and clearly, but more importantly, I listen to others, even the ignorant, because everyone has a story to tell.' It sounded vaguely familiar to me at the time. It still does. Almost as though it was from a prayer or something, but I'm reasonably sure it wasn't, knowing Kathy's thoughts on religion, which were very similar to my own. I determined to search for it on Google one day, before very much longer…

As expected, she and Barry gelled immediately and again, found they had something in common. Both had absent fathers and a grandmother with the rather unusual name of Marguerite. It never ceased to amaze and amuse me just how many of these bizarre coincidences happened in people's lives. I left the two of them to become better acquainted as I spent the following hour or so dealing with our American cousins in an effort to make two of my aircraft serviceable once more.

Once that episode had been dealt with, and without meaning to sound rude, I reminded them both of Kathy's engagement that evening, and 'we still haven't eaten yet'. To which Barry made his apologies for taking up so much of our time and started to rise from the chair. Before he had a chance to make a move, she turned to me and asked, "Why doesn't Barry stay for dinner?" Without waiting for his answer, she looked at him and added, "It'll only be something simple, we haven't had a chance to think about a Sunday roast or anything, but you'd be more than welcome…"

'Whose house *is* this?' I wondered. 'Had she moved in already? Were we suddenly a couple? The royal we?' Of course, I had no objections to Barry staying for a meal with us, but my mind was racing at how easily she had made herself at home. In less than 48 hours she knew more about my neighbours than I'd learned in more than a year! I even found myself liking the fact… Dinner was indeed a very simple affair. As Kathy topped up Barry's glass, I popped over to Connie's and picked out a pack of frozen chicken breast fillets from the freezer. Chicken, chips and peas would suffice. As I turned on the oven, I decided to open a bottle of wine.

At that precise moment, Kathy came out to grab herself another beer. "Starting early are we?" She joked.

"Cheeky bitch!" came my reply. I had already decided I would have a few glasses while she and Debbie were over the road. I knew Kathy's normal alcohol intake for an evening in the pub—three, maybe four pints, before moving onto vodka and Cokes, usually large ones—and felt it made sense to roughly match her. I always feel there's nothing worse than one person being tipsy, or drunk, or hammered, while the other person is stone cold sober. That truly is the worst possible scenario. The drunk partner thinks everything he or she says is hilarious, while the sober one wonders if they're 'that bad' when in a similar state.

The simple answer to that is yes. Most of us revert to being children at heart after a few drinks. That was the main reason Kathy and I always tried to drink 'local', so that neither of us had the hassle of driving home. It was a lesson we learned on our first night together, back in that hotel in Burgh Heath. It also explained why I tolerated the White Horse in Ystalyfera… Having said that, the walk home from Kathy's local meant passing one of her friend's houses, which was almost impossible without being dragged in for a few vodkas and the inevitable roly weed… Safe in the knowledge that Brian was fairly strict about Sunday closing times, plus the fact that Kathy would be mindful of her long drive home the next day, I guessed she would be home soon after eleven, so I planned on pacing myself and matching her drink for drink, even in her absence…

Dinner went well enough, without event. I managed not to burn anything, and the peas weren't boiled dry. Barry offered his gratitude and promised to repay our kindness next time his hostess came to 'our delightful little part of the world', which we accepted, then he said his good-byes and went home. This left us just over an hour for Kathy to get showered, made up and changed into something suitable for the evening and… OK, so it wasn't the planned open-air session on the cliff-tops, but it came in as a pretty fair second, and as a bonus, we had been invited to Barry's house for dinner in a few weeks. Could that present the opportunity I'd been waiting for?

31

My Sunday evening was in part, one of reflection. I thought long and hard about our future. Kathy's and mine. Did we want one? Had we already agreed to have one, albeit without the spoken word? I thought so. I believe she thought the same way at the time, but who could ever be sure? We both knew the day when that conversation would need to be had. We also knew that day would be sooner rather than later. But how soon? Tonight? Next week? Next time she came down? We had already agreed she would visit again in three weeks instead of two, ensuring she had my undivided attention and not have to share me with a Blackberry and a world full of Brannigan's helicopters… Half of the afternoon had been lost to my work and I found myself thanking Barry for keeping Kathy entertained.

We had also agreed future visits would always be this way around, her coming to me, not alternating as we'd done in the past. I suspect our mutual dislike of the village pub in South Wales may have swayed us both a little on that one. Plus, we both preferred Tilda's, its own pubs and my neighbours. It seemed the logical conclusion to the problem. I even offered to share the cost of petrol, which seemed only fair, but she told me it was of little importance as my 'olde worlde' generosity more than made up for the thirty pounds it had cost her for the required half a tank. It's true I spoil her whenever we meet.

Yes, I admit I'm old-fashioned in that way, but the fact I was earning twice as much as she was, it also made sound financial sense… How long, I wondered, before it occurred to her, to both of us even, that Kathy moving into Windy Cottage made even *more* financial sense… I had lived as a 'couple' just twice before, once during my failed marriage to Richard's mother—we had both been far too young at the time—and more recently with Ellie. I don't pretend to be the perfect partner, but I consider myself fairly easy to live with.

I pay my way and I'm happy to share the work-load of running a busy home… As I finished my third glass of Chablis, not for the first time that day, it was clear 'that' conversation had to be had very soon. Maybe that very evening, when she returned from The Beachcomber. But events soon put a stop to that. Right on cue, at twenty past eleven I heard the front door open—I had left it on the latch, we hadn't yet reached the point of swapping each other's house keys—followed by giggly voices.

Kathy had brought Debbie home for a night-cap: "She shouldn't be walking home all alone in the dark this late at night, should she, Paul?" Who was I to argue with a lady? Especially one in such high spirits. I didn't even bother mentioning that Debbie lived all of thirty yards away, or that the crime rate in St Matilda's Bay was less than zero. Had I been sober, it would probably have entered my head that Debbie had a violent husband who, at that very moment could be lurking in the shadows, waiting for just such a moment as that. Had I been sober, I would have remembered the dark figure Kathy had seen at the rear of Debbie's cottage. But I wasn't sober.

I was pleasantly merry, in a similar state to that of the girls, so I agreed whole-heartedly that she would be safer here with us and welcomed them both into the front room, where Kathy stole my chair and Debbie sprawled on the sofa. I wondered how much the latter had drunk, and how long since she'd last been that inebriated. I knew so little about Debbie that she could have been a recovering alcoholic and we'd just set her back five years...

"Ooooooh, wine! What a bloody good idea!" Kathy said, picking up the almost empty bottle. "Two more glasses please bartender, and have one yourself."

They both giggled. 'Plus, another bottle,' I thought to myself. "And..." Kathy was beginning to slur a little which made me smile. "And... I *did* mean just a night-cap my lovely, nothing else!" I knew exactly what she meant. It was a conversation we'd had several times, usually after a few drinks. Both of us had experimented in the past, with other partners. Without going into the full details, names or places, we had no secrets. As far as we were concerned it was just something most people did, given the opportunity. A threesome isn't something you can plan, unless you're in the adult film industry.

You don't simply phone a friend and invite them over to join in your fun and games. It's something that happens on the spur of the moment. A moment such as this quite often, hence Kathy's 'joke' warning. During those intimate discussions, she had admitted to being bisexual but at the same time preferring men. 'It was just something I tried once and found I enjoyed'. It emerged that should it ever happen to us, we were the perfect couple for it. I owned up to the fact that I would feel awkward doing anything sexual with another girl while Kathy was there, and she agreed she wouldn't be too keen on me doing it either, admitting she could be quite greedy and would want all the attention of both the man *and* the woman throughout the entire session.

We concluded that should the situation ever arise, the third person would have to be a lesbian, so that she would show no interest in me what-so-ever, and I wouldn't be tempted to try and turn the lady in question. Whenever this subject arose, I would always remind her of her original 'proud to be gay' claim. To which, she would usually wink and say 'twin beds?' It was something we'd laughed about quite a lot of the months we'd known each other, finally agreeing it was never likely to happen. From what little I knew of Debbie, she was most definitely not a lesbian, so Kathy was right yet again. Even though I can honestly say the thought *hadn't* occurred to me, until she herself made a joke about it, I instantly forgot about any such thing happening *that* night.

I was keen to find out how the evening had gone, without actually prying. Between giggles, they told how it had been just like any other girlie night out. They'd moaned about too much sport on television, slagged off men, all of whom were total bastards or wankers… Kathy *thought* they'd managed to keep the conversation on a low volume, but couldn't guarantee Rachel hadn't picked up the odd snippet. As I poured each of us another glass of wine, I knew I wasn't going to learn anything new about my neighbour until the next day. Debbie had, by then, curled up on my sofa and was only a matter of a few degrees short of being prone.

Her eye-lids looked heavy and she was struggling to stay awake. Kathy, far more used to alcohol than her new friend I assumed, tried to keep the conversation going a few minutes longer, but we both knew she was fighting a losing battle. I motioned to her to take our guests' glass and rest it on the table, pointing out that it was only white wine so unlikely to stain either sofa or carpet, but I still didn't want a damp patch to contend with. At this, Kathy lewdly pointed out that *she* usually slept in the damp patch so why should *I* care… Oh, the joys of alcohol… I went upstairs and grabbed the single duvet off of what was normally Cheryl's bed when she came to stay. By the time I returned to the front room, Debbie was only seconds away from snoring.

Kathy stood up and came to me, her arms wrapped around my neck, more in a show of affection than as an aid to staying upright. I'd never known her fall over from too much drink and I thought it highly unlikely she would that night either… "Take me to bed or lose me forever!" the lady commanded. As ever, my head was full of trivia and it rang a bell somewhere in its recesses… "Top Gun?" I asked.

"How the fuck would I know!" Came the chuckling reply.

"Give me two minutes, hun," I added, "I just want to make sure Debbie's door is locked." I wasn't about to let her go home to any nasty shocks in the morning… Still in t-shirt, I strolled along the lane to Debbie's cottage. All locked up, safe and sound. I looked up at the windows. Just a small one slightly open upstairs, nothing to worry about, par for the course in Tilda's… Colin's car park was virtually empty, but I couldn't be arsed to move my car that time of night. It could wait until the morning. I spotted a couple of tents down on the beach, silhouettes on the canvas.

No doubt making the most of the very last few hours of a warm week-end, probably waiting until Monday morning to return home to wherever… Better than getting caught up in the Sunday evening traffic no doubt. All was quite in the pubs. Customers long gone. Lights out, doors locked until the next time. I don't know what made me look around, but as I turned into my front garden, my eyes drifted back to the cottage two doors down and I could have sworn I saw a curtain move. 'Probably just the night breeze through the open window…' and thought no more about it.

The next morning, I awoke with a shock. Firstly, I was rudely awakened at silly o'clock by the familiar 'ping' of the Blackberry. I'm one of those rare people who doesn't mind having my sleep interrupted, but only on two conditions. If it's' by a good-looking woman in need of love and attention, or if it's only three or four o'clock in the morning. At that point, I can cheerfully go back to sleep for a couple of hours with no ill effects. Anything after five, and with my over-active brain, I struggle, knowing I will barely have time to return to my slumber before my work-day alarm goes off at seven… The sound of the dawn chorus, plus the early sun-rise told me it was nowhere near time for me to wake up. A glance at the red digital numerals on my radio alarm clock confirmed it was only 04.46, so far so good. I ignored the 'ping'—whoever it was could wait until I was officially on duty at 07.30—and turned over to give Kathy a cuddle…

Since meeting my current love interest, I'd become accustomed to having only about a quarter of my king-size bed to myself. I had soon learned that she was a sprawler. Arms and legs everywhere. So, it came as no surprise that while the back of my body could feel the warmth of hers tightly up against me, had I moved another inch away from her, I would be on the floor... That was the moment I was *truly* awakened with a shock. To the best of my knowledge, as we retired the previous night, she only had one head.

So, unless the Greek mythology fairy had paid us an unexpected visit during the night, we had company. Next to Kathy's head, was another... But this one had longer, more blonde hair. In the dim light that crept through the curtain, I could not make out the face, but surely, it could only be Debbie. I gently stroked Kathy's face until she opened her eyes. I pointed across her to the other head that was sharing her pillow. She turned to look, then turned back and smiled, holding one finger to her lips in a 'shhh' sign. Then she softly whispered, "I'll explain later." Then as an after-thought, "and no, you didn't miss anything." She reached up to kiss me, then lay back down, her arm wrapped around my body. I was still facing her as I tried to go to sleep again.

Her hand instinctively cupped my bum in that way that lovers do when sleeping in that position... I think I managed to doze for an hour or so, but was still up and about before the alarm clicked and Chris Evans' voice bade the world good morning. I carefully slid out of bed and reached for my jeans, slipping them quietly on in the hope that our house-guest didn't wake up and catch me in all my morning glory. I succeeded and made my way downstairs for my first cup of coffee of the day... My morning routine is normally to go down and set the filter machine in motion, then back up to do the customary ablutions as it does its job.

Rather than risk waking the ladies, I made do with a quick wee and a wipe of my face with a damp flannel. The rest could wait for once. I had the feeling Debbie might feel a little embarrassed to wake up and find me there, doing whatever we men do in the mornings. Far better for her to come down in an hour or two and see me at the laptop, happily moving an Accessory Gear Box from Sikorsky, USA, to Trinidad. As I drank my coffee and waited for the Internet to come to life, I had my first cigarette of the day. My mouth tasted like a gorilla's armpit and I couldn't *wait* to brush my teeth. But I had to...

Kathy appeared about an hour later, and with a cheerful 'Morning gorgeous', wrapped her arms around me and kissed my cheek. "Coffee's on hun, then you can tell me about..." My eyes rose upwards. She smiled and understood. She looked so wonderful in a huge extra-large t-shirt that she stole from my drawer and always wears in bed when she stays with me. So, soft and cuddly.

Why does it look so much better on her than it ever did one me? As she returned with her hot steaming drink, and a top up for me, I was so tempted to slide my hand under that t-shirt. I knew she was completely naked underneath... She sat opposite me, careful to keep her knees tight together, knowing there was little we could do until Debbie had gone home... "I think it was about two," she began. "It must have been about then because I hadn't really gone to sleep. I was just lying there, thinking what a great week-end it had been and listening to you softly breathing... All of a sudden, I could sense there was someone else in the room. I felt a hand sort of stroking my hair, no, not stroking it, just sort of feeling it. I imagine she was trying to tell if it was you or me. Then she whispered my name... 'Kathy,' she said, 'I don't want to be alone. Can I...?' She never completed the question because I lifted the edge of the duvet, slid myself further over to your side and just kind of let her in."

Kathy and I were halfway through coffee and toast as Debbie made her appearance about half an hour later... "I'm so sorry," she began. "I just... Well, I... I'm not used to drinking and..." Kathy stopped her right there. We could see the poor girl was clearly embarrassed and we didn't feel any desire to prolong her agony. For my part, I told her to forget all about it and have a coffee. "Toast?" I offered.

With that little piece of awkwardness out of the way, the three of us relaxed and chatted about nothing in particular for the next hour, until Debbie suddenly realised the time, stood up and said, "I must get out of your way." Then looking down at Kathy, added, "You're off home in a bit and I don't want to spoil what little time you have left together."

Without arguing with the lady—it was true, we *did* want a little quality time, there had been precious little of it that week-end—Kathy rose to her feet and answered, "Come on, I'll walk you home. I could do with the fresh air, and we can swap numbers, have a gossip every now and then..." With that, the two of them were gone.

Yes, it had been a great week-end. Strange in many ways when I thought about Barry, my singing, bumping into Sarah, then waking up to find two girls in my bed for the first time in ages. Strange, but all good...

I couldn't wait for Kathy to return with all the juice from the previous night. Surely in three hours, with the added incentive of alcohol, she must have learned something of my mysterious neighbour... I put on a fresh pot of strong Brazilian coffee and let it filter through the paper funnel as I lit a cigarette and waited for Kathy's return. I knew she would be away soon after lunch and wanted to make the most of our last two or three hours together. Apart from anything else, I knew she wanted to return to the cliff-tops to complete our favourite past-time.

What with Debbie, Barry and the pub, we had barely had five minutes on our own during her first visit to St Matilda's Bay. I suppose it was only to be expected. Naturally she had wanted the guided tour, and of course the neighbours were keen to meet the lady of whom they'd heard so much but never met. I was hardly in a position to argue. I'd been exactly the same on my first visit to *her* new home town. I'd been greeted with a glass of wine and introduced to her mum, three younger brothers and a little sister. I'd barely unpacked before I was whisked off to one of Kathy's friend's houses for an evening of vodka and a few smokes.

Despite not remembering coming home that night, the following evening was pretty much the same. Ystalyfera is situated about ten miles north of Swansea, near the foot of the Brecon Beacons. On the Saturday morning, our 'vodka party' hostess, a lovely lady called Jan, took us up the Black Mountain. It had been a glorious sunny morning and the view North to mid-Wales was amazing. Kathy looked as beautiful as ever and I could easily see why she chose South Wales over South London. The next morning, Sunday, she took me for yet another walk down by the river and told me some of the local history about a famous opera singer who had been born, raised and trained there.

Sadly, the man who taught her everything she knew, a late nineteenth century Svengali, had wanted her all to himself, unwilling to share the singer with her adoring public. One day he took the same walk that we were then taking, took her up to the railway viaduct and ended her life some fifty feet below. The viaduct is still there, towering over the valley with its cool, running stream and its waterfalls. Underneath, where Kathy and I were walking, there is now a small commemorative plaque, built into the rocks that line the river path...

With immaculate timing, Kathy returned just as I'd finished the morning's washing-up. I poured us both a coffee and we took it through to the front room. She was shaking her head in dis-belief. I asked her to explain. "Well to start with," she began, "last night, as enjoyable as it was, was a complete waste of time as far as investigative detection goes... And that's not easy to say this early in the morning. Each time I tried to steer the conversation around to her ex, or husband, whatever you want to call him, she deliberately changed the subject. In the end, she very politely said 'I know you're only trying to help, and I *do* appreciate it, but this is the first night out I've had in ages and I don't want *him* to spoil it, just like he's spoilt everything else that was good in my life...' so we never actually got to talk about it, or him, or her, much at all. All she wanted to talk about was what a lovely man you are (which I already knew of course) and how lucky we are to have found each other."

I waited patiently as she sipped on her coffee and smoked a cigarette. There was something she wasn't telling me. There had to be, otherwise, why the strange look when she came home? "So, basically, all we talked about was our childhood, musical tastes... Oh, and agreed that all men, with one obvious exception..." At this point the stroked my thigh and leaned over to give me a loving peck on the cheek, "...all men are arseholes!"

I was running out of patience and she could tell. She was deliberately teasing me. I knew there was something she wasn't telling me and Kathy knew just how to build up to a climax. She could read me like a book. I was ready to burst and she was holding on until the final second. It was a technique she frequently used during our love-making. I never asked how she learned it, and she never asked me how I became so good with my tongue... The past was the past and we were simply enjoying the present...

Finally, she revealed the punch-line, "As we got to her door just now—Oh, and I've got her mobile number by the way—I stood just behind her and as the door opened just a few inches, I saw a shadowy figure pass across the hallway." She paused for dramatic effect, but I think I disappointed her. I was thinking back to my own experience the previous night, when I was sure I spied a bedroom curtain twitch... "I'm absolutely convinced she's not alone in that house. I believe she's got a man in there!"

I told Kathy what I thought I'd seen last night and she agreed 'that settles it'. There was definitely something Debbie was hiding from us. Us and the whole of St Matilda's Bay... But who? Or what? I shared my thoughts with Kathy as we strolled along the lane, to the footpath by Tom and Alice's back garden, that would lead us to the cliffs. Maybe it was her father. Perhaps he secretly visits his daughter during the night to make sure she's OK. Or an old friend. A lover possibly. Perhaps that was the reason her husband beat her.

Possibly he had discovered her dirty little secret. Maybe Debbie wasn't the innocent party after all. The whole 'abusive husband' story could simply be a cover-up for her own guilt... We walked along the cliff-tops, smoking and chatting about the little blonde along the lane and her secret lover.

It was a fabulous warm sunny morning, just approaching lunch-time. Below us, forty or fifty people were already enjoying the beach, oblivious to the couple looking down on them from above. I was in just shorts and t-shirt and Kathy was wearing a little denim mini-skirt and a black vest top which showed off her olive skin to the best effect. She looked stunning. We lay on the grass, had a cigarette each and let nature take its course. All thoughts of Debbie and her mystery world were far from our minds as we came together in sexual harmony... Even the familiar 'ping' of my Blackberry couldn't spoil the moment. We lay there for several minutes, basking in the warm glow of ecstasy as the rest of the world carried on its business without us...

Eventually, I hit the pearl button and checked my messages. All but one could wait and that one I responded to with a brief 'on this shortly'. "I'm going to have to deal with this I'm afraid, hun," I explained.

Kathy smiled back at me, understanding. "But next time, we really will do a week-end when I'm *not* working!" The fifteen-minute walk home was one of those golden moments that two people share when everything is right in the world and nothing else matters. No, words needed to be spoken. At that precise moment in time, it was a perfect world. No, wars, no famine, no crime... Just us. Just Kathy and I enjoying *our* lives... With each other... As we reached the top of the footpath, ready to head down, I suddenly grabbed her arm and said, "That's odd."

Looking down into the lane just outside Windy Cottage, we could see Colin, Barry and Adam deep in conversation with Tom.... "In all my time here, I don't think I've ever seen those four together," I mused. "Tom rarely goes out unless it's to visit friends or to come along to mine. Adam simply talks to nobody.

"The only thing Barry talks about is gardening and I can't see the others being interested in his begonias, certainly not Colin... He struggles to keep his hanging baskets alive..." We tried to ignore this strange sight as we carried on down the over-grown footpath and into the village. By the time we reached my front gate, only Colin remained in view. With a cheery 'Hi, you two', he collected a few empty glasses from one of the benches and went back inside the Mariners.

32

That Monday afternoon really was unbelievably slow for me. All was quiet on the Brannigan's front which left me with plenty of thinking time. I tried hard not to think of Debbie's visitor, lodger, father... Whoever he or she may have been. And I also did my level best to ignore the strange sight of four of my neighbours chatting in the street... But I could not. My idyllic new home was rapidly turning into a den of mystery, and this time it was not just my imagination. Strange things were going on that I knew nothing about. And short of coming straight out with it and asking the blatantly obvious, there was very little I could say or do.

I could go round to Debbie's cottage and ask who the dark stranger was, and if I did and she denied it, I could hardly force my way inside to see for myself, could I? And what of the others? I devised a low-key plan. As soon as I had Kathy's call, to ensure she arrived home safely, I would pop over to the pub and ask something so outrageous that nobody would take me seriously...

Soon after six, my phone call came. All safe and well in the South Wales household, and Kathy told me she had even called Debbie to let *her* know the drive home had been uneventful. Although, this had been a part of the master plan. We needed to check that Kathy had been given the right number for the lady. Sure enough, Debbie had answered and even chatted for a few minutes... After promising to call her every day with an update, Kathy and I terminated our call. A fraction of a second before the tell-tale click, I thought I heard a very quick, quiet 'love you', but had no time to check, or answer.

Given the chance, would I have said it back? Or 'you too'? Maybe that was why she hung up immediately after, not giving me the chance to say it or not. Perhaps she didn't want to hear my reaction. It was still a subject we had managed to avoid over the months.... I signed off of my laptop at exactly six-thirty, had a quick cigarette and walked across to the pub. Colin and Rara were their normal selves, laughing and joking with half a dozen late weekenders propping up the bar. "Paul," Colin greeted me. "Good to see you mate. The usual?" To be honest, I'm not sure if I have a 'usual' but it's fair to say a pint of Carling would be my drink of choice, nine times out of ten. I nodded and smiled back at the bar in general...

It was just at that moment that my mobile rang. I recognised the number immediately, it was Ellie. I toyed with the idea of not answering, but within seconds decided she deserved better than that, stepped back outside the pub for privacy and hit the green button... "Hi," I tried to sound my normal cheerful self. Truth be told, a part of me still had very strong feelings for the girl I'd shared more than twelve very good years with. "Before you hear it from anyone else, I wanted you to know that Steve and I are getting married."

I could think of plenty of reasons for her to call me. Problems with her mother, or our shared pet hamster which she now had full custody of, but wedding bells? Ellie? I had to ask her to repeat it. Way back in 1999, exactly three months after we got together, Copa Karaoke had hosted a party to celebrate her twenty-fifth birthday. As a practical joke on all her family and friends, I had agreed to ask her to marry me 'live' on stage.

The look on the faces of nearly a hundred people who thought they knew us well was an absolute picture. Especially my partners in Copa Karaoke... "Ellie, will you marry me?" There was a hushed silence all around the back room of The Greyhound as she slowly walked towards me, climbed the three steps up to join me on the stage, took the microphone from me and responded loud and clear, "No." This was followed by 'Thank God for that' from me, a huge cuddle from the lady herself and cheers all round as they realised it had all been an elaborate joke. Over the three months we'd known each other and come to know our respective friends and family we had made it quite clear to all concerned that we were very happy as we were and had no intention of taking that next logical step as decreed by society. No, marriage, no children, just us, Bird and Bloke.

In later years, we even planned a non-wedding but that never quite came about. There always seemed to be something more important happening—genuine weddings, anniversaries, significant birthdays, etc.—that we were afraid of over-shadowing... And now here she was, planning to marry a man she'd known just a very short space of time. Well good luck to them both, I thought. If anyone deserves happiness it's Ellie, and I said as much before we ended the call. I sat quietly on the bench outside the Mariners for a few minutes and thought about my time with Ellie and the four or five other women who had been the main-stay of my romantic life prior to Kathy. It struck me that I had always been the warm-up for the main act. The Les Dennis to Les Dawson.

Always the bridesmaid, never the bride in a manner of speaking. It had never occurred to me before that very moment, but every girl I ever became really close to in my life and often spent several years with, had found their true love immediately after me. I had been their rehearsal, as I said, their warm-up. My first real girl-friend, at sixteen had been a neighbour, Christine. Having dated several other boys from Reigate Grammar school for just a week or two, we stayed together for eighteen months. Within weeks of us going our separate ways, she met the man she would later marry, and they're still together, with three lovely children. Maureen was next, the mother of my son Richard.

We were together for seven years but I couldn't blame her for leaving me. It was the time I found my true vocation, music. I was hardly ever at home thanks to the success of Cyclops Mobile Disco. She went home to her mother and later moved to Northampton and met Tony. Again, they're still together. Then came Sue. We met while we were both helping out a mutual friend, running the Prince Albert public house—now a MacDonalds—just south of Redhill. We were a couple for nearly ten years before we agreed to part.

Three months later she met Peter, moved to Spain and they now operate a very successful ranch near Alicante. Still together and as happy as ever. The same with Jeanne. We had eight wonderful years together but she always wanted marriage and children and that just wasn't for me. A year after we said our tearful goodbyes, she met and married Tony. They now have three teenage children and although she still moans about him being an arsehole—back in Surrey, we still met for lunch every now and then—they seem happy.

After Jeanne, I decided it would be the single life for me. I had my music and my friends, plus a lady called Sharon who I spent fun evenings with whenever we were both free. I no longer felt the need for a permanent love on my life. Then Ellie came along and changed all of that. The rest, as they say, is history. I returned to the bar…

"So, what were the Gang of Four up to earlier, Colin?" It just came out that way… "On some kind of smuggling mission, are we?" It just seemed like the most obvious thing to say in a Cornish village by the sea. To most, in particular our visitors at the bar, it would be another over-exaggerated story to tell their friends back in the office when they returned to Hampshire, or Berkshire…

Colin's reply came with an accent that was definitely in that general area. Heading west but not quite getting there.

Whatever reaction I was expecting to receive from him, his answer was quick and off the cuff, "Aaaar, got me another boat comin' in on the evenin' tide, me old friend." He laughed.

Judging by his 'local' accent, he'd been spending too much time with the Cockney Wurzels. The group at the bar laughed with us, clearly enjoying the early evening banter after a day on the beach. "Got me some of them Spanish dubloons for Adam, a crate of yo-ho-ho for old Tom and a couple of them serving wenches to cheer old Barry up…" This earned our landlord a slap on the arm from Rara. He turned back to the day-trippers and concluded, "I don't think the old boy's had the pleasure of a good woman in years! Ahaar…" To which I added, "Or even a bad one." My plan had clearly fallen flat on its face.

I decided I would try once more, with my wide-eyed innocent approach, as soon as we were alone… Half-way through my second pint—Colin had insisted I say for another—he took me to one side, "Listen mate, we didn't say anything because we didn't want to cause any offence like. But now you seem to have cottoned on, I'd better tell you the truth, but I promise it's only a bit of fun, no harm in it like…"

Ten minutes later, I was heading over to Barry Marlow's house. I politely knocked on the door. As he answered, he looked genuinely pleased to see me. We hadn't really had the opportunity for one of our man-to-man chats the past few days… "Come in, come in. What can I do for you, Paul? Fancy a cuppa while you're here?"

"I just want to know which is the most distant date. As in, how far into the future?" He looked confused, so I explained. "I've heard about your sweepstake my friend, very amusing. All I want to know is, has anyone gone as far as a year away yet? Two years? Three? Because whatever they've gone for, add a year to it and put me down for a tenner. Then I'll take *all* your money and buy myself another one. In fact, I think a matching pair would improve the look!"

Barry looked suitably ashamed and assured me, in the same way that Colin had, that it really was just a bit of fun amongst the bay villagers. I told him not to worry. My smile and acceptance of his coffee showed I meant it… "But I'm serious about one thing. I don't care how far ahead it goes," I took out a ten-pound note and thrust it into his hand, "you add a year to that and count me in!"

I was actually quite disappointed to find no-one in the village expected my palm tree to see Christmas... "Then we have a deal. Put me down for next summer, 1 June will do." I had to laugh as I walked home. But I would still prove them wrong!

I have to admit though, that Barry seemed to be taking *my* advice, even if I hadn't taken all of his... The coffee was much better these days. I called Kathy to give her Jo's good news, preparing myself for a good night's sleep, looking forward to the next day's end of shift, and the handover of all my work responsibilities for the following week. Unfortunately, her response took the edge of my relaxed mood, "Just Debbie to worry about then..."

33

"It wasn't easy guv, they're a fuckin' strange bunch. Mitch and I had a good nose about, keepin' 'em peeled like. Both the pubs seem straight enough. Both landlords been their donkey's, though one of 'em only opens in the summer which seemed a bit odd to me..."

"Skip the fuckin' 'nicities Smithy and give me what you've got, OK?"

"Sorry boss. Well, there's two or three oldies, been there forever like. Old couple with a little girl. She's the one that bloke saved in the storm last year. Then there's a younger bloke, probably mid to late fifties. Used to be a teacher but didn't hear much else about him, no idea how long he's lived there. The bloke in the end cottage might be worth looking at though. He's the one that saved the little girl when 'er mother died..."

"How old? Where's he come from?" The boss was finally showing an interest, which perked Smithy up a little.

"Used to live near Gatwick Airport, worked in an office, I think. Then suddenly gives it all up and comes down here... There... You know, St Matilda's. I'd say he's about sixty, maybe a little more. Seems to have a thing going with some girl from Wales."

Smithy's boss was still nodding, as if telling him to continue, which Smithy did. *"Then there's a young couple, I say young, maybe forty, forty-five. He works away from home sometimes but couldn't find out what or where, something to do with banking, I think. She stays at home, does a bit of gardening, probably bakes cakes and that. Mitch called her the Stepford Wife..."*

'Guv' was not in the mood for jokes and made it clear to his lackie, *"Who else?"*

"Then there's four young girls. Two of them work at the bar of the Mariners, and the other one does the same in The Beachcomber and also runs the mini-market by the beach. They all come from a village up the road a bit,

Harwick, a right dump. We had a nose round there as well, but couldn't get anything without looking too obvious. Didn't even have a pub we could ear-wig in. The whole place is dead guv."

"And the rest of them?" He was now getting impatient. This exercise didn't seem to be going any place in a hurry.

"The other girl lives in the village. There's a bit of gossip says she's got a fella tucked away, and someone else thought she might be a les. But we didn't see her at all. All the girls seem to be between eighteen and thirty-five, guv."

"That's a fucking great help!"

"The landlord in one of the pubs is single, always chatting up the ladies. The other ones married, or so I heard, but never clocked her. Then there's another old fella, must be seventy if he's a day, lives in the old railway station. Managed a quick chat with him but I don't think he'll be any help. Used to run the station for donkey's then bought it when it closed. Never goes to the bay or the pub, likes his own company and does his gardenin' all day. Kept going on and on about steam trains and the good old days..."

"And that's it?"

"Sorry guv but I reckon we're barking up the wrong tree. Must've been a visitor we picked up on that phone call..."

"Really?" Smithy's boss looked him in the eye and asked, "So, how come he used the phone again last night? From inside the Mariners Arms?"

Smithy looked shocked! Had they hit on the right place after all? He tried to remember who he'd seen in the pub. Evans had been there, but he couldn't recall any of the others apart from the landlord and the two barmaids of course. Then his superior spoke again, "Tell me about the girl. Didn't you say she comes from Wales? Wasn't that where the phone was used first time we copped it?"

"The bloke said it might have been South Wales, guv, couldn't be certain. Sounds like this is the first time we've actually pin-pointed it though..."

"Don't forget the one up the hill, guv." Smithy was quick to point out.

"...and you say this girl's down there now? That's very interesting."

34

Tuesday's handover was one of the easiest yet. Dave was on time as always, and apart from a French shipping agent sending one of my parcels to Sweden when it should have been destined for Australia, there was very little to tell him. Instead, we chatted about football and holidays and families... All the normal stuff men talk about. I reminded him to bring his wife down to Tilda's sometime during the summer and we called it a day. That conversation had reminded me. I had lots of planning to do. It was nearly July and I had to make the transport arrangements from Minnie and Cheryl to spend a week at each other's homes in the school summer holidays, now only about four or five weeks away.

I had to confirm dates from Kathy to come down again, hopefully in three weeks. Plus, her mum was insisting I had to go back up there again soon. Fine, but when? Even though I had no great love for Kathy's village, I adored her family and friends. To the best of my knowledge, none of them seemed to care that I was old enough to be Kathy's dad. Yes, it would be nice to see them again sometime... There was just so much going on. On top of that, Kimmy and Neil were coming down from Crawley 'sometime' in July. OK, so they weren't actually staying with me—Colin was putting them up on a bed and breakfast basis—but I still had to make time for them just the same.

I was looking forward to that, they're a lovely couple, one of several pairings that have come together thanks to the power of Karma Karaoke. And as if that wasn't enough, I'd told myself I would sort out the back garden in the summer, and I hadn't even looked at it yet, let alone made any plans. I could see I wasn't going to get much time to myself that summer.

As promised, Mickey turned up on the Thursday, only an hour late this time, and fitted my window and spyglass. He asked the very same question that Kathy had asked when I told her of my plans. Why both? The answer was quite simple. During the daytime, I would normally be able to check through my new window and recognise who my caller was by height or hair colour, even though they were unable to see me. However, at night, the situation was reversed. All I would see would be darkness, yet they would know I was in by my shadow in the light. Hence the spyhole. It made perfect sense to me but Mickey just shrugged his shoulders and carried on with his work. Very efficiently I might add. I paid him in full and gave him a twenty-pound note 'for a drink', promising to recommend him to anyone else I might hear of that needed any similar work carried out...

It had only been three days since Kathy left and although we had spoken several times on the phone—once for more than four hours—I was already missing her. She seemed very concerned about how I was reacting to my ex-girlfriend's engagement. I truthfully told her I was very happy for them both. It had taken time but I'd moved on. I could not have been happier with my life just then. As sad as I had been at the time, when Jo had said we had become more like friends than lovers, it had been true. Luckily, we were still friends and I was thankful for that... The day was cloudy but warm, so now I finally had the place to myself, I grabbed a beer out of the fridge and took it out to the back.

As yet, I had no garden furniture even. Not so much as one of those plastic chairs you can pick up at the 'pound' shop. I sat on the step by the French windows and started to visualise how it could look. I liked the idea of the home-made tree house and the gravel section surrounding it. Or maybe bark, to give the kids a softer landing in the event of any unfortunate accidents. A small patio leading away from where I was sitting, complete with a weather-proof table and chairs set. A brick-built barbecue for those long summer evenings to come, hopefully... But that still left a huge expanse of area which, Barry claimed, would make a wonderful lawn, 'specially with all the rain we get down here'.

I had already given in to him and had two small patches of grass in the front, which I had to admit looked very presentable, and exactly as he had said, only took up half an hour every now and then to keep them looking good. But that didn't alter the fact that I had no intention of having half a bloody football pitch round the back! Right, so a slightly larger patio than originally planned for, a bigger table and maybe six chairs instead of the customary four... Then maybe an Oriental garden with bonsai trees and various multi-coloured gravel spots... Another of Barry's suggestions.

As much as it annoyed me to admit it, he was usually correct in his assumptions... 'and protected from the wind by your cottage on one side and the cliffs on the other, you should have no growth problems' he had said. I took his word for that and as usual, he would be proved correct later that year. But I still wanted at least some of the garden to be of my own design. Now I've never been one for 'keeping up with the Jones's' but I do admit to the odd glance over the low dry-stone wall that separated my garden from Sarah and Adams, just to ensure the Jones' were not leaving me completely in the dust.

Apart from a sizeable shed and a few slabs around the back door, it was largely lawn. Immaculately cut, with stripes and everything, but still just a lawn. I felt that, carefully planned, and with some clever lighting, they might just look over once in a while and think 'yes, he's done really well with that'. I also fancied an illuminated walk, maybe from the Oriental garden to the tree. I know it sounds daft, but the moment I saw that one on Torquay's sea-front, I'd always thought it romantic and made up my mind to have one someday. In the past, I had never had a suitable garden for such a thing. Now was that time.

For the first time in about eighteen months, I was actually *feeling* romantic again. Kathy had breathed life back into me and I had something to look forward to, something to live for, rather than work, the pub and suspecting my lovely neighbours of God-knows-what. All seemed to be going right in Blokie's World for a change. Experience should have told me it wouldn't last...

The following four days and nights were quite possibly some of the worst I've ever known. Admittedly they weren't as bad as driving head-long into a horse, or falling off my motor-bike for the first time on ice—the bike went one way while I went the other, smashing myself into a public telephone box—and I would have to say not as scary as falling asleep at the wheel on the M1 or nearly drowning in a flood... But all of those had been over in seconds. Those four days near the end of June 2013 just seemed to be one long nightmare...

It began when I awoke to the sound of a siren. If I'm honest, it took a good few seconds to sink in. I'd barely seen a policeman in St Matilda's Bay, let alone a car. Or several police cars... And a fire engine... And an ambulance... I glanced at my alarm clock. The little red lights told me it was shortly after three in the morning. 'What the fuck...?' I leapt out of bed and slipped on my jeans. Through the curtains I could see flashing blue lights and red lights, plus (I guessed) two or three bright white lights which must have made the entire bay look like a Christmas tree.

Again, I thought, 'What the fuck?' I nearly tripped, trying to pull my jeans up one leg while balancing on the other... Was this really happening? Was I dreaming? This could just as easily have been a space-ship landing outside my window. The lights were blinding and my curtains were still drawn. I could almost hear the Close Encounters theme inside my head, but the noise from the sirens was deafening. Amongst the wail of two or three sirens, I could also hear voices, shouting, screaming, barking orders… Both legs were in my jeans by then and I rushed to open the curtains.

My eyes, still half asleep, blinked at the brightness and I immediately closed the curtains again. Turning to grab last night's t-shirt from the back of a chair, I put it on as I raced downstairs and out to the front of Windy Cottage. There were three police cars, two fire engines and an ambulance. All lights were still flashing but all sirens had now been turned off. All six of the emergency vehicles were crammed into a tiny space between my cottage and the lane proper. Why do the strangest thoughts come to me in the middle of the night? In the midst of whatever tragedy might be unfolding before my very eyes, I wondered what speed they'd been able to do around the lanes between Harwick and Tilda's.

I even wondered if our very own speed camera had been set in motion for the very first time. I visualised six blurred black and white photographs of number plates… As these ridiculous thoughts ran through my head, I raced down my front path and out into the street, straight into the arms of a bulky man in uniform. A black uniform. He wore a large yellow helmet. "I'm sorry sir, you can't go any further right now." The fireman warned me, and as he spoke, a policeman took hold of my arm and let me across to where Colin and Brian, both in dressing gowns were watching the activities.

From our safe distance over the other side of the lane, I could see the full horror of the red and orange burning flames leaping from every one of Debbie's windows… "Is she…?" I began… Nobody knew the answer to my unfinished question. A policewoman near me confirmed that nobody had, as yet, been brought out from the burning cottage. However, the flames had been raging so strong with a blinding heat that the firemen hadn't been able to attempt an entry so far.

Would they find one body or two, I wondered. How the Hell did I manage to sleep through the early minutes of this emergency operation? I know I can sometimes be a heavy sleeper, but this must have been going on for a good ten or fifteen minutes before I woke up. Two fire hoses were trained on the windows, alternately moving from the top floor to the bottom. There had been no sound from the house, but if Debbie *was* still inside, she would surely be over-come by smoke and fumes by now… I prayed that if she *was* still inside, her body had gone into shut-down mode and she had collapsed into a coma to escape the terror she would certainly be enduring if still conscious.

On the step of the cottage next to mine, Sarah was gripping her husband's arm. I could only imagine their conversation. It was no doubt similar to that of Colin and I, now joined by Brian's wife Pat from The Beachcomber. We all asked the same questions but none of us had the answers. Neither the police not the fire service had anything to say, they were all far too busy. A few yards further along the lane, two paramedics could do nothing but stand and watch and wait… And hope they would be required to perform their duty rather than send that message to the on-call coroner.

Pat asked, of no-one in particular, "Does anybody know if she's in there? Do they know if she's alive? She was only in ours the other night, so full of life…" Meaningless words but nobody knew what else to say. Thick black smoke poured into the night sky illuminated by two hastily erected flood-lights. Water ran in rivulets from Debbie's front garden. I walked to the edge of the Mariners and without really wanting to know, looked for Debbie's little Fiat 500.

It was there… "She's inside!" I screamed. "Her car's there, she must be inside!" I ran across the lane to the nearest police officer and repeated it. "Her cars over there, she *must* be inside…"

Despite my own recent luck in 'love', I still had very strong feelings for the little lost blonde, who came to St Matilda's Bay to escape a violent and abusive husband, only to find herself a virtual prisoner in her own home, and then… This. I fell to my knees in tears. This shouldn't happen to anyone, let alone someone like Debbie. Sarah saw me and ran across to comfort me… "Why? WHY?"

I begged for an answer between my sobbing. As with all the other questions that night, it remained unanswered. As yet, there were no answers… The heat from the inferno was unbearable. I had to go back to where Colin and the others still stood, like me, waiting for answers… Through the smoke, we could now make out the glow of fire through the roof tiles. The flames had reached the attic. My total inability to do anything constructive led me to think of my own attic, stuffed with years of memorabilia… When I had moved to St Matilda's Bay last year, I had simply packed everything from my old attic in Smallfield into cardboard boxes and stashed it away in my new attic. I had no idea exactly what was in them, but it had been my life up until that point.

Photos of my mother winning the football pools in 1968. Over two hundred pounds. A small fortune in those days. Pictures of my family at parties, weddings, Christenings… Drawings my son Richard had done at school. His exam certificates and end of term reports. The pictures had spent many weeks stuck to the kitchen wall with Blu-Tac, eventually being put away for 'safe keeping'… Had Debbie put things in her own attic for safe keeping? Would anything remain of them if she had? Would she live to see them if she did? I turned to look at Colin with no further words to say. It had been he who raised the alarm. Luckily, we hoped, he had woken up in need of the toilet and spotted the fire in its early stages. He immediately called 999 and the police—first to arrive—were here in less than fifteen minutes. The fire engines arriving a few minutes later… "I didn't even think to look and see if her car was there…" Again, I wondered how the Hell had I slept through the start of this horror.

I know it sounds crazy, but Sarah and I did the only thing we could think of at the time. She told Adam to put the kettle on as she asked anyone willing to listen if they would like tea or coffee. Myself? All things considered, I'm ashamed to admit I went inside and grabbed my cigarettes and lighter. Apparently, I was the only one who thought this insensitive, as both Colin and Patricia took one from my offered packet. "Debbie was a smoker, wasn't she?" said Brian.

"Is a smoker," I hit back… "Debbie IS a smoker!"

We must have been out there in the dark of night, illuminated jointly by the flames coming from Debbie's cottage and the spotlights aimed at it, for well over an hour before the firemen considered it safe to venture inside. Armed with fire-proof suits and ventilator masks, three of them slowly made their way inside, as others continued to aim the strong jets of water at the building, killing off the last of the flames and cooling everything down. The next five minutes were the longest of our lives. They seemed like a lifetime. Nobody spoke.

Nobody dared to, after the horrific sight we had just witnessed. Sarah had handed out mugs of hot liquid to anyone that wanted it. Colin had been into the pub and brought glasses of whisky out for Pat, Brian and ourselves. Adam remained on the door-step, just staring. Patricia, Brian, Colin and I just sat on the benches outside the Mariners and waited. Barry had joined us without saying a word. We smoked and we waited... I glanced up at Alice and Tom's bedroom window.

Neither of them had come outside. I assumed Minnie was sleeping through it all, or maybe she knew and was being comforted by her grand-mother. I'd spotted Tom in the window a couple of times. The first time I just raised my hand in a form of greeting. The thing you do when a wave doesn't really seem appropriate. On one occasion I would have sworn I saw him smiling, but I'm sure that was just a trick of the light... I thought back a few minutes to Brian's comment. I'm sure he regretted it the moment the words escaped his lips, but he was right. Debbie is, or was a smoker.

I thought of the many times my own mother had warned me of the dangers of smoking in bed. It was totally banned in her house as I was growing through my teens and starting the disgusting, yet pleasurable habit that had gripped me for over forty years. I've done some crazy things in my life, and plenty of stupid ones at that, but I can honestly say I have never smoked in bed. Not even the classic 'after sex' cigarette. I've heard too many horror stories down the years to risk that one. I recalled the first time I stayed at Kathy's and noticed a small hole in the sheet, clearly a cigarette burn, and wondered why? Why would anyone be stupid enough to risk their life in that way? I was relieved to hear it had not been Kathy herself but a friend that had caused the burn hole.

Despite Freddie Mercury's poignant question, I *do* want to live forever thank you very much. Just as long as I have all my faculties and I'm not a burden to anyone... But I can't speak for Debbie. She always struck me as an intelligent young woman but you never know, do you? After all, I had only ever had about three conversations with her, and two of them made no sense at all. It's true to say that Kathy probably knew her better than I did, and she only spent one evening with her.

If questioned... If pushed, I would have to admit that, for genuine reasons, she was a very scared little girl. Maybe she *was* the type of person who would have one last cigarette before turning out the light. Maybe she had shared it with her secret lover, the dark figure both Kathy and I would be willing to swear we had seen if needs be. Who knew? And so, we waited. The three firemen had been in Debbie's cottage for an eternity, or so it seemed to me. To all of us waiting outside as the night-time turned into day, it felt like forever but at the same time, just a matter of seconds.

Almost without any of us realising it, the sun was slowly rising over the cliffs to the East. It was going to be another glorious day in St Matilda's Bay. But for how many of us? It was almost half past five when we finally got the 'all clear'. There was definitely nobody inside the cottage, alive or otherwise. No, Debbie, or remains of. And no mysterious guest, or remains of. The relief amongst her neighbours was audible. We smiled, we laughed, we cheered. We thanked the emergency services. We did what anyone else would do in that situation, all the while wondering where the Hell she could be and how the fire had started in an empty cottage. We hadn't heard the last of it…

The following day, brought the inevitable interviews with the police. Did we know her well? Who were her friends or relations? What did any of us know about the young lady who had shared our village for—in my case at least—the past year? Very little was the truthful answer. I told them what little I knew, including everything she had told me about her husband and feeling very awkward about revealing he was 'one of them'… A fellow policemen. First thing that morning I had called Kathy and given her the shocking news. We had agreed it was best for all concerned that I told the police all I knew, or thought I knew. After all, I only had Debbie's word for it, "And you say her husband's a copper?" The Detective Chief Inspector asked me.

"Well, that's what she told me, yes. But as I say, I've only spoken to her a couple of times and if I'm being totally honest, she was pretty drunk on one of those occasions." The DCI gave me a 'look'. I couldn't quite make it out. It could have been saying he thought I knew more than I was saying… "And you can't say if Miss Jones was seeing anyone on a permanent basis, or otherwise sir?"

So, it was Miss Jones, was it? Well, that was news to me, and I said so. "That was the name on the lease Mr Evans, one Deborah Jones…" His look was now distinctly 'you've lived near her for a year and not known her surname?' but I ignored it. To me, this was nothing unusual. In my former home, I'd lived for more than ten years with Margaret, Derek, Jill, Maurice, Theresa and Ron as my nearest neighbours, even sharing drinks and barbecues with them, but never known their surnames… Thoughts of my morning call to Kathy were running over and over in my mind. We had talked about 'that' night and decided it was irrelevant. As Kathy herself said, 'nothing happened so who needs to know?'

The more worrying aspect was that I had asked her to call Debbie, to find out where she was, to make sure she's OK and call me back. Debbie's phone had been switched off. I called Kathy back a couple of times then we left it that she would keep trying and let me know if she got through. As yet, nothing, and it was now the middle of the day. Nobody leaves their phone off that long, do they? I explained to the police that both Kathy and I suspected there had been someone in Debbie's life but male or female, temporary or permanent? Of that we could not be sure…

There seemed to be people everywhere, despite a 'Road Closed' sign at the top of the lane leading down through Harwick. Due to the narrow nature of our lane, this move effectively cut off their village also. But it didn't seem to stop half the villagers making the ten- or fifteen-minute walk through fields and footpaths to see what was going on. In amongst the five or six policemen, currently asking the population of the bay its necessary questions, there had to be at least another forty or fifty people just wandering round… Down to the beach and back, possibly in an effort to appear as though they had arrived there by chance, which of course all of us knew was bull-shit because we see them in our pubs most nights.

Some of them were already in one of the pubs, or Connie's. I'm sure Raechel was having the time of her life, and Colin and Brian's tills would see plenty of action as well. Quite likely for the next few days I shouldn't wonder. Every cloud, as they say… What I *did* wonder though, was where the fuck Miss Jones was. While I'll admit to being less concerned having learned she wasn't in the cottage, it was still more than a little worrying that she'd vanished off the face of the Earth. And without her car. The police had checked all local taxi companies and nobody had picked her up. She had been last seen in Connie's shortly after lunch on the Friday, Rachel not only explaining exactly what Debbie had purchased but also how much it had cost and the colour of the carrier bag it was taken away in.

If ever required to do so, Rachel would make a fabulous witness. Trust me, that girl doesn't miss a thing! So, at some point between about two in the afternoon and two in the morning, she had just disappeared… Gone. I suddenly had an awful thought. If Debbie had vanished after dark, there was one place I was certain the police hadn't looked. As far as I was aware, I was the only person in the bay that knew of her midnight walks on the cliffs.

What if something had happened to her up there in the dark? She could have gone over the edge, or maybe met an attacker… I told the DCI about this and as I suspected, it was one place they hadn't looked yet, mainly because they were unsure how to get up there... "Maybe I should call for the helicopter," he suggested. I admit I was reluctant to give away our little secret, so I told a half-truth, "It would be the best way, Inspector. She never actually told me how she got up there." Which was true, she hadn't...

The remainder of Saturday brought no further good news. The helicopter came and went, finding nothing significant. Several of the villagers, myself included, watched as the black and yellow Sikorsky S92 made three or four sweeps up and down the coast-line, until it reluctantly returned to base. The police took away Debbie's car for forensic checks, finger-prints, that sort of thing. Considering the entire village had by now advised the police what a loner Debbie seemed to be, it was a logical move to make. In fact, probably the only move they could make. From what I could see from outside, they weren't going to get any prints from inside the house.

Obviously, they were going over it with the proverbial fine-tooth comb, but I thought it highly unlikely they would find anything of value. No, better news from Kathy either, the mobile phone still being switched off. Naturally I had given the police the number and I was sure they would be trying as well, triangulating or whatever it is the experts do when trying to trace a mobile phone, but something told me that if Debbie *did* switch it back on, she was more likely to answer a friend calling than an unknown or unlisted number. She may well be alive and hopefully well, but something was definitely wrong with her.

You don't just vanish for no good reason. I had also mentioned the curtain twitching and Kathy thinking she saw someone else in the house last week-end, but that probably didn't help a lot if I'm honest. It only seemed to put the idea into the inspector's head that she'd probably gone off with her secret lover, in his car... "Maybe for a few days away from here," he said... Somehow, I doubted it.

35

I didn't sleep at all well on Saturday night. Considering I had only had about three hours the night before, I should have resembled a log, but there was so much going on in my head that each time I closed my eyes, I kept having flashbacks. Memories of that night with Debbie up on the cliffs. The apology. The ramblings. Her night out with Kathy, waking up and seeing her in bed with us... I kept thinking maybe I could have done more for her. Instead of just letting her walk away I should have followed her and offered more help, sitting up all night talking it through, if necessary, but no. What did I do instead? Fuck all! Nothing but those weird fantasies of sex and drugs, violence and prostitution. I could have done more, *should* have done more, but the simple fact was that I hadn't.

I said as much to Kathy on my third call that night. She managed to calm me down. She rightly pointed out that it was Debbie who had walked away, not me. 'What else could you have done? Break the door down and force her to talk?' She was right of course, but it didn't make me feel any better. I still felt I had let Debbie down in her hour of need. After all, who else did the poor girl have to turn to? Despite all Kathy's kind words, it didn't change the fact that Debbie no longer had a home in St Matilda's Bay and worse still, we hadn't got a clue where she was or if she was safe...

I drifted in and out of sleep, finally giving up at seven and going back downstairs for coffee and cigarettes. I switched on the local news. Nothing. No, mention of a Miss Deborah Jones. Not even a word about the fire. I'd thought it strange that there had been no TV crews in the bay all week-end. The lane had been re-opened Saturday afternoon so there was nothing to stop them. But no, not a single one, nor any reporters from the Cornish Times. Just the steady stream of sun-worshippers coming to our normally peaceful bay for some July bathing.

Maybe, just a small maybe, the inspector had checked up on my statement regarding her husband and insisted on a news blackout until she was found safe and well. I gave myself a very small pat on the back for at least helping Debbie in my own little way. I just hoped she would thank me for it if ever I saw her again... I suddenly felt the urge to eat. With everything else going on around me, I'd completely forgotten dinner on Saturday night. My body must have kept going on adrenalin, caffeine and nicotine or something instead of food.

I realised I was starving. Wherever Debbie was, if she suddenly needed me, I'd be no use to her in this state. I needed food. It called for a bacon sandwich... Isn't it strange how the tiniest thing in your head can make you think of a loved one. The mere thought of a bacon sandwich reminded me of the time I'd gone to stay at Kathy's. Her mum and the kids had gone away for the week-end and left us in charge of the house, and Bruce the cat. It was just the excuse we needed to Christen the place, smoke a little more than normal—not always the standard pack you find in your local newsagents, I might add—and down a few vodkas.

The next morning, as usual, I was up at the crack of dawn and making coffee. I sat outside in the early morning sunshine, waiting for the little lady to wake up. It soon became obvious she was absolutely shattered—I took that as a huge compliment—and not in any rush to wake up. I had left her sleeping soundly, not even stirring as I stroked her hair. My thoughts had turned to food. I checked the fridge... No, bacon! Nightmare! So, I scribbled a note and walked down to the village shop, returning with eggs, sausages and bacon.

As I walked back up the hill that led to her house, I spotted Kathy sitting on the door-step smoking a cigarette. The way she greeted me, you would have thought she hadn't seen me for weeks rather than hours. Then she spotted the carrier bag.... 'Mmmmmm, bacon butties,' she said, taking the bag from me and proceeding to make the best bacon sandwiches ever!

Lo and behold, it was Old Mother Hubbard time again in Windy Cottage. No, bacon and no bread! What was happening to me? I was always so organised. There was always bacon in the house, just in case... Grabbing some cash off the table, I walked over to Connie's. I was greeted with Rachel's biggest ever smile... "Great news eh?" She beamed. I looked bewildered. What could have possibly happened to cancel out the previous two days?

"They've found her, Paul. Debbie's OK!" I was stunned. How did Rachel find out so early? There had been no police in the bay as yet that morning. I mean I *know* she has this uncanny knack of knowing things almost before they happened, but this? This time she had excelled herself, exceeding even her own high expectations. Had I missed something on the TV news, or in the papers? I thought I'd checked everything with no success, not a word about our missing neighbour... "Where?" I asked. "How did you find out?"

"It was Sarah," Rachel explained. "Debbie called her earlier, said she was OK and not to worry about her." I practically ran out of the shop and over the road, banging loudly on the door.

When Adam answered the door, he was smiling... "Is it true?" I asked him. "Debbie's alright?"

He confirmed it was true. Debbie had phoned Sarah about six this morning, told her she was with a friend and not to worry. She seemed upset about the house but had assured Sarah that she would be back soon to sort everything out... And then she was gone. I thanked Adam and apologised for the interruption, which he understood, 'knowing how concerned you were.' There was slightly more of a spring in my step as I returned to Connie's to finish my shopping. I could now relax and enjoy my breakfast. Or so I thought.

As I thanked Rachel for my shopping, she said, "Doesn't it seem a bit odd that she called Sarah? They barely spoke two words to each other..." As soon as I got back inside Windy Cottage, I called Kathy to give her the good news. She sounded pleased but also thought it rather peculiar Debbie should call a relative stranger when she and Debbie had swapped mobile phone numbers only last week... And the phone was *still* switched off... The plot thickened. Did Debbie and Sarah share a secret the rest of the village knew nothing about? If so, what was it? This wasn't over yet, not by a long chalk...

I learned something very important many years ago. As a special birthday present for my hard-working mother, I bought her a brand-new set of kitchen-ware: Food mixer, whisk, set of eight knives—one for every occasion—and even a new set of pans, fit for cooking, boiling, scrambling or poaching any food you could possibly think of. While appearing over-joyed at the thought put into it, and my generosity, within weeks I noticed she had reverted to the same old wooden spoon she'd had for years, the old pans, a knife that had been sharpened by an old man who came along our street with a grind-stone attached to a converted wheel-barrow... In fact, virtually every new gadget had been relegated to one of the kitchen cupboards.

My mother explained that they just 'didn't *feel* right'. She was used to her own tools. The tools of her trade. It is something I've noticed many times down the years. An expert tradesman or woman will continue to use the same hammer, or stapler, or indeed a wooden spoon, until it falls apart. Go into any shed and you will find tools all over the place. It will look a mess. That's because the owner is a craftsman, an expert in his field, and he (or she) knows exactly where the right tool is for the right job. And woe betide the partner who thinks it a good idea to give that work-place a good clean and tidy!

I've known couples come close to divorce because the husband thought it a good idea to tidy up his wife's kitchen, or vice versa with the man's beloved shed. A wise man once said 'Show me a messy work-place and I'll show you a hard worker'. So, bear that in mind next time you see a spotless kitchen, office desk or garage. You may well find that person puts appearances ahead of skill or work rate... As I came back from the garden centre that Sunday afternoon, my mouse wasn't where it should have been. Prior to my trip into Harwick, I had been checking the price of garden furniture, miniature plants and the like on line.

As I sat back down at the living room table, I opened the laptop and instinctively reached for the mouse. It was a good three inches out of position. I had to noticeably stretch my arm to reach it. It simply wasn't in its normal comfortable position. Someone had been in my house. For what reason I did not yet know. I looked around the room... Everything else seemed to be in its place, but I would make sure. I opened up a few drawers, all present and correct.

I could not be sure they hadn't been opened in my absence, or if anything had been moved but I was reasonably sure nothing had been removed. They were not things I handled on a regular basis. But my cheque book was still there. Before I went upstairs, I checked all windows and doors. The front door had been securely double locked as I came in ten minutes earlier. All downstairs exits were still secure and no signs of tampering. The bedrooms and bathroom were the same. I had crept slowly up the carpeted stairs, not wishing to alert any intruders to my approach should they still be present.

But all was quiet and I disturbed nobody... As I had left them, there were just the small windows in each room open on the latch and too small for anyone other than a midget to squeeze through. Returning to the kitchen, I checked the 'holiday dosh' jars that I kept in a cupboard under the sink. So-called because I never spend one- or two-pound coins. It was something Ellie and I started years ago, when we were not as well off as we later became. We found that by not ever spending such coins, we could save up to a thousand pounds or more in a year and that, to us, was two good holidays.

Even though I was now 'comfortable', old habits die hard and that was one I still lived by. The three old mugs—my jars—still had their coins in them. True, I couldn't swear a coin or two hadn't been removed, but on the whole, it did not look as though anything had been stolen. Two of them were completely filled and the third about half full, just as I remembered them... But I *can* swear that somebody had been in my house, checking up on me... But for what? I made myself a coffee, lit a cigarette—I was smoking far too much these days—and stood by the front window, watching the world go by. To all intents and purposes, it was just another sunny summer's day in a pretty Cornish bay.

Visitors came and went. Connie's was doing a roaring trade in ice creams and cold drinks. Both pubs were full to bursting as per usual. From my vantage point, I could not see the now boarded-up front of Debbie's rented cottage, but quite naturally, most passers-by stopped to look and wonder. Some would take photographs to show their friends when they went home. Should anyone ask, the whole village had agreed—even Rachel—to say it was some idiot with a far-too-hot chip pan. This would normally be accompanied by that shaky hand movement close to the mouth, suggesting he or she had been drinking.

There was no mention of Debbie by name. With no media coverage, nobody would suspect foul play, if indeed there had been any. The age or sex of the tenant was not mentioned by anybody. With nothing on the local TV news or in the newspapers, any casual observer would assume it was just 'one of those things', and the topic of conversation would immediately change... In keeping with the official police line of media black-out, they were more than happy for us to use this 'drunken accident' as a way of keeping visitors from asking too many awkward questions. I couldn't speak for any of the neighbours, but I for one was keen to see if any stranger asked more than the average amount of questions regarding the damaged cottage. It could prove to be a valuable clue as to what was going on in St Matilda's Bay, if anything...

Early that same evening, I called Kathy to keep her updated, although I didn't say a word about the mouse. I suspected she would think I'd just knocked it out of position somehow. Apart from anything else, I did not want her to worry about me unduly. She may of course have been right, had I told her and she'd had the opportunity to voice her opinion... But I didn't. Was that another secret I was keeping from her? Was that a sign? Maybe. Maybe I didn't want her to think of me losing it. Becoming paranoid... 'Still no word from Debbie,' she pointed out, 'and her phones still off.'

This didn't surprise me. Nowadays, nothing surprised me. If I'd looked out the window and seen Debbie outside the Mariners with a pint of Guinness in her hand, I don't think I would have even blinked. I think I'd just begun to accept everything at face value by then. Yes, there had been a fire, but it was quite possible Debbie had left a cigarette burning in the ashtray as she rushed to meet some man who was whisking her away for a naughty week-end. Every odd thing that seemed to be happening in my little village, could very easily be explained away... So, maybe I *was* becoming paranoid...

That evening, having nothing better to do with myself on a Sunday night, as soon as the main crowd had drifted away, I went across the road for a pint with Colin and the girls. There were still about twenty people eating and drinking in the Mariners. I didn't recognise any of the faces at the tables... No, doubt tourists waiting for the early evening exodus to die down. Along the bar I spotted a couple of vaguely familiar customers. Harwick villagers, I think. We nodded at each other as I ordered my 'usual' from Lala... As we chatted about nothing in particular, a gentleman came in and ordered a pint of best.

Lala was just bringing it to a light head when he stated, "Nasty business that..." He nodded in the direction of the fire-damaged cottage. Lala gave the stock answer, to which the stranger muttered something about 'bloody idiots, why do they...?' and took his pint outside before either of us could catch the end of his rhetorical question. Why *do* people think they are perfectly capable of cooking or driving or even putting together a comprehensible sentence when they've been drinking?

The simple answer is, of course, because they're convinced they can. Every drunk driver will swear blind he knew what he was doing. He might even try to claim he's a better driver when he's drunk, because he has to concentrate that much more... Bull-shit! Lala, along with every other villager engaged in serving the Great British public that week-end was no doubt praying for Monday to come and for St Matilda's Bay to return to some form of normality. At least until it started all over again next week-end...

36

"It's me, guv, Smithy…" He was calling from the only working public telephone in Harwick. The other two had long since been vandalised and nobody seemed to be in any rush to repair them. Like many other out of the way public facilities, lavatories, pillar boxes, etc, they hadn't seen so much as a lick of paint for many a year.

"I would know those dulcet tones anywhere, Mr Smith," came the man's reply. This, of course went straight over the underling's head.

"What?" He asked.

"Never mind, Smithy, what have you got?"

"I'm telling you there's something weird about this place guv." At this, the boss' ears pricked up… "Everyone I speak to say's the same thing. Some drunk bloke falls asleep with the deep-fat fryer going. Burns the place down. Nobody killed though, or so they think…. The tart in one pub, landlord of the other, even the old geezer renting out the bathing huts… It's the same fuckin' story every time! It's like they've shut up shop and…"

"…and?"

"Well, it all sounds rehearsed to me. Like they've got it off word perfect and don't want the rest of the world to know what the fuck really happened!"

"Smithy," the boss asked, "when did you develop a brain? If I want your fucking opinion, which I doubt will ever happen, I will fucking ask for it, OK?"

But it did start him wondering… Maybe he should risk venturing into St Matilda's Bay himself… Smithy slammed the phone down with a 'Fuck You!' and returned to his cheap hotel in town…

37

If I'd thought the week-end had been crazy, to say the least, Monday was simply bizarre. It had to be seen to be believed... Every Monday, the locals of Tilda's, along with Harwick and several other remote villages in the North of the county, receive their 'freebie' newspaper. "The Pigeon", 'carried to your door since 1897', it proudly boasts. Legend has it that, back in the early nineteen hundreds, when our lanes were even worse than they are today, as in un-passable for weeks, sometimes months on end, the local newspaper was dropped at each village by homing pigeon.

Quite how the pigeon knew where to drop them remains a mystery, but you know the West Country, they love a good story. Pirates, pixies, or piskies to give them their correct local name ... I'd glanced at The Pigeon maybe once or twice in my time here. To be honest, apart from the news, what little there was, it was no different to any other freebie paper: Births, deaths and marriages, a write-up on the village flower show, several pages of small ads, 'looking for dish-washer' on one page, followed shortly by 'dish-washer for sale' a few pages later...

I often wondered if these people ever spoke to each other... Plus, countless advertisements for local businesses, etc... I normally read it over my morning coffee, then threw it in the recycling bin. But not on this Monday morning. This one was different. In the bottom right-hand corner of the back page, I spotted:

STOP PRESS

Tragedy hit St Matilda's Bay again on Friday night. A fire broke out in one of its cottages, leased by a Miss Deborah Jones. The cause of the fire is as yet uncertain, but it took the life of Miss Jones. This follows the tidal wave that nearly destroyed the small community two years ago. Miss Jones' family have been informed of the accident.

I had to read it again to be sure I wasn't completely losing my mind... Deborah dead? Where the fuck did *that* come from? I put down my half-finished mug of coffee and raced round to Tom's house. Having been invited in and offered a cup of tea by his wife—when will these people ever learn? I thought the whole of the West Country knew my total dislike of tea by now!—I slammed the paper down on the table and asked, "Where did *that* crap come from?" They could see I was not a happy man. "Took the life of Miss Jones? We all *know* she's still alive for Christ's sake! And her family have been informed? What family?" I was seething and they could see it.

Tom came over to me and put his arm around my shoulders, "Now calm down old son," he smiled, that same smile I thought I'd seen at the window the other night, as fire all but demolished our neighbour's cottage.

"You know what local rags are like, always making mistakes. Look here," he pointed at the article, "they can't even get the date of the flood right. Why only a couple of years ago..."

"This is not a mistake Tom! It's a fuc... a bloody outrage! What if she *does* have family, or friends that might not have heard the news yet? And how could *these* idiots know 'her family have been informed?' Even the police didn't know who she was two days ago!" I picked up the paper and threw it down again, this time to the floor, for extra effect... I was struggling to control my temper, and my language. Even though I knew Minnie was already on her way to school—I'd seen the mini-bus pick her up earlier—I was also well aware that Alice did not approve of swearing at all, and especially not the "F" word... But it wasn't easy. And Tom's ever-present smile wasn't helping. "It's just.... It's irresponsible, that's what it is! As you say, they even got it wrong about the flood, saying it was two years ago..."

It took a very large Scotch and a phone call from Kathy to fully calm me down... "Will you listen to me without interrupting, Paul?" She begged me. I had already tried to explain my feelings and thoughts about local newspapers to her, but each time she offered an explanation or an answer, all I had done was interrupt with 'yes but...' or 'but you don't understand what that family must be...' I finally apologised and told her to carry on, promising not to say a single word until her ladyship granted me permission...

"Up here, we have a local 'rag' as you call it, and over the years, my mum reckons they've killed off more locals than bird flu and TB did." She was making light of it, to help me regain my composure. We could always make

242

each other laugh, however bad the outside world seemed to be. "I'll tell you how shit they can be. The offices of ours are in a village about five miles from here, Llantrisant, and right next door to the Queen's Head pub. This Christmas just gone; the pub was broken into. Nobody hurt, but three day's Christmas party takings, plus both charity boxes were stolen. The following week, when the local paper came out, the story was quite naturally their front-page news. You'll like this bit… All the details were meticulously written up, including an exclusive interview with the landlord, under the headline "No, Christmas Cheer for The King's Head". And that was right next door! They couldn't even get the name of the bloody pub right!" She laughed.

I had too as well. Once again, Kathy was right. I was getting myself wound up over nothing. Considering its readership of no more than about five thousand, it was highly unlikely Debbie, or any of her friends or family had even seen the newspaper, let alone the story… I let the line go quiet for a few seconds, to ensure Kathy had completed her narrative, then asked; "Do you think I'm being daft, Kathy?"

"Not at all, hun," she replied. "You've had a really stressful week-end, what with the fire, the police and everything. It can't have been easy for you, or *any* of you for that matter. I wish I'd been there for you." Me too, I thought to myself. Then it was my turn to speak without interruption, as agreed…

"Maybe I'm being paranoid, but I just find it hard to accept so many strange things happening to such a small village—population just eleven—in such a short space of time. Had it been over a longer period, or in a large town somewhere, maybe I would have thought nothing of it, but," I listed what *I* considered certain inexplicable occurrences in what had been less than three months, "I know some of these would sound trivial on their own, but when you put them all together… The fact that only Debbie and I knew the way up onto the cliffs. The retired teacher and techno-phobe who appears to have no noticeable income, but owns a computer. The financial whizz-kid who works away from home, but trusts a neighbour, me, that he's barely spoken to in a year, to look after his wife for a week-end, then just a few weeks later goes away again and leaves her at home alone. The girl whose husband, a policeman working just fifty miles away, is unable to find her. The man in black, who you yourself spotted creeping across the back gardens at the break of dawn. That same man—possibly—who watched me from behind a curtain, then ducked into a back room as soon as you appeared at the door. The way Tom had smiled as his next-door neighbour's house burnt to a crisp. The fire itself. Debbie dead or alive, depending on who you spoke to or what you read. The fact that she called Sarah, a woman she had barely spoken to before, rather than you, whom she had promised to stay in touch with. Her phone still being switched off (I assume). Four of the men in the village suddenly coming together for a chat in the street, when clearly, they had very little in common, and spoke to each other even less than Sarah and Debbie. Then the way they dispersed as soon as we appeared on the horizon. My apparent break-in, but nothing stolen…"

"Hunni," her voice was soothing, "we've been through most of this before. There are possible, quite logical explanations for all of those things. Apart from maybe Debbie's phone call, but even *that* could have a simple answer. Maybe she's closer to Sarah than any of you knew. Her phone could be broken so she used a friend's land-line possibly. Did you ask if the call came from her mobile?"

I had to confess it hadn't occurred to me to ask… "I know it seems odd so much happening the way it has, like you said, in such a short space of time… But to think the whole village is up to something sinister I think could be more down to your imagination than anything else babes. I honestly don't think you're paranoid, just a little upset and confused over all that's going on around you. I imagine in a small place like that, every little thing appears to be magnified…"

"I'm sure you're probably right Kathy, but…"

"Let's be honest here, hun… We all have secrets, yes even you and me. I know you've been honest with me all along, but I'm willing to bet my life savings that nobody else down there knows you lay awake at night imagining Adam as a spy, or Colin as a closet gay, or Debbie as a former crack whore…" I stopped her there. This was all perfectly true, but Kathy had a further theory she wished to expound:

"As I said, babes, we all have our little secrets, so try these on for size. I know my imagination isn't up to *your* high standard," she giggled, "but if you think about it, these are far more likely, if not completely moral, than some of the outrageous ideas you came up with."

I told her I was always open to suggestions, but I refuse to repeat her answer… That little burst of smuttiness out of the way, Kathy continued with her ideas… "How about either Barry or Colin being the absent father of Minnie? You said yourself none of her family had ever met the man. It's just possible that he, whichever it may be, felt the need to be close to his daughter without the parental of financial responsibility… How does that sound?"

I had to agree that it was a highly feasible theory, even though I struggled to see either man as a doting parent. However, as I was quick to point out, I was almost certain both men had known Maria, Minnie's mother in the village before her death. I also knew from Tom, that the man whose name was on the birth certificate—Martin Davies—had happily accepted financial responsibility all along, and still did.

"OK," Kathy conceded, "but you have to admit I've been giving it a lot of thought, eh?" This was indeed true. "Well, try this one then. You all think that Sarah is the perfect little wife, and maybe she is. Perhaps she's just a little too perfect for Adam. Possibly he likes to live on the wild side from time to time. Debbie would fit the bill. OK, I will admit she's not single if all she says is true, but she sure as Hell is young and available. Or was…"

Now that supposition, I had to admit, while not exactly liking it, was extremely possible… I found myself, once again defending the lady's reputation. A reputation which, in all fairness, I had to admit had only ever been damaged in my own vivid imagination.

Kathy and I left it there, before our brains became even more frazzled than they had been before. Mine certainly did not need any additional possibilities to consider, and I'm sure hers had more important things to occupy it than my problems… "The only problem I have with you," she explained, "is how I'm going to get through the next eleven days without seeing you!" I could feel her warmth right through the telephone line. The feeling was mutual and I told her so, then asking, "Have you ever heard of a thing called Skype?"

38

Tuesday saw me back where I belonged, where I knew what I was doing. Back on the laptop, working. Where the Hell had the last seven days gone? I was totally unprepared for the daily routine of 'working'. Having said that, a large part of me was relieved to have something else to occupy my mind. There was far too much crap floating around in there. As far as village life was concerned, apart from the on-going fire investigation two doors down, Tilda's had pretty much returned to normal. Minnie caught the school bus at eight-fifteen, Tom at the gate to wave her off. Colin was watering his hanging baskets. Brian was hosing down the path outside The Beachcomber, his wife no doubt inside supervising the tidying up after the previous night's session.

Rachel was her usual busy self, piling up the fruit boxes outside Connie's. Nobody could ever accuse that girl of being work shy. Adam, I believe had left the village first thing for an urgent visit to the city, though which city I was unaware of. Sarah, as I was later to discover, was tending to her back garden, trimming and pruning as and where required. Barry was yet to be spotted, but my palm tree looked in fine fettle. Other than a few stray visitors, the bay was back to its normal quiet and peaceful self. Of course, the gossip continued, which Rachel was happy to pass on to anyone willing to listen, but only to the locals, not to any of the day visitors. To them, it appeared that ignorance was bliss.

Even Rachel herself had by then tired of the gossip surrounding the fire. She had started telling all and sundry how annoyed she was at being away at the time and 'missing all the excitement'. Debbie had been spotted in St Ives. The fire at her cottage had definitely been started by a stray cigarette… In the kitchen. Or was it the bedroom? It was also a certainty that the firemen had smelled petrol. And someone was spotted leaping from an upstairs window, minutes before the fire broke out… All of this was largely ignored by yours truly, except to relay such absurdities to my co-conspirator in South Wales, in preparation for her next visit.

I had a very pleasant chat with Sarah over the back fence. She was attacking something with a spray gun as I began to measure certain areas of my own little plot, and at the same time trying to decide where exactly I wanted my two benches, one hammock swing and a miniature climbing frame complete with rope ladders and slide. The latter being in readiness for the next onslaught of Cheryl and Minnie, who although now approaching their teenage years, were still very much kids at heart… And who doesn't enjoy a climbing frame? Even at my age. Let's face it, it's only a small version of an army assault course, right?

"If you plan it just right," my neighbour offered, "they could get from the climbing frame to the tree house as an alternative to simply climbing the lower branches of the tree." I was quick to point out that the tree house was still only an idea, and nothing carved in stone as yet, though I was still keen on Barry's idea, and I'd always enjoyed a challenge. We both took a break from our labours and enjoyed a cold lemon drink, plus a cigarette for me. Sarah was not a smoker as far as I was aware but had no objections to me indulging 'out here, but never inside the house'. She turned her nose up at the thought.

Considering the possibility of the cigarette connection, I was pleasantly surprised that Sarah and I managed to get through the whole half hour without a mention of you-know-what, even though we could tell by the noises coming over the fence, that the investigation was still on-going. If it hadn't been for a 'ping', we would probably have stayed out there longer. As it was, I had Main Rotor Servo's and their attached Nuts and Bolts to move to Norwich, so Sarah returned to murdering the wild life of St Matilda's Bay.

For once, my nightly chat with the gorgeous Kathy was a purely personal one, with not a single mention of the recent activity in my part of the world, which made a very welcome change for us both. The only vague connection was when she suggested we could both do with a holiday. 'With everything going on,' she said, 'you haven't had a break for over a year!' Which was true. Unless you counted my visits to South Wales and Kathy's own trips to Tilda's, neither of us had enjoyed a proper break for over a year.

For someone who had, until recently, been used to two or three escapades in the sunnier parts of Europe—sometimes more—every year, I had been sadly lacking in that department. With me being a million miles from the nearest travel agent, and still not 100% happy with spending so much money on line, I suggested she collect a few brochures to bring down with her the following week. I could tell be the tone of her voice, this idea was very well received… It would be another milestone, another first in our non-romance. Whatever next I asked myself after we'd said our good-nights? A wedding on the beach… Honeymooning in Jamaica… OK, so I was back in the world of fantasy for a few brief seconds, but the idea didn't completely revolt me, I had to admit.

But the second after I thought it, I immediately dismissed it. That day, if ever, was still a very long way off. All we both wanted right now… *needed* right now, was to get away for a week in the sun and forget all about the events of the past two months. Frankly, that day could not come soon enough. It was weird when I came to actually sit down and think about it. For the past year, I'd been too wrapped up in my own 'problems', beginning with the house and garden, then culminating in village life, to even consider where Kathy and I were going. By the same token, I'd also involved myself so much in the activities of my neighbours to see just how close Kathy and I had become.

Admittedly, the thought of the two of us becoming 'an item', to use the modern idiom, had crossed my mind once or twice, but each time I tried to foresee our future, something happened in the bay to erase it from my mind. Was that telling me something? Was I subconsciously looking for a way out? Was I still afraid of commitment? I had absolutely no idea, but it was clear the lady herself was in no hurry to move on just yet. The only clue I had to her true feelings for me and our possible future, had been an enigmatic, "What you need is a good woman to take care of you down there."

As always, I had made a joke of it by replying that I would prefer a 'bad' woman as they're more fun. If I'm honest, Kathy would easily fit both those descriptions…

39

On Thursday, the delivery truck arrived with my furniture. I heard the familiar bleep-bleep of a vehicle reversing as I was working in the front room. It was almost certainly for me as nobody else ever seemed to have large deliveries in the village, apart from Colin and Brian, and the Marshall's Brewery lorry always came on a Monday morning. I stepped outside to watch the driver reverse and spotted Barry watching also, no doubt expecting more palm trees, or maybe a Californian redwood or something equally exotic. He smiled and nodded a 'good morning'. I waved in return... Feeling almost sorry to disappoint my neighbour, I helped the driver unload the delivery, leaving one of the benches in the front garden.

Almost as an after-thought, I'd decided to remove four or five of the plants nearest the palm, and put one of the benches under the palm tree. There had been several reasons for this decision: I could work on my laptop and enjoy the weather on a good day. Tourists almost expected a little old man sitting outside a Cornish cottage by the sea, possibly smoking a pipe... It added to the character. OK, so I'm not little, I don't consider myself old and I don't smoke a pipe, but I was the best they had as a suitable alternative. I just hoped none of the tourists expected me to open up my windows and start selling pasties...

Most importantly, from that position, with my back to the sea, I could openly keep an eye on all the comings and goings of my neighbours, drinkers in both pubs and with a slight tilt of the head, even those going in and out of the mini-market. I realise that sounds reminiscent of the 'little old lady peeping through curtains', and maybe it was, but at least I was being open about it and one way or another, I was determined to discover if any of my suspicions had foundations...

Later that same day, at least one of my reasons for positioning the bench where I had, proved effective. As the mid-day sun grew stronger, several people arrived in the bay to enjoy a picnic lunch on the beach, and quite a few more chose the traditional Ploughman's and took a seat outside our two hostelries. I counted more than a dozen people offering me a 'good afternoon' or 'pleasant day' greeting. Maybe I wasn't the little old man they had hoped for, but swap the pipe for a JPS SuperKing and they had their little piece of West Country tradition. I found myself half expecting one of them to produce a camera. Thankfully, none of them did... I soon came to realise that the elderly—and at sixty I had to accept the fact that I was no longer a young man, or even middle aged—were able to be 'nosey' without causing offence.

Had I been a teenager, sitting in my garden, smoking a cigarette and enjoying the odd can of lager, I would be looked down upon, or thought a layabout, a hooligan, and 'why doesn't he get off his lazy arse and to an honest day's work?' Even in my forties I would probably have been accused of scrounging off the state, sitting there with my laptop 'probably on that new-fangled on-line betting, lazy bugger'. But no such problem when you hit sixty and your hair's going a little grey at the temples... So, there I sat, accepting the occasional word from the visitors, acting like a local, or more to the point acting like the visitors to the bay probably *expected* a local to be. This is no slant upon the lovely people of Cornwall.

Basically, with one or two exceptions, we are all the same in our outlook and expectations of different parts of the United Kingdom and indeed the world. If I go to Paris, I expect to hear accordions. If I visit Edinburgh, I want to see kilts and bagpipes. Consequently, when people travel to the West Country, they want cider, pasties and Wurzel look-alikes. We call it tradition and every country has it in abundance. I like to think we are all proud of our roots. I smiled inwardly, wondering where I could obtain a length of straw to chew on for extra effect... And it was not just the passers-by who noticed me. Barry popped down for a chat about nothing in particular, but couldn't resist a quick look at 'that' tree. He showed no obvious sign, but I secretly hoped he'd been more than a little disappointed to notice its healthy look. Sarah asked if I fancied a coffee. I accepted.

Two minutes later, she arrived with two hot steaming mugs and sat down next to me for an hour or so, mainly discussing donkeys and asking how Kathy was. Even Colin came across from the pub a little later, armed with a couple of bottles of beer. I believe it was that day that I finally accepted that I was a true resident of St Matilda's Bay. The locals had actually started coming to me, rather than the other way around. In between the odd e-mail—yes, I was still working—we enjoyed a very pleasant half an hour in the warm sunshine. "Rumour has it," Colin advised me, "that the fire was started by a cigarette end dropped on the sofa." I hoped his source wasn't the star reporter for the local Pigeon. He also let me know the Cockney's were back next week. Was it really six weeks ago they were last in the Mariners? After the previous music night, when I was talked into singing with the Night Crawlers, he thought Kathy might enjoy it 'her being from London like'.

I said I'd mention it to her, without actually admitting she had already arranged to come down that week-end. It seemed she was having quite an effect on the village, and not just on me. Even Minnie asked to be kept up to date on her next visit, although I think that was more because she found Kathy an easier chess challenge than I was. The twelve-year-old had already beaten her twice, though yet to score a victory over the master…

I hadn't expected anything to strike me as 'odd' quite so soon, but on the Saturday morning, I noticed two things that, although only vaguely connected, made me pat myself on the back for thinking of placing the bench where I had. My little old man act was beginning to pay dividends.

In my life, there have only been three instances that I can recall, when I deemed it necessary to wear a suit. Job interviews, weddings and funerals. For that reason, I have only ever owned two suits. The first one, boring dark grey, saw me through about sixteen job interviews, though I never had a single job that required me to wear one after I was offered the position. The second suit was a much smarter and far more expensive one, though sadly out of date now, in dark blue which I managed to wear to seven weddings and one funeral. All of the above I do my very best to avoid like the plague… Thankfully, due to long term employment in the same company, I haven't had the need for an interview for nearly forty years.

I'm not even sure I could handle one these days. I understand there are often three or more people conducting the same interview now. I believe you sometimes have to face a manager, a supervisor and a representative from Human Resources, all firing questions at you. Human Resources? That could only come from the USA, presumably imported along with down-sizing and growth potential. What ever happened to Personnel, the department that you would go to whenever you had a problem or a grievance regarding management? Human Resources tend to be on the side of management to my mind. That, I'm told is progress. I remember, back in the nineteen-eighties, some bright spark on Tomorrow's World telling us that in twenty years' time, computers would be able to do the work of ten men. What they didn't tell you was what would happen to those ten men, or indeed women who no longer had the capability of earning a living… Weddings?

Meaning no disrespect to the people concerned, most of whom I love dearly, I have always tried to tactfully turn down the invitations. All of my close friends tend to know my thoughts on marriage and religion so more often than not, I tend to receive 'Evening Reception Only' invites from them. That way I can swerve past the church and head straight to the hotel or club and keep the dreaded suit tucked away in moth balls until the next time. As for funerals, I have only ever been to one, my mother's.

After the mess they made of that, I swore that unless the unthinkable happened and my off-spring went before me, the next funeral I attended would be my own… In short, my mother had the same thoughts as I had on religion, and made it perfectly clear she was to be cremated in the shortest ceremony possible, with no hymns and specifically 'not a single mention of God'. Ten minutes into the 'service', a man in a dark grey suit, not unlike my own interview one, began, "We are here today to celebrate the life of Violet May Evans…etc."

This was fine so far. All of our friends and family knew my mother's thoughts and her attitude to life in general. In short, we just wanted to get it over with and head for the pub as arranged, and in accordance with her wishes. But then he ruined it. He ruined my last moments with my mother… Despite numerous letters of apology for the misunderstanding, none of which I ever accepted, and the offer of handling the entire funeral proceedings at no charge, which I *did* accept, to this day I have never forgiven that man for uttering the words, "We are all children of God…"

Along with many others in the crematorium that day, I walked out of there and never looked back. I would dearly love to return there some day but I simply cannot do it. Our family understood and accepted my decision. One of my cousins returned to collect the urn later in the week and we scattered her ashes on Brighton beach, near Black Rock, now the marina… I have kept my word and not been to another funeral service since, although I did support Ellie, from outside that same crematorium, when she lost her beloved Gramps.

The dark blue suit still hung at the back of my wardrobe in Smallfield when I left there last year. I imagine it to be hanging on a rail in a one of nearby

Horley's many charity shops by now… One thing I have never done, and don't believe I ever would, is wear a suit to the beach. But one man does.

40

That Saturday, the first Saturday in July, I'd had a busy start to my working day. It seemed that every Brannigan's helicopter was having difficulties of one sort or another. Due to the vast majority of our aircraft being American, there was very little I could achieve until around lunch-time when our cousins across the pond woke up. Even then there was always the possibility that I would get little response over a week-end. Therefore, I spent the first hour of the day sending out e-mails for stock availability, quotes, etc., then sat back to wait for the answers I knew would not come for several hours. That was the time to resume one of my favourite hobbies, people watching. I'm sure I'm not alone in that. I just love watching the world go by and in particular, its occupants... I took up my new favourite spot on the bench in my front garden. That's when I spotted him, the man in the suit.

Often, in the past, I've sat on the sea front at Brighton, or in the park near my old home in Surrey, and watched. Watched the people passing by. Trying to work out where they were from, what they did for a living, where they came from, if they were married, how much they earned... Sometimes I would discretely follow one of them to see if he, or she, went to the shop or pub or market. If it was the pub, I would try to guess what drink they would order and if they would ask for the menu or just buy a bag of Pork Scratchings to keep them going until they returned home to the 'wife and kids'.

It was fascinating and I know I'm not alone in this hobby, which I readily admit can sometimes border on obsessive. But this man... This man in the dark, almost black suit, reasonably new, clearly expensive and almost certainly Italian... He did not belong in St Matilda's Bay. Definitely not in that trilby! Who wore a trilby these days? And the sunglasses? OK, so he was on the beach in July, but it was cloudy. Who did he think he was? He looked to me like an extra from the Blues Brothers movie set. He stood there on one of the rocks, the rocks that had been tossed like marbles to the under-cliff just over a year ago.

He was slowly working his way through a cigarette, surveying all around him, as if he owned it. Maybe in a way he did. Maybe he was from the council planning department, working out new ways to bring revenue into the area. A picnic area maybe, or an ice cream parlour right there on the sand. I couldn't imagine the elusive Connie being overly enamoured at the competition... Or possibly he was from the brewery, waiting for a quiet moment in the day, a chance to speak to Colin or Brian, or both. But if that was indeed the case, why come on a Saturday in the height of the summer season?

Neither Brian nor Colin was likely to have a 'quiet moment' for at least another eight or nine hours. It was now ten forty-five and by mutual agreement, both The Beachcomber and the Mariners Arms opened their doors at eleven. To me, this man in the dark suit did not look genuine. Not real. More like a parody. Like he thought he was Al Capone or something. I imagined a machine gun inside that briefcase he was carrying. I really should learn to control that imagination of mine. Does anybody still carry a brief case in these days of laptops? Had I been able to see them, I would have deduced his eyes settling on our little row of cottages. Surely not a property developer.

If he had been, I could have told him he was wasting his time. No, amount of money was going to tempt me into dragging Tilda's kicking and screaming into the twenty-first century! I believe my thoughts spoke for the others also... One thing I was sure of. With no church in the village, he certainly wasn't here for a wedding or a funeral. I strongly suspected he wasn't looking for a job either. Despite the warm climate, the man looked quite at home, very comfortable in his expensive almost black designer suit. I think I must have appeared to be staring because just at that precise moment, he raised his hat to me and gave an almost unnoticeable little bow. He smiled as I nodded back to him.

Something told me that behind the sunglasses, his eyes weren't smiling... On the stroke of eleven—you could set your clocks by those two—both landlords threw open the doors of the bay's two public houses. It was going to be another busy one for them. The sun may not yet have been shining, but that never stopped us 'Brits' from heading to the coast on a week-end in July... Immediately following an extremely over-weight couple—they looked American—the subject of my morning's interest was the third person to enter The Beachcomber... I continued my people watching for a further hour or so.

Nothing much to report though, just the usual stream of couples and families intent on enjoying the relaxed atmosphere of the bay, with its quiet spots under the cliffs, its little rock pools to the Northern side, ideal for crabbing... Little ones paddling in the shallow waters, mums and dads lazing on the sand, reading, drinking, smoking... Once again, I felt the warm glow of belonging. I had been there little over a year and already it felt like home.

Lunch-time came and went. My American suppliers had come up trumps and promised shipping details later that evening. Mr Suit, I assumed, was still in the pub. Sarah chatted briefly about nothing in particular as she strolled over to Connie's for supplies. She was a stunning looking young woman. Dressed in floral print flared summer dress, stopping just above the knee, she could easily pass for ten years younger than her (around) forty years... "Hi Sarah, Adam OK?" I called out.

I hadn't seen him since that day Kathy and I had spotted him chatting to the other men in the village... "He's fine thanks," came the reply as she carried on her merry way... Both pubs were now busy, car parks full, customers spilling out onto the lane, a few drinks being taken down to the beach, plastic glasses for the use of. I caught the odd glimpse of Lala and Rara rushing in and out of the Mariners, delivering meals, collecting glasses, always with a cheery smile. I wondered how Brian and Pat coped with no Rachel until the evening shift.

I supposed the bank balance made it all worthwhile. Judging by the big grin on Colin's face, I imagined *his* accounts were none too shabby either. Not for me though, that life. I'd had a brief spell running a bar in Redhill—it later became a Mongolian restaurant where you chose your raw ingredients then cooked the meal yourself. That lasted about two years. The site where the Prince Albert once stood was now the afore-mentioned fast food joint, MacDonald's. Those two weeks were enough to convince me never to go into the pub game. Up at six to do the pipes. Topping up the shelves.

Preparing the lunch-time menu. Rushed off your feet for twelve hours and into bed about one in the morning if you were lucky! Definitely not for me... Colin waved across the road as he delivered two plates loaded with ham, egg and chips to a couple sitting at one of the benches. No, visit today then, I thought. No, free bottle of beer and a chat. The outside of his bar was positively heaving. You could barely see the sandwich board telling all and sundry that the Cockney Wurzels were returning next Saturday 'By Popular Demand'. I had not yet mentioned that night to Kathy, but I knew it would be right up her street...

"Paul," the smiling voice greeted me. "Are you free tomorrow afternoon for a couple of hours old son?" It was Tom. He had brought Minnie with him and with no hesitation what-so-ever, she had sat herself down next to me, big silly grin from ear to ear. I couldn't help noticing how much she had grown over the past year. No, longer the silly little girl sitting on the floor of her grand-parents cottage playing with Barbie, or whatever the current flavour of the month was. Only last week, she had been within a second of beating me at chess.

Any day now… But it wasn't just her mind that was growing. It occurred to me how much she must be missing her mother right now, at that time in her life. Some very obvious swellings were starting to show through her yellow cotton t-shirt. I wondered how Tom and Alice were coping with her approaching woman-hood. No, doubt the teasing had already started at school. Tom, having grown up in the same era as myself, the nineteen-sixties and seventies, would naturally assume 'that kind of thing is women's work'.

To a vast extent, he was correct, but I wasn't convinced that Alice, whom I estimated to be just a few years younger than her husband and on the delicate side, was prepared to handle a teenager whose hormones were about to start raging, if they weren't already… Due to Minnie's fondness for me— 'Are you going to be my new daddy?'—she had taken to sitting on my lap from day one. However, over the past year, I had started to feel uncomfortable about that and slowly weaned her off of the habit. It hadn't been easy but I had managed to convince her that while I still adored my little Minnie, she wasn't a child any more.

Cuddles were fine, and we both loved our hugs, but she was *much* too much of a young woman to be sitting on my lap. She seemed to accept this, albeit reluctantly, and it hadn't affected our surrogate parent/daughter relationship in the slightest. I hoped I wasn't sticking my nose in where it didn't belong, but I made a mental note to have a quiet word with Kathy on the subject when she came down the following Friday…

"Nothing planned at the moment Tom… Why?" The three of us ambled down to the beach. Tom and I found a rock to lean on while Minnie slipped her shoes off and ventured down to the water's edge. She still wouldn't go to the beach on her own. It always had to be with Tom or I, although I did manage to talk her into going down with Cheryl once, on the condition I stood in the garden and watched them. I can quite understand it. As a full-grown man of twenty-six, I never once returned to my mother's bedroom after I found her lying there one cold December morning, staring at the ceiling.

I was living in that flat a further six months before moving to my new home in Redhill, but still would not go back in that room. My girl-friend at the time had to assist the removal men when the time came. No, doubt it was even worse for Minnie. My own mother had died peacefully in her sleep. Hers had been crushed against the cliff face and/or drowned—it never had been determined which had killed Maria—while Minnie herself had come perilously close to having her own life ended by that particular 'Act of God'.

Tom went on to explain that Alice's sister, now well into her seventies and being cared for in a nursing home in Exeter, had fallen into an even deeper decline. It was now thought she would not see another Christmas. For various personal reasons that Tom had no desire to discuss, his sister-in-law and Minnie had never met. Due to her current state of health, he didn't consider now a good time to rectify that. His grand-daughter had suffered quite enough the past year or so that the last thing she needed was to suddenly be introduced to a new member of the family, only to lose them six months later. I agreed, and readily offered to take care of Minnie 'tomorrow afternoon' for as long as they needed me to…

As we sat there, waving to a very happy little girl each time she turned to face us, I smoked a cigarette and out of the corner of my eye, watched Mr Suit come out of The Beachcomber and walk the few yards to Connie's, then on again to the Mariners and round the back into the car park. No, doubt he'd parked there earlier when the bay was not flooded with sun-worshippers. I thought no more about it. Minutes later, the phone rang…

"Hey sexy bum!" I knew the voice immediately. "Debbie's just been on the phone. She said sorry for not letting us know before, but she's perfectly alright. Her phone died last week and she hadn't taken her charger with her so she called the only number she knew down here from a public phone box. Apparently, Sarah's number is almost identical to hers but ending 8181." I supposed that was easy enough to remember. I always find my bank card number easy because the four digits are a line from one of my favourite songs.

However, I didn't see why 8181 was any easier to remember than anybody else's she may have. Kathy explained, "It's her birthday silly! January the 8th, 1981." Now it made sense. Anyway, the upshot was that Debbie had had to run off in the middle of the night to help out an old friend, but 'not to worry, she knows all about my ex and why I'm in Tilda's. I'll be back in a week or two'. This surprised me as she herself had told me quite explicitly that her father was the only person who knew the truth of her being here. Kathy reluctantly agreed it was odd. She then suggested I had a word with the fire service to see if we could get into Debbie's cottage and clean it up a bit before she came home.

I agreed to try, though I hadn't a clue where to start asking! Either way, it seemed like a better option than the only other one available to the poor girl... Staying in my spare room, or the pub and I said as much. I confess I rather enjoyed Kathy's response to that one, "The pub it is, then." Was that a mildly jealous tone to her voice? At that point I had to cut her short. I had spotted a couple of e-mails coming through that required my immediate attention. I made my apologies to both Kathy and Tom, gave one last shout and wave to Minnie and went back inside to re-start the laptop. Work was calling me. If nothing else, it stopped me questioning Debbie's phone calls and the mysterious friend who seemed to know as much about her secret life as we did, never before mentioned...

40

"How can we be sure that was Martin?"

"We can't guv, but they both vanished at the same time so it's gotta be a fair bet, hasn't it?"

"Possibly, but I need to be absolutely fucking certain, OK? If Martin's still around come September, we're all in the shit!"

"I know guv, but we can't just… Well… You know…" Smithy was getting anxious. This whole business was going way too far for his liking.

"D'you have any better ideas then, smart-arse?"

"No, but…"

"Then get it sorted, or I will."

41

Sunday morning was a busy one, but that suited me. I find the time flies by when I'm hard at it. Plus, I still get a huge buzz out of what I do for the aviation world. There is nothing quite like that rush you get when something you, and only you have planned, purchased, shipped and had fitted in the minimum amount of time. My opposite number in Norwich, Dave Fincham, the man who looks after my work when I'm off duty feels exactly the same way. We've both been doing it for more than twenty-five years and it still feels just as good as the day we started. We also believe we're a special breed in our field. Not that we're better than anyone else in the company, just better at what we do.

We've seen four or five other members of staff try it for a few days, even management, and they simply cannot hack it... Consequently, when I heard the knock at the door, I had no idea it had turned two o'clock already. Where did *those* seven hours go? I was reasonably sure it would be Minnie and Tom. The sight of a flat cap the other side of my brand-new frosted glass window pane confirmed this... "Stay right there," I commanded as I opened the door to them.

Two minutes later, I returned with a coffee and an orange juice, put the door on the latch and escorted Minnie to the bench, where we sat and drank and watched until we saw Alice and Tom climb into their car and disappear round the bend at the end of the lane, en route to Exeter... As soon as they'd gone, Minnie asked if we could go round the back. "I don't like the way everybody looks at us sitting here," she moaned. "I don't mean that in a nasty way, I mean they're all very nice and they smile and everything, but I just don't like it, sorry."

I told her she had nothing to apologise for and agreed it would be a good idea, as I'd just remembered my new acquisitions, which I didn't believe she was aware of. Given the choice, I admit I would have preferred to stay on the front bench and keep a watchful eye on the village, but I saw little enough of Minnie as it was and felt it unfair to deny her of this opportunity. As soon as we reached the back of the cottage, as calm as you like, she marched over to the climbing frame and off she went up one of the rope ladders. Unlike those in public playgrounds, I had none of that safety padding they are all bound by law to lay these days.

All I could offer was a patch of that treated wood bark that seems so popular in gardens lately. Personally, I cannot abide the stuff, but it was the nearest I could get to the real thing and figured it was better than nothing at all. In any case, the only people likely to use my miniature assault course were two twelve, nearly thirteen-year-old, fairly sensible girls. Never-the-less, for her first time I stood nearby and watched as performed manoeuvres of near gymnastic proportions, notably that thing almost exclusively reserved for girls of a certain age, whereby they hang upside down on a cross beam by the crook of their knees... As I stood there keeping a close eye on my charge, I noticed a 'suit' in Debbie's back garden, two doors down. Not the Mr Suit in the trilby, but a different 'suit', this one in a bright yellow hard hat. I rightly assumed he was some kind of fire safety inspector and decided 'now was as good a time as any' to carry out Kathy's suggestion.

"Excuse me," I called across. He turned to face me and removed his hat. "I'm a friend of the lady who lives there. I just wondered when we'd be able to get inside and start a clean-up campaign." It seemed the damage was superficial and no structural repairs were required, but it was a bit of a 'bloody mess' to put it politely... The official safety certificate would be sent to the landlord in the morning. "So, with the landlord's permission, I take it there wouldn't be a problem if me and some of the neighbours went in with a scrubbing brush or two?" It seemed not.

The very nice man in the slightly dusty suit and shiny yellow hat was even kind enough to give me a number to call so that I could clear the way with the landlord. I felt certain he wouldn't object to someone improving his property, no doubt saving him valuable time and expense. Therefore, if I had a few quiet moments on Monday, I would set about calling him and hopefully get the go-ahead. Surely it couldn't be that difficult... I returned to my chat with Minnie, who was by now making what appeared to be a risky move from the top of the climbing frame to one of the lower branches of the tree. I was tempted to offer a warning, then remembered how *I* felt when 'grown-ups' advised me not to do this, or not to try that... We all learn from our mistakes, and let's face it, Minnie was hardly going to break her neck falling four feet onto a pile of wood shavings, was she? I let it go.

The rest of the afternoon passed quietly enough. We had two games of chess, both of which I won, but only just, a walk along the beach, both paddling for a few minutes, and an ice cream each. The Blackberry had behaved itself as per normal. Even though I was on call from lunch until bed time, nothing much ever happened on a Sunday afternoon. I was expecting nothing at all until the shipping details came through at the end of the American day, about ten o'clock Cornish time. Before we knew it, it was nearly six and we were back on the front garden seat, watching the day-trippers making their weary way home... Mums yelling at the little ones. Dads wishing they could have 'just one pint' before the long journey home, along with thousands of other drivers.

It was never going to happen, it rarely did. Mums always seem to rule the family roost. Minnie spotted her grand-father's car pulling into the car park. She and Alice shared waves. "Can I go and meet them?" She asked. I saw no reason why she shouldn't and watched her carefully looking left, then right, then left again before crossing the lane, even though on a Sunday, vehicles rarely came this far down and certainly nothing would be approaching from the left. Too many pedestrians and no parking spaces. It was still good to see it though, when you consider the way some youngsters behave on the roads.

I imagined a lot of that was from her grand-parent's methods of education. Being of a similar age, I know for a fact as a child, I would never have run out into a road without looking, or try to jump the level-crossing gates before a speeding train shot through, or any of the other crazy ways children and teenagers seem Hell-bent on ending their lives with nowadays. Are their lives really that cheap to them? Do they ever consider the people, parents and friends, they may well leave behind following these unbelievable games of 'chicken'? I sometimes doubt it.

"I suppose you two have been sat here in the sun all afternoon," Tom greeted me as the two of them came across the lane. I replied in the negative, confirming that rather than waste the afternoon, Minnie and I had flown across to the Scilly Isles and swam with the dolphins. This seemed to tickle the young girl who went into fits of giggles. They wandered off, still laughing, to help Alice home from the car park, while I sat back down to enjoy my first cigarette in three hours. Deep joy... I planned to have a relaxing Sunday evening, hopefully with no interruptions from work, air-way bills excepted, neighbours or anybody.

I would, of course, welcome a call from Kathy but that was unlikely before about ten o'clock, her normal time… I had much to think about and up until now, not a lot of time for my own thoughts. Too busy with other things, but this evening would be 'me' time. I decided on a bath.

I've always loved a good hot steaming Radox bath. The water so hot you can barely put your toes in it, let alone anything else. I adore that feeling of crouching in the water, hands gripping the sides, then gradually, ever so slowly lowering myself into the bubbles until I'm totally submerged. I will then lay there, often for an hour or more, usually in darkness, but sometimes with just the dim glow of scented candles and enjoy happy thoughts. Thanks mainly to people like Minnie, Kathy and my family, most of my thoughts those summer days were happy ones. True, I had my dark moments, and with all that was going on around me, who wouldn't? But on the whole, life was pretty damn good right then…

42

Having completed my Brannigan's hand-over to my 'partner in crime' once again, I had my Tuesday afternoon all planned out. I've always been fascinated by things that go on all around me, even if they don't entirely affect me and the way I conduct my daily life. I've often wondered how many cats have shuffled off their mortal coil due to my curiosity. As a child I used to love watching how my mother cooked. So, much so that by the age of nine I was more than capable of cooking a Sunday roast for four people. As I entered my teens, I would watch a neighbour of mine constantly stripping down and repairing his beloved Suzuki 500cc motorcycle.

By the time I hit fifteen, I could do the same, and without the famous 'bit left over' that had many people scratching their heads in wonder, especially when constructing flat-pack cupboards and wardrobes from the now defunct MFI. I just had to know how things worked, or what was going on around me... It was precisely for that reason that I decided I wouldn't wait until Kathy arrived on Friday. I wanted to know 'right now' the extent of the fire damage. Apart from anything else, as much as I liked Debbie and was happy to help in the clean-up campaign, I was also hoping that Kathy and I would have time to do our own thing at the week-end as well.

We saw little enough of each other as it was. Erik, my builder friend had kindly offered to help with any structural work required and was also due sometime soon, so it would be good if I had some idea what he had let himself in for. Although not officially approved as yet, I was sure the landlord would be happy for him to carry out any necessary work when the time came. He was good at his job, and he was cheap. I could not see any landlord turning down the opportunity to save a few pounds. I devised a cunning plan.

Due to my afore-mentioned curiosity, I was well aware that Debbie, along with many other people, had a spare key hidden in her back garden. I have to say it was more cleverly hidden than most though. Not to be found under a flower-pot or on top of the door frame, but under the top flap of a squirrel feeder box attached to a tree near the bottom of her garden. I had inadvertently spotted her using it one afternoon some weeks earlier... My cunning plan included borrowing Barry's lawn mower as I was yet to have one of my own, and being the kindly neighbour that I was, pop round to trim Debbie's grass.

He'd been good enough to let me use it when my two tiny front lawns needed a trim. Should I be spotted by Sarah or Tom, it would appear the most natural thing for me to be doing, especially as I was the only person she seemed to be fairly close to in the bay. Plus, several people knew I had a soft spot for her... After about half an hour of mowing, and confident nobody could spot me, I removed the key from its hiding place and slipped it into my pocket. Sometime later, equally certain I wasn't being over-looked, I slipped the key into the lock and entered by the rear door. I slipped the key into that funny little receptacle that all jeans seem to have just above the right-hand pocket.

I had always wondered what the point of it was. After all, how many people carry just one key? It was normally a bunch, or at the very least two or three and they would surely not fit. Then a few years ago I suddenly recognised its value. Very handy when you're flying off to the sun. Then of course, you don't need the car key, or the shed key, the back door key, the office key, the filing cab... Well, you understand what I'm saying. All you need is your front door key, so it's the perfect place to keep it.

Anywhere else, it could easily slip out, but it doesn't seem to matter where you go or what you do, for that matter how drunk you were before you ripped them off and threw them in the corner, there it would be, safe and sound as always... Despite Debbie's cottage looking like a bomb had been dropped on it, it was actually nowhere near as bad as I was expecting. I could easily understand why the fire investigation team had agreed there was no structural damage. As a rank amateur, I estimated most of the work would be purely cosmetic, requiring little more than a good scrubbing and a lick of paint here and there.

The cottage was far from falling apart at the seams, just in need of some TLC. To put it bluntly, or in the words of Kevin Bloody Wilson: The joint's a fuckin' mess! In truth, the kitchen had been barely troubled by the fire. A fairly recent extension to the rear of the house, with its quarry stone tiled floor and solid oak door blocking the way to the hall, the only signs I could see were smoke damage rather than that of the flames. A good hour or two with a bottle of Cif and it would look like new again. The same could be said of the dining room and the spare bedroom upstairs. Also, the bathroom and lavatory. Debbie had obviously been meticulous about keeping doors closed. All the rooms to the rear of the house would only require a good helping of 'elbow grease' to restore them to their former glory. Smoke, like spilt milk, finds every little nook and cranny to creep through.

Keyholes and minute cracks under the doors had allowed it to spread. Virtually everything was covered in a dark grey dust... Sadly, it was a completely different story in the front rooms. Virtually all furniture, carpets and curtains had been reduced to ashes, notably the living room sofa, the suspected starting place for the fire. As an aside, I sincerely hoped our friend Debbie had kept her contents insurance up to date. Being a rented property, I was unsure how much of the 'property' was actually hers, rather than that of the landlord. Either way, it looked to my untrained eye that the cost of replacing everything would probably be into five figures... The front bedroom was pretty much the same. I had to assume the firemen rather than the occupier had closed all the doors. How else could the fire have spread up the stairs to the first floor, and even into the attic without any serious damage to the floor and ceiling joists?

No, doubt, the official fire service report would explain everything in time. I decided the kitchen was as good a place as any to start. If Debbie was anything like me, the first thing she would want upon her return would be a bite to eat and a cuppa. I suspected a cigarette would *not* be at the top of the list... Yes, I would get to work on the kitchen. Then when Kathy arrived, maybe we could try to do something with the main bedroom. I was not keen on the idea of her sleeping in my spare room, especially if the girls started on the vodka again...

Armed with my bottle of Cif, I began to clean the oven and hob. Remarkably, the smoke hadn't managed to penetrate the interior which was a bonus. I hate oven cleaning at the best of times, but at least this was all for a good cause. As opposed to mine, Debbie's kitchen had only one central light, which must have made cooking and washing up a nightmare. With just a very small window—typical of eighteenth and nineteenth century cottages— practically everywhere you stood, you were working in your own shadow. No, doubt this was why so many modern kitchen units come complete with additional fitted lights either inside the cupboards or underneath. I was about to turn on the light when I noticed there was a double switch. Maybe I was wrong.

Perhaps, somewhere along the way, the current owner or a previous one had added concealed lighting under the eye-level cupboards, a popular accessory in the late twentieth century as described above, or maybe it was for an exterior light outside the back door... I turned on both switches. As I did so, the central strip light above me crackled and flashed its way into life, and at the same time, an approximately two-foot square section of the floor opened up in the middle of the kitchen. How curious. I looked down into the darkness. There was a ladder leading down to what I assumed was a cellar. Maybe Debbie had a secret stash of wine down there, I thought. Nothing surprised me about that young lady any more. Just as I was about to explore further, my *own* lights went out!

43

Déjà vu were the words that first sprung to mind. As I woke up, all manner of strange things ran through my brain. I've had several uncanny experiences in my lifetime. In particular the first time I visited Jo's parent's house in Redhill. When asked to retrieve a bottle of Lemon Barley Water from the larder—yes, some people do still have larders—the first thing I spied was the orange lino— and yes, some people also still have linoleum! It was identical to not only the remains of a former floor covering in my own airing cupboard in Smallfield, but also the exact same pattern and colour as I recalled from my grand-mother's house forty years earlier. But probably the most peculiar instance I can recount, would be the very first time my mother took me to the Isle of Wight.

It was in 1962 and I had just hit the ripe old age of eleven. It was my first ever trip 'overseas'. At least it felt like it when we boarded the ferry to take us to what seemed to me like another land. All our previous summer holidays had been spent either with my Great Aunt May in Brighton—hardly a holiday as I already spent much of my time there—or in a boarding house overlooking Dreamland Pleasure Park in Margate. I think at the time, the ferry was possibly the most exciting experience of my life. I can still recall standing at the rear of the boat, the stern, watching the harbour at Portsmouth growing smaller and smaller… Then rushing to the front to see Ryde coming ever closer.

In my own mind, I was the captain of the ship, guiding it safely through shark-infested waters to a foreign land full of exotic animals and strange people who spoke another language to that of my own people. As we walked along the pier, one of the longest I'd ever been on—it even had its own railway station at the pier head—we both realised how hungry we were. Neither of us had eaten since a really early breakfast at six-thirty. It was now nearly one o'clock. Although we had accommodation booked in the town, it was only a bed and breakfast style boarding house, so lunch or evening meal was not included.

I watched a train leave the pier, take a left turn and vanish into a tunnel under the promenade. A tunnel leading to who knew where. As we exited the pier and headed into town, I suddenly turned to my mother and said, "There's a café just up that hill then turn left mum." She gave me the strangest look ever and I had to admit I had no idea where that had come from. This town was all new to me. At the time we had not yet acquired our first television set. That was to come four years later, in time for England's one and only successful World Cup campaign... So, I hadn't seen Ryde on the television.

Films tended to be more about America, or if set in England, usually centred around London, so it hadn't been there... Never-the-less, out of that famous curiosity of mine, I convinced her we should walk up the hill and turn left. Which we did. And there in all its glory stood a café. I'm not going to pretend it looked just how I imagined it to be, but it was still a café all the same. To this day I have no idea what that was all about, but it happened...

As I woke up to this feeling of déjà vu, I looked around me and saw the familiar windows, the same cream curtains, the same green and cream two-tone walls... Only the nurse had changed. Oh, and the visitor by my bedside. Kathy had replaced Ellie in that respect. The look of relief on her face was a joy to behold. But the joy was short lived. As I reached out for her, I realised just why I was back in a hospital bed once more. Not the same room as after the flood, but clearly the same hospital. My head, neck, shoulders, in fact everything above chest level hurt like Hell...

"What...?" Kathy called the nurse who immediately checked the collar that was holding my neck still and straight. Then passed me two pain-killers and a glass of water. Apparently, she was not surprised I was in agony after what happened, but 'the doctor saw no need to give you anything for the pain until you regained consciousness'. At the sight of my confused look, Kathy explained...

"The doctors think you were knocked out when the light fitting fell on your head. Luckily, Sarah found you and called the ambulance..." She reached out and squeezed my hand. I still didn't understand. The light fitting looked fine to me, and why would Sarah be in Debbie's cottage? "I'm only glad I thought to call her. I was so worried when you didn't answer your phone. I'd been calling all day. Then the next morning..."

"What?" I was stunned, in more ways than one... "What do you mean 'the next morning?' How long have I been here? What day is it?"

"It's Friday babes. You've been in here since Wednesday morning!" Kathy gave me hand another reassuring squeeze… Something about this wasn't right. Was she saying I'd been unconscious for what… More than forty-eight hours? Was that physically possible? Can a person really live that long in a comatose state without medical attention? I assumed the doctors had kept a close eye on me, but even so… I remembered going round to Debbie's after lunch, the pretence of cutting the lawn, finding the back door key, checking each room of the cottage, even the attic as I recalled seeing flames through the roofing tiles on the day of the fire… Something about *that* wasn't right either.

All the fire had been at the front of the house so how could it have spread upwards but not outwards, or backwards? And that light? I've never known smoke damage cause a light fitting to come crashing down. The kitchen was untouched by the fire. I should know, I was about to start cleaning it. Then I tried the switches… Two of them… The cellar…

"Kathy, was the cellar door open when you came in?" She knew nothing of a cellar as it was all over by the time she arrived. Sarah and the paramedics had been the only ones in the house that morning. "Can you do me a favour hun? No, two favours if you could please?" Her answer was in the affirmative. "Can you give Sarah a call and ask her exactly how she found me? And see if she came with me to the hospital? But before that, can you find me some food, I'm starving!"

An hour later, I'd had the collar removed. There was no damage, but because I was out cold the doctor didn't want to risk me causing any harm to it in my sleep. To all intents and purposes, I was as fit as a fiddle if you ignored the throbbing pains wracking the entire top half of my body. 'These accidents will happen," the doctor had said. "You really shouldn't go wandering around places like that on your own and without a hard hat too."

I apologised for taking up so much of his valuable time and asked why I'd been out cold for so long. "We all react differently to a bang on the head Mr Evans. I've known people get up straight off and walk away as if nothing happened. Then others have been known to take a week or more to come round. In fact, another twenty-four hours and we would have been considering a drip-feed for you." Apparently, they had been monitoring my breathing and brain activity—Kathy smiled as he said that and I knew what she was thinking—and I seemed to be coping fine on just the fluids supplied. He wagged his finger at me as if I was a naughty school boy caught scrumping apples. "As far as I can see, you've been very lucky. No, bones broken, so I see no reason why you can't go home after a few tests."

These included checking my eyesight and hearing. When he discovered both were as good as he'd expected them to be in a man of my age, I was given a release form and told I could leave any time I wished. I wished as soon as possible. I was never a fan of hospitals. I hated the smell, the food was generally either under-cooked or burnt and very little of it, plus they always served as a reminder that the short time we spend on this planet is not a rehearsal. I was not ready to meet my maker, whoever that may be, and had no intention of being so for a good many years yet. When Kathy returned with a brown bag of McDonald's take-away, I *knew* it was time to leave. To my mind, Mackie D's is only one step higher on the food ladder than that of hospitals. On the way out to the car park, she told me all she had learned from her call to Sarah.

As we perched on the wall munching on cardboard 'fries' and the only thing I find acceptable from that particular fast-food supplier, Chicken McNuggets, she told me how the phone call had gone, "According to Sarah, you must have gone into Debbie's place about three, because she saw you cutting the grass. When she could no longer see you, she didn't think to go round, just assumed you'd finished and gone back home. I phoned her about ten the next morning, because I couldn't get you on the phone. She told me what she'd seen so I asked her to go and check. She found the back door unlocked and you lying on the kitchen floor with a five-foot strip light fitting on the back of your neck.

"I'll be honest with you, Paul, she screamed when she found you—we were still on our phones—she thought you were dead! So, she knelt down to check and she could feel your pulse and see you breathing, but you weren't moving…"

"What about the cellar door? Did she say anything about that being open?"

"I asked her that like you said, but she said she didn't even know there *was* a cellar under the kitchen. But if there was, the door to it was definitely closed."

"What do you mean *if* there was?" I wasn't happy about Sarah's inference, or Kathy's way of repeating it for that matter.

"I'm sorry babes, she didn't mean anything by it I'm sure, but the doctor did say you might have some form of short-term memory loss or something. Nothing serious but it was a possibility…" I felt guilty and kissed her hand. Of course, she was right, but I knew there was a cellar door in Debbie's kitchen. It opened by the flick of the switch next to that of the strip light. And it was open the last time I looked, just before the world came crashing down on me. I was looking down into it. I saw the ladder leading down and then, Wham! "Well, the ambulance got there about ten-thirty and brought you here. That's about all we know, hun."

"It's me that should be apologising Kathy. If I hadn't been so keen to get things started, or if I'd waited for you to come, none of this would have happened. The doctor was right, I'm an idiot!" At least I was glad to get the all-clear. If I'd been warned to take it easy and not to put any strain on my neck, there was no way I would have climbed on the back of her Honda 250 for the forty-five-minute ride home to St Matilda's Bay. Don't get me wrong, she's a great driver but I'm just a lousy passenger. I'm the same I cars.

Where any form of driving is involved, I always want to be in control. As a pillion rider I still find myself wanting to brake or change gear. It drives her crazy to be honest. I also think it looks a bit daft when a six-foot man has his arms wrapped around the body of a five-foot two-inch girl, apart from... Let's not go there. But that's just me I suppose... I couldn't wait to get home and have a drink.

Determined not to appear ungrateful, as soon as we arrived in the village, I called in to thank Sarah for everything. "If it hadn't been for you..." etc. To which Sarah pointed out it was Kathy I should be thanking, not her. She only did what any other good neighbour would do, and she was pleased to see me home and looking so well after such an experience... "Well, thanks anyway Sarah, and if you're free tonight, I'd like to buy you a very large drink! We'll be in the Mariners about eight I reckon."

"I'd love to thanks, but I'd better stay by the phone just in case Adam calls..." We left it there. With a final 'thanks again', we walked back to Windy Cottage. Despite having what amounted to about sixty hours sleep, I was shattered, and it was only the middle of the afternoon. I blamed the pain killers and knew I probably shouldn't be throwing alcohol down on top of them but I really needed a drink...

44

That week-end in the middle of July was possibly one of the most alcoholic I had known since my infamous fiftieth birthday party when I fell asleep in the gents at the Crawley British Legion an hour before the party ended... As Kathy and I entered the bar, cheers went up all around. I was quite embarrassed that so many of Colin's regulars, mostly from Harwick seemed to know all about my unfortunate accident. I thanked Rachel, in my head, for spreading the word. How kind of her! It could only have been Rachel. It's what she does... Spread the gospel according to the less than saintly Rachel. Quite possibly I had suffered my injuries fighting off four or five armed burglars.

I may even be in line for the George Cross for such acts of extreme bravery! I said nothing, and accepted the pint of 'Carling Darling' that Colin placed on the bar in front of me, "On the house, mate, you deserve it. And the usual for the lady?"

I loved the way Colin assumed everyone had 'the usual'. In all the times I had partaken in alcohol in the Mariners, my 'usual' had varied between Guinness, wine, cider and lager. Even the odd large Scotch if I was in the mood. In fact, not too long ago, Kathy and I had a night on the vodka with him. So, much for my usual. Though in fairness, that time of year it was normally lager. And Kathy? Like me, her tipple varied with the mood or the weather or both. Either way, it was a bloody good night and several usuals were consumed.

As we left, earlier than normal, Lala reminded us of the live music night tomorrow. We promised to be there... As we walked back across the road, I asked Kathy if she would mind us having a quick look in Debbie's kitchen before, we turned in. "I just want to check something," I explained. "Just to make sure I'm not going senile."

She assured me I *was* going senile but would go along with it if it made me happy. She sat on the seat under my famous palm—no, it hadn't died yet, much to Barry's dismay—and smoked a cigarette as I went inside to grab the key.

Sure enough, there it was, still tucked in that marvellous little pocket of my favourite jeans. I grabbed my trusty torch from the kitchen and joined Kathy outside for a cigarette of my own. I didn't often think about it, but thanks to the smoking ban, it was only my second one of the evening. When I think back to how often we used to pop outside for one in the early days, it just goes to show how quickly we become institutionalised... Another curious thing occurred when we reached Debbie's cottage. The back door was locked again.

I found it hard to believe the ambulance staff had rummaged through my pockets, removed the key, locked the door then replaced it from whence it came. I also considered it unlikely Sarah would have a spare and hadn't she told Kathy she had found the door unlocked? I concluded someone must have called the landlord who would have rushed out to secure what was left of his property. Or maybe the locks had been changed? But no, the key still worked and we entered. The kitchen looked exactly how I'd left it three days earlier, apart from the remains of the light fitting pushed to one side. I had to check.

Opening the door leading to the hallway, I went through and turned on the light. It would not have been bright enough to work in, but it cast enough light to see what we were doing. I told Kathy to step back and flicked the second switch and the cellar door opened as before. Although it *wasn't* as before. Now there was no ladder. There wasn't even a cellar. Where the cellar had been, just three days ago, was now a wooden panel made out of floor boards. It was similar to those square pieces of decking you see in garden centres, about eighteen inches square and an inch or so thick. I crouched down to see if it moved. It did.

I lifted it up to find earth and hard-core. The cellar had been filled in. But why? What did Debbie have to hide? And if Debbie hadn't been back here, what did somebody else have to hide on her behalf? I stood back in amazement. Kathy joined me and held my arm... "It was there, I swear to you!"

Back in my own home, a large black coffee laced with Tia Maria in my hand, I reluctantly agreed that it may have been my imagination. I didn't think so, but it may have been. Half an hour later, all thoughts of cellars and ladders and neighbours were banished from my thoughts as we enjoyed each other for the first time in nearly three weeks. I can happily report my neck suffered no lasting ill effects as I lustily indulged Kathy's favourite passion... A further hour later, with her head nestling on my chest, I listened to her breathing—or purring almost—and her hand came to rest between my thighs.

I stroked her soft hair as slowly, she drifted away into the land of sleep. No, such pleasure for me though. The last time I glanced at the red digits on my bedside table, they read 04:27. As tired as I was—a combination of the hospital, the alcohol and best of all our love-making—I could not let my mind rest. It stayed on overtime for nearly three hours, with thoughts of cellars that weren't cellars, people who had other people's phone numbers and possibly keys for no apparent reason, strip lights that fall from solid ceilings, my rapidly increasing distrust of anyone and everyone I knew, bar one... I had, by now, spent the best part of three months having serious doubts about the validity of my so-called friends and neighbours. The more I thought about it... Them... The more I found myself suspecting one or more of them of God-knows-what.

I'd been down this road before, not so long ago. At that time, I'd slammed my brain into reverse gear and convinced myself I was being ridiculous, letting my imagination run away with me yet again. Now here I was, heading down that road with no reverse gear. This time I would follow that road, with or without Kathy as my passenger by my side, until I reached the end of the road. The main reason for this was the certain knowledge that as I stared down into that cellar—yes there *had* been a cellar—on Tuesday afternoon, I had heard something seconds, maybe fractions of a second before whatever hit me on the back of the head. I didn't think much of it at the time because there were always sounds.

As quiet as Tilda's may be, and it certainly was the quietest place I had ever lived, you never experience total silence. There is always something. A bird singing. A fox or badger on the prowl. The radiator pipes settling for the night. Your pet hamster waking up and running like a mad thing in that squeaky plastic wheel... Always something. Always a sound or two... I now knew as clear as day, the sound I heard wasn't a light fixing coming undone. The sound I heard, that fraction of a second before I blacked out, was footsteps... Very quiet, almost silent footsteps on quarry tiles.

The next morning, Saturday, we had a rare lie-in. We had agreed last time Kathy was down that this would be *her* week-end. Apart from the planned evening over the road watching and singing along with the Cockney Wurzels, we would do whatever the little lady wanted to do. On her last visit, I had spent so much time introducing my gorgeous friend to the locals as well as spending much of it working, that the only things we actually did together was visit the donkey sanctuary, make love and sleep. We had barely even managed a meal together as just a couple. There always seemed to be a neighbour round, or we'd be in the pub.

This time would be different. I would put all thoughts of dark deeds in the bay to the back of my mind, although I was sure they would come racing to the forefront the moment I closed my eyes. We had even agreed to abandon the idea of cleaning much of Debbie's cottage. Meaning no dis-respect to the lady, because I genuinely liked her and Kathy did too, but we didn't receive one phone call or a hospital visit throughout my indisposition. I considered that a little un-thoughtful of her and said so. Kathy agreed… So, after our customary early morning constitutional, not to mention coffee, breakfast and a cigarette each, I asked her, "So, what do you fancy doing today, my sweet?"

By lunch-time, we were in one of the many car parks that look down over the bay of St Ives. It was world famous for its scenery and artists who captured it on canvas, but even though Kathy had been to Cornwall once before as a teenager, for some reason her parents completely over-looked it. It had been her immediate answer when asked what she fancied doing. It took us nearly as long walking down to the sea front as it had driving there from home. Not that the walk is that far as the crow flies, but the lanes and alleyways that you walk down are a myriad of tiny shops and brightly painted cottages. Every turn you make introduces you to yet another stunning viewpoint… Another photo opportunity. Even from above we must have taken thirty or more photographs. From way up there, St Ives itself reminded me of a miniature village I once visited at Babbacombe, near Torquay in Devon.

To the left you could see the pretty white church. To the right you could see the railway line making its way to Lelant, the walk I'd made all those years ago. As Kathy took still more photos, what looked like a model train appeared from beyond the cliffs and pulled into the tiny station. Stunning views every which way you looked. And we'd picked the right day for the weather as well. I found myself wondering if it ever rained there. Obviously, it did, but never when I was there. I was blessed. We made our way down the winding streets, most of which were one way only as they were barely wide enough for one car let alone another passing in the opposite direction…

"Oh my God!" Kathy stopped and grabbed my arm. She could not believe her eyes. Yes, I explained, they really *do* make their own pasties and sell them through the front windows of their cottages. I had mentioned this to her some time ago, when I promised to take her there 'one day', but I don't think she really believed me. She quite naturally assumed it was just one of the many legends that surround the West Country. Like pixies—or piskies—and pirates and hundreds of shipwrecks. Finally, she was coming to realise I hadn't been making it up. It was all true.

"Even the pixies," I promised her. That one earned me a punch on the arm. I have to say I'm in two minds over Cornish Pasties. While a large part of me is saddened that the genuine pasty has now been over-taken in popularity by the Pepperoni Pasty, and the Chicken Tikka Pasty amongst others, I have to confess a love for the Steak, Ale and Leek Pasty that I'd been introduced to the last time I ventured down this way with my ex. It had been our only visit over- shadowed by atrocious weather. Until that final trip in 2009, we had always been lucky, but on this occasion, it had rained for most of the five days we were in Devon and Cornwall.

So, no drunken sand-castle building on Teignmouth beach to the cheering of the many on-lookers. No, windows wide open in bed-sit land for her under-garments to be discarded through... And for the first time ever, we actually ate in restaurants instead of our normal routine of gathering snacks and eating on the various beaches we stopped at. It was at one such restaurant that I was introduced to the Steak, Ale and Leek Pasty. Never had I tasted anything like it. We went back for more the following day; it was that good. However, I still lean towards tradition and try to keep to the real Cornish Pasties whenever possible.

A Full English Breakfast Pasty is all well and good as a novelty for the tourists down on the sea front, but for the little old ladies baking them in their kitchens, then opening up brilliant blue gloss shutters to serve the public, it has to be a traditional Cornish Pasty. We hadn't eaten since bacon and eggs three hours ago so we were ready for this. I bought two for the unbelievably low price of one pound fifty each. They were steaming as she popped them into little white grease-proof bags and wished us a happy day in St Ives and 'watch out for the pixies!' We both laughed as we strolled in the warm sunshine to find a convenient low white-washed wall to perch on and enjoy our lunch. "Oh wow!" was all she said as she swallowed her first mouthful. I agreed.

Despite my many visits to this little piece of paradise on Earth, it had been several years since I had enjoyed a real pasty. I worked for some time in Dorking—yes, that Dorking, the one with the girl in the flowing skirt—and one of its High Street shops used to proudly boast it was the Cornish Pasty

Company, claiming to sell, amongst other delicacies, genuine home-baked Cornish Pasties. Now while I'm sure they were exactly what they claimed to be, in accordance with the Trades Description Act, not only were they not freshly baked, but they tasted nowhere near as good as the one currently sliding down my throat and warming my stomach. And I was charged nearly three pounds for that privilege. Give me proper home-made any time… Oh, and as we sat there enjoying our lunch, I have to say the view was a Hell of a lot better than Dorking High Street too.

I had to warn Kathy of the sea front. "Sadly, even though it still has that pretty look about it, commercialisation moved in some time ago. In amongst the quaint shops selling hippie clothes, scented candles and dream-catchers, I'm afraid you will find pizza parlours, candy floss and souvenir shops." She understood and promised not to let it spoil the overall picture. It didn't. The cameras never stopped clicking, both of us taking care to avoid anything that didn't look like it belonged. We spent an hour or two just walking along the length of the bay, out to the church and back again.

We ambled up a few side streets where pavement artists were selling amazing canvasses of all the obvious views for two, three or five pounds each. Silly money. Kathy bought one of the Atlantic rolling in and crashing on the rocks to take home for her mum. It wasn't to my taste, but then very little to do with crashing waves was these days. It was shortly after four that we decided we had time for a pint before returning for our evening entertainment. Finding a pub that wasn't packed to the rafters with tourists wasn't easy, but we managed it.

The Badger Inn was a typically traditional pub with open plan bars and the required oak beams. It was then that I reminded the lady that we were in a holiday town, a tourist attraction… "To be honest, Paul," she said, "the whole place seems just like a theme park to me. If you ignore certain aspects, like the burger van parked over there, it's almost like showing how English summer life was a hundred years ago." I had to smile at this analogy. I had virtually the same thought when I first came to St Ives all those years ago. In parts, it really was like stepping back in time… That hadn't been what I meant when I reminded her, we were by the British coast. She soon found out why after treating us both to a pint, but still she never once complained.

Like everything else in Kathy's world, she just accepted a pint of lager was four pounds as opposed to the maximum three fifty you pay virtually anywhere inland, sat back and enjoyed it... It was nearly six by the time we made it back to my little Clio, and both of us realised just how unfit we were. For some reason, you never think about the return journey when you're walking down hill to enjoy an afternoon by the sea. Our legs were killing us!

Sensibly, we had booked a table for dinner in the Mariners for seven thirty. With an hour-long return journey, we just about had time for a quick shower and change before popping over the road. Showering together would have been the sensible time saving thing to do, but for blatantly obvious reasons, we decided against it just for once. The band weren't due to start until nine but we wanted plenty of time to eat, relax and get at least a couple of pints down our necks before they came on. We both elected to go for the traditional steak and chips—Kathy because it was her favourite meal and she never had it at home, and me because she told me I needed to keep my strength up.

I assumed that meant we might be in for a long walk on Sunday perhaps. Of course, I could have been wrong. Only time would tell... If I'd thought the last time this group appeared here was busy, it was nothing compared to this night. By eight o'clock, as Kathy and I were about half-way through our meal, the place was already heaving. Such was their popularity, that Colin had even hired extra bar staff. Rara's sister Mish—not surprisingly short for Michelle—was rushing around like a fly with a blue posterior along with the other two girls. There had to be at least seventy customers in already and it was still an hour until kick off. God knows where they all came from but the car park up by the old station must be doing a roaring trade.

Kathy said we should suggest Colin claims ten per cent commission off of the council. The general buzz of the people was getting ever louder as each tried to hold a conversation with his or her friends while others in turn spoke louder themselves in order to be heard. We gave up trying. At one point I thought she said if ever I deserted her, she would scream, but I found out later it was 'I'm so full I can't handle dessert, not even an ice cream'. Ah well... Maybe I should have suggested sending reinforcements because we were going to advance, but being only thirty-three she might not have heard of Chinese whispers...

The band were incredible that night! Even better than the first time. They played a couple of new compositions that had us all in stitches. Then a few of the old favourites, Chas and Dave in a Cornish accent. By about ten-fifteen, it was time for a break. They would be back shortly for the second half, ten-thirty until midnight... "Fucking brilliant!" Kathy said as we went out for some fresh air, then immediately polluted it with cigarette smoke. Luckily, a very friendly couple had shared our table through the first half of the show and they'd offered to hold our seats for us if we returned the favour. "I love it! Only a Cornishman would know what a Wurzel is, and only a Londoner or an Essex Girl would know about the Kursaal. And they make it rhyme in a song about dung heaps. Good shit man!"

"It's quite appropriate when you consider what a shit-hole Southend is these days eh?" I replied. One of my oldest friends, Jenna lives in Southend-On-Sea, to give it its full title. Married to an arsehole, but with a gorgeous son called Harvey, she's spent her whole life trying to get away from both him and the town. I don't think she ever will... The whole evening so far had been one long laugh, and there was still another hour and a half to go, if you included the inevitable encores. With still another ten minutes or so before they were due back on stage, we risked the wrath of our table companions and had another cigarette. Bad boys and girls. But they were fine about it. Kathy returned to the table as I went to the bar for more drinks.

This would be pint number four for both of us and we knew it would be vodka from now on. With this in mind, I asked for two pints, two large vodkas, a bottle of Coke and a Red Bull... "Plus, a tray please, hun." It had taken Lala nearly ten minutes to get to me, no favouritism there then I thought. The band were already taking up their positions on stage. "So, where's the boss, tonight? Not like Colin to miss something like this."

"He's got *things to do* apparently!" She did not look happy as she made the inverted comma sign with her fingers. "Like we haven't!" As she came back with a tray full of drinks for me. I gave her a twenty-pound note and told her to keep the change for a drink later. "Sorry, didn't mean to moan, he's great normally. He said he'll be down for the second session..." and then she was gone. I headed back to the table and put the tray down. Kathy smiled. I recognised that look she gave me. It was the 'we know each other so well' look, and I liked it. I liked it more and more each time we were together.

It always got me thinking, but now was not the time. I sat down and with a clink of glasses, we began to sink our latest pint. Better not take too long over it or the ice would melt in the vodka. A quick look at the clock told me it might be an idea to get another one in as soon as possible. At this rate you couldn't be sure when you'd next be able to grab one of the girls' attention. It was at that moment; I spotted a smiling Colin enter the bar from the rear. He gave each of the girls a friendly and apologetic cuddle. They'd be fine, they always were.

The Cockney Wurzels began their second set with one of Colin's favourite songs, the Irish classic Wild Rover. I don't think he'd ever heard anything like it in his life. Come to that, neither had we. To hear an Irish folk song sung in an East London accent and interspersed with Cornish 'ooo-ars' was a new one on all of us. In a rare quiet moment, I leaned across and asked Kathy how she thought they'd go down in her own little village. She just shook her head in disbelief at the thought of it. The next song was another of their own compositions called Nice One, Terrific, Blinding!

It was sung to the tune of Jeff Beck's classic Hi Ho Silver Lining and soon had all of us singing along to the new chorus and laughing at the strange tale of an unfortunate young man who has no luck with the ladies. For the last line of the chorus, substitute the usual lines for 'You think you've got it made, but still I can't get laid' and you'll understand why it went down so well. None of us saw the punch-line coming as the lead singer was lusting after this girl with a sexy bum in the second verse, when she turned around to face him, 'she had a fuckin' beard'.

Unbelievable. It raised the roof of the Mariners. The girls were up on the bar singing and dancing... For the final encore—it was nearly twelve thirty by then—they handed out little plastic Union Jack flags and gave several rousing choruses of Rule Britannia. It was just like being in the Royal Albert Hall, except this was a pub in Cornwall and I'd never heard the chorus sung in quite the way they performed it. It bordered on the racist, but in a fun way that nobody in England would take offence to. I'm fairly sure the line that follows Rule Britannia, Britannia rules the waves isn't normally 'Brit girls are better than the French coz French girls never shave'. What a wild night!

Kathy had the time of her life. We took our drinks outside for a final cigarette of the evening, or should that be the first one of the new day? The music was still ringing in our ears, but what a feeling. I don't care how famous a band is or how large the venue, you can't beat the atmosphere of a really good, no *great* live gig! The two of us were high on more than just the vodka. Loud music has that effect on both of us. It would be a long time before we slept that night. It had always been the same back in my karaoke days. Many a time after a really good show in The Castle or The Causeway, I would sit up drinking coffee and smoking cigarettes until the sun came up. I know karaoke is pretty low down the musical family tree but I still got a tremendous buzz from putting on a good show. And hey, if karaoke is good enough for Michael Buble on Ant and Dec's Saturday Night Takeaway, it's good enough for me!

As we strolled back home shortly after one, most of the village was in darkness. The Beachcomber had closed more than an hour ago. Lights were out in the Bonnell's cottage and of course Debbie's. Barry Marlow also tucked up in bed as usual. I could vaguely make out a dim light through the curtains of Alice and Tom's at the opposite end of the lane. Not a sign of life in Minnie's window above. The last few people were still leaving the pub as I put the key in the lock, opened the door and let Kathy in first, ever the gentleman. The last thing I saw before closing my front door was Adam, coming from behind the Mariners, crossing the road and walking up Tom's front path…

45

Sunday was peaceful, relaxing. And it needed to be. After all the exercise in St Ives the day before, then the evening's entertainment including large quantities of falling down juice, not to mention the bottle of wine we finished off before bed, we felt we deserved a day of rest. My own tiredness wasn't helped by the return of the night time brain activity. My poor little Kathy was so shattered she was actually snoring—yes snoring—within ten minutes of slipping under the covers. No, sex please, we're British. It was a really warm night and I'd opened the windows to try and let some cool air in but it had very little effect. It was so warm that even Kathy and I had agreed she would not sleep in her usual wrapped around me fashion. "You're like a bloody hot water bottle, you are!"

As she turned away from me and onto her side, thrusting her backside against my thigh. "Just think of the long cold winter nights then." I teased. "Mmmmm…" came the reply, along with a wriggle of that gorgeous bum. And that was it. Not another word was spoken that night, which left me to my thoughts. All the usual ones of course, plus I still wondered where Debbie was and why she hadn't been in contact since the incident with the light fitting. But now there was a new thought to ponder on. What the Hell was Adam doing round the back of the pub? If indeed it was Adam. It certainly looked like him, but I couldn't be sure in the dark.

But then if it actually was him, why would he be going into Tom's house that late at night? More importantly, why had all the people I'd come to know so well, the people that had been one of the main reasons for my move to Cornwall, become the subject of so many of my darkest thoughts the past three months? Surely the only guilty party in the entire scenario was Debbie's ex-husband, the wife beater. Wasn't that the case? Wasn't there a perfectly good reason for every other dubious looking event in the bay? Yes, of course there was. So, why was I so scared something bad was on the horizon? At that point, Kathy's nasal antics kicked in and I had to chuckle to myself…

After a late breakfast, we dressed and took a walk along the beach. It was already filling up with Sunday sun-bathers, though I suspect they were more than a little disappointed to find the sun hiding behind the clouds for most of the morning. On a quiet stretch of sand, a few hundred yards North of the main beach, Kathy stopped, grabbed my arm and spun me around. She looked me in the eye. It was a look that spoke volumes, but I was suddenly illiterate. I can't explain why, but I had the feeling she was about to say something Earth-shattering… And then she reached up and kissed me. A long powerful, yet loving kiss. It seemed to go on forever and at the same time, time itself stood still.

As we parted, she still held onto me. Normally, after such a kiss, one or the other of us would either go 'Wow!' or laugh nervously as though we were unsure what to say. We had come to know one another so well over the months that words were often unnecessary. Sometimes, there *were* no words to express what we were thinking or feeling. Or maybe the words were there right in front of us but neither of us wanted to say them. I remembered a telephone call we had a couple of weeks ago where I thought she had said 'love you' just before the line went dead. She hadn't given me the chance to respond.

Perhaps she didn't want me to respond. Possibly she was afraid of what my response might be. Or I could have totally misheard her. It was never mentioned or repeated. There were several reasons for that, all of which made sense, yet none of them made sense either, depending how you viewed it… One thing I knew for sure. That wasn't a goodbye kiss! It had more depth, more feeling, more passion and emotion than I had ever felt before. My entire body was still tingling several minutes after it. Still gripping me tightly, she was staring down at the sand below us. I cupped her chin in my hand and softly lifted her face, then pecked her softly on the lips and asked, "What's up, babes?"

I've been in similar situations many times in my life. Some of the outcomes were good, some not so good. Sometimes it even depended on your definition of 'good'. For example, during my ill-fated marriage to Richard's mother, I embarked on an affair with a girl in the office where I worked. She was only young, still a teenager and eleven years younger than me. Despite her innocence, she could tease with the best of them. Within weeks we were embroiled in a mad affair, grabbing every possible chance to be together. Lunchtimes, evenings if I could get away, quick kisses in the office when nobody was looking, the usual things that secret lovers do… One day I found an envelope in my pigeon hole. I recognised the writing.

It was hers. I took it back to my desk and surreptitiously opened it. Inside was a small folded piece of paper and on it she had written just three numbers. Nothing else, just 8 3 1. I had no idea what it meant. I do now of course, and any Take That fans will have noticed it on the Progress album. Eight letters, three words, one meaning. It was then that I knew I had got myself in way too deep. While I thought we were having fun, the poor girl was falling in love with me. Hence my comment about how you perceive the meaning of the word 'good'. My suspicions were correct. Whether or not that was a good thing I was yet to decide, or agree with…

"I know it's against the rules but we always said we'd be honest with each other. I can't just sit back and say nothing, Paul… I think I love you." For once, the Partridge Family were not uppermost in my mind. In fact, I don't think I even made the association at the time. I didn't think of Andie McDowell in Four Weddings either. I don't know what I thought to be honest. It certainly took my mind off the strange things in my head concerning my neighbours. As soon as the words left her lips, she kissed me again and then as our lips parted, she replaced hers with a finger… "Don't say a word… Please. Not now. If you say it back, I might think you're just saying it to please me. If you try to explain why you can't say it back, I might start to doubt you, or myself. Just please say nothing OK? Maybe I was wrong to say it but the time seemed right to me and so, well there it is. It's out there as they say… I'm not going to apologise for saying it because I meant it and…"

I put my lips to hers and kissed her to at least show my feelings for her hadn't changed because of what she had said. In my head, I already knew I loved her, but I wasn't sure if I should. All my feelings for Ellie, another girl young enough to be my daughter, came flooding back to me that second. Kathy looked around. There was nobody near us, no-one within earshot. She pointed at a fairly flat rock, told me to sit down and listen without interruption. It was the second time in as many months that I'd had such a demand.

The previous time I was forced to listen to the random ramblings of Debbie regarding her ex-husband, her dead friend, New Zealand and a dog. I suspected Kathy's tale would be far more interesting and beneficial, though I was still unsure whether or not I wanted to hear it. As I sat down and she started to speak, the sun peeped through the cloudy sky and shed a warm glow over the bay. The setting was perfect...

"Paul," she began. "I know what you're thinking. Let's be honest, most of the time we both know what the other one's thinking almost before it's been said. That's how close we've become isn't it? No, don't answer, just listen because you know it's true. Just as what I said is true and I think you knew that as well. Yes, we said we were just going to have fun 'while it lasted' and not get too serious, but we also said we'd never lie to each other and by not telling you, I'd be lying by default if you know what I mean. So, I won't do it. It's not important if you feel the same or not, or even if you don't say the words. As much as I'd love to hear the words, it's not important right now. I can tell your feelings by the way you react.

"The way you hold my hand and little things like the way you protect me from the wind and crossing the road or anything bad and that. I can tell by the way you hold me close and hug me long after we've finished making love. I'm no angel, you know that. We've never discussed the past, we agreed not to, but I'm not afraid to admit I've had one-night stands—I'm pretty sure you have as well—and after shagging we just walk away, but it's not like that with us. We still want to be close immediately after and long after. Even go for seconds sometimes. And that's another thing. I know you worry about your age, but let me tell you Paul, you're healthier and fitter than most fellas I've known that were half your age and without a word of a lie, you're the best lover I have ever had!"

That one shocked me. I never considered myself that good in bed... "You're soft and gentle, always putting me first, unless I take control lol, but at the same time you can be forceful when it calls for it. If that wasn't good enough for any of the other girls in your life, then they were at fault, not you. I don't know anything about your former sex life and I don't want to, alright? But what I do know is that they were lucky to have had you. Unless I'm some kind of sexual Goddess, which I wouldn't believe for a minute, I guarantee sex wasn't the reason your other relationships didn't work out for you! You have more stamina than anyone I've ever known. Now we come to your ex and the age thing.

"This will probably surprise you and you might not like some of the things I'm about to say, but they have to be said."

At this point I decided we both needed nicotine. I took two from the packet, lit them both and passed one to her. "I can actually understand how she felt. I

287

even sympathise with her. Because of nearly a year together, I can easily see how she fell head over heels in love with you. Any girl who gets to know the real you *would* do! Now I'm older now than she was then. I think you said she was mid-twenties when you got together…" I nodded.

"Well, I'm eight or nine years older than that and I can assure you that right now, as far as I'm concerned, it doesn't bother me in the slightest that you're thirty years older than me. And if we weren't having this conversation, I would tell myself it still won't matter in ten years' time when you're in your seventies. But we *are* having this conversation and I can't promise you that. When I'm forty and you're seventy, I might feel completely different, always assuming we're still together…"

I smiled at the possibility. "So, I can only imagine the Hell she was going through when it suddenly hit her that she'd made a mistake. That you were right all along when you said, 'What about when I'm fifty, or sixty' and she said it wouldn't matter, that the age difference wasn't important. Suddenly, one day in the autumn of 2011, she realised it did make a difference. Can you imagine how she felt, knowing you were right and she was wrong? Nobody likes to be proved wrong, especially with something as life-changing as that, and to make matters worse, she knew you thought of her as your last chance of happiness. In your own words 'someone to grow old with'. It must have been a nightmare for her. I'm sure she still loved you, even when you broke up, possibly still does in her own way, even though she's moved on. So, yes, I do sympathise with the poor girl, but she was right to do what she did. There is no point staying in a relationship that makes one person unhappy just for the sake of making the other person happy."

She took a few more drags from her cigarette before continuing… "The only thing I feel she did wrong, and if we try to make a go of it, I promise that won't happen with us, is not telling you. Leaving it until the day she left to tell you it wasn't working, that the relationship was going nowhere, that she was leaving you… That was the most unkind thing she could have done, giving you no chance to prove her wrong. Well, I can't promise I'll still be around in ten years' time, or twenty, but what I *will* promise you is that I will always be honest with you babe. If I ever feel it isn't working, you won't find me sitting up half the night chatting to people on the PC.

"You won't find me telling your friends what's wrong with us. And you certainly won't find me suddenly saying 'It's not working, I think it's best that we go our separate ways'. I hope that never happens, but if it does, if I ever feel things aren't right between us, I will say so and we'll sit down and talk about like mature adults, the way it *should* be done. I won't just pick up the ball, say I'm not playing anymore and run off home."

She took one last breath and concluded... "Now as much as I would love to hear the words, I don't expect them and I don't want you to say them just because it feels right. Only say them if it's true. But what I said back there, I meant it. In fact, I don't just think I love you Paul, I fucking *know* I do!" It was barely two minutes since we both stepped on our dead cigarettes, but already it was her turn to reach down for them and light two more...

I was right on both counts. It wasn't a random ramble like Debbie's, and she did love me. I stood up and held her close as we smoked. She was trembling. It must have been the hardest speech she'd ever made and it was said from the heart. I even had to agree with what she said about Ellie. At the time when she was leaving, and for weeks after she'd gone, I hated her. But I also still loved her. A part of me still does and probably always will. I think even Kathy knew that.

You don't suddenly stop loving someone you've shared twelve happy years with; however, it ends. Love and hate are simply two sides of the same coin. I told my friends, our friends, that even if she changed her mind, I would never take her back, and I meant it. It would have been hard to say but it was a rule I had always lived by. I'd seen other people try it and it nearly always failed. Whatever went wrong the first time would inevitably go wrong again, sooner or later. Yes, I now realised the torment the poor girl must have been going through those last few weeks. Kathy was right to say what she did and I admired her for it. I admired her for her honesty.

But at least this time, if we agreed to make a go of it, I knew she wouldn't just walk out at a moment's notice. I knew we would have a chance to put things right before we finally called it a day. As I finished my cigarette and threw it behind one of the nearby rocks, I looked her in the eye. We were both close to tears from the emotion of the past few minutes. With a nervous giggle she granted me permission to speak. I joined in the laughter, but my serious face soon returned as I knew it was time to return the honesty...

"OK, now it's your turn to listen. And again, you might not like what I'm about to say, but I hope you understand it." To save her the agony of waiting, I had to put her mind at rest on one subject before I approached the other. "First off, let me just say I agree with everything you just said, and more importantly I *do* love you, Kathy. I have done for a long time, but for exactly the reasons you've explained, I was afraid to admit it to myself, let alone you."

She fell into my arms and we held each other for the longest time. We felt safe with each other. It was warm, loving, comfortable, everything a close relationship should be. But if we were going to continue being honest with each other, I had to let her know my true feelings regarding the lovely village I now called home. The village she too may someday call home... "Now that we've cleared the air over that one, there are things you need to know about Tilda's hun..."

She already knew much of what I was about to say, but now was the time she needed to know everything. Everything I knew for certain along with my thoughts and my suspicions. The reasons I lay awake some nights long after she'd fallen asleep in my arms. Why I would never again be totally at ease with my neighbours until I got to the bottom of the bay's secret... "I need to talk to you about this, Kathy." I gestured towards the bay and hoped I wouldn't get 'Not that again' in reply. I didn't.

"It's what being a couple is about Paul, sharing things. If I agree with you, I'll say so, but don't take offence if I disagree. Nobody, not even a clever sod like you can be right all the time." She laughed and held me close again to show our unity. "It's been on your mind a lot, hasn't it?" I agreed and admitted I'd lost a lot of sleep over things that even I had to admit might just have been my imagination.

"Maybe it's true. Maybe I *have* watched too much Wycliffe and Midsomer. I know not every village is concealing a mass murderer, or a fugitive from the law, or a couple trying to hide their secret past as notorious brothel keepers... And I'm well aware that not every vicar hides a dark secret from his adoring parishioners..."

"We're alright on that score babe," she butted in. "We don't even have a church." We both smiled at the joke, and I felt a warm glow inside at the way she said 'we' rather than 'you'....

"Now then," I chided. "No, interruptions young lady! You had your say, now I'm going to have mine. You can give your opinions after, OK?" She looked suitably chastised as I continued.

"Let me just say first off that I'm by no means sure of much of what I'm about to say, but I want to put a list of salient points to you. Individually, they would probably go un-noticed, mean nothing. But collectively, in a village with a population barely into double figures it leads one to think. Before you say a word, I accept I possess one of the most vivid imaginations known to man— Kathy was well aware of my nightly fantasies of being the Invisible Man or some kind of Super-Hero—and I'm also sure that much of what I'm about to say would keep a psychologist in work for years, maybe give him a book or two. But when you put them all together, I think even a sceptic like you would have to admit I'm right to have my suspicions..." I started to count the following list on my fingers:

- We have Colin, a man who clearly loves the ladies but hasn't had a serious partner in twenty years. Maybe he's scared of failure, much in the same way as myself, or maybe there's another reason he remains a single man. Does he have another agenda? For evidence, I list that strange meeting with Tom, Barry and Adam that we both witnessed. Four men who have just one thing in common: Living in this village. The other three barely even drink let alone go to the Mariners. Then there was last night. The bar was busier than it had ever been since I arrived here, he even hired an extra barmaid for the night. Yet he was conspicuous by his own absence until after ten o'clock.

- Next, we have Brian. Why would a man of his age only open up his pub for a few weeks in the summer? What pub landlord have you ever known to prefer a bunch of rowdy holiday-makers to the relative peace and quiet of the locals on a winter's night? That doesn't seem right to me.

- Barry: The man who claims he used to be a teacher, yet never gives a genuine reason for giving it up. Oh, I know he moans about the state of education these days and how the kids get out of hand, bringing knives into school, abusing the staff and all that, but teaching is a vocation hun. Everyone knows the pay isn't great and the schools are over-crowded but teachers, like nurses, do the job because they love it! And why does a man who claims to hate everything hi-tech, he doesn't even have a mobile phone or so he says... Why does he have a computer hidden away? And it's not one of those old-fashioned things that looked like a portable telly from the 1980s, it's got a flat screen and all that. Fairly new I'd say.

- Then there's Debbie. Everything about that woman arouses my curiosity! I won't dwell on the early days, the late-night walks and stuff, but take recent events. I don't believe for a minute she left a cigarette burning in an ashtray then went out in the middle of the night never to return. And why would she not have her phone charged for several days. Then there's the call to Sarah the other day. They barely even talk to each other. I don't care about all that mumbo-jumbo about her birthday being the same as Sarah's phone number… That's bollocks! Surely it would have made sense to call you, someone she speaks to, had a drink with, a friend. Everybody keeps a back-up of phone numbers somewhere, right? And wouldn't you have thought she would have made the effort to find out how *I* was after the accident? Me, her so-called only friend in the village.
- And as for my next-door neighbours… One minute Adam says he's going away for a few days and would I look after Sarah for him because she doesn't like being on her own. The next minute he vanishes for days on end—Sarah tells me she hasn't seen him for over a week now 'but he phones me every day so that's alright'—yet it no longer seems to bother either of them that's she's all alone again.

It was time for yet another cigarette while I collected my thoughts. Had I known this moment was coming I would have written this all down for her, but I didn't. Having just listened to Kathy's heart-felt speech, the time just seemed to be right. It was now well after mid-day and the mid-July sun was getting stronger by the minute. I slipped my top shirt off and sat there in just a 'Beatles at Shea Stadium—Tickets $3.50' t-shirt and jeans. Kathy just wore an electric blue vest, no bra, still firm, and cut off leggings. As previously stated, neither of us would ever be considered style icons but we were comfortable and nothing else mattered…

Now we come to all the strange things that have happened which, as I said earlier wouldn't mean much on their own but… First there was that late night chat with Debbie up on the cliffs and her apology a few days later. Now OK, I have sympathy with any woman being abused by her bloke, it shouldn't happen but the fact of the matter is, it does. But her husband's a copper for fucks sake! I don't care how well liked he was, she could still have reported him. She could have gone to the hospital, have photos taken of the bruises and shown them to a trusted WPC or something. The police aren't above the law so there must have been something she could have done.

I don't care how popular he was, there had to be someone there she could have gone to, even another police station. And what about him. If he's half as good as she thinks he is, how come he couldn't trace her? This place isn't exactly a million miles from Plymouth, is it? I honestly don't believe we know the true story there. And there's that meeting of the four men in the lane. Was that deliberately held because they knew I was out of the way? As I said, they have absolutely nothing in common, so why would they suddenly come together like that, then split up before *we* arrive on the scene? Now I need to tell you some things that you don't know about..." Kathy looked worried for the first time. "There was a man down here last Saturday. Very shady looking. Wore a suit, a trilby and sunglasses and just stood on the beach... I mean, on the beach in a suit? Any other day I might have assumed he was the VAT man or someone from the council or something. But on a Saturday? I swear to you he looked like something out of a gangster movie.

Even his smile looked evil—yes, he spotted me, tipped his hat and smiled. He spent half an hour or so in both pubs, then left. Brewery man maybe? I thought it possible but again unlikely to visit on a Saturday. Then there was that afternoon in Debbie's cottage. To all intents and purposes, I was genuinely going round to do some tidying up, a bit of cleaning and that to save us sometime this week-end. I wanted to make sure we had as much time together doing what we wanted, not what we felt we *should* be doing to help a friend..."

Kathy gave me that look again and squeezed my hand for effect... "But I admit I was curious to see inside the cottage. For various reasons. Twice you thought you spotted a man round there, so it's not just me, is it? I knew any clues would have been whisked away or burnt to a cinder, but I thought just maybe I might find a man's razor in the bathroom or the toilet seat left up or something... The really strange thing was, it was only the front of the house that was fire-damaged, not the back at all. You'll remember I said there were even flames in the attic? So, how could fire spread through the whole of the front of the house without extensive damage to ceilings or floors? Because it was started deliberately!"

I paused for effect... "I don't care what the official reports say, I think three separate fires were started, one downstairs, possibly the 'cigarette on the sofa' thing was genuine. Secondly, I think someone did the same thing in the front bedroom, then again in the attic to make it *look* as though the whole house was on fire. Let's face it, I know you weren't here to see it, but trust me, everyone was out the front watching it, I saw them all..." I suddenly remembered the smiling face of Tom in his bedroom window. I would return to that in a few minutes...

"It's a well-known fact we all sleep in the front bedrooms here. So, think how easy it would have been for our fire starter, or even Debbie herself to set the place alight then slip out the back way. In the confusion of all the noise and lights and sirens, how easy would it be to climb the fences and vanish down that footpath that runs along the side of Tom's cottage? I know I like to think I'm the only one that knows about it but that's highly unlikely, isn't it? After all, if you really saw someone out the back that morning, at least one other person knows about that path... Anyway, back to 'that' afternoon. There's something else I haven't told you."

She looked surprised... "Not that I didn't mean to, or that I was lying by default to coin your eloquent turn of phrase," we still managed to keep our sense of humour through all of this madness, "but simply because I didn't want to frighten you or worry you. I swear to you there *was* a cellar under that trap-door and I *did* see a ladder going down into the darkness, and I think someone's been in there and filled it in to hide whatever I nearly found before someone jumped me from behind..."

"What?" She was genuinely shocked at that simple statement of fact...

"Yes, it's true, hun. I remembered it only yesterday. I heard footsteps behind me a fraction of a second before that light supposedly fell on me! Now there's just a couple of other things I need to mention. Firstly, on the night of the fire, I said we were all outside, but that wasn't strictly true. Tom wasn't out there, but he *was* over-looking the front from his bedroom window. Now maybe it was a trick of the light, you have to remember there were a dozen flashing red and blue lights in the lane that night, but I swear to God, as I looked up and saw him, it looked like he was smiling!"

Kathy shivered as I said that. "Yes, Tom. The one man I have had absolutely no suspicions of what-so-ever. The man who's gorgeous grand-daughter considered me as her new dad, or a second granddad. Whether or not he knew Debbie was safely away at the time is debatable, especially when you think about that newspaper report that everyone laughed off as a regular occurrence, but the more I think about it, the more certain I am that he really was smiling… And there's another thing hun, just as we were coming home last night, I'm almost certain I saw Adam coming out the back of the Mariners and going into Tom's cottage."

We had yet another cigarette. What with all this and Kathy's declaration of love for a man old enough to be her father, I suspected it would be far from our last… "I've saved this bit 'til last babes. And you're not going to like it I'm afraid." I related the tale of people and the tools of their trade, ending with the certain knowledge that despite my security at home, someone had been inside Windy Cottage and accessed my computer…

It had been quite a morning of revelations. Kathy and I loved each other and I, soon to be we possibly, lived in the village of the damned. We walked in silence back to the main beach. Obviously, many people had checked the weather forecast that morning and headed for the coast. The main beach was now packed with bodies. Adult males in everything from Bermuda shorts to Speedo's. A couple of girls sunbathing topless out of sight of the main throng.

Children covered from head to toe in Factor 50, running in and out of the sea, some with buckets of water to fill the moats surrounding the many sand castles… All of them oblivious to our recent revealing conversation or the hidden secrets of the bay they were now enjoying the pleasures of. We walked past them all and took a seat outside The Beachcomber. For once, we needed privacy for our drinks and knew for certain that apart from Pat and Brian, who would probably be too busy to venture outside, we would not be disturbed… Despite that, for the most part, we drank our lager in virtual silence. It wasn't so much that we had nothing to say to each other.

Quite the opposite in fact. It was more that we both needed time to consider everything we had heard. I had to decide if and when the time was right to suggest Kathy move down here, for I was sure now it was what we both wanted. She, no doubt was probably wondering if she liked the idea of sharing the next ten or twenty years with a crazy man. For that was what any stranger would have thought. On many occasions Kathy and I had discussed my theories on what was going on in the bay, but it had always been light-hearted banter and more often or not, she would call me her 'crazy man'. But now it was becoming serious. Not just serious between the two of us, but serious about my, and hopefully our suspicions…

46

After a second pint, we adjourned to the back garden of my cottage and took our places on one of the two garden benches. Making sure we were not been spied on, and couldn't be over-heard, "Are you sure they haven't got the place wired for sound?" Kathy joked, but it was hollow, nervous humour. It had to be considered a possibility. Not so much out here in the garden, but maybe inside... Putting aside our individual thoughts of her up-rooting herself from the foothills of the Brecon Beacons and planting herself firmly in St Matilda's Bay ad infinitum—that could wait and be safely discussed indoors—we decided what could be done, if anything, about my many suspicions and quite a few certainties... It was agreed the most important thing was to get back into Debbie's house and check that trap door again. Kathy was now coming around to my way of thinking, that it had been deliberately filled in to deter anyone, myself or others, discovering its secret.

My first thought, possibly spurred on by two pints of lager, was to go in tonight when it was dark, less chance of being seen, but as Kathy pointed out, it would not be easy without lights and we couldn't risk being seen flooding the back gardens with torch light. Her own suggestion was a repeat of my original excursion, feigning assistance to a neighbour in distress. As she pointed out, we cloud quite legitimately enter the cottage—I still had the landlord's permission—as a second attempt at restoring it to something like its original state, before the fire as it were. I had to agree this made sense...

"And this time," she added, "if anyone comes in to bonk you on the head, they'll have me to deal with!" I suggested if there was any bonking to be done it would be by us with no-one else involved. "But seriously, the way I see it, it was only a warning. I think they needed me out of the way to give them time to cover their tracks. Let's face it, I had my head down in a dark cellar so if they'd wanted to do serious damage, or even kill me, they could have quite easily. No, it was a warning. 'Keep out of our business or else!'"

Kathy nodded in agreement, adding that with two of us this time, they were less likely to attempt any attack for fear of being recognised. There again, I argued, to ensure they wouldn't be recognised... I didn't like to finish the sentence. The possibilities did not bear thinking about... It was agreed we would resume Operation Clean-Up the next morning. Kathy had planned to travel back to Ystradowen in the morning, but with no work until Tuesday she saw no reason to leave before about three or four, "I'd rather not leave it any later, you know how I hate riding that bike in the dark." It was understood.

We spent the evening nervously going over Kathy's comments about me, about my ex, about our future... We seemed to agree on most things about our relationship, even to the point of my saying she would be more than welcome to move in with me if that was what she wanted. We then went through the 'only if it's what *you* want' and 'yes but are you sure?' routine that I'm positive every couple go through at times like that. Each knowing what they want, but needing to be sure the other doesn't feel they are being pressured into doing something they had doubts about.

These were life-changing decisions after all, and who would have thought that at the ripe old age of sixty-two I was still having to make them? I made a simple statement, which seemed to be the right thing to say and do. Kathy's constant nodding interspersed by the odd 'yes' suggested I was right, "As far as I'm concerned, hunni," I said, "you can stay here right now! Or you can move in next week, or next month, whatever suits you best. I know you feel the same way, that was pretty bloody obvious by your speech on the beach, so whenever is good for you is good for me. I know there's stuff like your mother and work to sort out but..."

"Cheers babes!" She raised her glass of wine and we clinked. It was our second glass from our second bottle and we were starting to feel quite merry. "Mum won't be a problem. I know she loves me and everything but she's not my real mum and I know she could do with the extra space. She'll just have to get someone else to look after the 'fucking cat and the fucking fire'"

That had been a standing joke between us. The poor cat—it wasn't his fault—was so old he had to be lifted up to the sink because the only thing he would drink was tap water, and it had to be straight from the dripping tap, not from a bowl. If she'd left him to drink from the bowl, he would have died from dehydration months ago. And as for the fire, her mother for some reason nobody could quite understand, kept the fire going all day and all night, all year round. She insisted it was cheaper than running the heating and hot water off of oil or bottled gas, the way every other member of the little Welsh village did.

It was so bizarre to visit in the summer. There would be a roaring fire burning in the grate, and all the windows would be wide open to cool the house down. Go figure! No, Kathy wouldn't miss the cat or the fire… "And I don't think work will be a problem. I'll speak to the agency and see if I can transfer down here. I expect they need nurses locally as much as they do up there…"

Agency Nursing had its good points and it's bad. The good being you could pick and choose where and when you worked. The down side being you couldn't guarantee a steady income, which made mortgages or long-term loan agreements almost impossible. No, such problem for us though. I had a ridiculously high steady income, a five-figure sum tucked away in the bank and ISA's and no mortgage. Some time ago I had already calculated that I could live a comfortable life, either on my own or with a significant other, for at least thirty years. After that I might need to take up a part-time job as a multi-drop van driver, but until then…

"I'll have a word with the agency as soon as I get back." This was all happening mighty fast and I wasn't complaining. I found myself getting as excited as Kathy was at the prospect of being a 'couple' again. I knew her mother wouldn't be a problem. As Kathy had once told me, she wasn't even a blood relative. If I remembered correctly, she was the ex-wife of Kathy's step-dad, so neither bore any loyalty to the other. Don't get me wrong. They behaved like mother and daughter and Kathy even considered the three young boys and the little girl, her 'mothers' true children, as her own brothers and sister.

But the simple fact was, she had been good enough to put a roof over Kathy's head when it was needed, when nobody else offered, and in return Kathy looked after the cat and the fire. They were all very close and even made *me* feel like a part of the family, for which I will be eternally grateful, but at the end of the day, they all knew the time would come when Kathy would move on again and that time was now. Or at least in the immediate future.

"I think this calls for a celebration!" I declared. It was only eight o'clock. We hadn't eaten since breakfast and considering the lunch-time pints and the best part of two bottles of dry white, I thought it not a bad idea to grab some food. Being officially summer-time, the Mariners was now doing food seven days a week until ten o'clock so we trundled over the road for dinner and yes,

I'll admit it, quite a few more drinks. As I believe I mentioned earlier, almost certainly my most alcoholic week ever…

"Shall we?" Kathy nodded at the bar. It was a fairly busy Sunday evening. Amongst the daily stragglers, reluctant to make the final journey home in preparation for 'back to work Monday', I recognised quite a few Harwick regulars. Many of them these days nodded and even spoke as we entered the bar. It had taken me more than a year to be counted as a regular, but for some reason, Kathy shot straight to the top of the new member's list. I imagine being young and pretty wasn't exactly a draw-back for her, and she always made the effort to talk to anyone who was willing. She was just so damned nice!

As I've said many times before, even other women like Kathy. They don't see her a s a threat, just a mate, someone 'nice' to chat to… I knew exactly what she meant by 'shall we?' Quite a few people had asked the question in the recent past. After all, she was becoming a frequent visitor to Tilda's and seemed to have a permanent reservation at the Windy Cottage B&B so it was hardly surprising. Until now I had always said she was just a bloody good mate, but I think the people who knew me best had other ideas. Maybe they knew me better than I knew myself. Who could say… "Why not?" I replied. "If nothing else it'll be one up on Rachel! This will be the first bit of village gossip she *didn't* hear first!"

I think it was probably the cheapest night out we'd had for a long time. Some of the customers just gave us their 'congratulations' with a smile or a hand-shake, but others bought us drinks… The really odd thing about the entire evening was that nobody seemed in the least surprised. Perhaps outsiders can see what's happening better than those within, I don't know. Either way, everybody seemed genuinely pleased for us. In such a short amount of time, Kathy had become a part of the Tilda family. I liked that, and so did she. It showed when Rara raised her glass and called for a toast to the happy couple, 'though God only knows what she sees in an old git like him! Kathy and Paul everyone!'

Anyone would think we were getting engaged or married or something. All it was, was the mutual agreement to share my house, see a lot more of each other than we had in nearly a year 'together' and save the regular nightmare of the M4 and M5 motorways. Plus, I didn't have a fucking cat or a fucking fire… We, or at least I slept a whole lot better that night than I had for several weeks. Kathy of course was dead to the world in ten seconds flat. I spent about five minutes thinking about how often fate, or karma, or whatever you wanted to call it, had played a major part in my life. Not always in a good way, but more often than not, to my benefit. Que sera sera. I slept like a log...

47

Had it not been for the love and support of our friends—I was starting to embrace the odd 'we' and 'our' in thought and conversation—I may well have laid awake half the night planning our campaign for Monday morning. As it was, we awoke to the sound of birds singing and the sight of the sun rising through the curtains. It was only just after six, yet both of us felt we had had enough sleep. It was going to be another beautiful day in Cornwall. Those without children or work to hinder them would already be packing up their cars and caravans, heading for the long trek down the M5. But for Kathy and I, there was work to be done... I showered and dressed as Kathy prepared breakfast in her over-sized t-shirt.

With full bellies, we laid out our plan of action. The simplest way to gain access to Debbie's cottage was for us to walk quite openly round to the back garden and carry on cutting the grass, weeding the borders, sweeping the path... And wait for the right moment to enter the kitchen. We'd been busy for about twenty minutes when Sarah appeared next door. Her beaming smile told me she already knew about our plans... "Hey, you two, heard the news! That's great. You," she looked straight at Kathy, "will be an asset to this place. And if ever you have any spare time, you'll be more than welcome to help me with the donkeys. We can always...."

"Shit!" I exclaimed, dropping the weeds I had plucked from a flower bed, closely followed by "Sorry, back in five minutes, love you." The 'sorry' was aimed at Sarah. Kathy swore nearly as much as I did but I couldn't recall Sarah uttering anything worse than the odd 'bugger'. The 'love you'... I'll say no more. Stepping back a sentence, the sudden outburst was my sudden remembrance of the power of the internet. Combined with Rachel's knowledge, it was highly probable that there were people in China later that day reading "Awww, my new best buddy Paul is moving the lovely Kathy down to Tilda's! Yay!"

Rachel is one of those people you cannot help but like. In turn, she rarely has a bad word to say about anyone. She has more friends than anybody else I know, but sadly most of those are Facebook friends. Following the success of my house-warming party, she was now 'friends' with Stevie, Kimmy, Linda, Karen (sometimes known as Wendy following a drunken garden party) but worst of all my ex. Rachel has just two faults. One is that she gossips all the time, which we all just accept as Rachel being Rachel.

The other is that she acts without thinking. I would be willing to bet my house that the afore-mentioned message would be winging its way around the world the very second, she finished her shift in Connie's. I prayed she'd been too busy so far to send it out on her iPhone… I raced into the house and turned on the laptop. Two minutes later, I hit the Karma Group e-mail button, deleted Ellie and sent the following message:

Due to the power of technology, you may already know this, but just in case some of you are too busy working (lol) I would like to (hopefully) be the first to let you know that Kathy will be moving in with me into Windy Cottage next week, or maybe the week after. No, questions please. All I will say is that we're not getting married but we will be saving a fortune in petrol and phone calls. Love and kisses from us both.

Then I hit 'new', added Ellie's e-mail and forwarded the same message, preceded by:

As you were decent enough to let me know about you and Steve, I thought I owed you the same courtesy. Unless any of the others read that before you, I've tried to let you be the first to know. Please be happy for us. Paul

I then grabbed my mobile phone and texted her, "IMPORTANT: Please read e-mail now! Thank you."

I hoped that would do the job for all concerned. I may well have been wrong about Rachel but I wasn't willing to take that chance. I gambled on most of my old friends from Surrey and Sussex being at work and not seeing e-mails, or Facebook until the evening, particularly her. Whatever the reasons for us splitting up, I still felt I owed it to her to be the first to know I really had moved on. The text that arrived two minutes later made me smile, "About bloody time. Good for you. Bird."

As I returned to the ladies, they were still happily chatting away about nothing in particular as far as I could tell. "Sorry about that," aimed at Sarah, then turning to face Kathy, I winked and explained, "Left the tap running on the washing up." I tried to look suitably embarrassed for being a 'typically useless bloke'. Kathy fell in immediately, glanced across at Sarah, then raising her eyes to the sky, uttered one simple word which explained everything...

"Men!" Sarah just laughed and agreed, adding that she was sure Kathy would soon straighten me out. We looked at each other, both recognising the double entendre that Sarah probably hadn't even considered... Five minutes after she had made her excuses and gone back inside, I quickly explained my vanishing trick, which reminded Kathy she would have to do the self-same thing later that day.

"Thank God, Rachel doesn't know anyone in Wales or South London!" She said with a smile... A few moments later we were in Debbie's kitchen. This time, I not only locked the door from the inside, but also left the key in the lock. It was a little trick I'd learned in Smallfield to my cost. An earlier girl-friend of mine, Trish, had gone out one afternoon and without thinking, inadvertently taken both sets of keys. When I came home half an hour later and found myself locked out, I thought no more of it and popped next door where I knew Margaret had a spare key to the back door. It was something we'd done for several years.

Both couples being fond of frequent holidays, it was handy to have someone tidy up the mail and freebie newspapers that always clogged up your letter box... An open invitation to burglars. However, when I tried to unlock the back door, I couldn't get the key in. Through the glass pane, I could just make out our third set, the one with the gas key, shed key, laundry key, etc. dangling from the lock. I was stuck outside for two hours waiting for her to return... It was a little trick I found very useful since my suspicion of someone being in my home while I was out.

Ever since that day, I have always kept the back door key in its lock. I thought it extremely improbably any would-be burglar would try to enter Windy Cottage through the front door... Hence my use of the same trick in Debbie's back door. With Kathy also standing guard, I felt reasonably sure I would not be receiving any unexpected bangs to the head this time. We had come armed with a trowel, a rake and black bin-liner, quite natural for someone helping to tidy a garden I rightly assumed. With a flick of the switch the cellar door opened once more. I lifted the decking look-alike off the rubble and turning the rake upside down, prodded through the dirt. We looked at each other and smiled in some kind of victory as the handle only went about a foot down.

With Kathy holding the bin-liner open, I soon cleared the mixture of earth, pebbles and broken bricks from the opening until we reached yet another wooden panel, this one much sturdier than the first. Thankfully, it wasn't fixed. It was clearly a rush job. A make-shift temporary fix in an attempt to convince me, or anyone else who dared to poke their noses in where they didn't belong that this was nothing more than a blocked-up cellar, no longer in use. But we knew different.

I lifted the second panel from its resting place, two primitive batons nailed into the cellar shaft, and once more, as I had done just six days ago, stared down into the blackness. This time I *would* discover the secret of Debbie's cellar... With the kitchen blinds drawn, the door securely locked and Kathy on guard, I took the torch we had smuggled round inside the bin-liner and descended the steps. My final words to Kathy were, "As soon as I'm down there, close the cellar door and just wait, OK?"

I knew if any legitimate caller came to the door, she would be able to explain away the bag of dirt and the rake. She was very good at coming up with just the right story if needs be. I hoped she wouldn't have to, but trusted her in any event. Her final words to me were, "Be careful."

By the light of the torch, I could see the steps led about ten feet down. I descended them slowly until I hit terra firma. I can honestly say I had no idea what I was expecting to find down there, but I strongly suspected it was not going to be a row of dis-used wine racks. I swung the torch around until I could see which way to go. The answer was simple. There *was* only one way. Into a low tunnel, about three feet from floor to ceiling.

It reminded me of those television programmes when people explored the sewers of Victorian London, except this was dry and as yet rat-free. The walls of the tunnel were part brick, part wood and mostly earth and clay. I stooped to walk through it in a most uncomfortable crouching position. Whoever normally used this route to wherever had to be a midget. Either that or it was only used in emergencies. One thing was certain... There was no wine cellar down here. I continued struggling my way through the near-darkness for a few seconds until I came to what in road traffic terms would be a crossroads. I shone the torch back in the direction I had come from. It was only a few yards.

Yet here I was with a decision to make already. My brain didn't need this. It was already into over-drive, imagining Nazi war criminals on the run—well you read of such things—or maybe this was what you found on the other side of a priest's hole. After all, there was all that business way back when they tried to build a church here... Left, right or straight ahead. Seconds later, the decision was made for me. As a sometime asthma sufferer, I realised my chest was tightening and I found I could barely breathe. I turned back. This exploration would have to wait for another day. Maybe if we could afford to leave the cellar door open, I could make it to the end of one of the three tunnels, but certainly not today.

As I reached the top of the step ladder, I tapped lightly on the trap-door. Moments later it opened and I was greeted by the smiling face of my loved one. Before she had time to ask questions, I said we should quickly put things back the way they were. Noticing I was catching my breath, she asked if I was alright. I made the hand motion I always used when activating my inhaler. She understood. Two minutes later we were back in the garden. I made that same motion as I left her there, once again pretending to be weeding the borders, and went to grab my inhaler from home...

"So, where the fuck do they lead, then?" Kathy couldn't believe what I was telling her, though she knew it was true. I was trying to piece it all together. The position of the cottage in relation to the rest of the village. The angle at which the first tunnel, the one at the bottom of the steps, had run off... I closed my eyes and thought for a few seconds, "If I'm right, there's one leading off to the right, in the direction of Barry's house, one directly opposite that one, possibly heading for Sarah's, and the one in front of me started off with a bend, but it could have been going right under the lane..."

"To one of the pubs or the shop," Kathy deduced. I nodded, not really wanting to think what we were both *already* thinking. We were sitting on the rocks down by the beach now, both of us virtually chain-smoking. I had already decided it might not be safe to talk indoors. Kathy no longer thought of me as paranoid, or the crazy man, if indeed she ever did. Under the heading of 'better safe than sorry', by mutual consent, neither of us would ever mention my...*our* suspicions indoors again. We were lucky in that everyone knew how much we enjoyed the open air.

Even before we embarked on this mad escapade, we were well-known for our walks along the lane, up on the cliffs, down on the beach... Quite possibly some of them assumed we were both outdoor lovers in every sense of the word, which in fact we were, but that was no longer the main reason for our regular walks. It just seemed safer to talk outside. Walls have ears as the saying goes. Anyone who watched the entire series of Spooks in the early two thousands will know what I mean.

Listening devices, or bugs these days, if that show was based on fact, could be no larger than a pin head. Any expert worth his salt could hide one anywhere. I had even decided to turn off the mains electricity first chance I had and check behind all the switches and sockets. I know it sounds crazy—maybe I really *am* that crazy man—but something was going on in St Matilda's Bay. Something that most, if not all of the neighbours knew about... Except me. But I was determined to join that elite band of brothers, whether they wanted me to or not!

Apart from the odd tube of Smarties which may or may not have mysteriously vanished from Smith's Newsagents, Woodhatch, in the nineteen sixties as Mrs Smith was searching the top shelf for a big jar of humbugs, my career in crime had been minimal. Whatever my neighbours were up to, I wanted no part of it. I told Kathy my thoughts about the Nazi's and priests and she responded with just one word, "Smugglers."

I thought about it, we talked about it, and the more I thought, the more we talked, the more it made sense. Despite its long history of smuggling, with pirates, gold coins, ship-wrecks, etc., it was a proven fact that smuggling was still very much alive and well on the North coast of Cornwall. Of course, nowadays you swapped Spanish gold for heroin and cocaine, but the bottom line was always the same... People were making huge profits from smuggling in these parts.

With most of the recognised ports and airports sewn up by the police and customs alike—no more 'mules' swallowing condoms full of the stuff, or poking it up your backside—the clever smugglers were finding new routes. Only two years ago, in Agnes Point, just a few miles along the coast, police had executed a successful raid on a house and discovered heroin worth close to ten million pounds on the streets of the UK. Drugs were big business. The new 'pieces of eight'. The obvious differences being that way back in the pirate days, it was only one or two people getting killed, the rest simply got rich. With drugs, many people would have died from that shipment sniffed out by dogs at

Agnes Point had it reached its destination of dealers distributing death throughout the UK... But drug dealers don't give up their vile trade that easily.

There was too much easy money to be made, if you didn't get caught. And the truth of the matter is that the real dealers, the ones making the millions rarely do get caught. It's usually just the minnows that end up in jail for ten or fifteen years, either not willing to reveal the names of the superiors in the chain, or simply not knowing. Those at the top of the tree simply find another minnow or two and its 'business as usual' within days... Yes, Kathy had hit upon what now seemed to be the most logical conclusion. But if she was right, where did that leave Debbie? For that matter, depending where the tunnels led, where did it leave the rest of my friends and neighbours?

48

By the time Monday evening arrived, my mind was in a state of confusion. While I was over-joyed at the thought of Kathy only being gone for eleven days, then back for good, I couldn't stop thinking of where my neighbours fitted into this horrendous scenario. I gradually put the most likely possibilities in place. If she was right about St Matilda's Bay being a modern-day smuggler's cove, then it was no wonder many of them acted strangely in my eyes.

To the regular visitor, they would all appear to be perfectly normal, but to me, the odd man out, the new kid in town… It's fair to say I know very little about hard drugs, no more than I'd read in the papers or seen on the television news bulletins. My own personal experience was no more than dabbling with LSD as a teenager, 'dropping acid' and drifting away into a world of my own to the sound of Pink Floyd. I didn't even smoke my first spliff until I was well into my twenties. One thing I *did* know, was that people were making millions out of the stuff. And if millions of pounds, or Euros were changing hands every month, a payment of say five thousand pounds a month to a few people in a quiet Cornish village would be a mere drop in the ocean. I consider five grand more than enough for Mr and Mrs Average to live comfortably on, especially if they continued with their normal day jobs as well.

Hell, I was working my nuts of every other week for less than that. And these people had the added bonus of not having to hand a sizeable chunk of it over to the government. If our suspicions were correct, it was easy to see how the likes of Barry Marlow no longer had to spend six hours a day trying to educate thirty-odd screaming kids! With his regular absences, Adam would fit the bill of top man in the bay. Possibly his frequent trips to 'the city' weren't to London as we all assumed, but to Dublin or Amsterdam. Dublin had been the source of the Agnes Point supply, and everyone knows Amsterdam is famous for more than its diamond trade, canals, tulips and red-light district.

Plus, Sarah's charity work only goes to show what a fine upstanding couple the Bonnell's are, doesn't it? Then there was Debbie. Without meaning to generalise or come across as sexist, what young girl would turn down five thousand pounds cash in hand for doing no more than turning a blind eye for a few hours once a month as a couple of holdalls full of white powder vanished under her kitchen floor? The more I thought about it, the more Kathy's one word statement began to ring true. The tunnels leading off from beneath Debbie's kitchen definitely went left, right and diagonally left again following the bend I'd seen.

The obvious conclusions were that they led next door either way, to the Marlow cottage and that of the Bonnells. But without further examination, which I had solemnly promised Kathy I would steer clear of until she returned, I couldn't be absolutely certain. As for the other possibilities, there were several. Heading in my direction, I had to admit it could only end at Sarah and Adam's. Erik and I would surely have noticed anything resembling a false floor or indeed a damned great hole in it when we were re-building Windy Cottage.

Plus, from what I knew of Steve Taylor, his brain was so fried by the time he moved to his retirement home, he could not have been trusted by 'the gang' to keep his mouth shut. At that moment, I even considered the possibility that his illness had been somehow induced... In the opposite direction, if the tunnel didn't end at Barry Marlow's house, there were, as far as I could tell only two other possibilities. One was Alice and Tom's, and I simply could not bring myself to consider Tom as being involved in drug trafficking, not when you considered Minnie.

Tom doted on the girl, adored her. It was as plain as the nose on your face! And we all know how children get started on drugs. It's a well-documented fact that pushers wait near school gates and hand it out free of charge, knowing full well that in most cases it only takes one hit and they're hooked. They come back for more and this time it costs. As does the next hit... And the next, until that child is just another statistic. A small line on page thirteen of the Sunday papers. So, common is the story these days that it no longer *is* a story.

The fact that Joe Bloggs or some such similar nonentity had been kicked out of 'X' Factor this week seemed far more important... The only small detail that put the tiniest doubt in my mind was Alice. Her health was not good. Neither she nor her husband had fully explained what the problem was, and I certainly never asked, but just how much private health care would five thousand pounds a month buy? I tried to picture Kathy, or Richard, or my own precious grand-daughter with a life-threatening disease... What lengths would *I* be willing to go to in an effort to ease their suffering? The other, more feasible theory would be the tunnel stopping at Barry's, or not as the case may be, then by-passing Tom's cottage and heading for the woods deep in the hills leading out of the bay.

As with many other remote parts of Great Britain, mostly in the South, there were still thousands of trees uprooted by the storm of October nineteen eighty-seven lying where they had fallen. While the built-up, populated areas had been cleared away and back to normal within weeks, making millionaires of anyone who owned a chain saw or two, it simply wasn't economical in the wilds of Dartmoor, Exmoor and indeed the hillside woodlands between St Matilda's Bay and Harwick. What better place to conceal an exit from the tunnels? If it came out near the old railway track bed by the former station, the 'gear' could be transferred during the night to a parked car or van and be in London before the sun came up.

I doubt the old man in the station would hear a sound. The illicit cargo would practically be on the streets before Debbie had time to close the trap-door... No, it couldn't be Tom. Not with his grand-daughter to take into account. It was either Barry or away to the hills... But what of the other tunnel? The one leading, I assumed, under the lane to Connie's or the pubs. I immediately discounted Rachel for two reasons. For one thing, if she was making five grand a month, or whatever the figure might be, there was no way she'd be working double shifts in the shop and The Beachcomber unless she was a workaholic. Secondly, she wouldn't be able to keep quiet about it!

Unless her gossiping nature was all just a part of the act. That just left Pat, Brian and Colin. As much as I hoped it wasn't Colin, one of the nicest men I'd ever met, and from my home town to boot, I have to confess I could quite easily picture him being involved. No, kids or family to speak of. The drugs weren't hurting anybody in our idyllic little spot by the sea... The expression 'what the eye doesn't see...' sprung to mind. Unfortunately, if Colin was in the frame, that put Tom back in the line of suspicion. Why else would Adam, who rarely drinks, come out of the back of the pub and head over to Tom's house at one o'clock in the morning? It was not a pleasant thought and one that I put immediately out of my mind.

I didn't *want* to think badly of Tom, so I wouldn't. There had to be another explanation for Adam's late-night visit. Of course, I could not be certain he'd come from the back of the pub that night. Due to the live music, the car park had been packed so Adam could just as easily have been coming from there. But that still left the mystery of why he would be going to Tom's at that late hour… Now Brian Issom. With or without the involvement of his wife Patricia… I'm afraid I have to say Brian would be ahead of either Rachel or Colin if my theory of the tunnels, and Kathy's theory of smuggling *were* correct.

I've been a drinker for most of my life, starting at fourteen in pubs around the Redhill and Reigate area, many of which such as Greyhound, the Noah's Ark and the New Inn are long gone, but I've never known a pub landlord turn down the chance of making a few extra quid. I've seen gin watered down, house whisky's topping up the Bells and Teachers. I found it hard to believe the Issom's opened The Beachcomber for just a few short months as a hobby… So, there we have it. The St Matilda's Bay smuggling gang comprising Debbie, Barry, Adam, possibly Sarah and Brian. Problem solved. How easy was that?

Now all I had to do was pick the right moment to tell Kathy, plus the small matter of proving it without further risk to life or limb… Before she left Windy Cottage earlier that afternoon, possibly for the last time, we had agreed I would do nothing 'dangerous' until she returned on the Friday of next week. What she *did* give me permission do to was really rather clever on her part. I was to invent reasons to visit each of the cottages and somehow, if possible, carry out a detailed search of the downstairs rooms in each of them. As with Debbie's kitchen floor, once you knew there was something odd about it, it stuck out like a sore thumb. Surely, I would be able to spot a minute crack along the side of a floor tile, or a loose carpet tile… Maybe a stray rug that looked out of place in a living room.

I foresaw no difficulty where Tom or Sarah was concerned. I'd visited both houses on several occasions, though never looking for trap-doors of course. On reflection, Barry was going to be the tough cookie. Ever since I'd spied that flat-screen computer through a small crack of the living room door, that same door had always been closed. I was sure the kitchen wouldn't be difficult, but gaining admittance to his living room, presumably without his permission, was an entirely different kettle of fish. That was going to take some very careful planning… And I could see no possible way of penetrating either of the pubs, or

Connie's Mini-Market for that matter. Still, we had plenty of time, didn't we? On the subject of crime, I noticed I'd let my coffee go cold. Now that really was a crime! In fact, it's almost punishable by death in the Evans household. So, pleased I got that microwave oven…

Due to the fact that I was back on duty the next morning—and I have to say I would be relieved to occupy my mind with something 'normal' for a change—I had arranged to speak to Kathy only via mobile phone and only from the relative safety and privacy of the beach until further notice. The calls would be short and sweet, limited to how much we missed each other, our future plans, etc., and not a word about you-know-what. We had also agreed that I could safely keep my eyes and ears open to the comings and goings of any boats in the bay after dark, or similarly any vehicles that didn't appear to belong there. To this end, I devised a plan, one that could easily be checked by my medical records should anyone choose to do so… About seven years ago, I suddenly developed a regular attack of night cramps.

My doctor seemed to think it was because of my constant use of a laptop, which kept my legs in an almost permanent static position for anything up to fifteen hours a day if we were busy. Three or four nights a week, when I lay down in bed, they would start, and believe me it was agony. I was in tears some nights as Ellie furiously massaged my shins and feet. It was often an hour or more before my muscles finally relaxed and we were able to sleep. My doctor prescribed exercise, a brisk ten- or fifteen-minute walk before bed to get the circulation flowing again. I suppose it was a little like that thing frequent fliers get. It was all down to lack of regular movement from the thighs down. I had tried the toe-wriggling thing but found it almost impossible to type at the same time.

So, from that moment on, I would walk to the end of Laburnum Court, take a left into Redehall Road, then do a circular route around Park Road and home again. This took about fifteen minutes and also gave me time to have my last cigarette of the day. For a period during those times, Ellie had succeeded in giving up smoking so in support of her, I would only smoke outside the house. Not fun when it was raining, hence the porch I erected in 2007, but I think it worked for her. She was never again tempted back on the demon weed until a few days after our separation. Stress I imagine…

So, back in Tilda's, each night at the agreed time of eleven o'clock, as soon as I'd finished my day's shift and shut down the laptop for the night, I took the footpath up onto the cliffs and watched. Watched for any signs of boats, signals, flashing lights over the sea, or even from the roof of one of the pubs... Anything that might suggest an 'all clear' signal for this month's delivery. Remembering earlier ventures up there and talk of how close Ystalyfera was, and how we could probably wave to each other on a clear day with a set of powerful binoculars, Kathy had said there would be another flashing light to watch out for.

At exactly eleven thirty every night from now until the following Monday when my shift ended, she would sit in the darkness of her own bedroom over-looking the ocean and flash her light constantly for five minutes. A simple YES or NO text from me would confirm or deny a sighting. Even if we were spotted—we had to assume, if the smuggling theory was true, they would have at least one look out—anyone would assume it was just a lover's romantic way of staying in touch. We had considered our own signalling code but decided against it for fear of being caught...

My need to keep my mind off of the exploits of my neighbours was resolved much easier than I had anticipated. Over the previous week-end, one of Brannigan's S92 Sikorsky helicopters in Lagos, Nigeria had suffered severe fire damage and was going to take about six weeks to re-build. This amounted to my having to raise an average of forty or fifty additional high-cost purchase orders per day as opposed to the normal twenty or so, more than doubling my regular work-load. On top of that, a full report of each item had to be e-mailed to our company insurers.

When you consider most of those e-mails were returned to me for further vital information, then submitted once again, sometimes three or four times, I barely had time for coffee and cigarettes, let alone spying on the criminal fraternity that surrounded me... Allegedly. The laptop was red hot all day that first Tuesday back on duty. It only began to quieten down after the Lagos operation closed for the day, about six in the evening. Even then I had the suppliers, Sikorsky to contend with. Situated in Orange, Connecticut, they were on Eastern Seaboard Time, five hours behind the UK, so I had questions and deliveries to contend with right up until shut-down at eleven... As much as I loved my job, still do, it was a relief to finally switch everything off and relax.

I'm lucky in one respect. I'm one of those people who can switch of my work brain just like that—imaginary snap of fingers—as easily as switching off the laptop and not worry about work-related things again until seven thirty the next morning. I'm confident enough in myself to be sure I have done everything within my power to complete my day's tasks to the best of my ability. I have many testimonials from operational Chief Engineers and company directors to qualify this. As far as Brannigan's is concerned, I sleep soundly. Its other things that keep me awake at night.

Kathy, smugglers, invisible men... All manner of weird and wonderful things penetrate my brain in the hours of darkness, as previously described in lurid detail, but helicopters and their numerous problems have never been one of them... So, there I sat on the cliff tops, shortly after eleven that Tuesday night waiting for... Something. Anything. A clue to what was sullying the village I had fallen in love with. The village I had given up everything I knew and loved in my previous life to become a part of... As I sat there in silence, all I could hear was the sound of the waves crashing against the rocks.

I was gradually coming to enjoy the sounds of the ocean once more. It had taken me a year to enjoy that sound again without picturing so many people who would never again enjoy our sandy beach. I felt sure as soon as could put this smuggling business to bed, I would be able to forget past tragedies and move on, back to enjoying life in the bay, the way it had been last year, but this time with a partner...

49

"You did what guv? Wasn't that a bit risky?" Smithy was amazed at his superior's brazen attitude.

"It's gotten beyond risky matey-boy! You and that other half-wit, what's his name? Mitch, is it? Well, you got nowhere, did you? It was time for direct action. Time is running out and I've even heard a whisper, nothing official like, that they're moving the show forward. It could be as soon as next month!" The boss was clearly agitated and running out of patience with the people in whom he'd put his trust... "Anyway, this is England and everyone has to wear a suit from time to time. No, fucker took a blind bit of notice..."

"So, did you get anywhere? What's the next move? If we've only got about four weeks 'til..."

"From what I could tell, there's three or four possibilities. Now that girls out of the picture we've got an old boy near the beach, some kind of local hero, rescued a girl from that fucking flood last year. He's a possible, and he's got a new girl-friend, half his age. She comes from Wales so you never know. Next to him there's a young couple. It could be either of them. Couldn't find out much though. Then there's another bloke in his fifties. He's a maybe. Other than that, they all seem to have lived there forever, except for one of the barmaids. Rara, they call her. What kind of stupid name is that? No, idea what her real name is... Probably Raquel or some other stupid name of the television. She's a bit of a mystery. But that's it. The others are out of it I'm certain."

He flicked a cigarette from the pack on his desk, lit it and carried on, "Get hold of that Mitch character again, pick up a couple of the girls and get yourselves down there this week-end. Pretend you're a nice romantic foursome off for a dirty week-end. I'll be there," he stopped and checked Smithy's intended interjection, "but you don't know me, right? We don't say a single word to each other, OK?" Smithy nodded.

"I'm going to try and get the girl from the shop chatting. A couple of drinks should loosen her tongue a little. Not that it needs loosening... That girl knows everything that happens down there from next Thursday's weather forecast to the inside leg measurement of the fucking window cleaner!"

"Window cleaner?"

"Oh, do shut up, you twat! It's just an expression!" He stubbed the cigarette out in an over-flowing ashtray, half wishing it was Smithy's face. Better still, Martin's.

"So, if we find out for sure which one's Martin guv, do we...?"

"You do nothing! Nothing, understand! We meet back here on Monday and I'll decide our next move... There's a lot riding on this my old son, and if we don't find Martin and get him out of harm's way, the fucking balloons gonna go up!" He slammed his fist down hard on the desk to emphasise the point, sending the ashtray and its stale contents flying... "And if that happens, something very brown and fucking smelly's gonna hit the ventilator!"

50

Luck wasn't on our side that Tuesday night. Or the next night for that matter. Both of our plans had failed to bear fruit. On the Tuesday night, I sat there for over an hour and smoked three cigarettes, more out of boredom than anything else. It's odd, but a few years earlier, I would have happily sat on that exact spot for hours, simply enjoying the sights and sounds of Cornwall. But now, with everything that was going on down below me, I wanted something to happen... For things to take shape. Kathy had come up with the perfect solution to it all but there seemed to be nothing we could do to speed things up, to spur the smugglers on, or even prove her assumptions correct. As I looked out from the bay, across the Atlantic Ocean, or was it still the Bristol Channel? I couldn't be sure... Either way, there was not a flashing light to be seen anywhere on the water.

Neither was there from any of the buildings in the village. Only one window over-looked the sea and that was at the far end of The Beachcomber, out of sight from my vantage point. So, Pat and Brian could be light-flashing all night long and I would never be any the wiser. However, logic decreed that if *they* were flashing out to sea, surely someone would be flashing back. But they weren't. And as for 'Plan B', due to what I can only assume was a trick of the light, literally, every single light along the full length of the South Wales coast was flickering.

For all I knew, Kathy was quite possibly one of them but I would never be sure. Not tonight, not ever. Either that or she was playing a joke on me and had asked all her friends to flash their lights at eleven thirty that night. I pictured her Facebook status inviting everybody to... No... Highly unlikely... Wednesday was even worse. Again, following yet another manic day on the laptop, I took myself up onto the cliffs at the allotted time, only to find that not only was it a cloudy night—I had noticed from down below but thought it still worth a try—

317

but also there was a rolling mist covering most of the bay, making even the bright lights of Swansea impossible to see.

It resembled the big screen adaptation of Stephen King's classic horror story, The Fog. I half expected to see zombie-like sailors from century old shipwrecks creeping up the beach and into the village, ready to wreak havoc upon anything that stood in their way... Severely frustrated, I returned home, had one final coffee, strong black with two sugars and made my way to bed.

The more I thought about it, the more I came to suspect what little I was doing was by no means anywhere near enough. If indeed drug traffickers were using Tilda's to bring their merchandise into England, who was to say it would happen around midnight? It could just as easily be two, three, even four o'clock in the morning, and it simply wasn't possible for me on my own, or even two of us once Kathy moved down here, to monitor the shipping lines of North Cornwall all night. If only there were someone else who could help us. Someone we could trust... I could think of several suitable candidates, all of whom lived some three hundred miles away and most of whom had work and families that they couldn't just abandon for God knows how long on a whim.

I thought about testing the water with one of the girls. Not Rachel obviously, but maybe Rara or Lala. I certainly considered Lala trustworthy, especially after my drunken diatribe regarding my thoughts on Debbie a few weeks earlier. Lala had agreed to carefully find out more about our mystery neighbour for me and as far as I could tell, had not repeated either our conversation or my request to anyone else in the bay. Yes, I would discuss that possibility with Kathy as and when I had the opportunity.

In the meantime, I would stick with our original 'shot in the dark' plan and do my nightly stint on the cliffs for the next for the next eight or nine days until she arrived. In addition to that, I had also started working on 'Plan C'. Yes, there as a 'Plan C'. It revolved around finding ways to examine the back rooms of all my neighbour's cottages. It came to me in a flash, really quite simple as most of the best laid plans often are... I took each of them in order, starting with the most difficult: Mr Barry Marlow. I concluded that if I should succeed there, then the next in line, Sarah and Adam would seem that much easier and so on. A bit like shooting someone if the films are to be believed... That would save Alice and Tom until last, and by far the easiest. Minnie's adoration for her surrogate father, or second grand-father gave me licence to virtually come and go as I pleased, so from now on, until my search was complete, I would do just that…

Barry: I considered the best approach would be the usual one. When it came down to things horticultural, he could talk the hind legs off of one of Sarah's donkeys. And it was about time I put some enthusiasm into that back garden or at the very least appear to be doing so. So, far, all I'd managed was two benches and a climbing frame. Hardly Kew, was it? No, it would soon be time to call again for Mr Marlow's expertise and learn a few new words of Latin. Hopefully, we could avoid the subject of palm trees.

Sarah and Adam: Running a close second to Nigella Lawson in the domestic Goddess stakes, I decided to approach Mrs Bonnell, rather than her husband. In fact, he was so rarely at home these days, according to Sarah, that I probably didn't really have that much of a choice. Something else the lady had in common with Nigel Lawson's little girl. Sarah it would have to be then. I was hit by a brain-wave. If Kathy was to be moving in next week, what better time to have a 'Welcome to Tilda's' party especially for her? Of course, I could hardly expect my little lady to organise her own party, could I? Maybe I could do with some valuable assistance from the lady next door. I was sure Sarah would be more than happy to bake a special cake for the occasion. While I'm a dab hand in the kitchen—breakfasts, fry-ups and roast dinners no problem—I simply cannot bake to save my life. But I was equally certain our own resident Nigella could.

Alice, Tom and Minnie: I had the perfect excuse to call round there. In fairness, due to local activities and the on-rush of my new 'serious' relationship, I must confess I'd spent very little time with Minnie lately. We hadn't played chess for more than a week, and I'd only taken her to the beach once recently. I decided some quality time was the order of the day. As with the other two, the kitchen would be easy to access. A sudden need for a glass of water could hardly fail.

Once inside each of the cottages, I would have to play it by ear and somehow try to wangle my way into their living rooms, all situated in the back. I have no idea why I assumed each tunnel entrance would be at the back of the other cottages. Maybe because Debbie's had been. I rebuked myself and swore to make the effort to check all downstairs rooms if possible. Unlike many other towns and villages, our row of cottages had by no means been erected in a straight line. An old childhood expression that I hadn't heard for many a year, higgledy-piggledy, would describe them… This I decided would be my task for the following Tuesday, Wednesday and Thursday. I would see how far I could get before Kathy arrived with all her worldly goods.

Debbie: No, I was not going back in there until Kathy returned the following week, even if she *did* reappear. I had promised her that and there was no way I was going to wake up in a hospital bed again. Or worse.

The week flew by. Work was busier than ever, at least three times the usual thanks mainly to the continuing re-build of the S92 in Lagos. My nightly walks carried on, although as the week drew on, they were more for the pleasure than anything else as precious little was happening out at sea. Once the midnight hour approached, I even found myself looking around the cliffs from time to time, half expecting Debbie to come wandering along and calmly sit beside me, smoking a few of my cigarettes and chattering away about nothing in particular.

Well, nothing that made any sense to me at any rate… On the Friday night I heard a fog horn, which was somewhat out of the ordinary especially as it was a clear night… Kathy and I managed to maintain our daily telephone calls, interspersed with the odd text, which were getting naughtier every day we were apart. In recent times, I'd almost reverted to being a teenager again, enjoying the thrill of text sex. Crazy at my age, but true. Roll on next Friday! All of our calls were, by necessity about ourselves, our future, planning holidays, how to spend next Christmas… That part was easy as it was all genuine.

We really *did* appear to have a future—for how long, neither of us could be certain for any number of very good reasons—and we were definitely going to have a holiday once all this issue of the smuggling was resolved, always assuming we were both still around to enjoy the fruits of our labours. The Greek Islands were mentioned and I never say no to them. Once or twice we each had to bite our tongues moments before asking something about bay activities that we had no wish to be over-heard. But to keep it natural, Kathy made a point of asking how Minnie was, what plans Colin had for music nights and even taking the piss out of Barry and his opinion on my still-very-much-alive palm tree.

I mentioned my offer of holding quiz nights in the Mariners, so we managed a good ten-minute chat about music trivia. 'No, Bob Holness did not play saxophone on Baker Street, and neither did Rod Stewart play harmonica on My Boy Lollipop' I confirmed, wondering where and how these rumours started. I did however confess to singing backing vocals on the nineteen seventies hit Chirpy Chirpy Cheep Cheep, but I prefer to keep that to myself, for obvious reasons. All in all, it was a perfectly normal lover's conversation. To an outsider, everything in the garden would appear to be rosy. But all of that would change on the Saturday morning!

I had managed a visit to Alice and Tom the day before. I timed it perfectly as I saw the school bus pulling into the lane. It was just after 3:45 and I saw Minnie climb down onto the grass verge. As soon as she spotted me, she came running my way and gave me a huge hug. I apologised for not having a lot of spare time lately and asked if she fancied an ice cream down on the beach. Having checked with her granddad, we found ourselves in Connie's ten minutes later, buying two Magnums. Rachel was as chipper as ever, asking Minnie how Alice and Tom were, then turning to me and instructing me to give her love to Kathy when we next spoke, adding, "Tell her, we'll all have to get together and have another girl's night out when she's settled in. We haven't had a good one since Easter."

I promised to do so, then just as Minnie and I were about to leave the shop, I turned back and said to Rachel, "I'm thinking of having a 'welcome' party for her sometime next week-end. Nothing mad like the house-warming, just the neighbours and the girls for dinner or something, maybe a Barbie if the weather holds. I'll let you know…"

I silently assumed she already knew of my plans. With that we were out of there. I didn't want to stay and discuss it. Frankly, there was nothing to discuss. It had been a very recent decision and no plans had yet been made. It just seemed the sensible thing to do at the time. Tell Rachel and it would save me the effort of handing out invitations. Mean but true… On the beach, I was bombarded with questions about Kathy. Clearly the jungle drums had reached little ears as well as grown up ones. 'When is she coming?' 'Will she be staying?' 'Were we getting married?' 'Could she be a bridesma…?'

"Woah! Little lady!" I stopped her in her tracks but kept the laughter in my voice. "Slow down, will you! She hasn't even moved in yet and you've got us married off already. At this rate we'll have three kids before Christmas…"

"Now that," she stated with the certainty of a child who by now had probably had two or three years of sex education, "Would be physically impossible! It takes nine months to have a…" So, she knew all about the art of having babies, and hopefully how *not* to have them, so why had nobody told her it was time to buy a bra or two! Kathy…?

"OK," I was still laughing, "let's leave it there, shall we? Yes, she's moving in next Friday, but there are no plans to get married just yet. We need to get to know each other a lot better first. We might not even like each other as much when we see each other every day."

It was something we had spoken about and to that end, Kathy had agreed to keep some of what she called 'her junk' at her mother's house until we knew for sure it was what we both wanted. Looking back, I recalled Ellie doing the same thing. To this day there are still things at her mum's place that I never got to see… As usual, Minnie and I walked down to the water's edge, took our shoes and socks off and paddled for a few yards. Christ knows why we do that! The water's always bloody freezing and it takes forever to get the sand from between your toes without taking half the beach indoors with you. But still, we do it.

Minnie always shrieks with delight each time a little wave catches us. I always shriek with the cold. But I would always do this with my little Minnie, because she was one of the main reasons I was here in St Matilda's Bay. It had taken nearly a year for her to trust the sea again, but she made it, and I would share that with her until the day she felt she was too old for such little girl things. No, doubt in a few very short years, she would be doing the same thing with a boy of the same age. I hoped that day was still a long way off. Little girls seem to lose their innocence so young these days. Having spent so much of my life in Brighton and Crawley, I had seen it first-hand…

On the Saturday morning I had checked the Blackberry. It showed nothing that couldn't wait an hour or so. Thankfully, most of our people in Nigeria have the week-ends off so I was having a welcome break from the re-build. I'd had my first cup of strong black coffee to kick start the day and was just about to pour the second when I heard the post arrive. Picking up the small bundle from the mat, I noticed the usual bills, junk mail and this month's "Specials at Domino Pizza".

For God's sake, the nearest Domino's was more than twenty miles away. I know those cardboard boxes hold the heat pretty well but… That's when I spotted it. A plain white envelope with a stamp on it. Yes, a real live first-class postage stamp! I hadn't seen one of those for ages. I think the last one was over a year ago when I received my final settlement bill from the solicitor in Truro when the deal for Windy Cottage had been completed. Does anybody use stamps any more I asked myself? I couldn't even tell you how much a first-class stamp costs these days. Thirty pence? Forty? Fifty? Obviously, they did if the envelope in my hand was anything to go by. I remembered as a boy, the thrill of receiving letters or cards in the post, usually around Christmas and birthdays.

As children, it was about the only time you *got* something through the post. The rest of the year, everything was always for your parents, and usually in a brown envelope. Nowadays of course, being the computer age of the twenty first century, you simply log on to Moon-Pic.com and your card to a loved one arrives as if by magic the next day... I took the unusual 'gift' through to the kitchen with me, poured that second cup of coffee, lit a cigarette and held the envelope in front of me. I know it sounds daft, and of course it would have been so much quicker and easier just to open it, but it was all about the anticipation.

Receiving a genuine letter these days was a novelty, a rarity even. My name and address were clearly typed on the front, complete with the correct post code. The slightly askew stamp was blue, had 1st in the corner, and four black wavy lines running through Her Majesty's face and onto the envelope itself. To the left, I could just make out that it had been franked, or post-marked if you like in Plymouth, Devon. Now personally, I only know one person who lives in Plymouth, a lovely girl with a colourful past to put it mildly. Her name was Kerry and like Jenna in Southend and Debbie right here, there had been an abusive man in her life. I came to know her quite well on a dating site.

The fact that she was even on such a site suggested she was looking for a way out. I got to know Kerry really well, even meeting her twice, once in Bournemouth and once, at very high risk to both of us, in her home town. I did my best to rescue her from the animal that was ruining her life but despite saying she would leave him so many times that I lost count, she's still there in Plymouth, and still with him the last I knew. We haven't spoken for about eighteen months but she has my number. Even though I'm now with Kathy, there would still be a spare bed for her if she needed it.

On the subject of violent and abusive partners, there was one other person I knew, or rather knew of in Plymouth... Debbie's husband, or ex-husband as she prefers to call him. I took a few sips of coffee and stubbed out my cigarette, then opened the letter... I felt a strange child-like excitement as I ripped the seal open. I remembered trying to guess which of my aunties or cousins had sent me which of the five or six cards I would receive each birthday. I was always fairly sure which one was my nan's by the spidery writing in real ink. I was equally sure it would contain a ten-shilling postal order. It always did...

If you know what's good for you, and for the lovely Kathy, stop asking questions and poking your nose in where it doesn't belong. It will be better for all concerned if you take my advice. You have been warned!

There was no 'Dear Mr Evans' or 'yours sincerely' and it certainly wasn't signed. It was just a plain and simple warning. A warning I was very tempted to heed, but deep down inside, I knew I wouldn't. More importantly, I knew Kathy wouldn't... The main question was, how should I react? Did it really come from Mr Jones? Or was it from someone much closer to home? It sure as Hell wasn't going to scare me off. I would carry on my normal life in the village wherever it came from, and that included asking questions and poking my nose in. If they thought I scared that easily they had another think coming. They seemed to forget I grew up in the nineteen sixties, the early days of Doctor Who...

Nobody ever caught *me* hiding behind the sofa! But in fairness, I had to warn Kathy. If the threat had come from a copper in Plymouth, I don't believe it would have been in the form of a letter. I was more likely to have my door kicked in, closely followed by a similar action to my head. The more I thought about it, while once again chain-smoking, the more it became obvious that it could not be from Mr Jones. Had it been, he would obviously have known where his wife was staying and gone straight to the root of the matter rather than via one of Debbie's neighbours. No, this was from one of the smugglers, in effect one of my so-called friends... My neighbours!

51

While in some respects, technology has moved us forward in leaps and bounds, in others it hinders us more than we thought possible. Had that letter arrived on my door mat thirty years ago, I could have taken it to the police. They would have checked the typing, noticed a faint nick in the curve of the letter "s" and been able to identify the exact model of typewriter it had been written on, where and when it was purchased and the age and sex of the writer's next door neighbour's mother-in-law at the blink of an eye. But with technology, ever type-face or font looks the same as the next one. Every sheet of paper comes from a batch of ten million reams, sold in every Staples or PC World in the country.

No, DNA where the perpetrator had licked the stamp because they're all self-adhesive, as are the envelopes. Unless whoever sent me the threatening message had been stupid enough to cover it with his finger prints, we were pretty much fucked, to put it bluntly. Consequently, no point what-so-ever in taking it to the police. Not that I would have anyway. No, unless Kathy had other ideas, which I very much doubted, life in Windy Cottage would continue as per normal. I would go ahead with my plans for the 'welcome' party, and at the same time inspect my neighbours' houses, if possible, and take it from there.

Whatever threats were handed out, it only made me even more determined to continue to ask my nosey questions, probably even more so in spite of the perpetrator. I placed the letter carefully on the table, noting its precise position in relation to the pattern on the table cloth—in the event of any uninvited visitors—collected my mobile phone from the kitchen, left the cottage and walked down to the beach. It was not as warm and sunny as the previous week-end but that failed to dampen the enthusiasm of the Great British public. It was only just after nine o'clock and already there were forty of fifty people on the beach...

Walking to the same spot as the lovely Kathy had made her declaration of love just a week ago, I dialled her number. She was normally an early riser like myself, but in any event, she would almost certainly be up and about by now. Probably not dressed, but awake. She picked up on the second ring. Once the niceties were out of the way, I told her about the letter. Rather than being worried or frightened, she positively enthused, "That just goes to prove we were right then, doesn't it?" She could barely keep the excitement out of her voice.

I liked the way she gave me half of the credit for the idea, when the smuggling idea was completely her own. "We have to get down those tunnels and see where they lead. I liked your idea of the woods, but I don't believe Debbie's in this all by herself hun. There has to be back up. Either from Adam or one of the pubs." We'd both agreed Rachel wasn't involved. Tom, we had doubts about after that late night visit, but surely not Rachel. Everybody loved Rachel. In any case, it was impossible to check the shop or the pubs. There was just no way we could get in there. It was different with the cottages.

People expect neighbours to pop round from time to time, but you didn't just turn up at the back of a pub and ask to borrow a cup of sugar, did you? Even we weren't that brazen… In my other hand, I felt rather than heard the 'ping'. I made my excuses, promised to call her later whether I had news of not, and terminated the call. The last thing Kathy said was 'Ignore aggressive people babes, they're vexations to the soul'. Where did she come up with these profound statements? It was the second or third time she had made such a point. I knew I'd heard it somewhere but as yet, could not pin-point it.

But for now, there was work to be done. On the way home, Colin was outside the Mariners putting up brightly black and gold parasols advertising Strongbow, one of the few ciders he *didn't* sell… Odd. He waved and bid me 'good morning'. I called back in similar vein. "How's Kathy? Alright, I hope. Not long now, eh?" Was there something in his tone or was I imagining it? I tried to ignore the inner feeling nagging away at me as I replied, "Just six days to go mate, but who's counting?"

"How many hours and minutes?" I laughed and headed back up the garden path, pulling the bunch of keys from my pocket as I did so… I don't know exactly when it began, but recently I had developed something resembling a sixth sense. The moment I opened the door, I knew something was wrong. I walked through to the kitchen and hit the filter coffee button. The key was still in the back door lock. I lit a cigarette and went into the front room. I wasn't in the least bit surprised to find the letter had been moved. Not by much, maybe a few millimetres, but it had been moved. As I said to Kathy later that night, "These bastards are clever babe! We're gonna have to watch our backs from now on."

Someone had clearly been making sure I'd not only received the letter, but read it. Now I wanted to see the reactions of everyone in the village. To see what they thought about my cavalier attitude. One of them had tried to warn me off but without shouting 'you don't scare me you crazy fuckers' from the roof tops, there was only one way to do it. 'Plan C' was going to be set in motion right after lunch…

Sausage, egg and chips, an old pub favourite from Brighton café days did the job for once. I had one more thing to do before I went poking and probing into the lives and homes of my neighbours. I Googled 'vexations to the soul'. It had to be a quote from somewhere. Shakespeare possibly. 'Vexations' sounded like something the Bard of Avon would have written. It was certainly not a word you would normally find in the vocabulary of a thirty-something. And there it was. A poem allegedly discovered in an American church nearly a hundred years ago, called Desiderata:

Go placidly amid the noise and haste, and remember what peace there may be in silence.

As far as possible, without surrender, be on good terms with all persons. Speak your truth quietly and clearly; and listen to others, even to the dull and the ignorant, they too have their story. Avoid loud and aggressive person's, they are vexations to the spirit.

If you compare yourself with others, you may become vain and bitter; for always there will be greater and lesser persons than yourself. Enjoy your achievements as well as your plans. Keep interested in your own career, however humble; it is a real possession in the changing fortunes of time.

Exercise caution in your business affairs, for the world is full of trickery. But let this not blind you to what virtue there is; many persons strive for high ideals, and everywhere life is full of heroism. Be yourself. Especially, do not feign affection. Neither be cynical about love, for in the face of all aridity and disenchantment it is perennial as the grass.

Take kindly to the counsel of the years, gracefully surrendering the things of youth. Nurture strength of spirit to shield you in sudden misfortune. But do not distress yourself with imaginings. Many fears are born of fatigue and loneliness.

Beyond a wholesome discipline, be gentle with yourself. You are a child of the universe, no less than the trees and the stars; you have a right to be here. And whether or not it is clear to you, no doubt the universe is unfolding as it should.

Therefore, be at peace with God, whatever you conceive Him to be, and whatever your labours and aspirations, in the noisy confusion of life, keep peace in your soul.

With all its sham, drudgery and broken dreams, it is still a beautiful world.

Be cheerful. Strive to be happy.

Kathy may not have been word perfect, but the sentiment was there just the same. I even found why it seemed so familiar to me. Amongst the seventeen thousand, four hundred and thirty-seven entries on Wikipedia—at the time of writing—was one that advised of a single from the mid nineteen sixties by someone called Les Crane. I can only assume I'd heard it on my transistor radio. For any younger readers, that was the iPod of my teenage years. I was tempted to Google Les Crane to see what he was up to fifty years later but who knew where that would lead to? Right there and then I had smugglers to deal with…

"Come in my boy, come in…" Barry's welcome was as warm as ever. Apart from our slight disagreement over my desire to grow one of the few palm trees on the North coast, we had always been nothing but polite and friendly with each other. I would never class Barry and I as close friends, not yet at any rate, but as neighbours go, I'd had a lot worse in my time. "So, you're finally getting round to sorting out the back then. I was beginning to think you'd lost interest old son…"

Was that a subtle hint that I might have other things on my mind? Bigger fish to fry maybe? Or simply that he was keen to get started on another project. Any tradesman worth his salt loved to give his expert advice. It was good for the ego. Without being openly conceited about your successes, it always felt good when someone followed your lead, or chose to do things in a similar way to than of your own. I don't believe I've ever boasted about anything in my life, but I do know what I'm good at. My entire life I have only ever done things I could excel in. If I tried a new job and found I wasn't up to scratch, I would move on to another, and another, until I found one I *was* good at.

I know I'm good at what I do for my current employer. If I wasn't, they would not have re-hired me a year after my redundancy. And I know I'm good at presenting karaoke shows… Or I should say 'was', as I retired from them over a year ago. The proof of that was clear to see. Not only was I told so on a regular basis, but if ever we covered for another outfit, our following would be bigger than theirs. Plus, right up until last year, I would still visit other shows to see if they were doing anything I felt Karma should.

All I found were others copying what we'd been doing. So, yes, along with my two brilliant partners, and my former partners in Copa Karaoke, I was the best. There are many things I would have liked to do with my life but never did because I had either tried it and failed—so never again—or it was blatantly obvious I would never be good enough. I would love to have been Ray Davies, writing and performing brilliant music, but it was never going to happen. Instead, lower down the ladder of success, I made sure Barley were the most popular 'local' band in the South. The best. The same could be said for Cyclops Disco. And we were, yet again, the best in Godstone, Oxted and the surrounding areas of Surrey.

Like many small boys, I grew up hoping to be a famous footballer, playing alongside nineteen sixties super-stars like Denis Law or Jimmy Greaves but again, it was only a dream, so therefore I was more than satisfied to manage a youth team from the Sovereign Club in South Park, Reigate. They won the Sunday League in 1972 and in my own little world, that gave me something in common with Sir Matt Busby. We all have hopes and dreams and I believe it is our duty to strive to achieve those aspirations. But at the same time, you have to know your limitations. Just be the best you can be at what you do.

Take pride in your work, hopefully without conceit, and it will reap its own reward. That was how I viewed Barry Marlow. Whatever else he may have done in his life: School teacher, failed or otherwise… Smuggler, soon to be caught if true and I had my way… In my eyes, he would always be an expert gardener and I was happy to accept his advice… With no prompting from me, he took me through to the kitchen—a good start—sat me down at his breakfast bar and offered me a coffee, which I gladly accepted. I had to admire his kitchen. I had been in it once before but I'm ashamed to admit I'd never really taken any notice. Having said that, I had not been looking for secret passage ways at the time. Unlike my own kitchen, which is purely functional—Erik and I had chosen a simple but effective B&Q flat-pack design—Barry's was quite stunning.

The cupboards were of solid oak, with lead-light panels in each door, meaning you had to keep the contents neat and tidy, unlike my solid 'pine-effect' ones which hid a multitude of sins such as out of date Baked Bean tins. Each of his units had its own secluded interior light which illuminated upon opening. This I noticed as he retrieved the coffee and sugar jars. Again, unlike mine which stood at the back of my worktop next to the kettle. Energy economics I called it. Some would say lazy or even use the correct term, which I believe is ergonomics but I wouldn't swear to that one.

Note to self: Check the dictionary in future before trying to use clever words... His all-round worktop and breakfast bar was of polished marble. All of this luxury I could understand. The breakfast bar was clearly the hub of the cottage. The place people met, drank coffee and chatted about the chosen subject of the day. In my case, gardens... As we enjoyed what I have to admit was an excellent Brazilian mixture, I carefully glanced at light switches—the kitchen had four of them, positioned just inside the back door—and of course the floor. Four switches I thought to myself, hoping he wasn't as good at mind-reading as he was with a trowel... One for the double six-foot strip over-head no doubt.

One for the six under-cupboard mini-strips I assumed... But what of the other two? Possibly exterior lighting. I reminded myself to check when I later made the excuse to view his own garden. That left one unchecked. As we continued to talk of suitable all-year-round plants and the best months for bedding them in, my eyes drifted down to the marble tiled floor. Each one perfectly matched the grain of the worktops. Each one impeccably grouted. I could see no obvious cracks or gaps. All of this took but a matter of seconds, but as he turned to pour me another cup, I quickly gave the floor close scrutiny. I would have sworn there was no secret trap-door... This meant I needed to devise a way into the only other room in the back of Mr Marlow's cottage and possibly the front also. That damned dining room. The one with the PC in it that he 'doesn't own'.

The room whose door has always been closed ever since I spotted it months ago... Out in the back garden some ten minutes later, he was busily explaining—mostly with the aid of Latin names as always—which blooms were which, where they should be planted in relation to the sun and wind, etc. while I was checking for tell-tale signs of outdoor lighting. There was an extravagant waterfall leading down to a pond, complete with what I thought were coy carp, but couldn't be sure. Attached to a tree nearby were two coloured spot lights, one red, one green. Could they account for the other two switches? It seemed unlikely both colours would be fed by the same switch, though not entirely impossible. While no expert on gardening itself, I considered myself reasonably artistic when it came to the use of lighting. In *Paul's* world, the red and green would be on separate feeds to give a completely different effect, depending on your mood, or your guests.

The green would obviously enhance the look of the lilies in the pond and the various exotic grasses that appeared between each of the surrounding rocks, while the red would give a magical fairy-tale look to the scene, along similar lines to my planned walkway, perfect for visiting children for example... But then, Barry may have completely different ideas. I tried to imagine how the scene would look with both lights on at the same time, but failed. Strolling around this oasis and admiring how every inch of space had been carefully designed to the best effect, it wasn't difficult to check for additional needs for electricity.

I had already noticed a halogen security light above the rear entrance, but surely that was fed direct from the mains or possibly by a sensor. However, as we walked further away from the house, he described in great detail the magnificent Japanese garden, with its marble and onyx gravel, if that's the right word, complete with miniature oaks, willows and monkey puzzles, all of which would look like a fantasy as the sun set and the seven various lanterns came to life. There was even a small section where he'd cleverly used real toy marbles. Damn it!

I left the garden in two minds. One was full of admiration for a job extremely well done, and the other a feeling of deflation in the knowing I'd learned nothing more than a few new words of Latin. Everything about Barry's garden was planned to perfection, from the miniature garden to the carefully planted borders, the ornamental octagonal planter, cleverly disguising the man-hole cover for the water mains, even the ivy weaving its way up the rear wall looked... I don't know... Just right. The man was a horticultural genius! 'And this year's winner of Best Garden in the village is...' Back in the house, I brought the subject back to my own garden.

In between graphic descriptions of each flower bed, Barry had thrown in the occasional 'they would grow well in yours' and such like. I asked him if he would be good enough to write down some of the names for me as I planned another visit to the garden centre this coming week-end... "Or maybe you know a good web site to buy them on line? I suspect some of those would be too exotic for Harwick…?"

"Of course, I can my boy," came the reply. Finally, this was his admission to owning a computer. I was no longer interested in why he had one but insisted on denying it. I know longer cared if it was littered with porn, legal or otherwise… All I wanted to do that moment was enter that back room and check the floor… "I can come back with you right now if you like." Foiled again.

Back in my own cheap and tacky flat-pack kitchen, with its authentic looking but never-the-less still artificial wood-grain parquet flooring and its 'marble effect' work top's, I lit a cigarette and poured myself a large whiskey. Now I'll be honest and say I don't normally drink the hard stuff that early in the day—it was still only three o'clock—but I needed it. On the former subject of being the best at what I do or not doing it at all, I now had to accept the fact that I would never be James Bond. Truth be told I suspect I would even fail the 'Dixon of Dock Green' entrance exam! My skills as a sleuth would put Peter Sellers to shame.

I was that bad, it was making Murder She Wrote look like the work of a genius! I had left Barry's house with a smile more false than that of a circus clown, bursting with enthusiasm as fake as my pine cupboards. Hopefully he hadn't noticed. As an after-thought, just as I was walking away from his door, I turned and said, "Oh, I nearly forgot the other reason for my coming round. I'm having a welcome party for Kathy next week some time, I hope you can make it…" He said wild horses wouldn't stop him. Why was it that I was starting to read between the lines every time anybody gave me a simple answer? Why couldn't I just accept that Barry Marlow simply wanted to be a part of the welcome committee for the new love of my life? Why did I take it to mean 'Of course, I'll be there Mr Evans. I need to keep a close eye on you… Both of you!'

52

Not to be deterred, I downed the whiskey and as I often did in such stressful situations turned to my favourite comfort food. The good old reliable fried egg sandwich. I know it hadn't been that long since my last egg but I can't deny my affection for the little beauties. With some people its cheese on toast. With others, particularly the female of the species, its chocolate. But for me, there is nothing like an egg, properly fried with added salt and a dab of HP sauce. And it has to be just right. This was another thing I've been told I'm very good at. First, prepare your bread with butter, not any of those 'It looks just like butter but tastes like shit' alternatives the so-called experts try to force upon us— Quorn instead of real meat is tantamount to sacrilege in my book, nearly as bad as alcohol free lager—then you should add a light sprinkling of salt on both slices.

This saves you valuable seconds later and ensures your fried egg sandwich is piping hot from the first bite. Next, add a few drops of HP to one slice, spreading it evenly all over. Add a few drops of sunflower oil to the pan... It has to be very hot. You crack the egg and pop it in the pan for just a few seconds. As the egg is starting to fry, you take the spatula—preferably wooden as the albumen can stick to plastic—and very carefully nudge the sides into an approximation to the shape of the bread. Flick the hot oil lightly over the yoke to seal it, then flip it over, turn off the heat and flip it back again almost immediately. Your perfect fried egg is now ready, complete with crinkly brown edges if you had the oil as hot as suggested. Pop it on the bread, spike it with a knife and spread the flowing yoke to all four corners. Place the other slice on top and Bob's your uncle.

Mary Berry, eat your heart out! One word of warning... This should only be done either on your own, or with someone you are very comfortable with. I find a good guide-line is the moment you realise you're not afraid to pass wind in front of that person... The reason for this is that if done correctly, as above, there is a better than evens chance of the yoke dribbling down your chin at some point in the procedure, so not exactly the desired impression to put across on a first date… Satisfaction guaranteed. Heaven on a plate! I was now ready to face Sarah, and possibly Adam if he had finally returned from wherever he'd allegedly spent the past two weeks…

The best laid plans of mice and men, as someone once said, though I've no idea who said it or what the Hell it meant. Do mice really make plans? Plans to do what? Eat cheese? Avoid the cat? No, reply from the Bonnell's. Adam still away no doubt and Sarah quite possibly organising a Jumble Sale for the Women's Institute, or more likely on reflection, putting in a shift at the donkey sanctuary… This was not a problem. I walked three doors along and called at Tom's.

He and Alice, along with Minnie were out in their back garden. I had heard the laughter from the front path and without invitation walked around the back to locate the source of merriment. It was Minnie in a bikini—I really *must* remember to get her and Kathy together for a girlie chat very soon—ducking and diving, trying to avoid the spray from Tom's hose as he alternately sprayed his lawn and his grand-daughter. On the subject of ducking and diving, watching this idyllic Cornish village scene, in the warm sunshine, under the craggy but beautiful bracken strewn cliffs, it was impossible to imagine Tom as anything other than a doting grand-father. I hoped I was correct in my assumptions.

"Paul old son, lovely to see you!" This was echoed by Minnie's squeals of delight, possibly more at the spray of water cooling her slowly tanning skin than at the sight of me. I still received my customary cuddle though, leaving damp patches on my faded jeans. That reminded me, 'I really must dig out my shorts. This was turning into a glorious summer.' As the little girl ran off for yet another shower from her grand-father, I bent down to kiss Alice's cheek for which I was rewarded with one of her usual warm smiles. "What can we do you for?" My host added.

I explained about the forthcoming welcome dinner for Kathy, offered the necessary invitation and wondered if they might have any spare chairs I could borrow for the 'do'. I was thinking on the hoof. I knew their house so well, although I hadn't been inside since discovering the tunnels. I knew for certain they owned a magnificent oak dining room table, big enough to seat eight, and chairs to match. I doubted they would refuse me. I went on to say the plan, if the weather holds, was to do a barbecue, in which case just a few plastic garden chairs would suffice, but 'knowing the fabulous British weather...'

Alice fell in straight away, "Borrow whatever you like Paul, you're always welcome, you know that." The smile was still on her face and I was glad to notice she no longer finished such sentences with 'after what you did for Minnie...' As proud as I was of that moment, it could be an albatross around my neck sometimes. I still received the odd request from local reporters for an update on my progress in the village, though thankfully never from The Pigeon.

As for the others, along with Alice and Tom, you could only say 'Oh, it was nothing' or 'Anyone would have done the same thing under the circumstances' so many times. Thankfully, it was now a thing of the past in our conversations... I then had a flash of inspiration. Alice was sitting comfortably in a cushioned garden chair. Tom was still busy with the hose as we spoke, and Minnie was absolutely soaked and would no doubt be banned from the house until she dried out...

"Would it be OK if I grab a glass of water, please?" They were hardly likely to refuse their 'hero' were they? Alice told me to help myself, which I did. The back door, leading into the kitchen had been propped open all this time, giving me the chance for the odd sneaky peek, but now I could have a proper look inside. It wasn't going to be as easy as I'd hoped. A quick look around, as a pretence at locating a suitable glass, showed me just one wall switch, obviously controlling the central ceiling lights, and the floor was covered with a criss-cross patterned linoleum in red and black.

It appeared to be tacked down at intervals of about six inches throughout the entire circumference. Either it was a very clever disguise, or exactly what it seemed. Unlike Debbie's kitchen, a concrete-based extension to the cottage, all of the others including my own, were the standard original build, based on wooden joists and floor boards. I 'accidentally' knocked a spoon off of the side. This made Tom look up—he hadn't before which suggested innocence—but as I picked up the discarded piece of cutlery, I was able to closer examine the tacks. They were real.

I found a tumbler in the 'cupboard over the sink' just as Alice had advised, filled it with cold water and returned to the garden... That just left the other downstairs rooms. I prayed I would find nothing suspicious in there. Of all the people in the village, these were the ones I wanted in my sights the least... Out of the blue, as is so often the case, Minnie opened up a window of opportunity, "Can we go inside and have a game of chess please, Paul?"

I have no idea if whiskey is a stimulant for the brain cells, or if I'm just naturally quick-witted, but my immediate response was, "What? In this weather? Why don't I bring the set out here and give you a game on there?" indicating the patio table. All seemed to be in agreement and two minutes later I was in the back room of their cottage. I had played Minnie several times in there before and had always admired the room. If you can picture your granny's house as you remember it from your child-hood, that was Alice and Tom's dining room.

The big oak dining table, complete with lace table cloth, doilies for place mats and even silver serviette holders that Alice kept immaculately polished. I couldn't help but wonder how many people ever got to see them these days. In one corner of the room stood a stereo radiogram—I had no doubt that had I opened the sliding doors beneath it I would have discovered a stack of 78's by Glenn Miller—and along the far wall, a magnificent carved sideboard. Nobody has sideboards any more. It's all wall units and fitted cupboards nowadays. This particular model was an absolute gem.

The work of a true craftsman from days gone by. I had a little side bet with myself that given the time to explore, I would find a secret hidden compartment or two. In the opposite corner of the room to the radiogram stood another little master-piece. A small, delicately carved and highly polished chess table, with inlaid squares of dark and light wood to represent the black and white squares of a chess board... All of this I knew from earlier visits and many other games of chess with the little girl. We had always used the special chess table for our games in her grand-parent's house. There was something quaint and 'olde worlde' about it.

We both preferred the table to the transportable board that leaned against the wall beside it... I estimated I had about two minutes to check the floor before one of the family wondered where I'd got to. The carpet was of the fitted wall-to-wall variety in a red, yellow and orange Paisley design. As with the kitchen, it appeared to be fixed all around with no obvious signs of having been lifted recently. No, upturned corners for instance. This pleased me, but I reminded myself I would still need to check the front room to be absolutely sure of their innocence.

I collected the box of chess pieces and the spare board and returned to the waiting Minnie satisfied in the knowledge that my dear friends almost certainly had absolutely nothing to do with any dark deeds that may, or indeed may not have been plaguing our peaceful little bay… Minnie and I played three games— I won them all, just—before the 'ping' of my Blackberry forced me to leave. Although I had arrived under false pretences, I thoroughly enjoyed that afternoon. They really were three of the loveliest people you could wish to meet, and so genuine. Or so I thought at the time…

53

Having returned home, I switched on the laptop and spent the next half an hour moving an Air Data Computer, that's the famous 'red box' to you and me, from Norwich up the East coast to Humberside by taxi. A few confirmation phone calls and it was job done. I opened up e-mails, hit 'new' and typed in 'KA'. The drop-down box displayed seven possible contacts including the obvious one. I was so tempted. Tempted to give Kathy the good news about Tom but I didn't dare. It would have to wait until later. I had already checked every light switch, socket and fitting for bugs.

I had no idea what I was looking for but convinced myself I'd know one if I saw one. I also removed and replaced every door handle in the place, in fact everything I could think of that was easily removable in a matter of seconds, I had checked, but with no success. I told myself if there was a camera or some kind of listening device in my house, I would have found it by now, but it was still not worth the risk. It seemed the obvious place was in the laptop itself, now that I was convinced the cottage had been penetrated by the enemy, but there was no way I was going to strip that down, not if I wanted to keep my job. No, it was a phone call, albeit still risky, or nothing. I turned off the laptop with Googling Les Crane, poured myself a cup of coffee, lit a cigarette and went outside to sit under the palm tree and watch the sun go down...

Connie's was doing a roaring trade, with many of the children departing the beach demanding one last ice cream 'before we go home please daddy'. A few of the die-hards were still sun-bathing despite the drop in temperature over the past hour, but most were packing up their things and either heading back to the car park, if they had children, or heading for the pub if not. I received the usual few nods from the passers-by, but saw nobody suspicious. No, return of Mr Suit. I was so tempted to ask Brian or Colin who he was but was no longer sure who I could trust.

Then I thought about Rachel. Hadn't he popped into the shop en route from one pub to the other? I was no longer sure. I was no longer sure about anything other than Kathy and my desire to spend many long years in her company. To that end, I made a decision. I was going to offer her the chance to back out of all this behaving like spooks. I would broach the subject tonight... I sat there for a full two hours contemplating how to get the message across without looking like a quitter. In that time, I kept a close eye open for any sign of Sarah, but by eight thirty she still hadn't returned. As the sun began to set slowly to the West, I picked up the phone and headed down to that same spot on the beach to call Kathy...

"What?" She was clearly taken aback by my suggestion that maybe, just maybe, we should abandon this venture. "No, fucking way babes! We've nearly cracked it. That letter *proves* we're getting close. It's no fantasy any more Paul, no paranoia, this is real life!" I went on to explain the whole scenario as I saw it...

"I'm only thinking of you, hun. I'm not a young man any more. I've faced danger and death three of four times in my life, it no longer frightens me, but you..."

"Stuff that darling!" was the response. "If we can put a stop to even this little cog in the giant drug wheel, I'll die a happy woman, believe me!"

"OK, I'm with you there, but I need you to think this through before we decide once and for all to carry on." She said nothing, so I continued... "If we pull this off, three things are going to happen. 1) Some, possibly most of our friends and neighbours will wind up in prison for the next ten years or so. 2) The dealers, bosses, whatever you want to call them will simply move ten miles up the coast and start all over again in a matter of weeks. Look at Agnes Point. And 3) Those same bosses aren't just going to sit back and think 'ah well, it's only five million', are they? They're going to want to find out who fucked up their operation, if they don't know already!"

After a few seconds, Kathy came back with, "Fine, so we move to Sardinia, or Corsica or something..."

"How about Sicily, make it easy for them!" We both laughed at the attempt at humour, but it was hollow... "You're serious about this, aren't you hun?"

"Dam right I am babes! Fuck the consequences!" She said. "If we're going down, we'll go down screaming and fighting!"

I thought about that. Why not? Kathy was right. So, we may not end the drugs supply to the UK, but it would sure put a dent in that cog for a while… "Fuck it! Who wants to live forever anyway?"

That side of the conversation concluded with an inspired piece of ad-lib from Kathy, "…and if any of you bastards are listening in, we got the warning thank you very much. Now take one from us! If anything underhanded happens to either of us, the whole world will know what we know at the push of a button, thanks to more than a dozen trusted friends and the power of Twitter, so you can all go fuck yourselves you shower of shit!" Spoken like a true lady…

Then just before we returned to more important matters such as Kathy's move to St Matilda's Bay, sometimes latterly known as Smuggler's Cove, I added, "You may well have a few tame coppers and customs men in your pocket but somewhere out there in the big wide world, someone will believe us. You have been warned!"

"So, how the fuck are you going to move thirty-three years of your life from there to here on the back of a Honda 250?" It was a problem neither of us had considered until just that very moment. Had we been a normal couple, meeting, going on dates, getting to know each other until finally the time came to share a home, it might have crossed our minds. But Kathy and I are anything but normal. We're just two crazy abnormalities who came together on the internet nearly a year ago. A pretend gay and an ageing rocker. We never had time to think about the logistics of the move. We had been too busy having fun, making love, drinking vodka and the small matter of trying to catch an international gang of heroin traffickers…

"Shit!" was the lady's one word reply. The obvious answer was for her to bring down the immediate necessities… A few clothes, a toothbrush and herself. We could go and visit her mum a few weeks later and throw the rest in the Clio. How hard could it be? We orally shook hands on the deal, said a few private things the rest of the world had no need to know, but may well do if our suspicions proved to be correct, and said good-night…

In my determined effort to act as normal as possible, on the way home from the beach I stopped off at the Mariners for a pint. Colin seemed the same as ever, smiling and joking with the customers, then beaming a big 'Hi' over my way as I walked into the bar. He certainly didn't look like a man who had been listening in to private conversations just a few minutes earlier. I ordered a pint of 'the usual' and invited him and Lala, currently serving an elderly couple a few feet away from me, over to mine the following week-end, for the welcome do... "Nothing mad, just a few friends and a bite to eat in the garden during the afternoon if it stays dry."

Lala chipped in with "I'll bring the vodka." Colin, meanwhile added 'Plus, a coach-load of nutters from Crawley and several tents'. I tried to explain it wasn't going to be that kind of a party, to which the lady turned her nose up and said 'Fair enough, we'll just have to drag her over here for the evening then' and carried on serving as if I wasn't there, bless her. I asked Colin to let Rara and Mish know it was an open invitation to the whole village even though they were Harwick girls themselves, then took my Carling outside to reflect upon the day and watch the world and its wife go by, most of whom were heading for the car park up the hill and home after another glorious day in our tranquil setting...

Five days to go and I'd be a 'couple' once again. Should that be *we'd* be a couple? As per every other time I went through a relationship breakdown, however long or short, I had convinced myself it would never happen again. But it always does. Partners seem to be like alcohol. You can take so much that when you're finished and can take no more, you swear it's the last time... Ever! Until the next time. I kept my eye on Sarah's house to see if she returned while I was on the bench but she didn't. Not to worry. I would track her down tomorrow. She couldn't vanish forever.

Colin came out to collect the empty glasses and I couldn't resist asking, "No, sign of Debbie's car yet then? Why would the police keep it this long, especially now they know she's OK..." Totally unfazed, he came straight back with, "Probably taken it *to* her, or maybe she collected it herself, you never know from one day to the next with that one. Strange girl..." He was still muttering as he re-entered the pub with about nine empty pint glasses attached to his fingers. Very good, I thought, and I wasn't thinking of his dexterity with beer glasses.

Sunday was possibly the quietest day I'd known on the work front. By ten o'clock that morning, just three e-mails to check and nothing that couldn't wait until Monday morning. No, doubt the calm before the storm, so I would just have to make the most of what remained of the week-end. It was sunny and warm again so I finally dug my shorts out from the back of the drawer.

Armed with the Blackberry, I took my trusty cup of strong sweet black out to the back garden and relaxed on the bench over-looking next door. I was determined to catch Sarah somehow... Everything comes to he who waits and

341

sure enough, just before lunch the lady herself appeared from out of the back door, looking very casual in knotted shirt and denim shorts. Not at all bad for a forty-something I had to admit. In an effort not to appear too pushy, I let her open the conversation…

"Hiya, enjoying the sun?" I waved the Blackberry in response, adding that I was making the most of it while I could. "You do that Paul; I hear we're in for showers this time next week." Bugger! Never-the-less, it did give me the opening I was hoping for.

"Talking of next week, are you and Adam free next Sunday afternoon?" I explained why, to which she responded that she wondered why she hadn't been invited yet. She, not we. That told me two things. Firstly, that she'd been shopping in Connie's and secondly that Adam almost certainly wasn't going to be around for yet another week. "Are you sure you're OK on your own Sarah? You know I'm only next door and I remember the last time…"

"That's just Adam. He worries about me. He never normally goes away for more than a day or two but…" She then went on for the next two minutes dropping the name of a well-known German bank that was in crisis and the price of a barrel of oil the past few weeks. All stuff she could have picked up from Sky News or the Sunday Times supplement, but she was also aware that I could do the same thing, so it was an easy alibi to offer for her husband's absence.

I very quickly came to the conclusion that either all of my neighbours were bloody good actors or only a few of them were actually involved in the drug business. I had to accept that it was quite possible that Colin was, and the girls not. That Adam was and Sarah was not. Possibly even Tom, but not Alice… It wasn't getting any easier. The one thing I knew for sure was that just as soon as Kathy returned to St Matilda's Bay, I had to get back down into those tunnels and find out exactly where they led…

"If you're not too busy, why don't you pop round for a drink?" A clear invite from my neighbour. "Promise I won't bite." Was this woman flirting with me? Is this what she's normally like when she goes without… Well, without whatever she and Adam do on the rare occasions he deems to come home. Under different circumstances, I may well have been tempted and I admitted as much to Kathy when we next spoke, but all things considered, anything along those lines was strictly off limits! No, harm in a little innocent flirting though eh?

"Cheeky!" I grinned. "I don't see why not. But I should warn you, there's not enough meat on me to be worth biting. Even the mosquitoes don't bother." I half expected her to keep it going with 'maybe just a gentle nibble then' or worse, but she didn't. I would like to think she knew me well enough, not to mention my impending partnership with Kathy, not to take it any further than we had. I too resisted the temptation to accept her offer with anything remotely like a double entendre.

It would have been so easy to hit back with 'I'll be up your back passage in a flash', but thought better of it. Instead, I decided a simple 'Cheers mate, I'll be right with you' would suffice and at the same time defuse any sexual tension that might have arisen. Not for the first time lately, I found myself relieved that the person I was talking to was not a mind reader...

Sunday afternoon in Sarah's back garden passed pleasantly enough, with no further flirting on either side and no mention of Adam either. In fact, all she wanted to talk about was Kathy, which was fine by me. I could talk for England at the best of times, but when it came to that girl, there was no stopping me. However, I was careful not to mention Ystalyfera specifically, just 'a little village near the Brecon Beacons'. I was taking no chances. After our telephone conversation, it could just as easily have been Sarah listening in as anyone... If anyone.

The two glasses of wine I consumed may have loosened my tongue a little but I was still alert to any way she might try to trip me up, or give away anything I shouldn't. I had taken my one and only opportunity to check on the kitchen floor. I was beginning to feel more like a bloody building surveyor than an amateur detective! Having polished off one large glass of very fine dry white wine, I was offered a second.

Sarah was sprawled on a sun lounger, while I contented myself with a simple folding chair. It seemed like the gentlemanly thing to do as I offered, "I'll go," then as an after-thought, "if that's OK?" She showed no sign of being unwilling to allow me into her cottage, but just smiled in acceptance, happy not to have to move from her position in the sun. I reached down to collect her glass, wishing I could read what was going on in those eyes and beyond...

Given no clear direction to the fridge gave me a few extra seconds in the kitchen. The floor was similar to Barry's, though I didn't think as expensive. Maybe I wasn't the only one to shop at B&Q. Once again, I could see no obvious cracks in the grout and the only light switch on display, like Tom's, had to be for the over-head. I say 'on display' because it had occurred to me that some of the other cottages may not have been re-designed in the same way as that of Miss Jones. I could think of no logical reason for wandering off into the back room, so I poured the wine, replaced the bottle in the fridge door and returned outside.

I was becoming more and more frustrated. There was so much that Kathy and I knew, plus a lot more we thought we knew and even a few things we strongly suspected without a single shred of evidence, but we could prove absolutely nothing without an extensive search of everyone's houses and those damned tunnels. I did have one stroke of luck though. After her second glass had been devoured, the lady said she needed to lose some of it. I took this to mean Sarah was in need of the loo. I took my chance. "That'll make room for some more then…" I took her glass and followed her into the kitchen. "We must do this again sometime. My treat though."

As she made for the stairs, I quickly poured the last of the wine into our glasses and headed for the dining room. I knew I only had seconds, a minute at the most, but it was possibly the only chance I was going to get so… Most of the floor was covered by an exotic rug, with dragons and snakes and various Oriental patterns. Surrounding that were highly polished floor boards, nothing else. How easy would it be to roll the rug back, lift a few of the boards and… I heard the sound of flushing upstairs and hurried back to the kitchen doorway. I had deliberately left the dining room door open to deaden the sound of my sudden exit. As Sarah arrived at my side, I deposited the wine glass in her hand. "Your wine milady." I joked.

She took a sip and replied, "Why thank you Evans. Chilled to perfection I see." So, she'd taken the trouble to find out my surname, had she? Back on a serious note, I motioned towards the back room, hoping she wouldn't notice the door was now a few inches further open that she'd left it… "I *love* that carpet, Sarah! Japanese, is it?" She happily took me by the hand and led me back into the room I had so recently vacated. I couldn't help noticing her hand was slightly damp. It's odd the way things penetrate your mind. Well, my mind at least. I couldn't help but hope the dampness was due to the fact she hadn't fully dried her hands after washing them…

"Mongolian, I believe. It's something Adam insisted on bringing back from our honeymoon cruise. Costs a bloody fortune to have cleaned. Ugly think I think, but he adores it." I deliberately went down on my knees to examine it closely. I touched it, stroked it, made a few of the right noises, then lifted it slightly pretending to check its thickness, all the while trying to get a look underneath... I had to admit I actually liked it, and told her so, but then I always did have somewhat bizarre tastes in many things. "Really?" She said. I felt she was asking more about my taste in the bizarre rather than the fact that I liked the rug itself. I left it there and we went back once more into the garden and the warm sunshine...

"I really should be going after this one, just in case duty calls." I waved the 'ping' machine to accentuate the point.

"Are you sure you wouldn't like to stay for dinner? I haven't cooked for two in ages, it would be a plea...."

"Sorry, I can't Sarah. Another time maybe but I have two or three calls coming through about seven or eight and I'll need to be by the laptop." The look she gave me seemed sincere. If I hadn't had my current doubts about her, among others, I would almost have believed she meant it. In fact, she probably *did* mean it. Having noticed fresh lever marks on one of the floor boards under the Mongolian carpet, I bet she would happily keep me there. Anything so that she could keep a watchful eye on this man who kept poking his nose into everyone's business. But for all that, I swear she really sounded so sincere. Only time would tell...

54

In a dimly-lit room, shortly after midnight, five men and three women were discussing the current position:

"So, the letter didn't work then?"

"Not in the slightest. If we're not careful he could screw up the whole show. He has to be stopped."

"I agree, but that was a clever move on the phone. Probably bull-shit but we can't risk it, not this close. We need to think of another way to stop him. If this got out all over Twitter it would put all our carefully laid plans at risk. That cannot and will not be allowed to happen!"

"What else is there? The fire didn't scare him off. Neither did the smack on the head. Maybe you should have hit him harder!"

"Too risky. Anyway, I think he's satisfied about the so-called cellar now. Him and the girl were in there again the other day, we caught them on CCTV. Didn't stay long and the kitchen was spotless. I think we fooled him there…"

"But he won't give up, you know that. He was round at mine checking the floors you know. He thinks I was born yesterday. We have to put a stop to this now!"

"I like him… I think he could be useful to us in the future if we could just get him on side."

"You've got to be joking! He's even worse than that girl in the shop. He'd be telling all his old mates back in Crawley…"

"We'll see. We'll hold him off until after the August job, then put it to the vote. I think it could be handy to have another one on the team, less chance of being caught out if we're all batting on the same side."

"You're the boss… I suppose with the girl-friend coming this week-end, he'll be tied up with her for a few days, that should keep him out of our hair for a bit…"

"I'm not so sure. Strikes me she's even worse than him! Seems to get off on the thrill of it all. Poor girl has no idea of the danger they've got themselves into. She could get herself killed if she's not careful…

"OK, we'll leave it there. Keep a close eye on them both and we'll meet again next week. And this time, try not to make it quite so bloody obvious. At least in four weeks it'll be all over."

"Until the next one…"

55

Damn! I wish it was Friday already. There was so much to do in such a short space of time. Everything would be so much easier if Kathy were here already. Or even if we could just *speak* without feeling like the whole of Cornwall was listening in. Thank God for fire damaged helicopters. As least that kept me occupied for most of Monday now the West African's had come back to work, though Christ only knows how I'm going to get through the evening! I had now spent seven nights up on the cliffs over-looking the bay, 'walking off those dreaded night cramps' and it had all been a complete waste of time.

Apart from a couple of fishing boats I had seen nothing worth mentioning when we had our daily chat. Not that I would have dared to say too much even if the entire Bristol Channel had been sending secret messages to our roof-tops. At least now I knew it wasn't paranoia… Someone really had been in my cottage checking the laptop. Well, that had been a waste of time. The only message of any interest was the one I was reading that very moment, and I suspect they were already aware of that one. It came from 'a.friend@ some internet provider I'd never heard of.com' and it read, "Final warning my friend. Back off now or you may not live to regret it!"

Any normal reader may well have been scared shitless opening a message like that, but it no longer bothered me. Kathy and I were going to see this through to the bitter end, whatever the cost! I replied with a sarcastic 'No, idea what you're talking about *friend'*, but the message bounced straight back at me saying 'the internet domain cannot be found, etc.' Clearly a one-off sent from an Internet Café. Could this be a clue? I checked the time… Just after eight a.m. I went to the front window to see who was about. Connie's was already open, had been since seven no doubt, Rachel's normal starting time.

I could see movement inside the Mariners so I had to assume Colin was busy setting up the bar for another day. Too early for the girls though. They would arrive about ten and to the best of my knowledge, Harwick didn't have

348

an Internet I. From where I stood, I had no clear view of The Beachcomber or either of its occupants. I glanced in the opposite direction, but there was no movement from any of my neighbours. I rushed to the back to check the rear gardens. All clear. Then back to the front.

Somehow, I needed to find out who was missing from the bay, apart from Adam of course, my number one suspect who hadn't been seen 'officially', at least not by his wife, since the end of June. It was now Monday, 15 July. That date suddenly rang a bell with me. I had to check the calendar. Yes, as I thought, tomorrow was going to be Lisa P's birthday. In all the drama of Kathy moving down and chasing drug smugglers, I was at risk of forgetting my priorities. Mental note to self: Never forget your old friend's birthdays…

Spur of the moment plan: Go outside and catch Minnie waiting for the school bus. Surely either Alice or Tom would be at the door. That would eliminate two more suspects. I might even spot Sarah, or Barry… I slipped a proper shirt over my 't', lit my first cigarette of the day and did just that…

"Morning Tom, I was hoping to catch you." Stage one completed. Now to dangle the worm and see what I might catch. "What with everything else going on around here the past few weeks, I keep forgetting what the arrangements were for Minnie and Cheryl…" There, a genuine question with just a hint of how busy I'd been what with one thing and another. But he didn't bite. However, his response left his position open to suggestion.

"Same here old son. I'll check with the wife and let you know. She's the organised one in this house." With a manly laugh he was gone. I gave Minnie a peck on the cheek and waved her off to school. There was only two weeks to go before the summer holidays. Again, I was reminded of my responsibilities. Even with everything that was happening in the village, I had promised the girls a week down here and a week in Northampton. I wasn't about to let them down. My only concern was for their safety though. Could I really risk having two young girls around when it could all kick off any day now? Shit! If only I knew for certain when the drop was going to be made.

There was only one possible way to find out. It was by no means a certainty, but if I could get to the end of one of those tunnels, I might just overhear something to give me a clue. A gang meeting in the back room of The Beachcomber for example. An actual date would be *too* much to hope for, but one of the gang might just let slip something about 'only a couple of weeks away now'…

Walking back down the lane, I tried to check the other two cottages between Tom's and my own—I no longer counted Debbie's—for any sign of movement, but again, nothing. I carried on down towards the beach and sat on the edge of the two-foot drop to the beach at the end of the lane. There were steps either side for pedestrians to go down, but the centre had been deliberately cut away to stop people, mainly teenagers, driving down onto the sand... From where I sat, I could clearly see Pat and Brian tidying up

The Beachcomber from the Sunday night session. Unlike Colin, who liked everything spick and span before he went to bed— 'Can't be arsed facing all that stale beer and shit in the morning!'—they were usually too knackered to do all that hard work at one o'clock in the morning, preferring to start the day with some good hard slog, or so I'd heard. It takes all sorts as they say... That just left Barry and Sarah unaccounted for. Either of them could easily have slipped into town to set up the phoney e-mail account. Surely that had to be the way it was done, but it was a Hell of a drive just for one threatening message.

Never-the-less I couldn't imagine any other solution. In their delicately balanced situation—they must surely be fully aware of how close we were now—to set up anything out of the ordinary on their own home computers would have been nothing short of professional suicide. One swoop from the drugs squad and it would be the end of the road for their multi-million-pound caper. None of them were stupid. They had proved that adequately by working out what Kathy and I were up to. They were unlikely to throw it all away on such a school-boy error...

"Go to the other phone babes." It was all I needed to say for Kathy to understand our mobiles may no longer be a safe method of communication. While we were more than happy to keep them on their toes with our idle 'twitter' threats—it may even bring one of them out into the open—there were certain things I needed to say that I didn't dare risk being over-heard... On my last visit to her home in South Wales, I had jotted down the number of the public phone box positioned right outside their house. We found it useful with Kathy living in a house full of noisy but loveable children. It was easier to her hear what I was saying, and on a more personal level, she was able to describe in lurid detail exactly what she had planned for the next time we were together.

There are certain things a mother does not want to know about her daughter, even if she *had* been as bad, if not worse in her own younger years. Enough said, I think... It was quite a peculiar set up, that public telephone. Due to the fact that Kathy's mother had purchased the property—formerly the village Post Office—and all its land, the phone box now actually stood on *her* land. This meant the Royal Mail had to pay *her* a monthly fee to keep it there…

"Things are moving on Kathy," I began. "I had an e-mail this morning, anonymous of course, but saying pretty much the same as the letter. So, you were right yet again hun, this really does prove we're onto something. It also means they *know* we are! It was sent at 07:48 today. I know for certain where most of the villagers were at that time, but I've yet to see either Sarah or Barry today and of course Adam still has to be the favourite." I briefly explained the rest of my morning's activities and she seemed to be in agreement with me.

To put her mind at rest I assured her I was in Harwick. Apart from anything else, St Matilda's Bay didn't even have a public box. No, doubt the locals killed or maimed the GPO when they attempted to install it, in the same way they got rid of any church people all those years ago. I had enjoyed the walk to our neighbouring village. Despite its run-down state, it felt safe.

"Tell me something Paul," this came out of the blue. "Apart from a church or a Post Office or a public phone, the usual things that most villages have, what else is there that St Matilda's Bay doesn't have? I don't mean an all-night diner or a Tesco's Superstore…" I had to think about that one. She'd already killed off any chance of my usual witty response.

"Surprise me…"

"Well, you've been there over a year now so you should know better than me, but in my…" she paused to calculate the days, "I make it about twenty days, and nights, I've never yet seen a policeman, the good old-fashioned booby on a bike that they proudly boast about on television. Doesn't that strike you as odd for a seaside town? Even though it's tiny, it still attracts big crowds and both the pubs can get a bit rowdy on a Friday or Saturday night." I had to admit she was right. The only time I'd actually witnessed a man in blue was the night of the fire. Of course, there had been the CID visits, but certainly no 'country copper'. Apparently, there had been the day Colin said they'd come and taken Debbie's Fiat away for testing, but I never saw them…

"No, you're right, hun, they never come down here, only in an emergency. So, what do you think that tells us?"

"The way I see it, it means they either already keep a close eye on the place, maybe they already know something's going on but can't quite pin-point it…" I chimed in with the alternative, "Or our friends are paying them to steer clear!"

"Exactly my lover." For a brief second, I forgot about our local villains and enjoyed the 'my lover'.

Kathy's next question threw me. "Would you ever take Ellie back?"

"Where the fuck did *that* come from?" I couldn't help but ask.

"Well, it's the one thing we never talk about," the lady explained. "I know we always said the past is the past and not important and all that, but you'll never believe this, my ex called me earlier."

I wondered where this was leading. While Kathy knew quite a lot about my ex, I didn't even know *her* ex's name, let alone their reasons for splitting up. Until that very second, I honestly couldn't care less. Kathy knew I had always had a hard and fast "No, going back" rule when it came to past relationships. In all honesty, despite my very strong feelings at the time, if Ellie had phoned me the following week, claiming it had all been a mistake and she wanted to come back, the answer would still have been no. I tried to keep my voice steady as I said as much to Kathy.

"That's exactly what *I* said, babes," she replied. I don't know if she heard my audible sigh of relief, but I swear most of Harwick did. "He was an arsehole first time around so why should this time be any different? I just laughed and put the phone down on him." It was then my turn to laugh.

Following five minutes of 'dirty-flirting', the little lady warned me to be careful, very careful not to do anything until she got there. Then we would pick our moment and check every inch of those tunnels and find out exactly where they ended. Hopefully even over-hear some of the gang's plans. She agreed it was a long shot but we had very little else to go on... We put our respective hand-sets back in their cradles and I strolled back home to catch up on my work. I knew there was enough there to keep me busy well into the night.

I was taking a chance just walking into Harwick with so much going on in Lagos, but it had to be done, and after all, the whole trip had taken little over an hour. For the first time ever, I had lied on my 'OUT OF OFFICE' message, claiming to need an emergency dentist visit and 'back in one hour'. As I left Harwick and headed down the one-way lane to Tilda's, I marvelled at the fact I'd even found a public phone that worked in that back of beyond place! And for my next trick, try to spot a passing motorist make the speed camera flash as they drove past it... The two I spotted both failed.

I will hastily skip over the rest of my day. Suffice to say I was stuck on the laptop until well after midnight—must remember to claim my overtime—and crashed into my bed thoroughly exhausted. I didn't even have the time or the energy to do my last cliff walk of the shift. But it was all worth it, just for those few short minutes talking to Kathy. I couldn't help wondering how many minutes we would have together in the future. If the population of my little bay had anything to do with it, precious few was my best guess...

56

Another long hard shift bit the dust shortly after ten o'clock on the Tuesday morning. Apart for a reasonably quiet Sunday, it had been non-stop. I'd certainly earned my overtime that shift. Dave and I always tried to complete our hand-over as early as possible at the best of times, but having checked through his six and a half days of e-mails, he recognised this had been one of my busiest on record and was happy to relieve me, even though he knew he was in for much of the same for the next seven days. I vowed to do the same for him the following week, shortly after breakfast with Kathy for the fourth morning running... Hopefully. To date, the longest time we had spent together had been three nights and four days. Each of them had been full of fun, laughter and I have to admit quite a substantial quantity of alcohol, but more recently we can add thrills and excitement to the equation.

As of this coming Friday, 19 July, there would be other things to consider: Shared bills, cleaning, washing, ironing... But I wasn't ready to start thinking about that just yet. There was the chaos of finding places to store Kathy's former life in my little cottage first, and the small matter of keeping ourselves alive!

Determined to keep up the appearance of normality, I went over to the Mariners for one of my favourite lunches, Steak and Ale Pie with chunky chips. I'm a man of simple tastes. The most exotic dish I've ever sampled was a paella in Benidorm. I shall say no more on the subject. It was a week best forgotten for many reasons, too numerous to be worth a mention. The bottom line is that I'm very much a meat and potato man, with a few eggs thrown in, though not normally at the same time.

I do enjoy a good Indian but even then, it's normally with Bombay potatoes rather than rice. With no racist intentions, I'm simply not a man with a taste for foreign food. This is why I like eating in the pub over the road. The closest Colin gets to foreign food is a lasagne, and even that's frozen and 'nuked' for serving as opposed to his normally home-cooked fare... Tuesday lunch was generally a quiet affair. Very few holiday-makers and just the odd visitor from the nearby villages. It meant Lala usually had time for a chat, but I saw no sign of her this day. She hadn't mentioned anything about time off, but then why should she? Was I just becoming more suspicious of anything remotely out of the ordinary? Quite possibly.

In any event, the food was excellent as always—not poisoned and no visible signs of broken glass enclosed—and Colin had even supplied me with extra chips. 'You'll need to be keeping your strength up' he smirked as he placed my plate on the table. He'd long ago stopped asking the standard 'any sauces', knowing full well I prefer my food exactly the way it comes, with the exception of fried egg or bacon sandwiches, neither of which were on the Mariners' menu, and neither of which could possibly be consumed by a true Englishman without a dab of HP.

Tuesday afternoon arrived with no further threats to either life or limb. Neither had I succeeded in spotting either Sarah or Barry, or for that matter even Lala, returning from their morning task of sending threatening letters or e-mails. Yes, I reluctantly had to add my favourite barmaid to the list. If all was fair in love and war, she may well consider her five thousand pounds a month worth waging war with me, whom I would like to consider as her friend... As things stood, and again I emphasise there is little or no evidence to substantiate any of this, I had Barry, Sarah and Adam down as my prime suspects.

Pat, Brian, Colin, Lala and Rara as 'possibles', and bringing up the rear, my two rank outsiders: Rachel and Tom. For the record, under the heading of stating the bleedin' obvious, I considered Alice a non-runner. Unless she was the modern-day Ma Baker of the gang, barking orders from an easy chair, I couldn't see how Alice could possibly be involved, or even wish to be...

I changed into shorts and t-shirt and spent the rest of the day in the garden. Not much people-watching to do on a week-day so I chose the back garden, settling myself down on the bench facing the sun and the rocks leading up to the cliffs. Not a position I would normally choose, but it offered very little distraction and I had much to think about... I'd been out there no more than ten minutes when something caught my eye. Recent experience told me not to make any sudden movements and attract the attention of whoever it was, but without even looking I felt someone was watching me from up on the cliffs.

As the sun peeped out from behind one of those wispy white clouds you see so often on a summer's day, the glint of its rays caught the glass on something. I suspected the lens of a telescope. I gave it a couple of minutes and sure enough each time the sun disappeared behind the edge of the cloud, so did the flicker of light. There seemed to be no sign of him, or her moving away from the secluded spot fifty of sixty feet above me, so a few minutes later I casually went inside, only to return with a glass of Lucozade and wearing my sun-glasses. Despite my increasing years, most of my body parts are still in perfect working order, as Kathy will confirm, and that included my eyes.

Somewhat unusually, having finally given in to wearing distance glasses for driving at the age of forty-five, I found my failing eye-sight return to normal ten years later. Even now I can easily read a car's number plate at more than the regulation thirty metres. It is a total mystery to me optician... Mindful to keep my head at a slight angle, I focussed on the rocks once more. From behind the comparative safety of tinted glass, it was easy to spot the source of the twinkling reflection. What *did* surprise me was that it looked as though rather than coming from the top of the rocks, possibly someone looking down on me from a prone position, it seemed to be two or three feet down from the apex. I kept my eyes focussed until the sun went behind the cloud again. It was only then that my keen eye confirmed it wasn't a telescope at all.

I struggled to keep the knowing smile from my face as I took a large swallow from my glass. All of a sudden, everything that had happened to me in Debbie's house that day made sense. They, whoever they were, knew exactly when I'd entered the back door and exactly when to strike because they'd watched the entire episode on CCTV. The smile left my face though as it also dawned on me, they now knew the both Kathy and I had returned to Debbie's kitchen only last week. There was only one thing to do, and for once I had to do it alone...

It was risky but I considered it a chance worth taking. As soon as the sun set, I took myself along the lane, past all the other cottages without a single glance at any of them, past the entrance to the footpath to the side of Tom's house, onto the lane and around the bend. I'm not going to pretend it was easy, but a few yards up the hill, I found a gap in the hedge and slowly worked my way through the bracken and gorse until I found the course of the footpath, just past the end of Tom's garden.

From the position of the trees at end of our gardens I had a rough approximation as to where the camera was situated... God only knows how they'd managed to fix it to the rocks without anybody below noticing. Then I remembered all but Mr Taylor, the former owner of my cottage was quite possibly involved, and with the state of his health, I doubted he spent much time in his back garden. I still held out the hope that Tom wasn't a part of all this, and consoled myself with the thought that the gang would have waited until his family were out for the day, or at least a few hours. It would have been easy enough for them to find out... Ask Rachel. But how long had this been going on?

Certainly, more than a year or I'm sure I would have noticed someone abseiling down the cliff and drilling holes in the rocks. And those tunnels weren't new. The whole operation had probably been in place since the Agnes Point raid, or even earlier. I remembered watching war films where prisoners of war would dig two or more tunnels in case one was discovered. Why wouldn't a well-organised gang like this not do something similar? I had to admire their ingenuity if nothing else. The only thing missing from the tunnels were the rails to run the little trucks along while removing tons of earth... I found the camera easily enough. Now all that remained was to figure out a way to disable it. There was no way I was going to climb down there, as fit as I was for my age. I'm totally ignorant of spikes or crampons or anything to do with rock climbing.

The only rock I knew a bit about was the Kinks or Guns 'n' Roses. I had to find another way. Yet another thing for me to think about that evening, along with preparing my home to become *our* home—at the moment all the bedroom wardrobes were crammed with *my* clothes—and the minor detail of halting the progress of the next drugs run, preferably with Kathy and I in a position to celebrate the fact... I so wanted to drive into Harwick and give Kathy the news but I feared it would arouse suspicion if I was seen leaving the village that late in the evening.

It would have to wait... Safely back indoors, I decided with only two full days to go, I had to make a start on sorting out the bedrooms first thing in the morning. I hoped nothing happened around the bay that I needed to know about, but right now, my priorities lay firmly with Kathy. I wasn't going to have her move in and live out of a suitcase. That decision, however, was taken out of my hands...

57

I awoke on the Wednesday morning to the sounds of someone moving about down-stairs. Had I been James Bond, there would have been a convenient tin of aerosol deodorant and a cigarette lighter by the bed, or a gun under the pillow. I literally had no defence against whoever had invaded my property and was probably at the very moment creeping up the stairs armed with a crow-bar, or sawn-off shotgun, whatever the weapon of choice was for a twenty-first century hit man. In previous threatening situations, albeit never as serious as this one, I had always been able to talk my way out of trouble.

Somehow, I didn't think shallow words, or 'Would you settle for a pillow fight?' would do the trick this time. Why was it, even with the end of my life approaching did I always find humour in everything? I suspect I have an in-built defence mechanism. My body may well have been in good shape, but I was becoming ever more convinced I wasn't right in the head. What the fuck would Kathy make of *that* one I wondered? I just had to hope I would live long enough to find out…

"Wake up ya lazy bastard! Coffee's on."

"Shit Kathy, you scared the life out of me!" But that didn't stop us rolling on the bed and enjoying the biggest hugs ever. She could feel the tension in my body as we held each other as though we hadn't seen each other for months. Over coffee and cigarettes, she explained how everything was packed and ready to go by yesterday evening and she saw no point in waiting another two days. The plan had been to ride down right after the rush hour, but she had gone to bed bursting with excitement and been unable to sleep. Doze, wake up. Doze, wake up. At three o'clock she had decided to just get up and go, leaving a note in the kitchen for her mother.

"Apart from anything else, the motorways are dead that time of the morning." I was tempted to add that so are most normal *people* but as we hadn't considered ourselves normal from 'day one' I saved my breath. Just lately I'd been a very light sleeper, alert to every little sound in the bay and was astonished to find I hadn't heard the sound of her Honda 250 roaring in first thing. "That, my lover, was because I cut the engine halfway down the hill and coasted in." Inspired!

"I swear to you I was going to sort it all out... I promise hun! It was the first thing on my 'to do' list this morning... Honest!" She emptied the contents of her rucksack onto the bed as I cleared a couple of the drawers and one section of the wardrobe. All of my winter clothes could be stored away in the spare room for now. I would worry more about the space issue nearer the winter. Luckily Kathy is a jeans and t-shirt person like me most of the time. I'm not even sure I've ever seen her wear a dress. I knew of one denim skirt and two pairs of shorts, but the rest of the time her legs would remain covered.

I considered that a crying shame as the lady possesses gorgeous legs! Not to mention a fabulous bum! And of course... No, I'll say no more... Consequently, everything she had with her—there was also a pannier crammed with more t-shirts, socks and undies—was stored away neatly in the small space provided. I knew from past experience, that once we returned to South Wales for a complete clearance operation, four out of my, *our* five wardrobes would be Kathy's and I'd be left with just the one, but that was fine. I rarely wore a dress either so the only hanging space I required was for my one and only suit.

From what I remembered of her room at her mother's house, most of her worldly goods would be her collection of dragons and skulls. I did warn you I had an attraction for strange ladies, and Kathy was and still is one of the strangest. But in a good way. Being an old cottage, there were plenty of little nooks and crannies to tuck the collection away and show them off to best effect... In the future, assuming we had one, I would enhance the trinkets with subtle lighting. She had only been living with me for an hour and already it felt right...

I had been sadly lacking in the shopping department that week. For most of the past four or five days I had been pre-occupied with work, CCTV cameras and smugglers. I had neglected to top up on the bacon and eggs department. As with the wardrobe re-organisation, it had been on my list. The fridge and cupboards would have been full to bursting by Friday afternoon, the time of Kathy's planned arrival. 'Always expect the unexpected Paul. Wasn't that what we said from the start?' She got a slapped arse for that one, cheeky cow!

I promised we'd do a massive Tesco's top-up later, but for now, I would nip over to Connie's for the essentials: Bacon, eggs, hash browns, a new loaf of bread and a couple of packs of JPS. Rachel was her usual bright, cheerful, chatty self. 'Bet it's good to have Kathy here full time, eh?'—Don't ask! I don't have a clue—I love a woman who wakes up with a smile on her face. In any other time in my life, I felt she and I might have got together, but as close as we were, Rachel and I would only ever be mates. As I strolled back across the road, armed with a carrier bag full of goodies, in the early morning sunshine, all seemed to be right in the world. It was a gorgeous morning.

The beach was clear, reminding me of a desert island, somewhere in the Caribbean. The sea was a deep blue which only enhanced the effect. The birds were singing and I had a beautiful lady waiting for me at home. Once again, I had that feeling of euphoria, the warm glow that spreads through your entire being. The feeling that makes you believe you can take on the entire world if needs be, and win. It was a feeling I'd known before in my life, but it had never before been so strong.

Over breakfast, I outlaid my plan of action. I had no doubts in my mind that Kathy would fall into my way of thinking, certain that she would have a few ingenious ideas of her own to help tackle the on-going problem. I told her of my discovery on the rocks above the back garden and repeated my thoughts and plans, recent suspicions, plus the runners and riders, my favourites and Alice, the non-runner, "First off, I need to get back into the tunnels. We have to know exactly where they lead. If we can eliminate even one or two people, we could gain ourselves some valuable allies. But that means disabling that camera. I think it's safe to say they have someone monitoring it at all times, but I think if we can somehow put it out of action for just a few minutes, I think I can slip into Debbie's kitchen and out of sight in seconds. I'm fairly sure they wouldn't risk trying to repair in broad daylight. I already have an escape route planned, but I need that camera to go off line…"

"Leave the camera to me," she beamed, "I have a plan."

We couldn't wait for darkness to fall over St Matilda's Bay that day. We spent the morning at the supermarket, a fifteen-mile drive away, and even took the pretty route home via the cider farm. I'd only ever been there once before but thought Kathy would enjoy it. I was right. It was fascinating watching the whole process from the apples arriving by donkey cart, going through the processing and the presses, finally arriving on the shelves of the souvenir shop in gaily-labelled bottles. It kept our minds occupied for a couple of hours.

Back home, we put the shopping away like a normal couple, glad that we had postponed the Iceland trip for another day. I wasn't convinced frozen food would have survived two hours on the back seat of my Clio in the warm Cornish sun. We took advantage of Colin's 'All Day Menu Throughout the Summer' with a light lunch of ham, egg and chips, washed down with—surprise, surprise—orange juice and lemonade. Any other time, we would have chosen steak, lager and several vodkas for Kathy's first ever meal as a resident, but there was work to be done and clear heads were the order of the day.

Our response to Lala's look of amazement was that we planned an evening celebration and didn't want to risk 'getting pissed and missing out later on'. This seemed to satisfy the lady's curiosity. Even Colin came over and laid the palm of his hand on my forehead to check that I was 'feeling OK'. We kept up the appearance of normality throughout the afternoon and early evening by spending an hour or so on the front bench people-watching, another hour round at Tom's as Minnie arrived home followed by a walk along the beach.

To an outsider, we would have looked like any other happy couple enjoying the early days of a new relationship. It was our belief that whoever almost certainly had us under constant surveillance would think the same. Surely, we wouldn't be planning anything to undermine their operation the very day Kathy moved in, would we? How little they knew, or so we hoped…

As the sun went down, our plan came into fruition. As I had hoped, there was still no sign of life next door. Adam had not shown his face in the village, at least not during daylight hours, for nearly three weeks, and now his wife had also performed her own vanishing trick. We strongly suspected this was because the day for the next drop was imminent. However, this was to my advantage. With the key in my pocket and the torch in my hand—extra batteries and bin liner also in pockets—dressed in black shirt and my suit trousers, the only dark clothes I possessed, I sat on my back door step and waited… I double checked everything was working. I had no intention of repeating a stupid episode from my past, when I went down into Reigate caves, armed only with a box of matches. And a half empty one at that. By the time the matches had run out, I was completely lost. The firemen who came to rescue me three hours later were not impressed… Meanwhile, back on the door step, I spotted Kathy's signal, a very quick flash of dim light from the cliff top. I climbed over the two fences that separated my cottage from Debbie's unlocked the back door and slipped inside, leaving the key in the outside lock. I hit the switch to release the trap door, then wedged it open with a broom handle. Ten minutes later, just as I was putting the last of the rubble and earth mix into the bag, I heard the key turn in the lock. I switched on the torch and headed for the 'crossroads'.

Taking a left turn, I pulled my secret weapon form my trouser pocket... A ball of gardening twine, the kind of thing Barry would no doubt have miles of, tucked away in his shed. Having attached one end of it to one of the slats of the wooden tunnel floor, I made my way through the darkness in the direction of Sarah and Adam's property. I estimated the length of the tunnel to be about fifteen yards. As I had suspected, it would prove to be the shortest of the three tunnels. At the end, I swung the torch around and found an opening, complete with ladder.

Quietly climbing it—I could not be *sure* Sarah hadn't come home—I noticed a wooden panel, identical to the one under Debbie's kitchen floor. In my mind, I already knew this would exit into the Bonnell's back room, under the polished floor boards where I'd spotted the lever mark. I listened for a few minutes but heard no sound. Returning to the foot of the ladder, I cut the twine, returned to the cross-tunnel section, untied it, wound it around my hand and placed it in my left pocket.

I then repeated the procedure with the forward tunnel, the one that started with a bend. This one was much longer as I knew it would be. As I approached the end of the tunnel, I fancied this one to be in the region of fifty or maybe sixty yards. I heard voices and music. I was almost sure I was right underneath one of the bay's two pubs. But which one. I climbed yet another ladder and tried to recognise the sounds. I could hear glasses chinking and several people talking but couldn't recognise any of them. It all had an echo effect from my position just a few feet below.

There was a glimmer of light but that gave no clue. I had a very strong temptation to see if the wooden panel would lift but the sensible part of my brain talked me out of it. I carried on listening to see if I could hear Lala's voice, by far the loudest of the girls I knew, but no. It was all just a jumble of noise. I couldn't even make out a conversation, a word or two even, let alone identify a specific person's tone. Frustrated by the knowledge of being so close, yet so far, I cut the twine and returned again to the cross section of tunnels beneath Debbie's kitchen.

I released the twine from the floor board and having loosened my trousers, tucked it into the front of my shorts and waited a few seconds, just in case I heard anything from above, though not knowing what the fuck I could have done if there *had* been anyone there... Not a sound. All was going well so far. Now for the final tunnel, the one I expected to be the longest of the three, the one we suspected would end in the woods on the hill. In my mind's eye, I had already pictured the ladder at the end of this one. Twice, maybe three times longer to reach its greater depth... I was beginning to resemble the Hunchback of Notre Dame as I crouch-walked along the last tunnel.

I wondered if I would ever walk in an upright position again. The torch-light alternated between floor and ceiling for the first thirty yards, eager not to miss an entrance to Barry's cottage, and at the same time hoping not to spy one under Tom and Alice's. I found both. Each time I crept up the ladders and listened intently for any sign of life. Nothing from Barry's, but the blurred sound of what I assumed to be a television coming from the shaft that led to Tom's house... It's strange how the mind plays games in your head. For some reason, I half expected to hear the familiar 'doof-doof' of the EastEnders theme tune as the soap reached yet another ridiculous, cliff-hanging climax.

I detest soap operas! I heard no such thing. Hardly surprising when I remembered it was around nine o'clock, but that's just the way my mind works... I felt no need to remain there any longer. Unlike the sounds of the public house, I knew exactly what, and who was above me this time. I didn't even bother cutting the twine, but continued my quest through the under-belly of the bay... My heart sank as I finally accepted the involvement of my oldest friend in the village. I hoped I was wrong. Maybe the tunnel had been there before Alice, Tom and their family had moved to the bay and they were completely ignorant of the fact... Reluctantly, I had to accept I was making excuses for my friends.

After what seemed an age, I reached the end of the line. There was no further to go. Faced with a solid brick wall in front of me, the only way was up. Unsure of what I would find at the top, I chose not to use the torch but made my way up the last ladder by touch alone. I couldn't risk a shaft of light shining out through the darkness and into the woods. If my theory was correct and the next date was close, there was every possibility the gang would be holding regular meetings to ensure everything was in place, which could well include making sure Kathy and I were well out of the way. What better place to hold those meetings than deep it the woods well outside the village, and out of our sight...

The climb felt like an eternity. Without the aid of my trusty ball of twine, I would never have had a clue how far I had come through the tunnel, or how far up the ladder I'd climbed. Above me was only darkness. This suggested there was more than just a pile of storm damaged trees blocking the final exit. Even in what is often described as a pitch-black night, once your eyes become acclimatised to it, you can still see a certain amount of light. The sun, our life force, never truly sets... As I neared the top of the ladder, I gave myself an imaginary pat on the back. I had been right. For once my suspicions had been proved correct.

Following the dismal failure of our plan to spot lights flashing over the sea at midnight, I allowed myself a broad grin as I heard voices from above. At last, the Gods were smiling upon us. This was the first stroke of luck in all our delicately planned investigations. It was more than we could have hoped for as we began our quest. They were *indeed* in these woods, and I hoped making their last-minute arrangements. I silently climbed as high as I possibly could and very nearly banged my head against yet another wooden panel. I missed it by inches.

This time there was no sign of light at all. I took this to mean that, unlike those under the pub and the four cottages, this one was far more solid. 'Oh, these bastards are clever!' I thought to myself. They had to have been prepared for a stray rambler accidentally stumbling across this tunnel entrance. They couldn't risk a simple twigs and branches affair for the main way in and out with their deadly cargo... But, I deduced, that should make it even easier for me to locate, once daylight returned. With careful measurements taken, it should be relatively simple to walk through the trees, with its decorative ferns and bracken, treading heavily until we heard the sound of wood below our feet... I waited and listened.

Again, the voices were muffled and deadened by the panel that separated the smugglers from me, but one voice stood out above the rest. He was clearly the boss, the big cheese. I could barely make out what they were saying, but I did over-over-here a few note-worthy words. I prayed I would recall those words when back in the safety of Windy Cottage and the arms of Kathy... The one thing I hadn't thought to bring with me was a pen and paper, so I had to put faith in my normally excellent memory. I say 'normal' because these were truly abnormal times… The words I heard were: Martin, fifth, ten o'clock, Mario, life and Evans.

The sound of my own name sent shivers down my spine. Most of the talking had come from a voice I didn't recognise. I had to assume the ring-leader, possibly even a major crime syndicate boss, down from London to finalise his operation. Of course, that could have simply been my over-active imagination bouncing back to life once more. But I *did* recognise the voice who had spoken the only words I succeeded in picking up. The voice that had spoken my name. It was unmistakably that of St Matilda's favourite landlord, Colin Hughes…

I quietly and carefully returned through the dark and still silent tunnel, untied the last of the string, tucked it into my right-hand pocket and up the ladder into Debbie's kitchen. Then I carefully replaced all the necessary materials under the cellar door and after checking to make sure the coast was clear, left by the front.

58

"Are you absolutely sure?" Kathy couldn't believe what I'd just told her. Although we both suspected there was a very good chance that Colin was involved, neither of us wanted him to be one of the top men in the organisation. The way he had spoken, louder than all the others, bar the boss from London, had made it quite clear he was the voice of Tilda's, the man holing it all together in the village. Possibly even the one who brought the idea down here... We both so wanted it to be Adam Bonnell, he had always seemed a bit on the shifty side. Or even Barry Marlow. Despite his openly friendly attitude towards me, not to mention his invaluable advice on re-designing my garden, I had never fully trusted Barry. But Colin? That *was* a shock!

The man who had welcomed me, welcomed both of us into his public house, treated us more like friends than customers... There had to be a mistake. But there *was* no mistaking his voice. Unlike the others in the village, I had often heard Colin speak loudly. It was just something pub landlords had to do on occasions. You could hardly speak in a whisper when asking for seven pounds and sixty pence over the sound of the Cockney Wurzels and the ensuing laughter...

"I'm afraid so, hun. No, doubt about it." Here we were, planning the last hour or so of Wednesday evening in his pub, to celebrate Kathy's arrival. I wasn't entirely sure it would feel like a celebration now, not knowing what we had now learned. But never-the-less it had to be done. We had no choice but continue the façade of lovers enjoying their first day together in what was now *their* home. "We have to go hun. It would look mighty fucking suspicious if we didn't..." Kathy agreed.

It was just after ten as we walked into the bar of the Mariners—I estimated I had spent about an hour under- ground, crawling through those tunnels—and there he was, smiling as ever, chatting to the customers as though butter wouldn't melt. And all the while plotting my down fall as an amateur detective, maybe even planning my funeral arrangements for all we knew. Having discovered the camera on the over-hang of the cliffs, I was now certain it was Colin who had either spotted me on CCTV, or had been advised of my entrance to Debbie's cottage by another member of the gang, followed me in and smacked me on the back of the head, then calmly ripped down the light fitting to make it appear an accident... At least this time, thanks in part to Kathy's ingenuity, they couldn't possibly be aware of my recent escapade, let alone how much I'd discovered.

At that point, we had seriously considered reporting all we knew to the police. On reflection, what did we have? A series of tunnels under a tiny hamlet in Cornwall. For all Kathy and I knew, with our limited knowledge of the area, that could be the norm all over Devon and Cornwall. We had no cast-iron evidence of wrong-doing by Colin or any of the villagers.

Even Colin's words were, in legal jargon, no more than hear-say. The most the police could possibly do with such slender evidence, would be to shut down the operation, fill in the tunnels and wait for the drug smugglers to start all over again. God only knows why, but we both agreed it would be far better to try and catch them in the act, and risk losing our new friends and neighbours, not to mention life and limb...

"Hello, you two! And a very warm welcome to St Matilda's Bay to you, young lady. May your stay be a long and happy one." The slimy bastard took Kathy's hand in his and kissed the back of it. My flesh crawled, but I managed a beaming smile which I hoped looked sincere, as did she... In a bid to show a united and happy front, we accepted his offer of drinks on the house. "I do like to give our new residents a proper friendly West Country welcome."

The little shit even put on a fake Cornish accent as he handed over two pints of Carling Darling. I don't think I've ever found smiling so difficult. We both knew only too well the welcome he had for us in quite possibly the very near future. I remember thinking how 'nice, polite and charming' several people, especially the ladies thought Dr Crippen was. The same had been said by many about a certain Herr Adolf Hitler. I've always been one of those people who called a spade a spade. Totally honest and rarely known to sham enjoyment or affection. I saw no point. If you like someone or something, you said so in my book.

Similarly, if you didn't you should make that equally clear. But by necessity, this had to be the exception. Kathy and I were in love. We had spent a year getting to know each other, our friends and family, our good and bad habits, like her snoring and my farting... On this special day in our lives, we had to look the part. It wasn't just for Colin, but for the girls and all the customers as well. It was only to be expected and we didn't dare let them down.

The last thing we wanted was to hear mutterings of 'that won't last long' before we'd even shared our first night together as a proper couple... In a bid to keep a genuine smile on my face, we took a table near the window and Kathy told me how *her* hour had been spent. I have to say it worked, especially the clever twist at the end of the tale. We spoke in whispers, the way lovers do, with the odd laugh thrown in. Anyone watching would have sworn on the Bible that we were recounting an evening of sexual pleasure...

Interspersed with the odd 'you're terrible!' and 'that's outrageous!' from me, for effect, Kathy explained how she followed our plan almost to the letter, "You were right. It wasn't that far over the edge. Once I'd activated the telescopic handle of the umbrella, I reached it quite easily. Even a little short-arse like me! Luckily, it wasn't too tight and I managed to nudge it down just a fraction as we agreed. I imagine, until they feel it safe to fix it, they'll have hours of fun watching the oak tree growing at the bottom of Debbie's garden."

This made us both chuckle and reminded me of the 'live' feed you used to get on Channel Four during the night in the early days of Big Brother, when absolutely nothing happened. Four hours of people sleeping. The perfect cure for insomniacs everywhere... "Then I had this brain wave." At this point, Kathy leaned across the table and whispered in my ear. I would swear, by now, the entire pub was thinking what a pair of naughty people we were. They had no idea!

"I slipped my leggings off, then my knickers, then I leaned over the edge and carefully dropped them onto the camera..." I confess, that even in the midst of danger, and with one of the ring-leaders just thirty feet away from me, I felt a familiar twitch in my shorts. How bizarre. I whispered back:

"I hope it wasn't the black Frenchies, I *love* them!" With a coy smile, she apologised and suggested we go shopping for some new ones, adding that it wasn't all bad news. She still wasn't wearing any, and in any case, it was all for a good cause. She would have loved to be a fly on the wall, or in this case the rocks, when they finally felt it safe to re-position the camera and found them... 'They'll think someone ripped them off and threw them over the side in the throes of passion,' she concluded. I recalled a similar situation from my past but I shan't dwell on it...

That girl always manages to make me smile, even in the face of adversity. While I'm risking life and limb crawling through dark and dangerous tunnels, searching for clues regarding desperate and hardened criminals, she's dropping her knickers 'on camera' the little tart lol... Noticing the rapidly encroaching closing time, we ordered another pint with vodka chasers and agreed no more talk of drug-smugglers, dodgy gardeners, disappearing neighbours or very bad pub landlords, we set about our celebrations. Now safely back in our favourite position, propping up the bar, we downed the vodkas and ordered two more.

Large ones. I had always thought myself pretty good with a one-liner or a come-back, but I had to admit that in Kathy I'd met my match. Faced with Lala's comment about our late arrival, she simply replied, loud enough for all to hear, "I'm sorry, but I wanted to Christen my new home." With that, we raised our glasses and gave a rousing 'Cheers!' to all around us.

On the Thursday morning, we busied ourselves with tunnel measurements and the words I had over-heard from Colin the previous night under their secret meeting place deep in the woods over-looking the bay: Martin, fifth, ten o'clock, Mario, life and Evans. The last one took no working out at all. Clearly, they had been discussing how I, Paul Evans, was causing them problems. Unless they were all closet fans of a certain well-known comedian who was appearing at the St Martin's Lane theatre on the fifth of whenever, I saw no other possibility. If only I'd been able to hear more of the conversation, I may have had some clue as to what they had in store for me, and even been prepared for it.

It was a pretty safe bet that something deadlier than a light fitting would be involved next time. But what with the echo effect in the brick and wood tunnel, combined with the sounds of constantly moving feet, several of which sounded as though one or more of them was walking onto the wooden panel, I had only been able to make out those few words. We considered each of them carefully:

Martin: We both agreed immediately that Martin was the boss, the man down from the city to over-see the plans for the next shipment of heroin and cocaine coming into the UK via our village. It seemed the only logical conclusion, especially when we considered the unknown voice. I confirmed it was definitely not Brian, Tom, Barry or Adam, and yes, it was definitely a man's voice.

I know Rachel sometimes shows masculine qualities but the voice heard was not female. Indeed, I would be willing to swear I hadn't heard a single female voice amongst the mumblings. I suggested that it could even have been Mr Suit, the man on the beach, but admitted I hadn't heard him speak so it was only a possibility.

Fifth: Surely a date. The fifth of August, a Monday, was only just over two weeks away, and quite possibly the day the boat was due. I also pointed out that it was the second week of the school holidays and either Cheryl would be down here in Tilda's spending time with her new best friend, or vice versa. They were already Skypeing each other about it. We agreed to make arrangements to ensure that was the week Minnie went to Northampton. If we were right in our assumptions, that Monday would not be a good time to have two twelve-year-old girls to worry about. Kathy made the valid point that it could also mean the fifth shipment this year.

After all, they may be criminals but they were never-the-less still businessmen. 'And women', I added. Again, my over-active imagination kicked in and just for a second, I was reminded of German invasions and the fifth column. I discounted that one without a second thought. No, it had to be a date and judging by recent activity, August looked to be the favourite. We could think of no other reason for the use of that particular word and moved on to the next.

Ten o'clock: No, debate at all on those three words, or should that grammatically be two if the apostrophe is taken into account? Either way, if we were right about 5 August, then obviously that was the estimated time of arrival, presumably ten o'clock at night. We both made a mental note to check the tides for that evening. Kathy quite rightly suggested that had it been Colin's voice, he could simply have been pointing out his need to be back in the Mariners by that time.

Mario: That was a tough one. Kathy, as always, the comic even at times like this—yet another thing we appeared to have in common—thought what I'd heard in the tunnel the previous night had not in fact been a gang of smugglers, but a group of friends playing computer games. I appreciated the levity she brought to the proceedings, life of late had become far too serious. Where had all the fun gone? Roll on 6 August and we could get our lives back to normal, hopefully. "How does Crete sound? It's lovely there in September."

I needed to plan happier times. It was something I'd always done. It's good to have something to aim for in life and in Blokie's book, holidays are always something to look forward to… The more the merrier. Kathy's response was as romantic as ever, and I thought *I* was the big softie in this relationship… "Even Butlins at Bognor would be great as long as you're there, babes." I had to agree, but given the choice… However, returning to the serious business of Mario. It was just possible the boss' full name was Mario Martin. It wouldn't have surprised me to find an Italian connection. I tried to recall a trace of accent in the stranger's voice but failed miserably. So, muffled was it, that he could have been Pakistani, Arabian, even Australian for all I knew. We attempted numerous other connotations, but nothing seemed to work. Moving on…

Life: Another difficult one. It could have meant any number of things. The imminent end of mine. Worse still, of Kathy's. That didn't bear thinking about! Or indeed both of our lives. The possible prison sentence if they were caught. Ever the joker, Kathy piped up with, "Complete the following famous Stevie Wonder hit—For Once In My…? Correct, Mr Evans! You have won Bully's Special Prize—A speed boat!"

I had to accept the possibility that I had misheard the word 'life'. It could just as easily have been knife, or wife. I could not be certain. Despite the synchronised laughter, this led us into the last word I had heard. My name.

Evans: Yes, it was *my* name. A name I'd grown used to over the past sixty years, and I hoped to live with it for many more to come. It may even one day be Kathy's name, but that was still a long way off and as the American's say 'If it ain't broke, why fix it?' There was no disputing I had heard my name spoken by Colin. It could mean one of several things. What are we going to do about Evans? Is Evans still a problem? This Evans chap, how should we dispose of his body? I wasn't keen on that one. Trying her best to stay optimistic, Kathy suggested he might have been saying 'Evans? He's no trouble. Just asks a lot of questions but he knows nothing'.

Now that one I *did* approve of. It even showed Colin in a better light than we had thought. That wasn't a bad thing. The one thing we both agreed on was that the villagers, and their boss, had not been holding a secret meet of the Lee Evans fan club.

"So," Kathy was summing up, "We have the famous— '*infamous*' I corrected my loved one—*infamous* London gangster, Mario Martin, arranging with his Cornish crew, none of whom are actually Cornish—isn't that rather curious?—to smuggle in several million pounds worth of hard drugs, on the evening tide of Monday, 5 August. And if Evans causes any more hassle, we end his life." I can't say I was too enamoured at the prospect, but I had to concede it was probably the correct one...

The most annoying thing of all is that had we taken the time to check one of the afore-mentioned possibilities more thoroughly, we would almost certainly have resolved our dilemma right there at that very moment. The one clue we struggled with the most, would have given Kathy and I all the answers we needed had we looked in the right place. We had been that close, that a simple stroll into Connie's one morning would have almost certainly have placed the final piece into the jigsaw.

59

Having successfully worked out the entire dastardly plan, kind of, although we had no hard evidence, or genuine proof of its authenticity, or indeed how we planned to scupper it, we spent the rest of the day wandering around the village, then a few minutes up the hill towards Harwick and back down to the beach. We walked hand in hand like lovers do, cheerfully bidding all and sundry a 'good afternoon', whether or not we knew them. To all intents and purposes, Kathy and Paul were enjoying the first day of the rest of their lives together.

In fact, what we were actually doing was working out as accurately as possible, without raising suspicion, the distances between Debbie's kitchen and both of the pubs, plus how far up the hill we would need to go before we knew roughly where the final shaft emerged into daylight... I don't know if Steve Taylor had been a closet gay, or a tailor in more than just a sound-alike of his name, but amongst the few possessions he left behind when selling me Windy Cottage was a tape measure. I had discovered it in an old chest of drawers some time earlier and decided to save it for a rainy day. I've never been one to throw things away. I wouldn't say I'm a hoarder exactly, but I confess to annoying more than one former partner with my reluctance to discard anything I think may someday come in useful.

It had taken Kathy and I more than an hour to unravel the four pieces of twine which I'd hastily stuffed in my pockets and shorts. It came as no surprise to yours truly how knotted they had become. As any of my former disco, band and karaoke colleagues will confirm, it matters not how tidily you put your leads away at the end of the night, there will always be one in knots when you began to set up the equipment the following night. I normally blame Murphy and his dastardly law for that one... I had explained to Kathy the final length of twine, the shortest of the four, as being the distance from floor to exit of the longest tunnel.

This was the most important one. If we were to search the woods for a hidden panel, it needed to be as close to exact as possible. Almost as important was the tunnel under the lane. We needed to know for certain which of the pub's it led to, although knowing what we now knew, it surely had to come to an end right under the Mariners... Having ascertained the approximate distances, we then needed a reliable way to make comparisons around the village. We could hardly crawl up and down the lane on hands and knees armed with a tape measure, pad and pencil.

Firstly, having made sure the CCTV camera had not yet been re-positioned, I had tried walking from the front of the house to the back as Kathy measured my strides. Without looking like I was on a route march, my paces came to between two feet six and two feet nine inches... Roughly. It was an Imperial tape measure. This was clearly not going to be an easy calculation. Then Kathy tried. Her height being several inches less than my six feet, her step was considerably shorter, as close to eighteen inches as made little difference. That was to be our guide.

There being no need to check the other cottages, all of whom we now knew had secret trap doors, we decide to test the Mariners' theory first. Starting from the very end of my garden—I couldn't resist a quick look, Kathy's knickers were still up there—we walked the full length of our garden, along the side path to the front, across the road to where my car was parked at the back of the public house. Using the extra distance form the end of my garden to compensate for the fact I lived about thirty yards closer to the pub than Debbie, and assuming any hidden trap door would have to be at the rear, we both silently made the calculations as we walked. We agreed to within five yards.

With The Beachcomber being the other side of Connie's shop, a good thirty or forty yards further down the lane, the tunnel underneath us *had* to end under Colin's pub. This came as no surprise, but what it did do was confirm that my measurements and Kathy's length of stride were pretty damned close. Having retrieved the desired CD from the Clio—there had to be a reason for us being around the back of the pub—we then strolled down to the beach. This was purely bluff, our intention being to fool anyone who may be watching us from behind curtained windows.

Having spent half an hour sitting on one of the rocks under the cliffs, laughing, joking and smoking, we then chatted away about nothing in particular as we walked back up the cul-de-sac and passed Debbie's front gate. It was at this point we stopped talking... 'One, two, three...' Kathy was silently counting her steps again as we approached the lane, turned right and headed up the hill. The final piece of twine had measured twenty-two feet. As we walked, just before the steady incline, we both tried to picture a spot on the hill somewhere in the region of three and a half times my height.

Why is it you can never find a surveyor when you need one? One of those cameras on a tripod would have made our job so much easier... Kathy stopped walking. We reached a spot that we both thought suitable, no more than fifty or sixty yards up the gradient. Allowing for the thirty of forty yards from Debbie's gate to the "T" junction, the figure in Kathy's head was now almost exactly the same as that of the longest piece of twine...

"I've been meaning to ask you," she said. "Why *did* you stick one of them down your shorts?" I knew the question would come sooner or later. I just hadn't expected to take quite so long. I can only assume the fact that I had allowed her to remove that particular one had dulled the lady's senses momentarily.

"I just thought you might enjoy retrieving it." I smirked. And she had. We just never got around to discussing it. "Seriously though, I needed to differentiate between the two tunnels. There was every possibility the one under the lane and this one would be similar. I wanted to give us a better than evens chance of getting it right, hence left pocket, right pocket and as my suit trousers failed to include a middle pocket..."

"Ooooooh," she cooed. "Looks like I'm hooked up with the second Einstein." We both resisted the temptation of making comparisons between my good self and a certain time traveller's dog... To our left, there was a fence between the woodland and the lane, presumably private property. To our right though, the woods appeared to be common land. No, fence or hedge to bar the entrance. Not even a ditch. Also, it was just far enough from the old railway station to be out of view of the old gentleman himself or anyone using the car park.

I'm sure the opening of that, earlier in the year, must have put a doubt in the minds of Colin and his cronies... There was no sign of any cars or walkers, certainly no CCTV cameras to catch us, so we ventured in... Starting from a central point that we both agreed closely matched our calculations, we walked in ever-increasing circles, careful not to miss an inch of the land below our feet and mindful of any unusual sounds. Nothing. No, solid wood trap door to be found anywhere. This was a severe setback, just as we had thought we were actually getting somewhere. To make matters worse, the only sign that anyone had been in there was the down-trodden under-growth created by our own body weight. In hindsight—such a wonderful thing—I cursed myself for not waiting until all above me had gone quiet and tried to lift the trap door.

Either Kathy's step had varied with the rise of the hill, or more likely I had seriously miscalculated the direction of the tunnel as it marched on past Tom's cottage. In the darkness of the tunnel, it hadn't appeared to waver off of its straight line from Debbie's kitchen, under Barry's and Tom's cottages, but the dark can be deceptive. Clearly one of us had miscalculated badly. Back on the lane, we tried to view the rooftops in the village to check the positions of the afore-mentioned houses, but the dense foliage of trees and bushes where we stood made it impossible. We would have to think again...

Back in the bay, wearing forced smiles, we sat on one of the benches outside the Mariners and waited for Lala to come out. On quiet days, normally mid-week, she would happily perform a table service at no extra charge. It was so quiet that evening that she not only brought us out a pint each, she even sat down to join us for ten minutes. She and Kathy spent the time discussing the planned girlie night out the coming Sunday. I had almost forgotten about the welcome meal.

I'd invited the whole village to Windy Cottage, *our* cottage, in three days and hadn't even bought the food, beer and wine yet. I had come to St Matilda's Bay the previous year, feeling its tranquillity and seeing it as a place I would happily retire to and live out my days in peaceful solitude, enjoying the company of so many friendly people, plus the excellent ambiance of at least one of its pubs. It just goes to show how little you know about people until you really get to know them. Now here I was planning to invite them all, friends, neighbours, smugglers, criminals into my home yet again. Time to make a shopping list...

The whole welcome party thing was an 'off the cuff' way of gaining entrance to all of my neighbour's houses and exploring their back rooms. In the excitement, it hadn't occurred to me that we were going to have to receive and entertain our guests for a few hours. Guests who quite possibly were plotting our down fall at this very minute, as we were plotting theirs... OK, so back to the supermarket Friday morning. In the meantime, I would print some hastily designed invitations: 'You are cordially invited to... etc., etc., etc.'

This task was completed soon after dinner and we dropped each of them through the respective letter boxes. All were aware, but now it was official. This coming Sunday afternoon from about two o'clock onwards, my house and garden would be full of drug smugglers. Fabulous! 'Welcome to Tilda's, Kathy...'

60

Friday morning saw us heading for the supermarket yet again. The shop was carried out in virtual silence. We'd had a relaxed breakfast, content in each other's company as ever, made the list of required food and drink and set off shortly after ten. I'd been deep in thought for most of the drive. I'd been thinking back to Wednesday morning when I thought someone was downstairs. Of course, it had been Kathy using the spare key I had supplied her with several weeks earlier, but I wasn't to know that at the time. What I *did* know was that someone had been in my house before, on at least two occasions, almost certainly using my laptop to locate my e-mail address and quite possibly plant some form of hi-tech listening device and it could happen again at any time.

I was scared. Not for me but for Kathy. For all her bravado, she was still just five feet two inches of little girl, no match for the type of people who hit six-foot men over the head with light fittings if they tried to stand in their way... "Penny for them?" She asked as we were driving home. I hadn't heard that expression since my grand-mother died and it sounded odd coming from a thirty-three-year-old girl in the twenty-first century. I found a convenient lay-by and pulled in.

"I'm afraid it's another one of those 'no interruption' things hun..." We'd had several of those over the year and we each respected the other's need for them. I began, "As you know, babes, there's things happening in our village that were going on long before you first came down here, quite possibly even before I arrived. Those tunnels alone suggest years of planning, even if only as a back-up to Agnes Point. When I first came here, I fell in love with the place and it, the people that is, seemed to like me. It hasn't changed one bit in my first year here. The neighbours are just as friendly as ever, the pub's still great... On the face of it, nothing *has* changed, but in here," I tapped the side of my head, "Everything's changed! All of a sudden, you're the only person I trust and that can't be right. What do we really know about these people? As you said

378

yourself, not one of them is local, not a real-life Cornishman. They all come from, I don't know... Plymouth, London, Redhill, Crawley... Surely that *can't* be right, can it? I'm living every day as though it might be my last, because of what I suspect, or feel, even *know* in here."

I repeated my earlier gesture. "And now you're in the same boat, by association with me. I think what I'm trying to say is that if it all gets too much for you, I won't blame you if you turn round and head back ho..."

"Enough!" Her voice was firmer and more decisive than I'd ever heard it. "Seriously Paul, I won't have any more of this. I knew exactly what I was letting myself in for when I packed my bags and rode down here in the middle of the night! No, illusions. I already knew most of what you suspected and now I know much of it is true, I'm in this to the end. Not just because I want to be, although I admit a big part of me is enjoying the thrill of the chase, but because I came into this with both eyes wide open and with one intention: To stick by you through thick and thin. We may not be married, quite possibly never will be, but trust me, I'm with you all the way babes, for better or worse!"

We hugged each other for a very long time, drawing hoots from the various vehicles that passed the lay-by, no doubt each of them thinking the same thing and every one of them totally wrong. None of them could ever have guessed at the root of our conversation that day. Although the idea of what they were probably thinking was very tempting...

We spent the afternoon making sure the garden was tidy and cleaning the barbecue in preparation for Sunday's little soiree. I genuinely hoped most would turn up, although I suspected a 'no-show' from Adam. Colin and the girls had promised they would call in from time to time but I had to remember 'It's Sunday and the pubs bound to be busy'. Pat and Brian said as much themselves. Despite the rather under-hand way I'd gone about organising it, I still found myself looking forward to it. Kathy was too. Maybe it was something to do with safety in numbers...

61

"Smithy! Get in here now!" The boss slammed the phone down and waited in clear agitation.

"What is it, guv?"

"We've got a date. 5 August, confirmed by my man in the Met. That gives us just sixteen days to locate and erase Martin."

"But I thought..."

"You DON'T think, Smithy! I do the thinking alright? With the girl dead, nothing's changed so she couldn't have been Martin. The whole show wouldn't be going ahead without him, would it you idiot? We have to start again. Did you get things organised with Mitch and the girls?"

"Yeah, all sorted. We're going down tomorrow. There's a caravan site a few miles up the coast, we've got one of them."

"What about the pub? I thought they did rooms." He was clearly not happy with the arrangements but there seemed little he could do about it.

"Fully booked guv. It is summer remember. Even the bloke on the caravan site stung us for a full week. Didn't like to argue and cause a fuss."

"Quite right," he agreed. "Quite right. Well, I'll be there myself tomorrow night for an hour or two, then I'll pop back Sunday lunch-time. But remember, you don't know me, right? We have to find which one is Martin and take him out of the picture!"

There was a distinct air of tension gathering steam in that room as the date grew ever closer.

"Got anyone in mind?" Smithy was fingering his hand-gun through his jacket. His trigger finger was itching.

"One or two... I've got my eye on the bloke at the end of that row of cottages, Evans his name is. Not been there long. Same with the couple next door. There's just a chance it could be one of the Harwick girls, but my money's on the other three."

"OK guv, we'll see you there tomorrow then." He started to leave the office when his superior stopped him:

"No, you won't!"

Several seconds passed before Smithy's brain clicked into gear, "No, boss, of course not..."

62

Saturday came and went without event. To a casual observer, it was just another summer Saturday in St Matilda's Bay. Breakfast, coffee, cigarettes, lunch in the Mariners, eventually—it was one of the busiest days in the village for no obvious reason. I had called Clair and Richard to make the necessary arrangements for Minnie's visit. Alice and Tom were happy with that, agreeing to have Cheryl back down here the following week.

Kathy and I would drive the girl up to Northampton on the Saturday—the family were all keen to meet the lady who'd put a smile back on my face—and then we were to have an evening with Lucy, just up the road in nearby Kettering. It wouldn't be an alcoholic one, which in itself would be a rarity, as we had to return on the Sunday in preparation for the fifth, even though we still had no idea how we were going to handle it.

Having discovered the full extent of the tunnels, and what appeared to be Colin's involvement, we had toyed with the idea of putting the police fully in the picture, but both agreed we had no solid proof of anything. It had therefore been our intention to play it by ear and hope to catch someone out before August the fifth, or alternatively on the day itself. At that time, I don't believe either of us had a firm plan, deciding to 'wing it' as an when we felt the time was right. After all, the nearest police car would surely be no more than fifteen or twenty minutes away…

In the evening I did something I rarely do. I checked the weather forecast for Sunday. It looked good for the barbecue. I wasn't looking forward to cooking and eating indoors, plus being outside, Kathy and I could smoke whenever we felt like it. Even though we both smoke indoors, out of respect for non-smokers, I try not to if I have visitors… With a possible guest list of twelve, plus Kathy and myself, we had bought two dozen large sausages, the same amount of quarter-pound burgers, several packs of baps and a large quantity of wine and beer. If I'm honest, we probably had enough drink to satisfy twice the number of guests, but it wouldn't be wasted, we were sure of that. Even with a 'use by' date of 'next week' it would have eaten them by then.

I have to say the afternoon went even better than expected. All except Adam and Rachel arrived between two and half past. Even Sarah, who apologised for her recent absence due to an ailing relative. She made up for it by presenting Kathy with a gorgeous green and red dragon in blown glass. Minnie played happily on the climbing frame in between stuffing her tiny frame with three burgers! Had I said twenty-four would be enough? We all took turns in watching her play and not one person mentioned the strange piece of black material perched high up on the rocks.

Alice and Tom brought folding garden chairs with their own drinks holders and happily consumed several cans of beer, in Tom's case, and two or three glasses of wine for Alice. Barry walked me round the garden as Kathy took over the cooking and in typical Barry style said 'Not been doing much lately then' and then to pacify me 'but I'm sure it will be fine when it's done.' Sadly, he was right. With no excuse I could possibly make in public, I had failed miserably in gardening, extending the patio or any of my other grand plans.

At least it was tidy... As promised, the team from the Mariners called in two or three times, chatted to everyone then went back to work, each time managing a beer and a hot dog. Even Pat and Brian popped over briefly, both in turn apologising for their brief stay 'but you know how Sundays are in The Beachcomber.' I hadn't expected them so it was a pleasure to see them and they hoped to see Kathy 'and you of course, Paul' over the road sometime soon. Since coming to the conclusion that tunnel number two only reached as far as Colin's pub, Kathy and I had even considered in confiding in the two of them.

We may well need all the help we could get when the time came. For that reason, I felt quite guilty that we rarely used The Beachcomber. I honestly could not remember the last time I drank in Brian's pub, and I knew for certain Kathy had only visited it the once, that girlie night out with Debbie. Damn! That seemed so long ago now... On the subject of The Beachcomber and girlie night's out, Lala reminded Kathy she was expected in the Mariners about nine.

She and Rara would still be working but it had usually quietened down by then as long as she didn't mind propping up the bar... Does the Pope shit in the woods? Brian had given Rachel the night off so she would be free as soon as Connie's closed. Rara's sister Mish was coming down for the evening and Christ knows how she did it, but Lala had even convinced Sarah to join them.

She failed to talk Alice into it though, even with her 'every girl deserves a good night out' routine…

By seven, things were slowing down at the welcome party. Most of the food had been eaten and several drinks had been enjoyed. People started to drift away. By seven thirty all but Alice, Tom and Minnie had gone, each promising to see us later. Brian had invited me over for a pint on the house by way of a thank you for the afternoon and I happily accepted. 'Good,' Lala had responded. 'We girls will have girlie things to talk about and that doesn't include you, big boy!' I never argue with that girl, and especially when she's poking me in the chest, God bless her… I was just about to grab myself another beer when Tom stood up and offered me his can.

"Waste not, want not old son. I've had more than enough for one day and I need to get these young ladies' home." I took the can of Carling from him and watched as Minnie's face dropped…

"Don't panic, hunni," I crouched down to cuddle her. "You know you can pop round *any* time. You don't even have to ask." This put the smile back on my little girl's face. Mine too for that matter…

As I tidied up the last of the rubbish from the garden and decided the cleaning of the barbecue could wait until tomorrow, I felt absolutely shattered. As if she'd read my mind, Kathy came over and said, "Go inside and sit yourself down, babes. This can wait. Anyway, I need to get showered and changed. I have a party to go to… Yay!" She gave a little twirl like a teenager off to her prom night and headed upstairs. I collapsed into my favourite armchair to finish my drink and reflect on the success of the afternoon.

Obviously, it had been nowhere near as rowdy as the Easter do, but I hadn't planned it to be. It had simply been a very pleasant afternoon with just a few close friends. I gave myself a well-deserved pat on the back for an idea superbly executed. What had started off as a ruse to check out my neighbour's cottage's, had turned into yet another highly enjoyable get-together with them. As I sank lower and lower into the chair, I forgot all the things that were going on all around me, taking over my life and for the first time in weeks, was thankful that I'd taken that turn off the coast road last year. I drifted away with a contented smile on my face…

I awoke sometime later in total darkness and all my muscles felt constrained. I'd had cramp many times before but never as bad as this. And total darkness? There was no such thing! And my lips felt tight... Numb... I could barely move them... "Aha, good evening, Mr Evans."

I knew that voice. I'd heard it somewhere before, recently... It was the voice of Mario Martin, or whoever the stranger had been at the end of the tunnel under the woods. I now knew why my lips felt numb, my muscles ached and I was in total darkness, literally. My hands were tied behind my back, my legs felt as though they were bound to the chair, I was sitting on—a dining room chair I thought, quite probably one of my own—I was blindfolded and had tape across my mouth. I couldn't speak if I tried. I made a feeble attempt at breaking loose but firm hands held me steady by the shoulders.

A vague hint of after shave wafted under my nostrils, but it wasn't one I recognised... I knew I was in my own house. Every house has its own smell and I recognised mine. I gave in gracefully. Whatever else they had in mind, they obviously weren't going to kill me or they would have done so before now. I was equally certain they weren't planning any form of questioning. Why else would I be gagged? But if this was my own house, where was Kathy? Had they harmed her in a way of getting at me?

Was she in fact tied to an identical chair next to mine. I had no way of being sure but I thought I would have smelled her presence, even if she *had* just taken that shower... The voice of Mario Martin resumed. It was calm and controlled. He knew who was boss and it clearly wasn't me, "I know what you're thinking and let me assure you the young lady is perfectly fine. She left the house about half an hour ago and I should think she's on her second drink by now, enjoying a nice little chat with the rest of the girls. Now I'm not going to remove the blindfold because I have no wish for you to see my face, though I doubt very much if you would recognise me.

"Neither am I going to remove the tape from your mouth. I have no wish to hear either your protests or your begging for mercy. Let me assure you Mr Evans, there is nothing you could say that would interest me. You may think you know a little, you may think you know a lot. The fact is, you know virtually nothing. You're aware of a few tunnels and I congratulate you for a job well done on that score my friend, but in reality, all you and your young lady friend have succeeded in doing is annoying some of my esteemed colleagues. Well, it stops right here. Now that we know all about your underground exploits, there is very little else you can do to trouble them. Nice touch with the pants by the way. She should be congratulated for that one. However, you didn't really think that was the only camera we had focussed on the rear gardens, did you? Not quite as smart as you thought are you Mr Evans?"

I was beginning to detest the way he used my name. Nobody had called me Mr Evans for a very long time. Only at grammar school and in job interviews did anyone call me by my last name… "So, you ignored my three warnings, and I'm truly sorry about you having to be hit over the head, but you will see in time it was necessary. I have to inform you; this is your *final* warning. Should you choose to ignore this one you will only leave me with one alternative and neither of us want that do we? From now on, you will keep your nose out of village business, whatever you perceive it to be and you will advise your girl-friend to do the same. I hope I've made myself perfectly clear this time.

"No amount of flashing lights on the cliffs, or 'tweeting' the world with your suspicions will change anything. We simply will not allow it to. Now we're going to leave you to ponder over this. In two minutes, my colleagues will cut loose your hands. The rest you can deal with yourself. I would strongly advise you not to try and follow us or indeed try to take off the blindfold until you hear the closing of the front door. I understand you have arranged a drink in The Beachcomber so I shall not delay you any longer. I shall bid you a very good evening. We shall not meet again, Mr Evans."

I had already earned my hero status in St Matilda's Bay. I had no desire to add to it. I felt the ties being cut behind my chair and the knife being placed gently on my lap. My arms were free. I waited until I heard the door close and recognised it as my own. I waited a further estimated five minutes before lifting the blindfold from my eyes and removing the tape from my mouth. Fast or slow? I chose slow, very slow, and thanked whoever was watching over me that I'd shaved just a few hours ago. As my eyes began to focus, I found I was indeed in my own house, the dining room to be precise. I took the knife and recognised that also as one of my own. Cutting through what I now saw were tie-wraps, I was fully released…

63

It took every ounce of my courage to walk over to The Beachcomber. I arrived there at exactly half past nine. As I passed the Mariners, I could see the girls, including Kathy laughing and joking at the bar, oblivious to my recent experience, the fourth and apparently last of the threats... After bringing my aching arms and legs back to life, I jumped in the shower to freshen up and hopefully remove any sign of restraint to by wrists. Mr Martin and his crew had waited until Kathy was safely tucked away in the bar then simply made their way into my home the same way they had presumably done when searching my laptop and literally caught me napping... Brian handed me a pint of Fosters—they don't serve Carling in The Beachcomber—and asked me how the rest of the day had gone.

Was I becoming suspicious of everybody in the village? Only yesterday I had been reasonably sure Brian wasn't involved in the smuggling caper, but now? Did I spot a hint of satisfaction as he caught me rubbing my wrist? I dipped my toe in and tested the water, "Yeah, it was great thanks. Sorry it's a bit late, I was tied up with stuff, you know how it is."

His reply of 'I certainly do, mate' made me wonder even more. I vowed there and then to trust absolutely nobody in the bay except Kathy until after 5 August, by which time all of this mayhem would hopefully be over and life might just return to normal. More to the point, I hoped Kathy and I would *have* a life, normal or otherwise. As much as I would have preferred not to worry her, she had to know about my bondage session if only for her own protection...

My host and I managed a few short conversations between the serving of customers. It was just the usual landlord / drinker chat. The weather, the state of the nation, how England might fare in the next World Cup... 'Quite well', we both imagined, 'as long as we don't get the Germans in a penalty shoot-out.' Somehow, they had managed a two-two draw with Brazil in a friendly only the other night. Along with a few other customers, we had good chuckle at that, as if it was any guide to their future prospects.

One man, at the opposite end of the bar looked vaguely familiar, but I couldn't quite think where I'd seen him before. That was one of the few drawbacks of living in a seaside town or village. Sooner or later, you were bound to bump into someone you'd met before in the pub, or on the pier. Maybe in a café or on the beach... The beach! That was it. He was Mr Suit. I barely recognised him in casual blue denim shirt and cream slacks. But what to do about it, that was the question. I couldn't ask Brian who he was. The chances are, he would deny knowing the man, proclaiming him to be just another week-ender, or worse still, he could report back to his boss and tell him 'Mr Evans is at it again'.

What other options were there? Wait outside, follow him to his car, assuming he had arrived by car and take down the registration number? And do what with it? Hand it over to the police informing them that 'the driver of this car was walking on the beach in a suit one week, and now he's drinking in the bar of the local pub. I suspect he may be the leader of a gang of drug smugglers...' Welcome to my world, where nothing is ever what it appears to be... There was only one logical option open to me... Tapping him on the shoulder, I smiled and asked, "Didn't I see you on the beach last week-end? Are you a regular visitor? Nice here, isn't it?"

I'm unsure what reaction I expected to receive to my blatant introduction, but it certainly wasn't to see him slam his half empty glass down on the bar and storm out of the pub with his head down, doing his best to hide his face... "Well, that's charming, isn't it?" I said to Brian and anyone else who cared to listen. "I was only trying to be friendly and look at the thanks I get."

My outburst had a double edge. It was designed to bring about a reaction from the landlord, which it didn't. 'Bloody tourists!' That was Brian's only comment as he set about tidying up the mess the spilt beer had made. My comment was also loud enough for the rest of the bar to hear. If it all went badly and I was found dead in a ditch somewhere between now and 5 August, I hoped someone might just remember that particular interlude. Self-preservation I called it. My suspicions of Brian took an upward turn as he made his way to the back room, being replaced by his wife for the next ten minutes. Pat, however, seemed her normal self during that period, as did Brian upon his return...

Kathy and I had much to talk about, but it would have to wait until the morning. I had thanked Brian for the drink and come home shortly after eleven, carefully watching the movements of any stranger I spotted on the short walk. The girl's do had barely started. An educated guess said that Colin would give up, go to bed and leave them to it about midnight. It's uncanny how often my predictions come true where girls and alcohol are concerned. As she crashed through the door just after two, she woke me from my sleep in the armchair…

"Have you been there all night, young man?" Kathy slurred. "You need to get out more, babes. There's a whole world out there and it's got pubs!" I didn't think even a fried egg sandwich would do the trick this time. I simply helped her upstairs and started to get her undressed.

"I'm quite perfectly able, capable to undress myself thank you very much young man!" She threw her arms around my neck in an exaggerated embrace… "But don't let me stop you." By the time I'd removed the last of her clothes— Damn! That woman has a fine body!—she was practically falling asleep in my arms. "That Sarah… She's really, really lovely! But I love you Paul Evans and don't you forget about it!" That was the last I heard from her until the morning. I went back downstairs and poured myself one last coffee and lit a cigarette. Oh yes, we had lots to talk about in the morning…

"Hey baby. Wake up. It's your last day of freedom!" I opened my eyes to see the most wonderful sight a man could wish for. A stunning girl smiling down at him, without so much as a hint of a hangover. A huge smile spread across my face. I pulled her down and kissed her. "I haven't a clue what time I came home last night, or even how I got here, so it must have been a good one! Isn't it great living so close to the pub?" I didn't even bother to explain the state she'd been in. She probably guessed anyway…

"Yep, you're right babes. Up and at 'em, I say. Things to do and only one more day to do them. I was out of bed like a bullet from a gun. Whatever thoughts she may have had about keeping me there evaporated immediately. We both needed breakfast and coffee. There was much to tell her…

"…and all the time I was just over the road getting pissed! The bastards must've been waiting for me to leave!" Yes, I'd given Kathy the good news about the night before. "So, what the fuck do we do now? We can't just sit back and let it happen…"

"I'll be honest with you, babes, I don't see what choice we have." For the first time in my life I felt beaten, defeated. I was thinking aloud, hoping Kathy might find some rhyme or reason to all this madness… "And they hadn't even harmed me, that was the part I still couldn't understand. OK, so they hit me over the head and put me in hospital, but there was no permanent damage. Why not? The only answer I could find was that they didn't actually *want* to hurt me. But that didn't make any sense. If I wasn't really the problem, why hit me? Why send me threatening messages, tie me up, gag and blindfold me, warn me off—and you—only to let me go again? So, where do we go from here? We can't call the police because they have the phones tapped. Probably the same with my laptop…" If Kathy's face had been a cartoon in The Beano, it would have a light bulb over it. "What?"

"That's it, Paul! We might not be able to *contact* the police, but there's nothing to stop us *going* to them is there?" The woman was genius. Sure, these people may well have a few tame coppers in their pocket but surely not all of them. If we were to drive into town, find the police station then just shout it loud enough for everyone to hear, surely *one* of them would sit up and take notice! I was already reaching for the car keys when she grabbed my arm and pulled me back…

"Not yet, it would look much too obvious. We'll do a bit of shopping over the road, let it be known we were planning a garden centre run or something, then have some coffee out the front and after an hour or two of smiley-happy times for the whole village to see, we simply stroll across the road, jump in the car and go." I hated the way she was always the smart one…

"Kathy, are you absolutely sure when we get to the car, you don't just want to drive away from here and never come back?" It had to be said. I had to give her one last chance to walk away from this nightmare I'd inadvertently dragged her into. Her 'Hell no!' response said it all…

64

The weather forecast for Monday July the 22nd had been for warm bright sunshine all over the South West, which is precisely why I wasn't at all surprised to find it was cloudy outside and I even noticed a few spots of rain on the front path. With forced smiles—Kathy and I were rapidly becoming able thespians—we took our places on the bench. Sipping at the hot sweet black coffee, we began our mock argument regarding the now famous palm tree. She was deliberately trying to wind me up about it, saying that maybe, 'just maybe Barry was right.' Thankfully, the rain had come to nothing.

"But he can't be!" I stood up to demonstrate. "Look at it! It's grown at least six inches since I got it! So, now it's not just the rest of the village, but my own girl-friend won't believe me. Charming! Why don't you go and put your name on the sweep-stake then if you're so sure it's going to fail?" This continued for a good five minutes before she told me to calm down and suggested we go to the garden centre and pick out some plants for the back. I replied that I was still waiting for Barry to come and show me what would be right in the sun and the shade, etc.

"Oh, shut up and go and get the keys," she said, laughing. "Let's just go now and *I'll* choose some. You've seen my mum's garden, well that was all *my* doing! See, you weren't expecting that from your little rock chick, were you?" I couldn't be sure if that was all part of the game plan or if I really had landed myself South Wales' answer to Charlie Dimmock, but I was happy to go along with it. I took the coffee mugs inside and returned with the car keys.

We were still arguing as we crossed the road, opened the car door and switched on the ignition... It was dead. I gave it one more try, but not a peep. It sounded like the starter motor had jammed. In the old days, when I used to buy second-hand cars for about two hundred pounds just to keep myself mobile, I remembered lifting the bonnet and tapping the nut on the end of it. That used to work. I knew it wouldn't now though. The motor car had moved forward somewhat in forty years. I didn't even bother opening the bonnet.

It wouldn't have surprised me if the whole engine had gone. I told Kathy to go to her bike and pretend to be looking for something in the pannier, whereas in fact she was to 'run your eyes over the whole bike and see if you can spot any damage'. She understood. Five minutes later, she returned with the news that her Suzuki 250 no longer had a spark plug. I grabbed the AA map from the floor by the back seat and we went back over the road. I don't know how we kept up the pretence but this time we were arguing about the best route to Exeter...

Back in the house, I lit two cigarettes and passed one to her. "That's it, babes," she flopped down in the chair, "we're fucked!"

"No, we're not!" My turn for the light bulb. "We know all our comms are being monitored right? But that doesn't mean we can't use them. There's no reason why we can't dial 999 and get them to come here, is there?"

"Brilliant! Of course, they'd know we'd made the call, but they could hardly stop every police car that came into the village, could they? Oh, you are a star, Mr Evans!"

"Please don't call me that..."

"Police please," she paused. "My name's Kathy Lloyd, my boy-friend's been attacked. What? Oh yes, it's Windy Cottage in St Matilda's Bay. Please come quickly..." She hung up the phone before they could ask any more questions.

Some people, when they hear a siren, can instantly recognise if it belongs to police, fire or ambulance... Something to do with the Doppler effect I believe. However, I'm not one of them. Kathy is, and knew at once they were on their way. Maybe, just maybe we might be able to put an end to this situation. Now all we had to do was convince the nice gentlemen that I wasn't in the middle of a wild fantasy.

Sergeant Kelsey Williams and WPC Natalie Wells were now side by side on my black leather sofa. I had asked Kathy to let them in so that I wasn't seen at the door by any of the neighbours who might have been alerted by the siren... "Come in, come in." Kathy had bid them. They seemed surprised to see me apparently fit and well, sipping at my strong black coffee and smoking a cigarette.

"Now then, Mr Evans," Sergeant Williams began. "Miss Lloyd said you were attacked. Could you be more precise please?" WPC Wells pulled her note book from her breast pocket and began scribbling furiously as I related the whole sorry tale. Not just the actual attack, the light fitting incident in Debbie's cottage, but everything. From the very early days of my suspicions of Barry Marlow and his non-existent personal computer to the recent disabling of both of our vehicles, thereby rendering us virtual prisoners in Tilda's...

"While I can offer very little in actual proof or evidence, I'm hoping what I *do* have will be enough to arouse your curiosity." I went on to list all my thoughts, actions, suspicions... Every possible detail I could remember... My early conversations with the afore-mentioned Debbie, regarding her ex-husband, apparently a serving police officer in Plymouth, the death of a 'friend', even the dog. I recounted my views on the fire, admitting I had been in the house after the effect—with the permission of the owner I hastened to add—and suspected there were actually three separate fires. I reluctantly advised them of the smiling Tom.

I still hoped he was not involved, but if the police were going to thoroughly investigate my claim, they needed the full picture... I pointed out it was during that period I discovered the tunnels and received the crack on the back of my head. I even told them about the 'Stop Press' article in The Pigeon, proclaiming the sad death of Miss Deborah Jones, which we now knew to be false. Unfortunately, my copy of said newspaper had since mysteriously vanished...

On the subject of things disappearing—and this surprised neither Kathy nor I—the warning letter, posted in Plymouth had gone, and all sign of the anonymous e-mail had been erased. Sergeant Williams made a half-hearted suggestion at taking away my laptop and checking the hard drive, but it was obvious his hopes on their IT experts re-locating it were not high. In any case, I was not keen on them taking it away. It would have caused serious repercussions at Brannigan's. I had not mentioned any of this to my employers. I valued my position in the company and was hoping to hold onto it for a further three years...

Kathy brought us all a mug of coffee as we continued. I was pleasantly surprised to find the police had not yet dismissed me as a crank. "I honestly *hope* I'm making a dreadful mistake, because I really like my neighbours. They've been great to me the past year and I don't *want* to think of them as criminals, but..." Sergeant Williams made all the right noises and asked me to continue. I moved onto what I considered hard evidence. The tunnels. At least that much I *could* prove. "…and why else would an entire village have a network of tunnels linking most of its properties?"

I told them of my explorations, which houses had exit shafts, and approximately where we thought the last one came out, somewhere in the woods. I then gave them the words I had over-heard, suggesting someone called Mario Martin had 'something' arranged for ten o'clock on Monday, 5 August. Kathy's suggestion of smuggling brought what looked like a faint smile to both of their faces, but the smiles vanished when I reminded them of the similar situation at Agnes Point…

I also told them of what I considered the odd meeting of most of the men in the village that lunch-time a few weeks earlier, and my almost certain sighting of Adam Bonnell walking from the rear of the Mariners to Tom's cottage in the early hours of the morning… Plus, the strange man in the suit on the beach, and how he'd left the bar the following week like a bat out of Hell, hiding his face, which of course I hoped Brian would confirm…

I took them through to the back garden to show them the CCTV camera, but wasn't the slightest bit surprised to find it was no longer in position. It had vanished. My mind rested easy in the knowledge that should they choose to check, there would surely be signs of it still on the rock face. I didn't mention Kathy's French knickers…

Lastly, I came to the night of my final warning… "And you say it was definitely not one of the people from the village?" I confirmed this as true, adding that I was fairly certain it had been the same voice I had previously heard at the end of the tunnel, near the woods… Miss Wells shook her wrist as if to ease some tension. This came as no surprise. We had been talking for nearly half an hour and she had copied it all down, as near as possible, word for word. Once again, my ever-active mind kicked into gear, wondering why note books had not yet been replaced with electronic tablets. Budgets I assumed…

"I can assure you, Mr Evans, we will be taking this seriously. The one point that has me convinced there may be something in what you say is the bit about the three fires. We had an updated report only yesterday suggesting exactly the same thing." The sergeant finished his coffee and continued. "We were due to come and interview all the residents next week… Natalie?" He turned to his colleague, who flicked back several pages and confirmed 'Yes, Sarge, Tuesday'. "What I suggest is that we go and speak to them all right now…"

"God no!" Kathy interjected. "If you do that, they're going to *know* we've been talking to you!"

"If you would let me finish, please, Miss Lloyd... Kathy," the poor girl looked suitably chastised, "I was going to say that as we are in the area, we could talk to all your neighbours right now and find out who saw what on the night of the fire. The report will be official by tomorrow night so it would be a perfectly natural procedure on our behalf, albeit twenty-four hours premature. As I said, I'm taking this very seriously indeed and would like to be able to take back a full and frank report to CID."

We had to agree that made sense. It would explain why they had spent so long at Windy Cottage. To spend a further half hour or so with each of the villagers should not arouse further suspicion. Kathy and I had been kind enough to give them a little background knowledge of the village. It would *not* however explain why they arrived with a siren blaring... "Siren sir? That wasn't us. There was another patrol car on the lane after some boy racer..." He was good.

Before leaving us, Sergeant Williams asked if we had any plans for the following two weeks. 'If there *is* something going on down here that we should know about, it could be handy having you on site.' I can't say I was overjoyed at the thought of becoming an unofficial police informant, but after what Kathy and I had been through the past few weeks, I agreed it made sense. I had only two concerns. One was for our safety, to which Williams assured me he would speak to the CID team and have a man brought down as on-site protection.

"Wouldn't that look a tad obvious?" I ventured to ask. "You won't even know he's here sir." The second problem, and in my mind the more important of the two, was my imminent trip to Northampton the following week-end.

"If there's any way you can postpone that trip for a few days Mr Evans, we would very much appreciate it..." As long as Tom and Alice had no other plans, I saw no reason why not. With Kathy's 'Bring it on!' attitude, combined with my curiosity and sense of duty, I said I would be more than happy to see it through...

65

Williams and Wells were as good as their word. Through the curtain—I suddenly felt like a nosey neighbour, the comic book 'little old lady' again—Kathy and I watched as they called at each of the cottages in the bay, then Connie's and finally the two pubs. In fairness to them, I considered them very thorough. Having left us shortly after mid-day, it was close to four in the afternoon by the time they done the full round. In keeping with our 'keeping up appearances' attitude, we even called in to Colin's for a lunch-time snack and a pint. All we could do now was sit and wait. We had both promised the police we would cease our private investigations as of that moment and 'leave it to the professionals'.

It was going to seem strange, but at least we could start to act like normal citizens again, with the added bonus that if we weren't going around asking awkward questions, there was just a chance there would be no more visits from Mr Martin. Perhaps we could lead normal lives, certainly up until that Monday in August...

"I feel quite deflated," I moaned, as we sat in the back garden enjoying a glass of chilled white wine from the bottomless box in the fridge. While I was happy that we finally had some assistance, someone who would hopefully have more luck than we had, I would have loved to have found that vital magic clue to solve the case. That's what I get for reading too much Tommy and Tuppence as a teenager...

"I know babes," Kathy agreed. "That was the only reason I *came* here to be honest." I mock-glared at her and received a cheeky wink in return.

Safe in the knowledge that all of our suspicions were now in the hands of the official investigators, the rest of that week near the end of July, less than a fort-night until 'judgement day', Kathy and I finally managed to lead reasonably normal lives. It was possibly the most normal week the two of us had in the year we had shared together, bordering on boring in fact. Well, I should say 'nearly a year' as we were hoping to celebrate the first twelve months on 9 August... I was back on Brannigan's duty the following morning so my time would not be my own for the next seven days.

Kathy made good use of the time she had to spend virtually on her own. She succeeded in talking Sarah into another evening in The Beachcomber and successfully managed to keep the conversation to suitable subjects such as music, make-up, men, life in general. There was, she told me afterwards, not a single mention of village activities, fact or fiction. I suspected certain aspects of the evening must have been hard for Kathy... She's not a great one for make-up, preferring the natural look. Her taste in music would rarely cross over to that of our neighbour either.

I recall seeing Barry Manilow and Billy Ocean in Sarah's CD collection. That would leave just men. I imagine Sarah now knows more about Kathy's ex's than I do, it being a subject we agreed long ago to leave in the past. Truth be told, apart from our immediate recent failures in the romantic stakes, the main reason we came together in the first place, we neither know nor care about each other's past 'loves'. I honestly don't believe we have anything likely to come back and haunt us but you can never be sure...

I lost her almost completely on the Thursday. Having risen early and found we had run out of bacon—a crime punishable by death in Windy Cottage—she spent more than an hour in Connie's arranging yet another girl's night out with Rachel, then spent the rest of the day with Minnie: The morning playing chess and the afternoon on the beach. This suited me if I'm being honest.

I had by then spent so long working from home on my own, with no distractions, that I was struggling those first few days to concentrate on my work. And Kathy is such a *wonderful* distraction! Having said that, some of the lunch breaks were quite memorable. It certainly beat sandwiches and coffee in The Landing, our staff canteen back in the Redhill office, though I have to confess I sometimes miss my fried eggs on toast in the Chef on The Road...

We finally had an evening to ourselves on the Friday. I had promised Kathy a meal and a few drinks across the lane with Colin as long as the laptop remained quiet, which it did... "Do you realise, it's now been three whole days since we..."

"Don't tell me senility has set in already, Paul! What about last night?" She teased me.

"You know perfectly well that wasn't what I was talking about young lady!"

We both knew each other well enough to know we were referring to St Matilda's Bay. Having grudgingly agreed we would have no more part in the affair, the subject hadn't even been mentioned once since the police had visited. We were expecting a follow up call from the CID officers any day, but other than that we had ignored the fact that there was still no sign of Adam. Sarah had barely mentioned him the night she and Kathy had gone out.

When Barry came round to see how the back garden was coming along—not well sadly—he was welcomed with coffee and a lengthy chat about reed grasses, in which my little lady was surprisingly well-versed. To this day, that girl still amazes me with her knowledge of the bizarre and the unusual. Our occasional visits to the Mariners were purely to socialise and catch up with the 'general' gossip, rather than specifics... All in all, it was a very pleasant three or four days for us, acting as a 'normal' couple for the first time.

The week-end passed in much the same way. It was very quiet on the work front with most of the items required to re-build the fire-damaged aircraft now on site. Barely a 'ping' to be heard both days. In fact, there was more activity on my *own* mobile than the company one, mainly thanks to the hastily re-arranged travel plans. I finally managed to re-schedule Minnie's visit to my family in Northampton for the Saturday after the original plan. She would now go on August the tenth instead of the third. "Totally my fault, I'm afraid,'" I lied. "I completely forget I had offered holiday cover at work that week-end... Really sorry."

All concerned were more than happy with the arrangements... Even Minnie, who saw the delay as an opportunity to see more of Kathy and I. The two girls had become quite attached since Kathy moved in. This only made us both even more determined to put all thoughts of Tom's involvement in the unmentionable to the backs of our minds...

The following Monday morning—July the twenty-ninth—we stayed in and around the cottage, half expecting the C.I.D. follow-up visit, although Sergeant Williams had suggested there was a planned call the next day. We were determined not to miss their call. We had found a way through one whole week without talking about tunnels, Mr Marlow's computer, CCTV cameras, the mysterious Mario Martin and his gang of drug smugglers... Better still, no more threatening notes of e-mails or even visits from the great man himself. It had been surprisingly easy when you consider my vivid imagination combined with the events of the previous months... Neither of us had seen or heard anything of our on-site protection officer, but we both considered that a good thing. If *we* were unaware of him, or her, then surely, they were doing a bloody good job. Kathy and I were brought back down to Earth on that Monday evening…

66

"For fucks sake Smithy, there's only a week to go and Martin's still out there! I'm convinced it's one of two people in that bloody village! Either that Bonnell bloke who's gone missing... I suppose it's too much to hope that by some fuckin' miracle that was your doing..." Smithy shook his head in denial... *"No, I thought not. Well, if it is Adam Bonnell, we have a huge problem coz we've no idea where the fucker is! But at least we can eliminate the other possible suspect... That bloke in the end cottage, the one who sprung me in the pub... Evans, his name is. You can leave him to me..."*

"Why can't we just pull the Bonnell woman, guv? She must know where her old man is?" Smithy rubbed his hands together in anticipation. *"I'm sure Mitch and I could make her talk."*

"Really? And how do expect to 'pull' her? Walk right in and drag her out kicking and screaming from the middle of a fuckin' holiday village in the height of summer?" He was not a happy man and thumped his desk so hard to emphasise his displeasure that he spilt his coffee again... *"Get me a towel then we'll go and sort Evans out. That should have some effect. We'll soon hear on the grapevine if he is Martin. And if not, that just leaves Bonnell. In which case, I suggest we all get ourselves the fuck out of this country on the next flight! I for one do not want to be around next week if we fuck this up!"*

67

Kathy and I had just finished the washing up and were contemplating watching a film we'd recorded earlier in the week, one of my favourites, Road House which she'd never seen, when my mobile phone rang. I didn't recognise the number. I suspected it was that nice woman telling me yet again how many thousands of pounds I was owed due to mis-sold PPI. For quite a long period in my life, I had simply refused to answer calls from unknown numbers. It wasn't just the fact that I was being plagued with unwanted calls, but some of them were even charging me for the privilege of screaming abuse at a recorded message.

As I hit the green 'answer' button I prepared myself to yell the two obvious words into the mouth-piece, the second one being 'off'. I know it's a waste of time because the bitch is invariably yet another recording, but it still gives me a modicum of satisfaction to say it... "Paul... It's Brian. Grab Kathy and get out of there right now! Front door. Trust me. Don't ask questions, just do it and get over here!"

As the front door slammed behind us, we heard the explosion. A mixture of gun-fire and the shattering of broken glass as our back door disintegrated from the close-range shells of what sounded like a sawn-off shotgun. We raced across the road and into The Beachcomber as fast as our legs would carry us. "What the fu...?" I began to yell when I realised the bar was half full of late-in-the-day holiday makers enjoying a meal and one last drink before they headed home. "Sorry..."

I nodded at the faces that turned to look at this madman who'd disturbed their evening peace and quiet. I grabbed Kathy's hand, moved swiftly through the bar, lifted the flap at one end and rushed through to the back room. I had no idea where we were heading but it had to be safer than staying out front of house. Pat, who was busy at the bar looked on in amazement as we vanished through to the back rooms. We were met with three doors, one of which was slightly ajar. Through the gap I saw Brian sat at a desk, apparently going through his accounts. We walked in and breathlessly slammed the door behind us... "What the fuck was *that* all about?"

Brian looked suitably perplexed at my outburst, claiming to know nothing at all about any call... "I don't even know your number, Paul. Show me the phone a minute, let me see." But in my haste to 'get out' of Windy Cottage I must have dropped it on the way... "I think we need to call the police." I didn't dare risk telling him there was already someone here... Somewhere... Either Mr Issom was looking for an Oscar nomination or he genuinely had no idea what was going on.

Forty minutes later, Detective Inspector Peter Kearsley and Detective Sergeant Andy Horlock were in the kitchen at the back of the pub... "I'm afraid it's a bit of a mess Mr Evans. You're going to need a new back door. Unfortunately, there was no sign of the burglars..."

I was about to say 'Burglars? They were no burglars! That was some mad bastard trying to kill me!' but a tap on the ankle from Kathy made me bite my tongue... "We'll have SOCO check it for you but I suspect if they're bold enough to break in in broad daylight, it's unlikely there'll be any prints."

"Do you suppose this could have any connection to the visit we had from your two uniforms the other day?" Very tactful is Kathy. Careful not to state the obvious and put Brian on his guard.

"I suppose it's possible," The DI admitted, "but we have had a number of similar incidents reported lately so I think it doubtful to be honest. On that subject sir, will you be free tomorrow morning? We have St Matilda's Bay down for a follow-up visit regarding the fire across the road."

I tried to gauge Brian's reaction to that comment, but found it impossible. Remind me never to play poker with the man... I apologised to him for the rude interruption and the two CID men walked Kathy and I back across the road. In the rush to get out, I'd not only dropped my phone, but also left the keys inside. Not that it was a problem, considering the gaping hole where my back door used to be... "Shall we go inside and check to see if anything's missing sir?"

I prayed for the second time that week that the laptop was still there, and it was. As was the TV, DVD player, camera and every other expensive piece of equipment Kathy and I had either purchased or brought with us... A large part of me had hoped to find most of it missing and that it really had been some crazy house-breaker, but I knew in my heart it would not be...

"Are you seriously telling me," my question was aimed at DI Kearsley, "That this was the work of some local burglars, Inspector?"

"Clearly not Mr Evans, but I preferred not to discuss this in public," came the reply. "I've seen the report you made to Sergeant Williams the other day and I strongly believe this is connected. We've made preliminary enquiries into your allegations but as yet, have been unable to link any of it to a Mario Martin or drug-related organised crime. That was *our* man who warned you earlier sir. He'd spotted someone suspicious in the back garden of Miss Jones' cottage. Sorry it was a bit 'last minute' but he wasn't absolutely sure it wasn't just a nosey neighbour until he saw two men climb the fence into next door's garden."

We sat down for coffee, and a cigarette each for Kathy and I, as Kearsley brought us up to date with the current situation, or as much of it as he was willing or able to divulge...

"There have been whispers of something happening in August, but your report was the first real evidence we had. Now that we have a date to aim for, we're checking shipping lines, passport controls at all ports and airports, the usual routine when we think something like this is on the cards. We're working closely with the Customs and Excise team and we're fairly confident of a result. There is still one problem though sir..." He looked first at Sergeant Horlock, then at Kathy... "You two."

In my time, I'd been a problem to several people. As a child, often playing truant from school for weeks on end, I'd been a problem to my mother. As a teenager, I'd been a problem to the parents of several teenaged girls in the Reigate and Redhill area of Surrey. I will admit to having something of a reputation, but the young ladies concerned never seemed to complain... Just their parents. In any event, it was purely rumour and speculation.

There was no truth in it what-so-ever... Throughout my working life, I've been a problem to various figures of authority, managers and directors alike, who were none too keen on my refusal to suffer fools gladly. If I thought someone wasn't pulling their weight, whether they be my juniors or seniors, I would let them know in no uncertain terms. In my thirty-eight years at Brannigan's, I've worked under seven managers and nine directors, of which all but two have moved onwards but not always upwards, while I'm still there. I believe that speaks volumes... To the best of my knowledge, with the exception of one broken street light and driving a Morris Minor convertible (5737 MT—

you always remember your first car) on bald tyres, I have *never* been a problem to the police.

"You still want us to stay, don't you?" I glanced across at Kathy, who did not appear averse to the idea—Crazy woman! His look confirmed my suspicion. "Would you mind if I had a few words with Kathy before we make any hasty decisions?"

Being on the spot, so to speak, and knowing what we thought we knew, up until that moment, we felt like we were on the fringes of a murder mystery novel. Not quite involved, but seemingly being able to assist the police with their enquiries. It was exciting… A thrill. But all of a sudden, somebody wanted us, or at least me, dead. That was a whole new bag of worms.

68

The meeting of minds had converged once more…

"I believe we now have the situation under control. It was touch and go for a while there, but I think my little chat with Mr Evans did the trick. He showed no sign of recognition which was hardly surprising as we'd never spoken before. In fact, I think we've only ever seen each other once and that was months ago…"

"So, are we satisfied it's safe to continue? With Adam out of the picture for the time being, that only leaves Barry and Colin…"

"I'm sure they can cope. There's only a week to go. Everything's in place, transport's arranged and believe it or not, the police being on hand should work in our favour. It looks like Mr Evans and his lady friend are content to let them get on with things. I can't say I was pleased to hear Potter, Smith and Mitchell were as close as they were, but I think that's also been taken care of. I suspect we'll be seeing more of those three next week…" He laughed and the others joined him.

"All still OK on the 'Martin' front, I trust, sir?"

"Perfectly," came the response. *"Everyone and everything is now in place. Barring any unforeseen circumstances, we're all set for the fifth."*

"What about that business at Windy Cottage? I wasn't expecting that!"

"Me neither, to be honest. I hadn't realised they were that close. We must keep our eyes and ears peeled very carefully for the next seven days."

69

"I'm not sure we want the likes of you two down here!" Colin had his serious face on as he spoke. Kathy and I had decided we would try to stay alive for a few more days in Tilda's and right now we needed a drink, and some company. The kind you can only get in your local pub. The frown turned to a broad grin as he added, "Only joshing guys. It makes a pleasant change to have a bit of excitement in the bay. 'til you arrived, nothing ever happened, now we've got guns and explosions and criminals and all sorts going on! The usual, is it?"

With a pint of 'usual' in our hands, we explained the full story, with the exception of anything DI Kearsley had advised us to keep to ourselves for the time being. We told Colin of the phone call, the shotgun blast—which he, the girls and most of the village could barely have missed—the spate of local burglaries, of which he and the listening Lala seemed to know nothing of...

Passing it off as just one of those things and 'I very much doubt they'll try it again', Kathy and I told them we would take it on the chin and move on. The police had arranged for a man to come and board up the hole where our back door used to be— "He's making a few quid out of us this month," Kearsley had pointed out—so just for tonight, we had re-positioned what was left of the door and nailed it into place. A cut-to-size piece of plywood had replaced the broken glass for one night only. Hardly secure but then if someone wanted to get in badly enough, they would anyway. Even with a dozen Chubb locks on a metal door, I seriously doubted we could have stopped them if recent events were anything to go by...

I think it's fair to say the following days were some of the longest of our lives. Kathy and I barely slept, even though there were two armed policemen discreetly camped out in our Windy Cottage. DI Kearsley had positioned them that same Monday night and they stayed the entire week leading up to August the fifth. The two men shared the guard, one sleeping in the spare room while the other crept around the ground floor systematically checking through the curtains for anything out of the ordinary.

We spent the nights laying in each other's arms trying to sleep but failing miserably. Not exactly the romantic start we had planned for our hopefully long-term relationship, but at least we were together. No, more scary phone calls advising one of us that the other was in hospital. We passed those long nights planning our future, always assuming we were to have a future. As soon as this was over, we would sort the girls out with their week in Northampton and another down here, then we were off. By the end of August, Kathy and I would be lying on a beach somewhere warm and sunny, drinking tequila, smoking endless cigarettes and, all things being equal, celebrating our part in the downfall of one of the country's leading drug barons.

Upon our return, Kathy would find work in a children's home somewhere in Cornwall, I would return to my laptop and we would finally lead the lives of a normal couple. We both wondered how many of our neighbours would still be in residence. Remembering those days and weeks following the 'great wave', it all came back to me once again that those same neighbours, particularly Alice, Tom and Minnie were one of the main reasons I'd chosen to uproot my entire life and move down to the West Country. It was different for Kathy. She had only known them a few weeks and although they had all taken her into their hearts, she didn't know them as well as I did. I'd spent more than a year getting to know them and now I would almost certainly have to start all over again.

There may well be no more valuable gardening advice from Barry, the donkey sanctuary could be losing one of its most loyal volunteers and we would almost certainly have a new name over the door of the Mariners. But then, *had* I really known them? I'd spent a year with a pub landlord who had a smugglers tunnel under his bar, a former teacher who no doubt had shipping routes and evening tides logged onto his non-existent computer... The list goes on. Maybe it would be better to start again, with a different batch of neighbours. Maybe even make a fresh start in another part of Cornwall...

"Fuck that!" Kathy gave me one of her 'I'm the boss' looks. "This is your home Paul, *our* home! If we get through this, and I'm bloody well determined we will, we are staying! I love you and I love this place! Neighbours come and go in all walks of life, so you learn to live with it. We are going nowhere young man!"

I'd been told...

The first week-end of August was bizarre. To begin with, it rained for most of the two days, which meant the usual influx of week-enders and day-trippers dwindled from the usual two or three hundred to no more than fifty on both days. There was an air of tension in the village, almost like a feeling of impending doom. Even the dawn chorus seemed quieter than usual. I briefly spoke to Sarah as she attempted to hang out some washing to dry. Looking skywards, she swore—that in itself was something of a rarity—and went back inside. All of a sudden, nothing about St Matilda's Bay was as it should be.

Even our resident 'protection team' were more on edge than they had been the past few days. Everyone seemed to know something was about to happen in the bay, but how many knew exactly what? Kathy spent the Saturday morning at Tom's playing chess with Minnie. As she passed Barry's cottage, he muttered something about 'fat chance of getting anything done today'. She assumed he was referring to his garden but could not be sure. Rachel barely spoke when I called into Connie's for a few bits and pieces, possibly the fewest words she'd ever said to me... Had I done something wrong? Had word spread about the bay of our investigations again?

Maybe someone had spotted one of our visitors peeping through the net curtains... Outside the Mariners, the sandwich board proudly announced The Strolling Bones—Tribute Band—Sat August the third. No, further information required. Kathy and I would go of course. One of our residents had agreed to sit quietly in the corner of the pub while the other would remain in the cottage. Tilda's life would continue as normal... The rain eased off long enough in the afternoon for Minnie to come and play in the garden for a couple of hours. We discussed our plans for Cheryl's visit, promising to take both the girls to the beach and the water park... In many ways, it was just like any other week-end, except for the atmosphere.

Every smile, every cheery word seemed strained. It was as though the entire village knew something they weren't telling us, which was hardly surprising all things considered. Knowing what we knew, it would have made more sense for them to act normal... Only Colin seemed his usual jovial self. It was a fairly busy night and he had stayed in the bar throughout the show. The group themselves were good. 'Mick Jagger's' voice was spot on. 'Charlie Watts' looked even older than the real thing and even 'Keef' would not have looked out of place in a remake of Night of The Living Dead...

A few pints and a couple of vodka's helped Kathy and I through the evening, even managing to sing along with some of the better-known tracks. Wild Horses, I found out was one of my lover's favourite songs of all time… "God only knows why that SuBo woman had to go and spoil it," Kathy announced in the break. I had to agree. While I admire the woman's talent, she should not be singing Rolling Stones songs…

For the first time that week, we actually slept right through until eight o'clock on the Sunday morning. Thank you, alcohol. Later that morning, following bacon sarnies all round—God only knows what Rachel thought we were doing with all the bacon we were getting through that week—Kathy and I went for a long walk along the cliffs. For me it was like stepping back in time.

Many years earlier, on one of my first visits to my favourite part of our wonderful country, I had walked the cliffs of the North Cornwall coast in the pouring rain. As much as I confess to being a devout sun worshipper, I also share a love for walking in the rain. As long as I have a nice hot bath to sink into when I get home, I find it exhilarating. On that occasion, way back in the late nineteen eighties, I'd put on my anorak—Yes, I know, but they're bloody handy in wet weather—popped my portable cassette player in my pocket, loaded up with Bon Jovi's greatest hits, and spent hours walking the cliffs in the rain, singing my heart out. I may not have the best voice in the world but at least I can sing in tune! As the few people I met that wet afternoon could testify to. There may not have been that many people about, but those who were, looked on in amusement as I tried to reach the high notes of Livin' on A Prayer… No, chance!

On Sunday August the fourth, Kathy and I were doing virtually the same thing. In turn, we picked a song we both knew and tried to sing each one at the top of our voices until we forgot the next line. Then we moved on to another old classic… It was fun and it took our minds away from the goings on in St Matilda's Bay, all of which was about to reach its climax in about thirty-six hours… At one point we stopped and looked out to sea. No, sign of Ystalyfera in the distance. The rain combined with the sea mist made it impossible to see even Swansea.

As we stood there, soaked to the skin, we both wondered if the boat was out there somewhere, en route from Ireland or Amsterdam or wherever, waiting for tomorrow's even-tide. I pictured a strange figure landing on a secluded spot along the beach, holdall in hand, casually strolling past Windy Cottage, then my next-door neighbour's house and into Debbie's. Who would ever suspect what was in that bag, or how many times the delivery had been successfully performed before? If I had anything to do with it, this would be the last time! We held each other tightly as though it might be one of the last times we ever had the chance. At that moment, I had never felt so alive in my life… Tonight, we would make it special…

70

I'm not too sure how we managed it with everything that was going on all around us, not to mention our two house guests, but that Sunday night, Kathy and I made love like we'd never done before. It was full of passion and excitement but most of all full of our love for each other... Many times, in the pub with friends, that old 'What would you do if you heard the four-minute warning?' question would come up. Inevitably, most people's thoughts turned to sex. But could you? Knowing that in less time than it takes to smoke a cigarette, life as we know it would be no more... Would your normal bodily functions... well... function? Personally, despite the advice of the doctors, I think I would opt for one last cigarette.

Let's face it, it could only kill you, right? But yes, even though we both knew our entire lives would surely be turned upside down 'this time tomorrow', it was amazing! Plus, for the first time in nearly seventy years of combined carnal pleasure, we were simultaneous. We fell asleep around three in the morning, having gone downstairs for one last coffee and smoke. We neither knew nor cared how the police would react to anything they may have heard, but I think the after-glow of our exploits said it all. A cursory 'good-night' from the one on duty were the only words spoken. We returned to bed and held each other until we slept. No, words were spoken by us either...

If I'd thought the week-end strange, Monday morning was just surreal! Everything in the village seemed to carry on as normal. And why wouldn't it? Of course, I was sure that was how it was meant to look. Colin was hardly likely to put the sandwich board outside the pub to advertise tonight's entertainment, was he? Special Tonight—Cocaine & Heroin for ONE NIGHT ONLY... It might just have given the wrong impression.

For once, I had to disappoint Minnie. She came round about ten asking if I would play chess with her and I'm afraid I lied. I told the young girl I had a bit of a headache plus a lot of work to do around the house. To take away the upset look I promised her faithfully that we would have a few games the next morning. Now all I had to hope was that she was still there the next morning, and not ushered off to some foster home following the arrest of her beloved grandparents on a drugs-related charge. In a perfect world, she expected to be spending the next two weeks in the company of my grand-daughter, but this was not a perfect world. This was St Matilda's Bay, where nothing was as it seemed... Plus, I was due back on duty on the Tuesday so even a game of chess may prove difficult. Everything was up in the air that Monday and neither Kathy nor I knew what to expect after whatever was to happen later that evening...

We spent the afternoon chatting in the kitchen, drinking bottomless mugs of strong black coffee and smoking countless cigarettes. Thanks to the calming influence of my new romantic interest, I'd got myself down to about ten a day a few weeks earlier. On that Monday, I'd smoked ten before lunch! And Kathy wasn't far behind me. We spent hours talking about our pasts and our futures. We found ourselves telling each other things we probably would never have spoken of had it not been for our current position. It was as though we had to know every little thing about each other, just in case. This was *our* four-minute warning... She told me all about her own tangled childhood, that she'd never known her true father but now had four surrogate dads.

I told her how my mum had gone away to have me, coming home to explain to everyone how she'd fallen in love with a pilot in the Canadian Air Force who was tragically killed in a freak accident. I later learned my father had been a bus driver from Crawley and that I was the result of a one-night stand. My mother later learned he had been married and was too ashamed to go and see him about me. Although that kind of thing has been going on for centuries, in the nineteen fifties it was still very much frowned upon. Kathy thought my mother a very brave woman.

She was and I loved her very much... We learned that by a strange coincidence, we had both fallen into an open fireplace as children and both had the scars to prove it. Having watched Road House only a few days earlier, we then went through the process of showing off our scars. Her appendix, much smaller than mine. My needle mark on the back of my right hand where I tried to push one all the way through, at the age of nine 'just to see if I could'. The two-inch scar on her elbow where she'd backed into a glass door... By five o'clock, we could stay indoors no longer. "Pint?" I suggested.

"Just one?" She replied.

"Hi, you two," we were greeted by mine host of the Mariners. "Glad you popped in; it saves me a coming over." We were intrigued, but Colin had to get back to the bar to serve a few customers. No, sign of Rara or Lala behind the bar. Perhaps they were away making plans for later. Possibly Colin was going to ask us to look after the bar for him while he shifted the goods through the tunnels to meet the van on the lane near the woods… He knew both Kathy and I had worked bars before and it would be a good excuse to keep us out of harm's way while the rest of the village completed the dirty deed… We took our pints of Carling Darling out to the benches and lit another cigarette each.

Having decided not to mention the glaringly obvious, we contented ourselves just watching. Watching to see any sign of planning in the village. Any sign of 'out of the ordinary' activity. To all intents and purposes, St Matilda's Bay that Monday evening was like any other idyllic spot in Cornwall. The weather was mild. Typically, the rain had stopped the moment the weekend finished.

People were coming and going, not in droves but in twos and threes. Some locals, possibly from Harwick, popping down to the beach for the late afternoon sunshine. A few tourists who, like me more than a year ago, had spotted the un-signposted lane heading towards the beach and chose to 'give it a go'. I wondered how many of them might be looking to purchase property in Tilda's after their visit. There may well be two or three cottages up for grabs in the following weeks. Maybe even a pub or two… And a mini-market…

So, much had happened to me in the past eighteen months it was hard to take it all in. I'd gone from being a loved-up fifty-something, happy in my Smallfield home with the lady with whom I assumed I would be sharing the rest of my life, enjoying my weekly karaoke shows with friends I'd grown to know and love over a period of fifteen years or more, to saving the life of an eleven-year-old girl, making me a local hero, moving to St Matilda's Bay, meeting the new love of my life and embroiling her in a drugs war. Along the way, I had met several new friends, friends I had fully expected to share the next twenty years or more with.

Friends like Colin, who served a good pint, put on great live shows on a Saturday night and supplied an excellent menu. Friends like Brian who's pub, though not as popular as Colin's was still a pleasant place to while away a quiet evening. Friends like Rachel, who despite her gossiping nature, was one of the loveliest girls you could wish to meet. Friends like Rara and Lala, the perfect barmaids, always willing to listen to their customers—even me on one occasion—have a moan and groan about life in general. Friends like Sarah and Adam, who kept themselves to themselves most of the time, but would still make the effort to be good neighbours when required.

Friends like Barry Marlow helping me design my garden. Friends like Debbie Jones who probably needed a friend more than anyone I had ever known, and I'd been that friend for a few short weeks, even thinking at one time we could have been more than just good friends. And of course, my closest friends of all in the village: Alice, Tom and Minnie who, more than anyone had been instrumental in my settling here…

"You did the right thing moving here babes," Kathy covered my hand with hers. She could practically read my mind. The faraway look had been quite a clue. She knew we were only about four or five hours from something that was going to change both of our lives yet again, possibly forever. She gently took my chin in her hand and turned my face to look at her. "I don't care what happens tonight, I'm glad you came to live here Paul. More importantly, I'm pleased you chose me to share it with. I will never regret that."

Damn! I loved that girl so much at that second. If the four-minute warning had sounded right then, at seventeen minutes past five on the afternoon of Monday August the fifth, I would have died a very happy man, with a pint of lager in one hand and the lady I loved in the other…

"You've got about half an hour to drink up and get yourselves home," said Colin as he brought us out another pint. So, this was it. We were to be kept out of the way until after the ten o'clock show was over. No, doubt my Clio and Kathy's motorcycle were still incapacitated. We hadn't even bothered to check, so meticulous was the gang's planning. All in all, we considered it decent of him to give us this opportunity. No, doubt he, indeed *they* had been down this particular road many times before. I'm sure he was aware of the risks…

Police, rival gangs, anyone could have penetrated the Tilda's gang and render the evening's activities dangerous, bloody or even fatal. In spite of my immense distaste for hard drugs and anyone involved in the trafficking of them, I had enormous respect for Colin right then for doing his best to keep us safe from it all. Of course, as far as we knew, he and the rest of the village were blissfully unaware that we had our own private police force on hand, one over the lane in Windy Cottage and the other at one of the benches a few yards away, enjoying a pint of very weak lager shandy and a chicken sandwich... Never being the type of person to shy away from a fight, Kathy jokingly asked if we were barred? 'Why else would you want two of your best customers to leave this early?'

"Please..." Colin sat down opposite us and alternately looked us both squarely in the eyes. "There are things going on here that you know nothing about. Oh, I know you think you know, but there's a lot you don't! Now all I'm asking you to do is go home and have your dinners. I will expect you back here at eight o'clock." With that, he was gone. Our 'lodger' had over-heard the entire conversation and was now heading for the beach, for privacy we assumed, frantically punching the buttons of his mobile phone...

At precisely five minutes to six, Kathy and I finished our drinks and were about to cross the road when Colin popped his head out of the door and added, "By the way, when you get in, pop the six o'clock news on." Then he was gone again. As we pondered this last comment, we noticed a sign had been stuck to the window of the main entrance to the Mariners: Closed for Private Party. The management apologises for this inconvenience and hope to see you again soon.

"What the fuck was *that* all about?" Kathy asked as we crossed the road. It was purely a rhetorical question but in my head the words 'Search me' came to mind. I liked to think Colin's warning was born out of genuine affection for us. I hoped that in the midst of peddling death, he didn't want a pair of innocent bystanders getting hurt along the way. Nice thought Colin, but what about the innocent children your filth was going to hurt in the very near future if this drug run succeeded? Have you ever stopped and considered that my friend? A glance at Connie's and The Beachcomber told us both were closed.

Clearly everyone was being prepared for the evening's delivery. I was sorely tempted to wander up the hill to the disused station where I was sure I would find a dark van with false number plates, waiting for the illegal imports to be rushed through the tunnels from the cellar of Colin's pub, with the aid of Sarah, Barry and possibly even Tom, out of the exit in the woods, across the road and away by eleven at the latest. Four hours later, cocaine and heroin with a street value of what...? Five million pounds maybe...? It would be safely tucked away somewhere in London.

By Tuesday it would be sifted into little plastic bags and found on every street corner across the South East, maybe further... What Mr Mario Martin and his gang didn't know was that Messrs Kearsley, Horlock, Williams and WPC

Wells, plus our two anonymous friends from the Cornish Constabulary were onto them and if all went well, their latest import along with the gang themselves would very soon be in police custody. No, doubt the police and customs officers had the lane blocked. The only other way in or out of St Matilda's Bay would call for the use of a helicopter, and I'd seen or heard no sign of one as yet.

Whether or not Martin himself would be implicated—Kathy and I suspected not—remained to be seen... In spite of our love and respect for our friends and neighbours, we couldn't help but smile at the fact that we had done our bit, as small as it was, to protect the young of our nation. We sat down and turned on the television, just as the familiar theme tune was kicking in...

71

"Good evening. I'm Gareth Thomas and this is the six o'clock news. In the main news today, the trial of alleged London organised crime boss Mario Martinez began at the Old Bailey today. Mr Martinez, originally from Italy, now residing in Mayfair is charged with the murder of high-class prostitute Caroline Savage and WPC Janice Pearce. Here's Chelsea Langham reporting from outside the Central Criminal Court where day one of what is expected to be an estimated two week-long trial ended just a short time ago... Chelsea?"

Mario Martinez? Kathy and I watched in amazement as Miss Langham went on to describe the day's events, neither of us realising our two-armed friends watching from the doorway behind us.

"Yes, Gareth," the reporter began. "Mr Martinez arrived shortly after nine-thirty this morning, dressed in a cream Armani suit and accompanied by his team of solicitors. He smiled for the cameras but said nothing. One of his legal team, Mr Christopher Puttick, read out a short statement: 'My client wishes to make it clear he was not even aware of Miss Savage's existence and is certainly not guilty of causing either her demise or that of the woman police officer'."

The reporter continued, "The Metropolitan police have revealed the case hinged on the evidence of an eye witness who had been in Miss Savage's bathroom at the time and can positively identify Mr Martinez as the man who murdered Miss Savage in cold blood, slitting her throat with a Samurai sword. WPC Pearce, who lived in the next apartment, had heard a scream and ran round to see what was going on. The alleged attacker simply cut her down at the doorway. Although the murder weapon has never been recovered, it has been positively identified by the witness as being exactly the same as one allegedly stolen from Mr Martinez' home just a day earlier." The reporter glanced down at her notes before revealing:

"The eye witness, a colleague of Miss Savage's, was a Miss Deborah Jones, sometimes known as Deborah Martin, real name Deborah Overton-Crouthers.

She had been protected by the police while they spent eighteen months building their case against Mr Martinez. I can reveal she had been held in an experimental 'safe village' in the Staffordshire country-side, a small village where all its residents are former members of the constabulary or the armed forces.

"For obvious reasons, there is a media black-out regarding the exact location of the village. Miss Overton-Crouthers will testify that through a crack in the doorway, she clearly heard Miss Savage's scream and saw the defendant slit her throat, then viciously beat her pet dog with the handle of the sword. We understand there have been several attempts on the life of the star witness. Thankfully, none of them were successful. In addition to Mr Martinez, there have been further arrests..." Miss Langham took another look down at her notes... "Mr Graham Potter, Mr Dennis Smith and Mr Reginald Mitchell, known associates of Mr Martinez, all of whom will face conspiracy charges. All three men were arrested last night, remanded in custody and will appear here at a later date... Detective Chief Superintendent Steven Kimber gave our team this brief statement earlier today:

"This was a particularly evil crime. The accused was a former partner of the deceased and once he learned that she was back in her chosen profession, he took the strongest revenge possible and we believe murdered her. Mr Martinez and his associates had been on our radar for some considerable time, suspected of being involved in protection, illegal gambling and controlling prostitutes, but we were never before able to find enough evidence to bring him to trial. This time, thanks mainly to Miss Overton-Crouthers, we are more than confident of a conviction. If convicted, we will press for the maximum sentence with no remission. The streets of London will be a safer place without the likes of Mr Mario Martinez. Finally, I would like to thank the people of our 'safe village' for their hard work over a very long period. That's all for now, thank you."

Back to Chelsea Langham, "So, to sum up, the trial of Mario Martinez began at ten o'clock this morning, here at the Old Bailey and is expected to run for seven to ten days. Now, back to the studio... Gareth?"

Kathy and I looked at each other in amazement. How could we have been so stupid? How did we manage to get it so wrong? To think we suspected our... But then, what choice did we have? At every turn we hit a brick wall or a blind alley. From the moment Kathy had mentioned the magic word 'smugglers' it had all made sense. However, knowing what we do now, so does the witness protection scheme...

"I took the liberty..." One of the armed police had two beers in his hand and offered them to us. "I thought you could use them. Plus, you have a party to get yourselves ready for."

They were all there in the Mariners: Alice, Tom and even Minnie. Well, it was a private party after all. Barry, Sarah, Adam—back from wherever he had been the past few weeks—Pat and Brian, the three girls... Peter Kearsley, Natalie Wells, Andy Horlock and Kelsey Williams... Even a few people I didn't recognise, whom I assumed were working behind the scenes... Several pints went down before we hit the vodka, but before that, Colin broke out the Champagne all round. At nine o'clock, a vaguely familiar face stood up at the bar and began offering his thanks to everyone involved and handing out congratulations... "I just want to thank you all..."

I knew that voice. I told Kathy as much as he started speaking. We both waited patiently...

"...for eighteen months bloody hard work which looks like paying dividends. We will know for sure in a few weeks all being well, but I think I can safely say we have done everything we possibly could." He turned to look at me. "I would like to offer my specific thanks to Kathy and Paul for finally taking my advice and leaving all this to the experts."

Yes, he was the man who had sent the note and infiltrated my e-mail account, finally taking me hostage in my own home to offer the final threat. At least now I knew why no violence had occurred, apart from that light fitting 'accident'. I also knew why I had been blind-folded. It wasn't just so that I wouldn't recognise my captors, probably Adam and Barry, but also to ensure I didn't spot the master-mind behind the 'safe village' experiment... The so-called retired St Matilda's Bay station master.

The daft thing is, as I pointed out to both he and Kathy afterwards, I could so easily have identified him. Had I taken the trouble to look closely at the disused station web-site, I would have seen photos of the former station master who bore no resemblance what-so-ever to our speaker, and had in fact died some fifteen years ago...

Colin came to join us some time after and offered his heart-felt apology, "I'm afraid it was me who bumped you over the head that day." Charming I thought to myself, but at least now I understood why. It hadn't caused any damage—I'm extremely thick skinned—and the sleeping drug introduced to my blood stream explained why I was 'out cold' for nearly three days... "It was designed to make it look more serious than it was," he explained. "Plus, it gave us all a chance to re-group and decide how best to handle you two."

We learned that following the fire at Debbie's cottage, which the team had started themselves to convince Martinez' so-called friends of her demise, the lady herself had been in Colin's spare room all the time, under the watchful eye of the absent Adam Bonnell. All of this explained one of my earlier mysteries. Tom, as a part of the team, had known about the fire and subsequently Debbie's sanctuary in the Mariners, hence the smile I'd witnessed that night...

The boss came over to join Kathy, Colin and I... "I just wanted to thank you personally and apologise for not being able to tell you more of what we were doing here in Tilda's. It took a lot of convincing certain authorities that it could work. We found this spot and it was ideal. Both Colin here and Barry were ex-Army, and Brian ex-Navy, they'd already signed the Official Secrets Act so they were no problem. Tom and Sarah are ex-job, former coppers with bloody good records so again, we were able to put our trust in them. Until you arrived on the scene, the only worries we had were the three girls. It took about six months, but we gradually talked them into signing the Act and they are now fully-fledged paid-up members of our little club..."

As I said, finally now it all made sense. Debbie's ramblings about her friend being killed, the dog and her violent ex-husband being the reason why she was hiding away in our little village... A very good cover story pretty much based on the actual facts. I certainly fell for it... No, wonder she was running scared. That part of her story at least was true... And of course, all those words I heard jumbled up in the tunnel now made sense also... The 'ten o'clock' and 'the fifth' hadn't been 'smuggler's time' as we suspected, but the date and time of the trial commencing. Martin was Debbie's alter-ego, presumably while working as a high-class call girl...

"Why would someone like that sell her body Kathy? I mean, she's bloody gorgeous! And the double-barrelled name suggests good heritage..."

"I can kind of understand it," Kathy replied. "I mean the money's good right? They can earn thousands a night, get treated like royalty, taken to Paris and New York for week-ends... It's not like hung around on street corners to shag anything for fifty quid a pop, is it?" The lady had a point...

The night was long and the drinking was hard. I congratulated everyone for a bloody good operation. We learned quite a lot more about St Matilda's Bay that night, things we would never have found on Google. The tunnels, for example, were exactly what I had originally thought... Considerably old, rather than being made to look that way. Some thirty years earlier, Tilda's had been heading the same way as Harwick after the closure of the tin mines. Properties were falling into dis-repair as less and less money was available. Slowly people moved away, never to return.

The few residents that remained saw their opportunity when an offer was made, by a forerunner of Mario Martinez possibly. With the right investment, plus a financial incentive, a nice little smuggling operation had begun in the nineteen nineties. Not drugs but alcohol. In those tough days of little work and even less money, there was a fortune to be made in imported alcohol and many of the local publicans were happy to make a profit from it. They had got away with it for about five years and then it all came crashing down on them.

Five-to-ten-year prison sentences for all except Steve Taylor who, due to ill health was given a suspended sentence and the village fell into decline once more. Then along came the mysterious benefactor. Firstly, he had acquired the railway station from the former owner's relatives—He considered it the perfect spot to oversee operations from just outside the village. Then, with government sponsorship, he re-built the bay, turning it into an outwardly typical Cornish tourist attraction and the rest, as they say, is history. Following a few trial runs, protecting lesser priority witnesses, Debbie had been their first 'at risk' customer and barring a few hitches had been a roaring success. One of those hitches had of course been me and my vivid imagination... Not to mention my big nose and equally imaginative lady friend.

"I take it Debbie threw that New Zealand thing in as a red herring then?" I asked.

"I still find it hard to believe she was on the game though; she just didn't seem the type to me..." This made Colin laugh out loud.

"Debbie?" He was still smiling. "On the game? You're kidding mate! The police had to talk her into chucking in a promising acting career. She was all set to join the cast of The Hobbit when they convinced her this job would be far more rewarding. So, she handed in her Equity card and started working under cover. Bloody fine little actress, that girl, I can tell you." I had to agree. She had us fooled. "Anyway, it was only a small part, and who wants to spend six months in New Zealand anyway, the beers rubbish!"

"So, tell me," I implored, "what of your little meeting up the hill when I over-heard that stuff about the date and time, and my name? You couldn't possibly have known I'd hear you. I could've blown the whole thing…"

He smiled, that knowing smile of a man who is always one step ahead… "Well, firstly, Mr Evans, I should explain you made two mistakes. One, I should congratulate you on your measurements. You were so close with your calculations of where the tunnel ended… But you should have turned around. Had you done so, you would have been staring straight at my little railway station."

But of course, in my own mind. I had *known* it couldn't be the old man at the station. My God, how easily I had been misled. There must have been a very slight bend in the tunnel—practically impossible to notice by torchlight— which, over such a distance, had led us way off course. No, wonder Kathy and I failed to locate the entrance in the woods. However, that didn't explain the five words I'd heard quite clearly that day…

"…and two, we deliberately made sure you heard just enough to keep you interested without giving away the real reason for our meeting. At that point we were still hoping you might back off and leave us to it. Scare tactics, so to speak." There was that smile again, the cocky bastard. But I still had one more ace up my sleeve…

"Aha," I crowed, "but you couldn't possibly have known I would hear you. We checked everywhere before I went down there again. None of your crew could have seen me, and Kathy had fixed the CCTV."

"Oh yes," he conceded, "your lady friend's undergarments. A very neat little trick that, and quite daring on her part." He gave Kathy an appreciative nod. "But surely you didn't think that was the only camera we had did you? Apart from the obvious one in the lane…" I gave a look that said 'of course I'd worked that one out' which in fact I hadn't, but should have.

Apart from the one on the cliffs, the only one I'd spotted was on Colin's pub… "there are seven in all around the bay. You should have a good look around in the morning. They're really quite easy to spot if you know what you're looking for."

I tried hard not to look like a complete idiot, but he was right. It never occurred to me there might be others. So, much for my Sherlock Holmes impersonation. All in all, despite our best efforts, we had missed several glaringly obvious clues. Not just the cameras, but the station master himself, Tom's smile—so out of character for a man who so recently had faced tragedy—and even the news of Martinez' impending murder trial.

Even Adam Bonnell's apparent prolonged absence, which seemed not to bother his wife in the slightest, when in fact he was just over the lane, doing his duty. I took a long swallow from my glass and decided detection was not for me after all. I suspected I would see my working days out moving helicopter spares around the world. I would never be Barnaby or even Jones. Certainly not Robbie Williams, or Bruce Willis, or Cristiano Ronaldo... I knew my limitations. I was the best at what I did and would continue to be so, at least for the next three years. And after that? Hopefully another twenty in the company of the little lady by my side, always assuming my grandmother had been right. The girl who had shown me how good things could be in the autumn of one's life. Plus, as a bonus, I wasn't going to lose all my friends and neighbours...

"So, all that remains is what to do with *you* two..." The boss was speaking again. I realised I still didn't know his name, but thought it best not to ask. I was sure he would divulge it if allowed. Kathy and I had seen off two glasses of shampoo, a few pints of lager each and several vodkas by now. She was back to her brazen self...

"I would say you have two choices Mr Whateveryournameis. You can either bang us both over the head and leave us to rot in the tunnels, or enlist us in your project..." I worry about her sometimes. Mr What Etc. pondered this puzzle and his response was no surprise...

"The way I see it Miss Lloyd is that you either join us or, with what you know, I would have to kill you!" His smile was contagious.

There was one notable absentee from the evening's celebrations but we understood Debbie was now in yet another safe house, somewhere on the outskirts of London. No, doubt she would soon be back under cover again... Maybe, this time a million miles away from the sex industry, but you never knew. I imagine in that job, you get what you're given, and to be fair, by my own experience with her, she was bloody good at it! I wondered if her acting experience ever included improvisation...

It was only when Colin asked if I still fancied starting the quiz next month—it had been my idea to try in September as the crowds dwindled—that it occurred to me how rarely I read the newspapers these days. Back in my former life, I had often run pub quizzes and always included a 'This Week's News' round... All the latest celebrity gossip, the latest story lines from the soaps, plus the occasional crime story... Had I bothered to pick up a newspaper or turn on the TV news in recent months, I would no doubt have noticed how close we had been with our so-called 'gang boss' Mario Martin. Mario Martinez' name had been plastered all over the front pages as the trial grew closer...

I'm one of those people who, like most men, carry very little around with me. Wallet, phone and keys. That's about it. Even less if someone's trying to blast my head off with a sawn-off shot gun as it turns out. Kathy is surprisingly in agreement with me on that one. Unlike most women I've known, her handbag carries little more than the bare essentials. No, sign of the proverbial kitchen sink in there... So, what kind of a man goes to the pub with two copies of the Official Secrets Act tucked away in his pocket? Were we really that predictable? No, doubt we had been, without our knowledge of course, the subject of stringent criminal record checks and passed with flying colours. Consequently, the station master had come prepared.

"Just in case the media come knocking on your door asking for the exclusive story of your involvement in the Martinez case and how his right-hand man nearly blew your head off..." I'm not sure I liked the way he smiled as he said that...

His final words that night were, "In future, Barry must learn to keep that bloody PC out of sight!" I understood his agitation. The sight of Mr Marlow's computer had been the one thing that started me wondering about my neighbours all those months ago. If it hadn't had been for that...

Before leaving the pub that night, I took Colin to one side. There was one thing that had bugged me from the very first time I met him... "Were you really living just the other side of Earlswood Common way back then?" The landlord simply smiled, winked and walked away...

A lot can happen in eighteen months, but I think it's safe to assume more has gone in in *our* eighteen months than most people experience in a life-time... Kathy and I are now fully paid-up members of the 'Safe Village' operation, although none of our friends or family are aware, or allowed to be. As far as anyone outside St Matilda's Bay is concerned, we are just a happy couple, living the dream in a pretty Cornish village. Kathy is now a 'stay-at-home' girl-friend, along the same lines as Sarah, who we learned is not related to Adam in the slightest, both having been recruited for the 'job'...

This keeps my little lady happy as it saves us the hassle of regular trips to whichever children's home, she may have had allocated to her. In any case, Minnie and Cheryl are more than enough children in our lives, thank you very much. We are currently enjoying the white sands of Cuba, exactly as we had promised ourselves. Upon our return, we will commence our duties as joint protectors of a young man who turned Queen's evidence to squeal on his former friends in a South London post-code gang, famous for organising football hooliganism and street riots. He would be safely ensconced in what was once Debbie's cottage for an undetermined period of time as the necessary evidence was gathered. I can see he's going to be a right bundle of laughs. Can't wait!

The next morning, Tuesday August the sixth, having logged onto my Brannigan's web-site, completed my hand-over from Dave and brought everything reasonably up to date, I took Kathy's hand and we walked outside. The warm sunshine felt good. It was going to be another fine day in paradise. All being well, we had the rest of our lives to enjoy Tilda's. We managed to find four CCTV cameras, but God only knows where the others were. I was sure we would be told, all in good time. We may even end up monitoring them at some stage.

Checking the number plates of every single vehicle that passed the 'speed camera' up the hill. Watching the back gardens of the five cottages under the cliffs... After breakfast, strong coffee and a couple of cigarettes, we began planning our immediate future. Before anything else, I had to call Erik and let him know his services would no longer be required. If the Safe Village Society were willing to destroy one of their own cottages, I was fairly sure they would be equally prepared to re-build it. Erik was of course more than welcome to come down sometime soon and enjoy some of St Matilda's hospitality though. I had already arranged my two weeks leave. Dave Fincham would, as always, be happy to cover for me. It meant a huge chunk of overtime in his pay packet at the end of the following month...

72

On our arrival at the hotel, we received two messages. One to say 'our friend had gone on holiday'. This confirmed Mario Martinez had been found guilty and would be spending the next thirty years at the pleasure of Her Majesty. We later discovered his accomplices, Potter, Smith and Mitchell had also received long sentences. The other message was a simple postcard saying 'Thank you for everything. You were a true friend. Please forgive my deception. I hope we meet again someday under much happier circumstances. Much love from Debbie xxx.'

Kathy and I smiled as the waiter brought us another tequila. It's only ten in the morning but who cares? We have a life to live and it starts right here! Of course, in case you were wondering, it goes without saying that the 'safe village' is in neither Cornwall nor Staffordshire, but I can assure you, it does exist. Where? If I told you that, as the station master said, I would have to kill you...

P.S. The day before we left for the Caribbean, Minnie finally beat me at chess.

P.P.S. The palm tree is still growing...